THRUST & THROTTLE

Tarnished Angels Motorcycle Club Book 4

EMMA SLATE

Tabula Rasa Publishing

Thrust & Throttle
(TARNISHED ANGELS MOTORCYCLE CLUB BOOK 4)

My childhood best friend is a big, bad biker—and an animal in the bedroom.

I should know because we've been hooking up in secret for weeks.

We crossed a line we swore we'd never cross, but the lust we'd buried for years finally culminated in a night of heated passion.

I know the taste of Duke's lips, but this is more than just desire. When we're together I see the promise of forever in his eyes.

Duke is the only man who makes me feel safe enough to be vulnerable, but I'm terrified I'm going to screw it up and lose it all.

He won't stop until he has every piece of me, including my

heart. He wants me on the back of his bike, my name inked on his skin.

He wants me to be his Old Lady.

He wants me pregnant.

Chapter 1

"Hey doll, do me a favor," Mia said as she placed three pint glasses of beer onto a serving tray. "Take these to my husband and your boys. I'm a little short-staffed tonight."

I grabbed the tray from the counter. "No problem."

The tiny brunette smiled gratefully, lines of exhaustion bracketing her mouth. "Thanks. I appreciate it."

I walked through the bar, balancing the tray of drinks on one hand like a pro. It was busy due to Mia's drink specials for the evening, and the place was packed with a wide array of customers. The Tarnished Angels MC often hung out at Shelly's because Mia owned it, and was married to the club's president, but it was in no way a biker bar.

As I approached Colt and my two best friends from childhood, I attempted to avoid collision with several patrons.

"You're the best there ever was," Savage quipped, a bright, infectious grin stretching across his handsome face. He raked a hand through his blond hair.

"Yeah, yeah," I quipped. "I'm just giving Mia a hand, keeping you big, scary bikers hydrated."

A young woman with nearly jet-black hair in five-inch stilettos and a skirt so short it showed the curves of her ass was arguing with her roided-out boyfriend a few feet away. I hadn't noticed them until she began to get loud.

"Fuck this, *asshole*. You're drunk and I'm not putting up with this. I'm out of here," she yelled.

I turned my head just in time to see the guy she was with grab her wrist and drag her toward him. The young woman yanked her arm free. She wobbled on her heels and collided backward into me, causing me to nearly lose my hold on the tray.

"Willa." Duke grasped my elbow to steady me. His touch caused a zing to swoosh through my belly.

"Thanks," I said, righting the tray. Some beer had splashed over the rims of the glasses, but I managed to keep them upright. I looked up just in time to see the meathead reach for the girl's hair.

"Enough," Savage growled in the direction of the arguing couple. "Keep your fucking hands off her."

"Hey, fuck you, dickwad," the meathead snapped. "She's *my* fucking girlfriend. I'll touch her if I want."

Savage's blue eyes narrowed, and he looked down at the young woman who'd regained her balance. "Go on. Get out of here."

She blinked, and as she turned to leave she shot him a flirtatious grin. "Thanks."

"You stupid bitch," the drunk yelled as the girl started to walk away. "You better not leave. Meet me outside." He stepped toward her, but Savage reached a large hand out and stopped the jerk dead in his tracks, like he'd run into a brick wall.

"You want to let her go," Savage commanded, his voice dropping.

"Shit," Colt muttered. "Here we go."

The roided-out guy was too drunk to be scared and slapped Savage's hand away.

Duke quickly moved in front of me, his tall, brawny frame protecting me from the brewing altercation.

Savage's grin was feral as he cracked his knuckles. "Oh, this is gonna be fun."

"Tell Mia you're sorry," I commanded, hands on my hips.

Savage removed the towel from his fat, bleeding lip, swiveled on his bar stool and said, "I'm sorry we broke your jukebox."

Mia stood behind the bar, icing Colt's knuckles. She glanced at Savage and grinned at him. "You didn't technically break it. The douche who put his hands on that girl broke it."

"But only because Savage flipped him over and threw him onto the jukebox," I pointed out.

"I was a valiant knight in shining armor, coming to a lady's rescue," Savage remarked. "Thanks for having my back, Prez. I should've guessed that guy had friends."

"It's been a while since I've been in a good fight," Colt remarked.

"You'd think a brawl in a bar would be bad for business," Mia joked. "But videos of you guys have already hit social media. I expect another rush within the hour."

Colt looked down at his wife, who he towered over. "You know what's good after a fight?"

"What?" Mia demanded.

Colt leaned down and stage whispered, "A good fuck."

Mia's brown eyes flashed with heat. She took Colt's hand and placed it on the pack of ice and then addressed the other female bartender. "I'll be back in a few minutes." Mia pushed against her husband's side, all but shepherding him off the floor toward the back office.

"Lucky bastard," Savage muttered. "I need a good fuck too."

Duke—who'd made sure I was well out of harm's way before he joined the fight—sipped from his pint of beer. "I think you just might get lucky…"

"Yeah?" Savage perked up.

"She's back," Duke said.

The young woman with dark hair that Savage had gotten into a fight over stood near the entrance, looking around the bar. Finally, her eyes landed on Savage. She walked toward us with purpose, rocking her heels like a runway model.

"Hi," she said to Savage.

"Hey," Savage greeted.

"I just wanted to thank you for what you did." Her brown eyes were wide and beseeching. "I broke up with him."

"Yeah?" Savage drawled.

She nodded.

Savage rose from the bar stool. "What's your name, darlin'?"

"Elizabeth," she said. "Can I—will you let me buy you a drink?"

"Nah. How about I buy *you* a drink?"

She grinned and the two of them walked to the other end of the bar.

I looked at Duke. "I bet he'll be in her pants in under five minutes."

Duke cleared his throat and gestured with his chin. I

turned. Savage already had his arm around the woman's shoulders, and they were headed toward the restrooms.

"So, what about you?" I asked, filching Duke's pint of beer from his grasp and taking a sip.

"What about me, what?" he asked.

I leaned forward ever so slightly and peered into his dark eyes. "Do *you* need a good fuck?"

"You offering?"

"Yes."

He ran his fingers through his brown hair. "I told you I don't want to be your dirty little secret."

"That hasn't stopped you from fucking me the past few weeks."

"Willa," he growled. "You know I love fucking you, but I also want to walk in public with my arm around you, claiming you as mine. You know what all this means to me. Being with you behind my best friend's back puts our friendship on the line. For all of us. Either we do this out in the open, deal with the shitstorm it causes and it is what it is, or we need to end it now, stay friends, and move on."

"Move on," I said quietly. "You can move on? Just like that?"

His eyes seemed to flicker in the low light of the bar. "I've buried my feelings for you for years. I can do it again if I have to."

His words sliced into me, and I suddenly remembered where we were. "This isn't the place for this conversation."

"There's nothing more to talk about, Willa. You either want to be with me publicly, or you don't."

"Hey, Willa," Crow greeted as he approached us. "Sorry to interrupt."

I turned to the Tarnished Angels prospect and forced a smile. "It's fine. Hi, Crow."

"Someone named Jessica is outside. Says she's friends with your sister."

I frowned. "She is friends with my sister. Best friends. And Waverly is supposed to be at Jessica's house right now."

I looked over my shoulder at Duke and he nodded as I headed out of the bar.

My sister's best friend was a cute, petite sixteen-year-old blonde, who at the moment looked like she could pass for twenty. Her hair was curled and teased, her lips were seductively red, and her low-rise jeans showed a hint of her pink thong. Her bared midriff revealed a pierced navel.

"Jessica?"

She flung herself into my arms. "Thank God, I found you!"

"What's going on?" I demanded. "Where's Waverly?"

Jessica pulled back and grimaced. "That's what I have to tell you—and you're not gonna like it..."

Chapter 2

Jessica looked over my shoulder and stared at Duke.

"You can trust him. He's my best friend," I assured her.

"Wow," she murmured and then she realized what she had said aloud. The glow from the bar's outdoor lights illuminated the color suffusing her cheeks.

"Focus, Jessica," I said with a wry snort.

"So, we kind of went to a party," she said and then paused.

"And?" I went on.

"A party at a warehouse. There was a light show and music and…"

"Drugs?" Duke supplied, his voice harsh.

"Yeah, drugs." Jessica winced. "We didn't take anything, I swear. But we were dancing and the cops showed up. Everyone scattered like roaches, only Waverly and I got separated. She's with Dylan, though."

She unzipped her leather belt bag and pulled out a cellphone and handed it to me. "Her phone. She asked me to hold it for her."

"So, my sister is out there with some strange kid named

Dylan who she met at a rave, and you have her phone and she hasn't called us?" I asked, my ire rising to the surface.

"Not some strange kid," Jessica said. "Dylan."

"Is that supposed to mean something to me?" I snapped.

"Dylan's her boyfriend."

"*Boyfriend*? Waverly doesn't have a boyfriend," I scoffed.

"Oh, she has a boyfriend," Jessica insisted. "And they're together right now. I called his phone, but it went to voicemail."

"And he hasn't checked in with you?" I demanded. "I do not like this. I do not like this at all."

"Do you have any clue where they might be?" Duke asked.

"There's a diner on the other side of town called Boots. It's kind of their spot."

They have a spot?

"Why did you track me down?" I asked. "Why didn't you go to Boots yourself or better yet, wait for her to get into contact with you?"

"Boots is…well, it's in a part of town I'm scared to go to alone."

"And this punk took my sister?" I shrieked.

A hand settled on my shoulder and I immediately sank into Duke's strong chest, my back pressed to his front.

"Did you drive here?" Duke asked.

She shook her head. "I took an Uber."

"Where do your parents think you are right now?" I demanded.

Jessica nibbled her lip, suddenly looking a lot younger than she was. "Your place."

"Son of a bitch," I muttered.

"I'm going to have one of my brothers take you home. I want to make sure you get home safely," Duke said.

"Oh, that's okay, I'll—"

"Not up for discussion, kid," Duke growled. He stepped away from me and went inside the bar.

"I'm in a lot of trouble, aren't I?" Jessica asked.

"Yup."

"You're going to tell my parents, aren't you?"

"Yup."

"You're going to slaughter Waverly," she said.

"And then I'm going to find a way to bring her back to life just so I can kill her again."

"I thought, maybe, because you're her sister and not her mom, you'd be cooler than my parents about this. Clearly, I was wrong."

"You guys just don't get it, do you?"

"Get what?"

"I've been a teenager. I've lied and snuck around. I've gone to parties. I know you want your freedom, but you can't lie about where you're at. God forbid something really bad happened to either one of you tonight."

Was I overreacting? Maybe. But Waverly meant everything to me.

"If we'd told you the truth about the rave, would you have let her go?" Jessica demanded.

"Not the point," I stated.

"Kind of the point." She cocked her head to the side. "Are you really mad about the party, or are you mad because she didn't tell you about Dylan?"

My gaze narrowed. "Thin ice, Jessica. Thin fucking ice."

A few moments later Duke returned with Crow and Savage.

"Crow is going to give you a lift home," Duke said as they strode toward us.

"On a motorcycle?" Jessica's eyes widened in excitement.

"Fuck no," Duke barked. "He'll drive you in Mia's car."

Crow swirled a keyring around his finger. "Let's go."

Jessica dogged after him like a lost puppy.

"We better get going," Duke said. "I don't want Waverly and Sheet Stain to go somewhere else and force us to spend the entire night tracking them down."

I nodded.

"My bike or Duke's?" Savage asked.

"Duke's, I guess." I blew out a furious breath of air. "Weren't you getting frisky with Elizabeth?"

"I was," Savage drawled as he turned to look at Duke. "This fucker interrupted me right when it was about to get good."

I wrinkled my nose. "I don't want to know."

"I got her number. She'll meet me later. So all is not lost."

"Glad to hear it," I remarked dryly.

The three of us trekked to the corner of the parking lot with all the motorcycles. Duke handed me a spare helmet and then climbed onto his bike. I clasped the strap around my chin and then got on the bike behind him, scooting close and wrapping my arms around him.

He tensed ever so slightly and then relaxed.

"You know where this place is?" I called out.

"Yeah," he yelled back as the engine of the motorcycle came to life. "Hang on."

We zoomed out of the parking lot. It wasn't the first time I'd been on the back of Duke's bike. I was comfortable there. Like I belonged.

I'd ridden on the back of Savage's bike, but it wasn't the same. It had always been different with Duke, and that was why I'd been terrified of ever letting myself think about the possibilities of what we could become.

The three of us had been friends since we were kids. They were my family. We worked well as a group, the three of us—but only because we'd sworn not to let anything romantic get in the way.

But one night a few weeks ago, Duke and I crossed a line.

And I wasn't ready for it to change everything. It wasn't just about Duke and me. It was about my friendship with Savage. But it was also about Duke, Savage and me as a collective unit.

My situation with Duke was a mess.

Now my home life was a mess.

We pulled up to the curb just outside Boots, and Duke cut the engine. Savage rolled in behind us and did the same. It was clear the neighborhood was rough. The sidewalk was cracked, trash littered the gutter, and there were a few feral cats skulking around the alley. Half a block down, there were seedy looking men gathered in a cluster outside a liquor store.

"What the hell is she thinking?" I demanded, climbing off Duke's bike.

"Hormones." Duke grimaced. "Speaking of. Gimme a minute."

"Why would you need—" My gaze dropped to his lap, realizing that I'd been curled around him, the heat of me pressed against his back. "Got it."

I quickly turned away to give him the illusion of privacy.

"How do you wanna do this?" Savage asked approaching me, a gleam in his eyes. "You want me to go in there and scare the shit out of this kid?"

"Tempting," I said with a flicker of a smile. "But no. Let me handle this."

I walked into Boots first, Savage and Duke trailing behind me. Heads turned in our direction and there was a momentary pause in conversation before the diner roared to life again.

As I surveyed the room, Duke pointed at the booth in the far corner. Waverly was easy to spot because of her bright red hair. She was sitting with her back to the door so she had no idea that I'd arrived.

I strutted up to the table and casually slid into the seat across from her.

My sister was in the middle of sipping a soda through her straw when her blue eyes—heavily caked with black eyeliner and shadow—widened at the sight of me. She immediately began to cough as she set her drink aside.

"Willa!" She hastily grabbed a napkin and dabbed her watering eyes.

"Fun night?" I asked, reaching across the table to pluck a fry from her dinner. I dunked it into the blob of ketchup on her plate and then stuck it in my mouth.

"What are you doing here?" she demanded.

As I swallowed my French fry, I finally noticed what she was wearing. My mouth gaped. "That's *mine*."

She glanced down at herself and then quickly looked at me. "I borrowed it."

"Borrow implies that you asked. I don't recall you asking if you could borrow my leather corset."

Her mouth pinched. "You would've said no."

"Damn right. You're fifteen years old."

"I'm old enough to dress myself. What crawled up your ass and died?"

"What crawled up my ass, you ask? How about the fact that you lied to me about spending the night at your best friend's house when you really went to a rave so you could meet up with your boyfriend."

Her eyes widened.

"Next time, don't leave your phone." I reached into the tiny purse I wore slung across my body, fished out her cell, and placed it in front of her.

She grasped it. I noted the bright red nail polish on her fingertips. When she'd left to go to Jessica's for the night, they'd been painted black.

"Next time?" Her hand curled around her cell.

"Right, what was I thinking?" I clocked my forehead with the palm of my hand. "There won't be a next time. You're grounded until you're thirty."

"You don't have the authority to ground me," she lashed out.

"Your best friend tracked *me* down. Not Mom. As far as you're concerned, I'm judge, jury, and executioner. Speaking of executions…where is this boyfriend of yours?"

"Bathroom," she muttered. "Please don't embarrass me."

I raised my brows. "Like you have any grounds to make requests here."

A dark-haired teenage boy wearing jeans, a black T-shirt, and black Converse strode out from the back hallway into the dining room. He paused but a moment when he saw me and stood taller when Savage and Duke rose from their stools at the diner counter. They corralled him and shepherded him toward the table without a word.

He slid into the seat next to Waverly, who didn't move over for him. Instead, she tucked herself into his side. He raised his arm and placed it around her shoulder.

My gaze narrowed at him.

Calm green eyes peered back at me. Not pugnacious, not ready for a fight. But merely staking his claim.

"Dylan, I presume?" I asked.

He inclined his head. "You must be Willa."

"In the flesh."

Duke and Savage pulled up two vacant chairs from a nearby table, turned them backward, and sat down next to us. Dylan still didn't look uncomfortable despite two inked, muscley bikers making their presence known.

"What happened to your lip?" Waverly asked Savage.

"Bar brawl." Savage shrugged.

Waverly rolled her eyes. "Shocker."

"Don't start, squirt," Savage snapped.

Before the two of them could get into it, I interjected, "So, here's what we're going to do. I'm going to ask some questions, and if you answer them to my satisfaction, I won't drag you out of here and make a scene."

Waverly didn't move, and then suddenly she blew out a puff of air. "Okay. Sounds fair."

"Why did you lie to me about sleeping over at Jessica's?" I asked.

"I didn't lie," she said. "I just didn't add that we were going to head to a rave before I slept over."

"She said her parents thought she was sleeping over at our place. So...try again."

Waverly sighed and rolled her eyes. "I knew you wouldn't let me go."

"Correct." I looked at Dylan. "But there's more, yeah? I had no idea you even existed until tonight."

"I wasn't ready to tell you about Dylan." Waverly sat up and glared at Duke. "I can't believe you told her."

The breath froze in my lungs, and I slowly turned my head to look at Duke. "You knew?"

Duke rubbed his chin. "I knew."

"And you didn't tell me?" I snapped before returning

my focus to my sister. I'd yell at Duke later. "Why didn't you tell me about Dylan?"

"Why are you talking about me like I'm not here?" Dylan asked.

"Dude," I said to him. "You really want to be quiet right now."

Savage glared at Dylan who showed no signs of fear, but he did immediately clamp his mouth shut.

"Jessica found me at Shelly's to bring me *your* phone that you lost at a rave you weren't supposed to be at with a boy who looks old enough to get a tattoo without parental consent!"

My voice had risen to the point that we were actively drawing attention. The waitress behind the counter stopped wiping up a spill and stared at me.

"I think it's time to go," Duke said, standing up from his chair. Savage did the same.

"I'm so pissed at you right now," I seethed. "You didn't tell me she had a boyfriend!"

"I begged him not to, okay?" Waverly said.

"Why?" I demanded.

"Can we please talk about this at home?" Waverly asked, pitching her voice low. She suddenly sounded in control, and not at all like a recalcitrant teenager.

I took a deep breath and stood up.

Dylan rose from his seat and then held out a hand to help her.

"Shit," I muttered. "Did you have to bring her here? This isn't exactly the safest part of town."

"My uncle owns the place," Dylan explained. "Everyone in the neighborhood knows me. We're safe here."

"But *I* don't know you, and right now I'm the only one that matters," I stated.

Dylan's eyes were steady and earnest. "I'd never put Waverly in danger."

"You took her to the rave," I pointed out.

Waverly piped up, "It was my idea. He didn't want to go, but I said I was going, so he came to make sure nothing happened to me." She stood in front of Dylan to protect him from my wrath. She was a good six inches shorter than him, so it was a comical gesture.

My heart softened when he stepped closer to her and wrapped his arms around her, obviously not caring about anything in the moment except her.

I was starting to have a smidgen of respect for him. But I didn't know this kid. And I didn't know how far their relationship had advanced.

"I'm taking my sister home," I said.

Dylan released Waverly. "I'll call you tomorrow."

Waverly nodded and then stood on her tiptoes to kiss his cheek.

Savage headed the pack and Waverly followed him. Duke and I brought up the rear.

"You knew?" I asked him again, quietly this time. "And you didn't tell me? You broke the code."

"You're lecturing *me* about the code?" he replied, equally as quiet.

I flinched.

The four of us stepped out into the night. Savage walked over to his bike and picked up the spare helmet and handed it to Waverly. She took it and put it on.

"I'm sorry you were worried," she said to me.

"But not sorry about lying," I said.

"I…" she sighed. "I don't know what to say."

I needed another ride to clear my head. Why had Duke kept Waverly's confidence? Why had Waverly asked him not to tell me? Why did she keep it from me?

Keeping it from Mom, I understood. Keeping it from me? No.

My sister was growing up. I just wanted to be there to make sure she made good choices along the way.

"Hey," I said to her as she climbed onto the back of Savage's bike.

She lifted her gaze to mine.

"I'm sorry you felt like you couldn't tell me something. Something really important."

I didn't wait for her to reply. I wanted to let that sink in as they drove us home.

"We'll see you guys there in a bit," Duke said. "Willa and I have some shit we need to talk about."

"Fun times," Savage said.

"Did you know that Waverly had a boyfriend?" I asked Savage.

"Nope," Savage replied.

"Good. At least one person hasn't screwed me over tonight," I said lightly.

Savage cranked the engine and a few moments later, he pulled away from the curb, Waverly's arms around his middle. I stared off in the distance, watching the taillights of Savage's bike fade into the darkness.

"She skipped school a few weeks ago," he said.

"I remember," I said, facing him. "She called you."

"Yeah, she called me. I picked her up and put the fear of God into the kids she skipped with."

"Was Dylan one of those kids?" I asked.

"No." He rubbed the back of his neck.

"What? Out with it."

"Dylan is her tutor."

"Excuse me?"

"She was having trouble in some of her subjects, so the school assigned her a tutor—Dylan."

I blinked. "Are you saying what I think you're saying? That *Waverly* is the bad influence?"

"I wouldn't say *bad* influence… She's rebellious and pushing boundaries, but not a bad influence."

I swallowed. "Is she—is she doing drugs?"

"No."

I let out a slow exhale.

"I wanted her to feel like she could come to an adult that wasn't going to rag on her, you know? So that if she really got herself into some shit, she would feel okay reaching out instead of trying to handle it herself."

"She could've talked to me," I muttered.

He wrapped an arm around my shoulder and pulled me to him. "Hate to break it to you, but you're more like Waverly's mom than Angel is. Which means she's going to hide shit from you because that's what kids do with their parents."

"Shouldn't the school have called to let me know that Waverly needed a tutor?"

"They called Angel."

"Mommy Dearest forgot to pass along that message," I said bitterly. "And Waverly didn't say anything."

"You know what you're really pissed about, don't you?"

"What?" I demanded.

He smiled softly. "That she's growing up."

Chapter 3

"I'm not sure I like this," I said.

"Like what?"

"Insightful you." I cocked my head. "Adult you."

"What about reliable?"

"You've always been reliable," I pointed out. "Every time I've needed you. You were there. Especially that night…"

"Willa." We were on the sidewalk outside of Boots, but that didn't stop him from moving his large body toward me.

Even though I wore heels, Duke still had a few inches on me. He cupped my jaw and bent his head, his mouth inching closer to mine.

"I thought we weren't going to do this," I whispered.

"To hell with it," he growled.

His lips were just about to capture mine when my phone rang.

"Son of a bitch," he rumbled, lifting his head and dropping his hand from my face. He didn't step away though, choosing to remain close.

I pulled my cell out of my purse and saw Waverly's name flashing across the screen. With a frown, I pressed the answer button and put the phone to my ear. "Hello?"

"It's gone!"

"What's gone?"

"Our *home*. We just got here and the RV is gone. I called Mom, but she didn't answer. Savage went with me to knock on Mr. Edisto's door. He said Mom was here around six with some guy in a red truck. They hitched up the RV and drove off! My backpack with all my books are in there. Not to mention all our clothes!"

"Put Savage on the phone," I said, knowing there was very little I could do to stem the flow of a teenager's meltdown.

There was a moment of shuffling and then Savage said, "Hey."

"Hey," I said quietly.

"I'm gonna take her to the clubhouse. You guys can crash with us while we figure shit out."

I exhaled. "Thanks."

"Did you have anything of value in the RV?"

"No," I admitted. "Thank God."

The first and last time I'd hidden money in a home I shared with Mom, she'd found it and blew it all on useless crap. After that, I opened up a bank account. I didn't have a lot of money, but it was safer there than anywhere near my mother.

He hung up and I shoved my phone into my purse. I looked at Duke. "Did you hear that?"

"Yep."

"My mom's a real piece of shit."

"Yep," he agreed. "Come on, let's get you to the clubhouse."

"We have no clothes," I pointed out.

"Nope." He handed me the spare helmet.

"We don't even have our toothbrushes."

"We can get you new toothbrushes."

I set the helmet on my head and then clicked the belt. Duke made sure it was fastened tight enough and then dropped his hands. I shook my head and climbed onto the back of his bike.

He cranked the engine and then tore off away from the curb. I had my arms wrapped around him, but the thrill and excitement of my position never diminished, no matter how many times I rode with him.

Duke made me feel safe and free at the same time.

Just outside city limits, we turned off the main road onto a winding dirt path. The clubhouse lights shone brightly against the night.

South Paw stood at the gate and opened it when he saw us coming.

Duke parked in the gravel lot next to another bike that I knew instantly was Savage's. There were only a few other bikes and no cars in the lot. Old Ladies and kids weren't here tonight.

I climbed off the motorcycle before Duke cut the engine, and I waited for him. We walked up the pathway to the clubhouse porch steps, our arms brushing.

My body was a live wire when he was near. The night we were together, something changed for me. Now I couldn't stop thinking about him or what we'd done in bed together.

I pushed open the front door of the clubhouse. Waverly was sitting on the couch, her Doc Martens resting on the coffee table. She was eating something I couldn't decipher, but it smelled delicious.

"Didn't you just eat?" I asked, taking a seat next to her.

"This is comfort food," she said. "I've been abandoned by my mother."

"Oh, we're resorting to dark humor, are we?"

"If we didn't laugh, we would cry," Waverly pointed out.

"What is it?" I leaned forward to inspect her plate.

"Crow made chicken fried steak and mashed potatoes last night," Savage said from the recliner on the other side of the room. He took a sip of his beer.

"Crow did this?" I asked in amazement. "That kid knows his way around the kitchen."

"You want something to drink?" Duke asked me.

I shook my head.

The four of us were quiet as Waverly finished her food. My mind turned over ideas about how to find a place for us to live that would be both affordable and safe. That would come, but Waverly and I needed to have another discussion—one I didn't want to speak about until we were alone.

"That was really good," Waverly said as she polished off the last bite. She got up and rinsed her plate before sticking it in the dishwasher.

I studied my sister as she moved around the kitchen, putting things away. Though I didn't like the outright deception and lying to me about her whereabouts this evening, I couldn't help but realize that she definitely wasn't a kid anymore. And it wasn't just because she'd stolen my leather corset, or that it actually fit her. No, it was the fact that she moved with assurance and grace. I realized that a war of teenage independence was raging within her.

I hadn't had the chance for that. When I'd been a teenager, she'd been a young kid, and I'd been old enough to take on the responsibility of looking out for her. I'd become a mother long before I'd wanted to—but it had been out of sheer necessity.

And I'd do it all over again. All of it. Just to make sure she was fed and safe. It was clear now that I'd have to. My mother had shirked her maternal duties.

"You tired, kid?" Savage asked Waverly.

"Stop calling me that," she said reflexively.

Savage snorted. "I will when you stop acting like a child."

"Savage," I warned. "It's late. I'm tired. Waverly's tired. And this doesn't really concern you."

"It doesn't *concern* me?" His mouth nearly gaped. "For fuck's sake, Duke and I are basically her brothers. She got herself into some shit, and the three of us had to stop our night to bail her out. Now you guys are homeless and it falls to me and Duke to look out for you—like hell this doesn't concern me!"

"Oh, this is fun." Waverly wrinkled her nose. "Did I ask for two overprotective biker boys to act like big brothers? No. Did I ask you to trek across town and embarrass me in front of my boyfriend? Also no."

"Embarrass you? Embarrass *you?*"

"Savage," Duke growled. "Walk it off."

With a huff, Savage stood up from the recliner and stomped down the hallway. A moment later the screen door slammed shut.

The three of us didn't say anything for a while and then Waverly piped up, "I don't have any pajamas."

"You can borrow one of my T-shirts," Duke said.

"Me too, please," I said.

He smiled, his dimples popping. "I'll get them. The theater room downstairs has a pull-out couch. Fresh sheets and pillows are in the closet down there. And there's a half bath, too."

"Thanks, Duke," I said.

"Yeah, thanks," Waverly said. She nibbled on her lip. "I really didn't mean to make anyone worry. I just…"

Duke wrapped an inked forearm around Waverly's shoulder and roughly pulled her to him. "We get it. We were teenagers once too."

"Once, eons ago," she teased. "Now you're old. Like, *old* old."

He ruffled her hair and let her go.

"I'm the same age as your sister," he pointed out.

"Yeah and twenty-four is old," she sing-songed.

"I'll meet you down there," I said to her. Waverly nodded and then headed in the direction of the stairs that would lead down into the theater room.

When Duke and I were alone I turned to him and said, "Thanks."

He pulled me into his arms and held me longer than was necessary. He only released me when we heard the screen door slam again. Savage appeared in the hallway, looking a lot calmer than he had moments ago. The smell of weed wafted from him.

"A blunt?" I demanded. "Seriously?"

"What can I say? That little squirt brings out the worst in me. It's how I cope," he said nonchalantly.

"She's sorry, Savage. Can't that be enough?"

"No. No, that can't be enough," he said, his eyes turning violent. "She's like my own kid sister and I was sick to death worried about her. She's not just your family, Willa."

I went to him and wrapped my arms around him and pressed my face to his chest.

"So, you're an ass because you care?" Duke asked dryly from behind us.

"Pretty much, yeah," Savage said, dragging me closer and burying his face against my blonde hair.

"You're not called Savage for nothing," I pointed out. I pulled away and shot him a smile. "You're always there when I need you. The both of you."

"We got you," Savage said. "Waverly, too."

"I know." I squeezed his hand and then went downstairs to the theater room. Waverly had already opened the couch and was sliding the pillows into their cases.

"I would've helped," I said.

"I know. But I wanted to get it done." She tossed a pillow onto the mattress and sat on the edge of the bed. She started undoing the laces of her heavy boots. "Is Savage still pissed?"

"Sometimes his concern comes off as anger."

She sighed. "Yeah. I didn't think that you'd—and they'd—well, I didn't think about how this all could've played out. I really thought we were going to go to this party and Jessica and I would be able to sneak back to the RV, and no one would be the wiser."

"Mom's gone," I said quietly. "It's you and me now. We can't—I can't—no secrets, Waverly. No lying. Okay? We have to be a team."

"Team." She kicked off her boots and looked at me, nodding. "Where are we going to live?"

"Don't know yet," I said. "We'll figure it out. We always figure it out, don't we?"

She gave a tentative smile. "We do."

There was a soft knock at the top of the stairwell a moment before Duke came down. He held a stack of folded T-shirts and towels. On top were two plastic toothbrushes in their packaging and a tube of toothpaste. He set them down on the bed.

"You guys find everything okay?" he asked.

"Yeah," Waverly said.

"Good. See you guys in the morning."

He turned to head back upstairs, but Waverly called out, "Wait!"

Duke stopped. Waverly ran to him and flung herself into his arms. "Thanks, Duke."

He enveloped her in a bear hug and said, "You're going to be the reason I go gray early, I swear it."

Waverly pulled back and grinned. "Challenge accepted."

He tousled her hair like she was six years old, shot me a smile, and then left us alone.

"You want the orange or the pink toothbrush?" I asked her.

"Orange," she said. "Why does he have brand new toothbrushes for us?"

"Ah…"

"For their random hook-ups the mornings after?" Waverly pressed.

I cocked my head to the side. "How'd you know?"

"I'm fifteen. I'm not stupid."

"Fifteen, right." I opened my toothbrush. "Are you having sex with Dylan?"

"Willa!" Waverly's face flamed immediately, blushing the color of a ripe beefsteak tomato.

I raised my brows. "It's a valid question. He's your boyfriend. You lied about him. You lied about sneaking out, and you were literally just talking about people hooking up. Is it wrong to assume?"

She ripped open the packaging of her toothbrush, her eyes downcast. "No. You're not wrong to assume. But no. I'm not having sex with Dylan."

"Are you doing other things with Dylan?"

Her head whipped up. "Willa!"

"This is serious. I know it's embarrassing, but if you can't even talk about it, then you shouldn't be doing it. Sex can have consequences—"

"I know about the consequences," she snapped. "It's like you're forgetting about Mom. Do I have to remind you that she's been a less-than-stellar role model when it comes to the subject of sex?"

"So, you're still a virgin?"

"Yes."

"Okay." I tried not to be obvious about the relief I felt.

She filched the tube of toothpaste and traipsed toward the bathroom. "So," she began, "are you sleeping with Duke or what?"

Chapter 4

"I'M NOT SLEEPING WITH DUKE." The lie fell from my lips. I'd been saying it for years, because for years it had been true. A twinge of guilt moved through my chest as the moment evolved.

My sister stared at me for a while and then said, "Maybe you should be. He loves you, you know."

"Of course, he loves me. It's Duke."

"That's not what I mean, and you know it."

She sauntered into the bathroom, and I followed. I stood in the doorway while I watched her slather her toothbrush with far too much toothpaste.

"I'm curious what makes you say that." I crossed my arms over my chest and leaned against the doorframe.

"Duke has been in love with you for like, *ever*. The way he looks at you when he thinks no one is looking is the definition of *pining*."

I raised my brows as my heart beat in my chest. I was trying desperately to hide the truth from her, but I wasn't sure I was succeeding.

"I think it's kind of cool." She turned on the faucet.

"To have someone know you that well and still love you for who you are."

God, if only she knew what secrets Duke and I shared.

While she brushed her teeth, I changed into one of Duke's T-shirts, along with a pair of his boxers.

Waverly came out of the bathroom, her face washed and clear of makeup. She suddenly looked younger; innocent.

By the time I was done in the bathroom, Waverly was beneath the covers, her eyes closed. I turned off the light and made my way to the pull-out couch. It was a thin mattress, and I could feel the springs digging into my back, but I was grateful to have my sister next to me and that we were both safe.

I had stopped being mad at my mother years ago. Being angry wouldn't change the truth. She was a crappy parent who put herself first and foremost as a method of survival. Sometimes things happened to people they never recovered from. Mom was one of those people.

Waverly fell asleep quickly, but I lay awake. I tried not to toss and turn so as not to disturb her, but finally, I gave up the fight. I got out of bed and quietly trekked up the stairs to the first floor of the clubhouse. The kitchen and living room lights were off, and I listened for noises coming from any of the bedrooms. There were none. Whoever was here was bedded down for the night.

The second floor was a different story. I heard the sounds of passion coming from behind the closed door of Savage's room. I deduced that he'd called the brunette he'd met at Shelly's before my sister had turned the night upside down.

I gently rapped on Duke's closed door. He opened the door a crack. When he realized it was me, he quickly hauled me into his room. The lamp on the bedside table was on, and it illuminated an unscrewed bottle of Jack Daniel's.

He closed the door.

"You're not asking why I'm here," I whispered.

"There's a reason I didn't go to bed," he countered.

I smiled and gestured in the direction of Savage's room. "I thought it was the moaning and grunting that kept you awake."

"You forgot the occasional ass smacks," he quipped.

I placed my hands over my ears. "Earmuffs."

He chuckled. "You don't want to hear about Savage's sexcapades?"

"Not even a little bit." I dropped my hands from my ears and wandered over to his bed. Without pause, I climbed into it.

Duke sauntered over, settled down next to me, and propped up against the wall. He reached for the bottle of whisky and held it out to me. I shook my head. He took a sip and then screwed on the lid before setting it down again. He shut off the lamp. Without a word, he pulled me into his arms and rolled us over so he spooned me.

After a few deep breaths, I slipped blissfully into sleep.

"Willa," Duke whispered.

"Hmm?" I asked, keeping my eyes closed. I was in that perfect state of being awake but completely able to go back to sleep.

"It's five in the morning," he said. "You might want to get back downstairs before anyone realizes where you are."

My eyes sprung open and I shot up, accidentally colliding my skull with Duke's.

"Fuck," he hissed.

I rubbed my head. "Shit, I'm sorry."

"It's fine," he muttered.

"Thanks for waking me up."

"You know, if this was out in the open, you could've stayed here until you woke up. We wouldn't have to sneak around."

I scooted down the bed until I got to the end and then stood up. "It's too early for this fight."

"Not a fight, Willa. A conversation."

The lamp came on and I winced. "Then it's too early for a conversation."

I walked around the bed and leaned over and kissed his lips quickly. But before I could make my escape, he grasped the back of my neck and hauled me closer. I fell into him, our mouths tangling with an illicit goodbye.

Duke released me, looking far too cocky this early in the morning. I knew what he was capable of when he was fully awake, and he had that look about him now. I needed to get back downstairs before I demanded a quickie.

It didn't help that he dipped his hand into his boxers and began stroking himself.

"I have to get downstairs," I whispered.

"You don't have three minutes?"

"Three minutes? Three minutes for what?"

"For us both to get off. Touch yourself, Willa. I want to watch."

"Duke, I—"

"You're wasting time," he growled. "And I'm already close. Woke up with your gorgeous ass pressed against me. You know what I wanted to do to wake you up? I wanted to slide my hand into your panties, play with you until you were nice and wet, and then I'd slip my finger all the way inside you, and then add another. And when you were slippery and hot, tender, needy, *begging*, I'd gently remove my fingers."

His eyes were on me as he stroked himself harder.

With a dry swallow, I glided my hand into the boxers I wore, pressing my fingers against myself.

"You know what I'd do next?" His voice was raspy, like it was taking all of his concentration to paint a dirty picture.

I shook my head.

"I'd take off your panties and then I'd grasp your hip, holding you in place, while I thrust into you from behind. I'd rock against you until I was all the way in, until you couldn't tell where you stopped and I began, but then I wouldn't move. I'd throb so deep inside you that you could feel it, and you'd wriggle that hot ass against me, needing me to get you off."

My skin was on fire as my fingers danced across my swollen flesh. Our gazes were locked on each other as I stood in front of him.

"And I'd get you off, Willa. I'd make sure you were so well satisfied that when I pulled out of you, you cried at the loss of me. You deserve to be sore between your legs. You deserve to remember what a night of hot fucking feels like when you're living your life during the day, trying to keep it all together for everyone around you. But at night, and in the morning, I'd remind you that you had nothing to do but lay down and let me make you come."

"Duke." I groaned out his name.

"Yeah, babe. Say my name. Think of me fucking you from behind. Think of waking up every morning to me filling you."

I was so close. His words were liquid fire that shot straight to my core. I imagined it was his fingers touching me, not my own.

He grunted softly, his hand working himself harder and faster, until his breath hitched and he was coming. His release triggered my own and I came.

When the tremors subsided, I slowly removed my hand from the boxers I wore and headed for the exit. With my heart racing, I made it down to the theater room without seeing anyone.

Waverly's soft, steady breathing let me know she was still sound asleep. I climbed into bed next to my sister, Duke's words playing over and over in my head.

Chapter 5

"Morning, sleepy head," Mia said, greeting me with a smile thrown over her shoulder.

I blinked as I sat down on a kitchen stool. "What time is it?"

"A little after nine. I thought for sure we'd woken you up, what with Captain barking when we came in and Scarlett crying."

"Did you close Shelly's last night?" I asked.

Mia flipped a pancake in the pan and shook her head, brown hair sliding off her shoulder. "No, but it was a late night, what with the second rush. Scarlett was up at the ass crack of dawn, too. I'm a train wreck."

She set the spatula down and went to a cupboard, opened it, and pulled out a mug. She poured hot, fresh coffee into the cup and set it down in front of me.

"Thanks," I said.

"You look like you need it." She winked and turned back around.

I grabbed the carton of cream on the counter in front

of me and poured a hefty amount into the cup. "Have you seen Waverly?" I asked.

"She's helping Joni get some stuff out of her car."

"Joni's here?" I asked.

"Yeah." Mia finished the stack of pancakes and set them down in front of me. "Eat."

"Smells amazing," I said. "Thanks for this." I doused the short stack with butter and syrup and then cut a bite.

"Duke called Colt last night," she said, reaching for a blue coffee mug and leaning against the counter, facing me. "After he brought you here."

"Did he?" I asked, bowing my head. "So, you know…"

"That your mom took off in the RV with all your earthly belongings and now you and Waverly don't have a place to live. Yes."

"Blunt is your middle name, isn't it?" I asked with a sigh.

The president's Old Lady looked at me with understanding. "It's not easy to ask for help. Believe me. I know. So, I'm going to do what the other Old Ladies did for me when I needed a hand. I'm going to force you to accept the help because that's what family does."

She pulled a set of keys out of her back jeans pocket and set them down in front of me.

"What's this?"

"Keys to your rental," she said. "Brooklyn and Slash were the last of the club to live there, but he bought her a house and she's in nesting mode in their new place so the rental is empty."

"I've been there," I said. "It's cute."

"Waverly can have her own room. So can you," she said gently. "It's safe and clean, and you can stay as long as you want. But the price is better than anything you can find on the market right now."

I raised a brow. "I don't want you to cut me a deal on rent…"

Mia shrugged. "It's my house and I'll do what I want."

"I'm paying," I insisted.

"Of course, you are." She smiled. "As someone else who hates charity, I get it. Believe me. Now, eat your breakfast."

"Yes, Ma'am," I said, relief curling in my belly. Waverly and I would have a place to sleep. A real place, too. With a roof that wasn't literally taped together to try and keep the rain out.

That was the thing about the Tarnished Angels. They took care of people they thought of as family.

The front door of the clubhouse opened, and Joni waddled inside carrying two canvas bags. Waverly followed with another few bags.

"Hey," Joni said to me. "You're awake. Awesome. Now I can see if my jeans fit you."

"Your jeans?"

Joni lifted the bags. "My pre-pregnancy jeans. We're nearly the same height, so I figured it was worth a shot. There's some other stuff in here too."

"Wait," I said. "I'm not following."

Waverly set the bags down by the couch and then sauntered over to the counter. She took my fork and cut herself a bite of pancake. "Mia gave me her pre-Scarlett clothes—her words not mine—and Joni is giving you her pre-pregnancy clothes. So now I won't have to wear the leather corset you're mad that I stole from you."

I grabbed her nose and gave it a tweak. "Jerk."

"You gonna finish these?" she asked.

I dropped her nose and shook my head, pushing the plate toward her.

"Can I show you my favorite pair of jeans?" Joni asked. "They'll make your ass look great. I should know. They caused this to happen." She pointed to her stomach.

"What caused what?" the vice president of the Tarnished Angels asked, striding in from the back, holding a baby. He marched to Mia. "Your husband wanted me to give you this."

Mia took the baby. "Hungry, needs changing, what?"

"Yes," Zip said. He looked away from Mia to his pregnant wife, a roguish grin on his face.

"I stand corrected," Joni drawled. "It wasn't just the jeans. It was those jeans and *that* smile... That's why I got pregnant."

I hastily tossed the jeans in question at Joni. "You keep them. I don't want that kind of energy."

"Suit yourself," Joni said, folding up the pants. "But I'm not allowed to wear these again until I'm ready for another baby. Because knowing Zip, it'll be a one shot, done deal."

Zip wrapped an arm around his wife's shoulders. "I love it when you compliment my sperm."

Waverly choked on her food.

"Look what you've done to the poor kid," Joni said.

"This poor kid is taking these pancakes to go," Waverly said, picking up the plate and beelining it to the theater room stairs.

"Thanks," I said to Zip.

Zip frowned. "For what?"

"For scaring Waverly away from ever having sex."

"Oh man," Mia whined. "Scarlett just blew out her diaper and got it all over me!"

"Quick, get her back here," Joni said. "We can double whammy her. She won't have sex for years."

Mia sighed and wrinkled her nose as she kept the baby pressed to her chest. "Excuse me while I go deal with the consequences of my actions."

I wasn't sure how I felt about the fact that the Old Ladies —and by proxy—all the Tarnished Angels knew what my mother had done. If it was just me, I'd figure out a way on my own. But I had Waverly, and she'd been through enough upheaval. The fact was, we needed help.

My phone rang as I buttoned up a pair of Joni's jeans. They fit like a glove and I was instantly in love. I fished underneath a pile of clothes to find my cell and answered it.

"You're either calling to tell me you're changing the café menu and I have to update your website, or you're calling because of the Old Ladies group text and you know about me chasing my fifteen-year-old sister around the city last night, only to discover she has a secret boyfriend and then later get news that our mom hitched up the RV and bounced, and that Waverly and I are moving into Mia's rental."

"It's not to update my website," Brooklyn said. "And I'm going to need more details on all of that. I just heard that you were moving into Mia's rental and I was wondering what I can do to help. I'm sort of in the nesting phase of my pregnancy and I'm worried I'm about to start crocheting table cozies."

I chuckled. "You could just crochet scarves."

"We're in Texas. There are like three days a year you need a scarf. We're getting off topic."

"I don't need anything," I assured her. "We're good."

"Okay, but you ask if you need anything, alright?"

"I will."

She sighed.

"What? What's that sigh mean?"

"It means you won't ask for help even if you need help because you're inherently stubborn and independent."

"Sure, that's the reason. We don't need to unpack that trauma over the phone."

"We could unpack it over coffee and a quiche. I'll be at the bakery Monday morning."

"I'll swing by after I drop Waverly off at school," I said.

"Bye, girl."

"Bye."

I hung up and tossed my phone aside.

"Your ass looks amazing in those jeans," Duke said.

I whirled. "Don't sneak up on me."

He raised his brows. "I wear boots and there's no carpet. There's no sneaking."

"You're not allowed to just comment on my ass," I said.

"We're sleeping together in private." He took a step toward me. "Doesn't that warrant me complimenting your ass?"

I hastily put my hand over his mouth. "Someone might hear you."

His brown eyes twinkled with devilish humor and then he kissed my palm.

I yanked my hand away, tingles shooting through my body.

"How'd you sleep?" Duke asked.

"Fine." I blushed.

I wasn't the blushing type, and I'd known Duke forever. But what we'd done...

"Glad to hear it."

"Did you just come down here to compliment my ass or was there another reason?" I asked, my lips quivering in humor.

"You want to get breakfast?"

"Mia made pancakes."

"When am I going to see you again?"

"Probably tonight when I call you and Savage to help me put together an IKEA shelf."

"That's not what I meant."

"I know what you meant and the answer is I don't know. I kind of just became a full-time caregiver and, oh shit, I forgot to tell Laura an emergency popped up and I won't make it in for my shift. Fuck."

"It's been taken care of," he said.

I rubbed the back of my neck. "Of course it has. This is what happens when your entire life is wrapped up with the Tarnished Angels."

"The club fronted Laura the money for Leather and Ink. She gets club money; she gets club life. That's the way it works."

"She's the best boss," I said. "Super understanding, what with who I run around with."

"Back to my question," he said.

"I don't know." I put my hand to his chest.

He covered my hand with his and sighed. "Call me when you need help with the IKEA stuff."

"You promise to read the manual?"

"I promise to pretend to read the manual."

I smiled and leaned in to kiss his cheek. "Thanks."

"We'll bring the pizza and beer."

I reluctantly dropped my hand. I would've liked to stay in that moment for a while longer, but my sister was upstairs, along with everyone else.

"Has Savage's lady of the night left?"

"As far as I know they haven't even come out of his bedroom yet."

"That poor girl," I said with a laugh. "She'll be ruined, you know."

"You think so?" he asked.

I started folding clothes and putting them back in the bags. "Definitely. I heard the noises coming from his room. Ruined for all others. I'm sure of it."

"What about you?" he asked.

"What about me what?"

"Did I ruin you for all others?"

"Hey, can we *please* go!" Waverly asked as she traipsed down the stairs. "I have to call Dylan and I'd like to do it in private."

"Who said you're going to be talking to Dylan?" I demanded.

Waverly's eyes widened and her lips began to quiver. "My mother abandoned me."

"Okay, but you can't play that card again for the next six months," I stated.

Her face straightened immediately and she saluted me.

"Shit, one problem," I said. "I just realized I don't have my car."

Duke removed a set of keys from his leather cut and handed them to me. "Gotta love prospects."

"How do I get that kind of power?" Waverly asked.

"The price is too high," I joked.

"Savage and I are bringing pizza over to your new place tonight," Duke said to Waverly, wrapping his arm around her neck. "Any requests?"

"Pineapple and ham."

"Ew. No," I said.

"One purist pepperoni and the other adventurous. Got it," Duke said.

"I'm the fun sister," Waverly said.

She turned back around and marched up the stairs.

Duke opened his mouth to say something and I said, "Don't. Just don't."

Chapter 6

"WE GET TO LIVE HERE?" Waverly asked.

"Yes."

"Seriously?"

"Seriously. You've been over here before."

"Yeah, but this was Brooklyn's place." Waverly's mouth was agog as she whirled around the living room. She bumped into the couch that had once belonged in the clubhouse. "This is way nicer than the RV—which, let's face it, isn't hard to beat."

"It's also nicer than that motel we had to stay in for two weeks."

"Oh, I forgot about that," Waverly said.

Good. It means she doesn't remember the roaches.

"You get your own room," I said.

"No."

I nodded. "You do."

"Which one do I get?" she asked.

"Which ever one you want," I said, my throat constricting with emotion.

"No fighting over the bigger room?"

I smiled. "No."

"No Rock Paper Scissors?"

"Nope."

She launched herself at me. "You really love me, don't you?"

"More than anything." I patted her. "More than anything."

Waverly pulled away and grabbed my hand, dragging me in the direction of the bedrooms, which were dramatically different sizes.

"I don't feel right about taking the bigger bedroom," she said quietly. "You're going to need a desk to work."

"So are you," I said.

"But you wanted to buy a dual monitor for your web design business." Her lip quivered. "Mom leaving really fucked up your finances, didn't it?"

"It'll be fine," I lied. "Better than fine. Whatever furniture you want, you get, but…"

"We probably won't be able to go to New York for my sixteenth birthday." Her shoulders slumped.

"Probably not," I said. "But we'll make it happen at some point."

She blinked watery blue eyes at me. "Really? Or will something else derail our lives before we get to go?"

"Who knows," I said. "But that's the fun of it, right? The roller coaster of life?"

"Roller coasters make me puke."

"That was only once at Six Flags, and it was because I let you have an entire funnel cake first."

"It's weird, you know," she said.

"What is?"

"All my best memories are because you made them happen. Not Mom. You."

"You're killing me, kid," I groaned. "Seriously. I'm going to start crying any minute now."

"Tears make me uncomfortable," she teased.

"Then I'll make sure to bawl."

She laughed, but the look on her face said the moment was impactful.

"Come on, let's go pick out some cheap furniture that Duke and Savage have to put together."

I locked up the house and we headed down the front walk that was lined with blooming yellow and pink flowers.

"Where were you this morning?" Waverly asked as she buckled herself into the passenger side of my car.

"What do you mean?"

"I rolled over early and you weren't there. And you definitely were *not* in the bathroom at the clubhouse."

"Oh," I said, feeling my insides heat. "I was hanging out with Duke. I couldn't sleep."

"Hanging out, huh?"

"Why do you say it like that," I demanded. "We *were* hanging out. I don't have to defend myself to you."

"Who's defending?"

"Have you called Jessica?" I asked, deliberately changing the subject.

"No, I'm mad at her. Are you going to call her parents?"

"Yes," I said automatically.

"Her parents won't let us hang out if you do that," she pointed out.

"It's probably for the better," I said. "You guys should chill out for a while. We've got a lot of stuff to get sorted with Mom gone…"

She looked out the window as we drove. "What do I tell the school?"

"Nothing," I said. "You tell them nothing because if

you tell them anything about Mom, they'll get CPS involved and that's a whole mess we don't want, okay?"

"She drove off with my books!"

"I'll go in Monday morning and talk to your principal. Books can be replaced."

"What are you going to say?" Waverly asked.

"I'll tell him that you left your backpack on the bus and it was stolen. If we can get through the next couple of months without them knowing Mom bailed, we have some time to figure stuff out before the school year this fall."

"So, you want me to *lie* to my teachers and my principal?"

"Yes."

She grinned. "Okay. I can do that."

I pointed a finger at her. "Just no lying to me, yeah?"

Waverly grabbed my finger and gave it a little tug. "No lying to the big sister who is buying me Swedish furniture that's impossible to assemble."

"We better get going. We still have to hit the grocery store."

"Can I drive home from the grocery store?" she asked, her blue eyes wide and pleading.

"Yes. But no speeding."

"I don't speed."

"Waverly."

"Fine. No speeding."

∼

"You don't have to do this," Waverly said.

I forced a smile. "This isn't for you. This is for me."

"When did cheap furniture become so expensive?" Waverly demanded as we strung up the twinkly lights. We were in the middle of turning the biggest bedroom in the house into a fairy fort like I'd done for Waverly's seventh birthday.

"No idea," I said.

"We should've just asked Duke."

"We should've just asked Duke what?" I queried.

She raised her brows.

"Is that expression supposed to mean something to me?"

"You don't think I heard your breath hitch when you handed over your credit card for the mattresses? We bought the lowest end twin ones and they were still a lot of money."

"And you think, what, if we asked Duke for some financial help we'd be better off?"

"Wouldn't we be? He's got the money. You know he does."

"I don't know anything about Duke's finances," I lied. "Besides, friends don't ask friends to loan them money. And I don't want you worrying about money. I've got it covered."

"I worry about money because we've always had to worry about money," she pointed out. "Mom really tried to pitch the idea that living in an RV would be an adventure, but that thing she bought… An RV is only an adventure if it's actually nice and you take it to see cool places—which I guess is what she's doing now with some random guy instead of us."

"I'll get another job," I said. "I'll get a bartending gig. Something that pays cash."

"Why don't *I* get the job?" she asked. "You already work really hard, Willa. This shouldn't all be on you. I can pitch in. Let me pitch in."

"You're sweet to offer, but I want you to focus on school, which you should be doing—and not getting

47

distracted by your boyfriend's green eyes when he tutors you."

"You know Dylan's my tutor." She sighed. "Yeah, I probably should've told you that one, too."

"Yeah, you should've. But I won't rag on you for it. I don't like ragging, contrary to popular belief."

"But you're so good at it, big sister turned maternal figure."

"You're far too smart and quippy."

"What about a summer job?" Her cornflower blue eyes were earnest. "I can find something. I know I can find something that pays under the table."

"What can you do?" I asked with a smile.

"You're mocking me," she accused.

"I'm really not," I assured her. "I just want—hell, there will be plenty of time to work. Okay? Let me handle this."

The doorbell rang.

"That's Duke and Savage," I said. "Will you answer it? I'll finish up in here."

Waverly left the bedroom, and I went to the cardboard box full of fake flowers.

I heard their voices in the living room, followed by the closing of the front door.

A knock resounded on the doorframe, and I looked to find Duke staring at me.

"Hey," he said.

"Hey."

"Pizza's here."

I sent him a small smile. "Yeah, I gathered as much."

"Got your favorite beer, too."

"Thanks. I'll be out in a second. Just want to finish up."

Duke pushed away from leaning against the doorframe and came into the room. Without a word, he marched over to the box and lifted a yellow flower and wound it around the twinkle light strand.

"It looks like Waverly's seventh birthday," he commented.

Color suffused my cheeks. "Ah, yeah."

"I still think about that birthday cake you made her," he said with a grin, tinged with memory and fondness. "Yellow cake with chocolate icing and star sprinkles."

"Lopsided and undercooked because the oven heated unevenly."

"The smile on Waverly's face when she realized what you'd done for her," he said, his voice soft.

Emotion from years past caused my throat to constrict, and tears blurred my eyes.

"It was a good birthday, Willa," he said.

I nodded and found a way to get my feelings in check. "Yeah. I guess it was."

"And you wanted to recreate it by making a fairy fort?" He took another flower—red this time—and twined it around the strand of lights.

"We were shopping all afternoon," I said. I looked at the doorway and couldn't see Savage or Waverly from my spot, but I pitched my voice lower anyway. "I could only afford brand new mattresses, but no frames to go with them. They won't even be delivered until next week, so we're sleeping on an air mattress." I gripped a flower in my hand, the synthetic petals crimping in my palm.

"We went to the craft and fabric store to get all this." I gestured to the blue toile fabric. "Waverly picked this out. And then we went to the thrift store to buy dishes and cookware. Found her a desk and a dresser, but my car isn't big enough to get them here."

"I'll get one of the prospects to handle it," Duke said, taking out his cell phone. "Which thrift store?"

"You don't have to do this," I said.

"Do what?" He looked up from his cell.

"Help. That's not your job. I mean, Jesus, Duke, it feels like all I do is ask you for things."

"You didn't ask, I'm offering. Which store?"

I told him.

"Crow will take care of it, okay?" he said.

"Thanks."

"You look sad." He took a step forward and reached for me, but at the last minute he dropped his arms, as if he remembered we weren't alone.

"I am sad," I said quietly. "So fucking sad. Mom still hasn't checked in. I called her once and left a voicemail, and I wouldn't care that much if it were just me, but Waverly, you know? Doesn't even get the courtesy of a goodbye or an explanation."

"That would mean Angel thinks of other people aside from herself." He hooked an arm around my shoulder in a friendly manner, and suddenly, I wanted to be able to press myself against him and let him hold me. But if I did that… it would mean I was admitting that things had changed between us. And right now, I couldn't handle any more change.

My life was nothing *but* change, and the only thing that mattered was ensuring Waverly had some stability. I had to be her port in the storm.

"You still pissed at your sister for the shit she put you through?" Duke asked as we headed to the doorway. I hit the bedroom light.

"Pissed is the wrong word. Scared, I think. She's at that age, Duke. It could go either way. And I'm just—maybe it's wrong that I didn't come down really hard on her. But she's sorry, and we have bigger fish to fry."

Duke and I entered the kitchen. Savage and Waverly were standing at the counter, eating pizza.

"We should've waited," Waverly said with a mouthful of food. "But then we didn't."

I smirked. "Nice explanation."

Duke dropped his arm from around me and I walked to Savage. He instantly hauled me against him and embraced me.

"Smells good," I said. "Thanks."

"Yeah, thanks," Waverly muttered before diving back into her piece of pie that was halfway gone.

"Dude, chew," Savage said to my sister, laughing and then taking a sip of his beer.

Duke went over to the fridge and pulled out two bottles. He took his keyring with the bottle opener on it and quickly flicked off the beer caps. He handed me one and I took a drink.

Savage flipped open a pizza box and the smell of pepperoni and cheese wafted to my nose.

I picked up a paper towel and then a pepperoni slice and handed them both to Duke. He set his beer down and took them from me. Then I took my own piece and dug in. It was perfect, especially after the day I'd had running all over town trying to put together a house with little to no financial resources.

"Just so you know," Savage said as he swallowed a huge bite of pizza. "LP and I are okay."

I frowned. "LP?" I looked at my sister. "What does LP stand for?"

Waverly grinned. "Little Punk."

I let out a laugh. "No better nickname for you."

"Can I have a sip of your beer?" Waverly asked with a teasing twinkle in her eye.

"Chill, LP," Savage said. "At least until you find a way to get a fake ID."

"Savage!" I shoved away from him.

He shrugged. "If you can't beat 'em, join 'em."

"She'll never make it to adulthood," I complained. "Not if you aid and abet her."

"Someone's gotta teach her," Savage said. "Might as well learn from the best."

"Yeah, that would be me," Duke said. "I'm the one who taught her how to defend herself."

"And that knowledge almost got her kicked out of school," I pointed out.

"I'm standing right here," Waverly complained.

Her cell phone vibrated across the counter and Jessica's name appeared on the screen. Waverly looked at me. "Can I take this?"

I sighed. "Sure."

Waverly picked up her cell phone and put it to her ear. "Hey, girl. Gimme a sec." She grabbed another piece of ham and pineapple pizza and trekked toward the bedroom. The door closed and I could no longer hear my sister.

Savage looked at me, a teasing grin on his face. And then I looked at Duke.

My boys. My family.

And the only reason I'd gotten through the crazy things life had thrown at me over the years.

"No fake ID's," I said to Savage.

"Yeah, yeah."

"I mean it," I warned.

"Oooh, hot teacher voice. I like it."

"Savage," I snapped.

"No fake ID's. I promise."

The washer beeped. I set my pizza crust down and

wiped my greasy fingers on a paper towel. I changed out the sheets and put them in the dryer. I pressed a couple of buttons and a few seconds later they were tumbling. By the time Duke and Savage left, they'd be dry.

This had felt like the longest day of my life.

I was halfway done with my beer when I realized Waverly was still in the bedroom, though I had a sneaking suspicion that she had long been off the phone with Jessica and was now talking to Dylan. I still didn't know how I felt about him—after all, it wasn't like I *knew* him, or had spent any amount of time with him.

Savage poked my forehead. "What's got you upset?"

"Waverly's boyfriend," I said. "I don't know anything about him."

I took my beer and went to the couch and plopped down. Duke grabbed another few beers and Savage picked up the pizza boxes and brought them over.

"I could find out about him," Savage said.

I raised my brows. "By tracking him down and intimidating him?"

"Nah, that would be so…henchman-like." Savage set the pizza boxes onto the coffee table and then sat next to me. "I could do a background check."

"That's a little extreme, don't you think?" I asked. "Let's do this the old-fashioned way and just get to know him."

"The kid is smitten with Waverly. I don't think he's going anywhere," Duke added, sitting on the other side of me so I was sandwiched between them. "We gotta know more about this guy."

"I'm surprised you didn't already get him checked out," I accused him. "After all, you knew about this long before the rest of us."

The bedroom door opened, and Waverly strode out. Her cheeks were flushed, and I narrowed my eyes at her.

"So, how's Jessica? You guys okay?" I asked knowingly.

"Yeah, we're fine." She bit her thumbnail. "Dylan called while I was on the phone with her. I talked to him for a bit."

Savage grinned and pointed at her face. "Yeah, we can see that."

"Savage!" She flushed harder, turned around, and marched back into the bedroom. The door slammed shut with teenage embarrassment.

I elbowed Savage in the ribs. "Nice going. I thought you guys were okay."

"We are okay." He smiled. "I was just doing my job and embarrassing the hell out of her like the brotherly sort that I am."

"But you don't have to make *my* life harder, do you?" I demanded, swiping the beer from Savage and taking a sip before handing it back to him. "If you'll excuse me, I'm gonna go do some damage control."

Chapter 7

I knocked on the bedroom door and a moment later Waverly called, "Come in."

The main light was off, but she'd plugged in the twinkle lights. She was lying on the air mattress, her black Doc Marten covered feet sticking out of the fairy fort.

"Hey," I said as I squatted down and grabbed her foot.

"Hey."

"You sound far too morose after just having spoken to your boyfriend," I teased. "Scooch over."

She wiggled her body over and I flopped down next to her.

"Talk to me," I said.

"I hate how he teases me," she mumbled.

"So, tell him that."

"Yeah. Like he'd listen."

"You might be surprised," I said. "Is that all this is about?"

"Savage is overprotective," she said. "I get it. I'm like his little sister. But I have a boyfriend. And I want Dylan to be comfortable around you…around them. But I don't want Savage teasing me in front of Dylan. You know?"

"Ah," I said. "I think I get it now. You want to seem really cool in front of your boyfriend, who you know I won't let you see if I don't get to at least hang out with him long enough to ascertain if he's worthy of you."

She sat up and tossed the pillow she was hugging to her chest to the bed. "That was a lot of words. I need you to promise to keep Savage on a leash anytime Dylan's around, okay?"

"What makes you think I can keep Savage on a leash?" I asked in amusement. "His biker name is literally *Savage*."

"How'd he get that name, anyway?"

"You'll have to ask him," I said evasively.

"Will he tell me?"

"Probably not."

"Dang. Now I really want to know."

I wrapped my arm around her shoulder. "I do want to meet Dylan. Like really meet him."

"Yeah," she said glumly. "It was his idea, actually."

"Sounds like he's trying to be a good influence on you."

"I'm terrified it might actually work," she said with a laugh.

"Hey! You guys better get out here and entertain us or we're leaving!" Savage shouted.

"Why do we let him hang around?" Waverly asked as she slid off the air mattress.

"Because he brings us pizza," I said.

"Right, that. Very important. Can you promise me something?"

"Anything."

"When you meet Dylan, can it just be the three of us? I don't want—well, I'd really like not to scare him off."

I grinned. "The fact that he's still calling and wanting to officially get grilled by me says a lot about his character."

"He got past my rough exterior," Waverly said as she opened the door. "He's something special."

~

Monday morning, I was jarred awake by my vibrating phone. With a groan, I fished for my cell and found it underneath my pillow.

DUKE

My hand is wrapped around my dick and I'm thinking about you.

"Who's texting you?" Waverly asked.

I quickly shoved my phone back underneath my pillow and then yawned wide enough that my jaw cracked. "Brooklyn," I lied. "Reminding me to come to the bakery after I drop you off at school."

"Hmm."

My phone vibrated again. I discreetly reached underneath my pillow and glanced at my cell, but the screen was dark.

It took my sluggish brain a moment to realize it was Waverly's phone that had buzzed.

"Who's texting *you*?" I asked.

"Dylan." She rolled onto her back, her face lit up from the screen.

"Ah, young love," I quipped.

"We're not in love," she stated reflexively. She hastily sat up and moved her tangled hair out of her face. "I'm gonna shower first, okay?"

"Take it," I agreed.

I turned off my alarm that was supposed to go off in fifteen minutes and then I typed out a reply to Duke.

ME

You can't text me shit like that.

A moment later, my phone vibrated.

DUKE

Why not? You make me hard. And if you were here right now, I'd roll you over and slide—

"I got the coffee started," Waverly announced from the doorway of the bedroom.

I jumped and my phone slipped out of my hand. "Thanks!" I squeaked.

Despite not wanting to be my dirty little secret he seemed to be embracing it, toying with me so that I kept coming back for more of him.

I got up, shot a text to my mother on the off chance she'd answer, and then knocked on the bathroom door.

"Come in!" Waverly called.

"You mind if I brush my teeth?"

"Go for it," she said. "Man, I'm not going to lie. I know Mom was trying to sell the awesomeness of the RV and trying to get me pumped for a summer road trip, but those twelve-minute showers before the hot water ran out were not fun."

I didn't have the heart to tell her why we'd moved into an RV in the first place, so I said, "Yeah, those showers weren't fun. You know what else wasn't fun? The tight quarters."

"We're still sharing a room," she pointed out.

"Makes sense though," I said. "Then we can use the spare room as an office with two desks."

"It is a better use of space," she agreed. "You were right about the fairy fort. Camping in it is kind of awesome. But don't tell anyone I said that. It would ruin my street cred."

Grinning, I shoved my toothbrush into my mouth and started brushing.

"I'm going to have to rebuild my entire wardrobe," she said, shutting off the water. "Mia's clothes fit, but they're kinda…"

"Kinda what?" I asked in amusement.

"Adult. I don't adult. Still, it was really nice of her to lend me some stuff."

"I'm sure she wouldn't mind if you Waverly-ed it up."

"Whatever that means." Her arm stuck out of the shower to grab the towel hanging on the rack.

"I just meant you'll find a way to make the clothes feel like yours, with your own style and personal flare."

"Oh, flare." She pulled the shower curtain back and stepped out onto the bathmat, her red hair slicked back away from her face, the towel wrapped around her body.

She glanced at me and grinned, suddenly looking impish. "There is one thing you forgot to do to make this weekend in the fairy fort perfect."

My face fell. "I forgot something?"

"You didn't bake me a yellow cake with chocolate icing. But I was thinking, we could do that later? When I get home from school?"

She sounded so hopeful.

"You want to put Brooklyn's lessons to use, huh?" I asked. "Thank God someone in this family has some skill in the kitchen."

Waverly bumped her hip against mine.

"I'll bring home the bacon and you can fry it up."

"It's like you've got a wife in the 50s," she quipped.

"I'll get the supplies and pick you up from school. Okay?"

"Okay. Just…you and me, right? No one else?" she asked.

I frowned. "No one else? What do you mean?"

"I mean no Duke and no Savage."

I cocked my head to the side. "Why Waverly Jean, I do declare. You actually want to spend time with your older sister?"

"Shocking, I know," she teased. "But I actually like you."

"You do? Huh. Who knew."

"Come back tomorrow, my answer might have changed."

"Little Punk," I groused, causing her to laugh. "Bathroom's all yours."

"Willa," Waverly hissed, hoisting her new black backpack over her shoulder and glaring at me.

"What?" I demanded.

"Stop walking that way."

"Stop walking what way?" I asked.

"You know." She mimicked an exaggerated hip wiggle only seen on model reality shows or the fashion runway.

"I don't look like that," I said.

"Oh, please. Did you have to wear a leather skirt and heels?" She rolled her eyes and pointed to the group of high school boys sitting on a brick wall. "They're staring."

"Got it." I slumped my shoulders and then shuffled like Lurch from The Addams Family toward the entrance of Waverly's school.

"Willa!" she snapped.

"I don't know what you want from me," I said. "And we're kind of on a time crunch here. Your first bell is in fifteen minutes. Let's get inside and talk to your principal."

"Did you have to wear that?" she muttered as she scuttled ahead of me.

I sighed. Waverly would've been upset if I'd worn jeans and a hoodie.

"Cut the 'tude, dude," I called after her.

"You know what," she whirled, "I'll handle this myself. Okay? I'll talk to the principal and if I have problems, I'll let you know. I'll see you later."

"I'll be here at 3:30," I promised her.

She gave a haphazard wave and disappeared inside.

Chapter 8

It wasn't even eight in the morning and I felt like I'd already had a day. I shot off a text to my boss at Leather and Ink and asked her to give me a buzz when she had a moment, and then I drove to Pie in the Sky.

A cheery bell jangled in greeting as I walked into the bakery that had recently expanded to include a café. Jazz was behind the counter, her brown braid slung over one shoulder, a welcoming smile on her face as she handed a customer a to-go cup and a paper bag full of baked goods.

He set the paper bag on the counter so he could reach into his pocket and pull out a few bills, which he then dropped into the tip jar.

"That smile of yours," I said to her as I approached the counter. "How much of it is genuine and how much of it is caffeine induced?"

"About fifty-fifty," she admitted. She cocked her head to the side. "Brooklyn said you were coming by this morning. But why are you—Jesus, you're wearing those *heels*! Aren't your feet killing you? And that leather skirt... I'd ask to borrow it, but I'd swim in it."

"Is that your way of saying I look nice this morning?" I teased.

"Nice," she agreed. "And ready for world domination."

"Ah, just the aesthetic I was going for."

"What do you want this morning? Caramel, mocha, hazelnut?"

"Yes. With a ton of whipped cream and an extra shot of espresso, please."

"That kind of morning?"

I rubbed the bridge of my nose. "That kind of weekend."

She frowned. "What happened?"

"Are the girls in back?"

"Brooklyn is in the kitchen making quiche. Brielle is in there too, icing a wedding cake. I'm making you a surprise concoction and then I'll bring it to you. Do not tell them anything until I'm there to hear it. I need this story from start to finish."

"Okay, General."

"If you're calling me a title, can you call me Admiral? They have better outfits."

I headed into the back kitchen. It smelled like sugar and eggs. Brooklyn was standing at the large island, chopping tomatoes. A carton of 48 eggs rested next to her. A huge metal bowl with a large handle was off to the side, ready to be placed underneath a professional mixer.

Brielle's blue eyes were intently focused on a six-tiered wedding cake at another station. A piece of red hair escaped from behind her ear and fell forward. With a grumble, she blew it out of her face.

"Hey, girl," Brooklyn greeted, quickly glancing up at me before diving back into cutting veggies. Her fair cheeks were flushed from the heat of the kitchen.

"Hey." I grabbed a stool and moved it into the corner so I wouldn't be in the way.

Brielle set down the pastry bag full of white frosting and wiped her hands on her apron. "I kind of hate you a little bit."

"Me? Why?" I asked with a laugh.

"Because you look like *that*."

"Like what?" I demanded.

"Like a vixen on steroids."

"Uh, thanks?"

"You do look quite…" Brooklyn paused as she surveyed me. "Unusually put together."

"I was supposed to have a meeting with Waverly's principal. Hold on, though, I'm not allowed to say anything until Jazz is back here."

"Is this an exciting story?" Brooklyn asked. "Please let this be exciting. I need some excitement in my life. Slash has entered overprotective mode."

"He just loves you," I pointed out.

"Yes, yes he does." She grinned. "But he texts constantly, asks about swollen ankles, and demands to know if I've had enough water. He's worse than my OB."

"You're not seriously complaining about your dreamboat of a husband. Your hot, inked, will-do-anything-for-you dreamboat of a husband," Brielle said.

"Not seriously complaining, no. But if he had it his way, I'd be on bed rest until the baby is born. I'd go completely bonkers."

"I still think it's sweet," Brielle said.

"Speaking of sweet," Jazz said as she came into the kitchen. She held a to-go cup of coffee without the lid and a plate with a doughy biscuit looking thing.

"What is that?" I asked, pointing to the plate.

"A *kolache*. It's got cheese, eggs, and hashbrowns in it. Hearty, savory breakfast," Jazz explained.

"I was promised quiche, but I'm intrigued by the *kolache*." I smiled. "And what is that?"

Jazz raised the coffee. "This, right here, is a work of art."

The work of art in question had a two-inch-high crest of whipped cream.

"It's a mocha caramel swirl with three shots of espresso and a mountain of whipped cream," Jazz said, setting them both down on the wooden island.

I got up off the stool and moved it closer. "Thanks, Jazz. I might need a shot of insulin after this, but I think it'll be worth it."

"Most definitely," Jazz agreed. "Kaley and Beatrice just clocked in. So, the front is covered while we get the skinny on your weekend."

"How am I supposed to drink this?" I asked, reaching for the coffee.

"Didn't think of that," Jazz said, nibbling her lip. "Let me get you a spoon."

"Nah, it's fine. I'll lick it like an ice cream cone," I said in amusement.

"Okay, enough about the coffee," Brielle said.

Brooklyn continued to chop vegetables while I relayed to them what had happened with Waverly. I told them about my mother's complete abandonment, lack of communication, and the fact that she'd taken all of our belongings with her.

"What about your laptop?" Jazz asked. "Are you going to have to buy a new one?"

"No. Thank God. I had it in the trunk of my car. I haven't left anything of true monetary value unattended with my mother in years. I learned that the hard way when she found the cash I'd stored in an air vent in an old apartment."

"When did you move into the RV?" Brooklyn asked slowly.

"Right after your wedding," I explained. "We were kicked out of our rental."

"You didn't say anything," Brielle pointed out.

"Yeah, why do I get the feeling you purposefully kept that to yourself?" Jazz demanded. "And seriously? How were you able to keep that shit on lockdown? That's like a really big life event."

"But not for us," I said, wincing. "We've moved around so much it's like second nature at this point. My life—and Waverly's life—have been nothing but a constant state of chaos for as long as I can remember. And telling you guys every time something happens because of my mother... well, it would just sound like a lot of drama."

"It *is* a lot of drama," Brielle said.

"No offense," Jazz said to Brielle. "But you come from a stable, loving family. Not all of us have that."

"That," I agreed, finally taking a bite of the *kolache*. "Good God..."

"Glad you like it," Brooklyn said. "I was playing with the recipe."

"I just don't understand how you're so calm about your mom bailing and the havoc she caused because of it," Brielle said. "You're like, not at all wigging out. And it sounds like you've already got everything sorted."

"I am nothing if not adaptable. And frankly..."

"What?" Jazz pressed.

"With Mom gone, Waverly and I actually have a chance at some normalcy. Mia's place is cute and clean."

"It is adorable," Brooklyn agreed. "And I definitely wouldn't have had a problem staying there if not for this little one." She pointed to her belly. "We just needed a little more space."

"Yeah." Jazz snorted. "More space, which is why Slash bought you a big old house with a bunch of rooms that he wants to fill with his little biker spawn."

Brooklyn laughed. "It takes two to make that happen. You get that right?"

"I'm pretty sure he has your full cooperation." Jazz winked, causing Brooklyn to blush.

"How's Waverly handling the transition?" Brielle asked.

"Like she always does. With a healthy dose of dark humor and teenage angst. Look, guys, we're okay. We know how to live in the perpetual fight or flight response. I just hate feeling like a charity case. Mia saved the day with the roof over our head, which I'm grateful for. Of course I am. God forbid I'd have to live in a shitty motel with Waverly. We've already done that. No need to repeat it."

The three of them exchanged a look.

I sighed. "Like I said, my mom isn't the most maternal or responsible. We've lived in a shitty motel, shitty apartments with roaches, and one shitty house that was one step away from being condemned, and a secondhand RV that smells like nicotine and lost dreams."

The three of them didn't respond, and the conversation fell into awkward silence while I ate my breakfast and drank half the coffee.

"So financially..." Brooklyn began. "Are you guys okay? Do you need anything?"

"Yeah," Brielle said. "I mean, I can't really offer you anything in way of financial assistance because I dumped my nest egg into this place." She gestured to the bakery and café. "But if you need something, like you want me to paint walls, let me know."

"Yeah," Jazz agreed. "Whatever you need."

My throat constricted with emotion. "You guys, stop. I can't even begin to… No. We're good."

Between the new mattresses and setting up a small, minimal house, my meager savings had dwindled. I no longer had enough money to buy the dual monitor I wanted. But Waverly came first and there was no resentment on my account because of that.

"Can we please talk about something else," I begged. "My pathetic excuse of a life is embarrassing."

"Did Waverly's boyfriend crap his pants when he saw Savage and Duke?" Jazz asked. "Oh, to be a fly on the wall of that diner."

I chuckled. "No, actually. The kid stood his ground. He's the one that suggested to Waverly that he meet me officially. In an actual boyfriend-coming-to-dinner capacity."

"How are you handling the lying and sneaking off to a rave?" Brooklyn inquired. "Is she grounded?"

I sighed. "I kind of let it slide. Not really *slide* per se, just…well, with Mom bailing, Waverly has the ability to spin completely out of control. You know? I don't want to push her to that. I'd rather her feel comfortable enough to come to me."

"She was suspended," Jazz said. "Wasn't she? A little while ago?"

"Yeah." I rubbed the back of my neck. "I don't know what I'm doing, you guys. I mean, I'm the adult. I get that. I was always the adult, even when Mom was here. But it's different now."

My phone chimed in my purse. "Ah, I need to grab that. It's probably Laura."

As far as bosses went, she was the best. She completely

understood life derailing at the drop of a hat—she had a kid of her own.

"You let me know what shifts work for you, okay?" Laura asked. "And seriously, if you need to take some time off to get stuff sorted, that's okay too. Your job will be here when you get back."

"Thank you," I said, feeling completely overwhelmed by gratitude toward the people in my life.

I hung up with her and was about to set my phone down when I got an email notification. I opened it and scanned it quickly. It was a proposal request for a web design rebuild for a small marketing firm.

Things are looking up.

"What are your plans for today?" Brooklyn asked.

"Not much, actually. Just kind of killing time until I pick up Waverly from school."

My phone chimed again. Duke's name flashed across the screen. My cheeks instantly heated when I remembered his text from this morning.

I was both relieved and disappointed when his text merely said:

DUKE
Buy you lunch.

ME
You treated last time.

DUKE
Willa, I don't give two shits about lunch. I'm trying to get you in the same room with me so I can kiss your—

My phone rang, and it startled me enough that I dropped it onto the wooden island.

"Crap," I muttered. I picked up my phone and answered it. "Hello?"

"Ms. Gravestone," a masculine voice said.

"Yes, this is she," I replied.

"This is Principal Schneider. I'm calling about Waverly."

I got up off the stool and headed for the corner of the kitchen. I felt the eyes of my friends following me. "Is this about her books? She accidentally left her book bag on the bus and—"

"It's not about her books. I tried calling your mother, but I had to leave a voicemail."

"She's out of town," I said. It was the truth, though not the full truth.

"Waverly explained that. Ms. Gravestone, your sister is being suspended—"

"Suspended! Again? Why? What did she do this time?" I yelled.

"For fighting. As you know, we have a zero-tolerance policy for fighting and she—"

"Who was she fighting? What was the fight about?" I demanded.

"I'd rather discuss this in person, if you please."

"I'll be right there." I hung up and clutched my phone in my fist.

"Willa?" Brooklyn voiced.

I turned and said simply, "I have to go."

Chapter 9

I PARKED in the school parking lot and cut the engine. I grabbed my purse from the passenger seat and then climbed out of my car, slamming the door, and marching into the school. Classes were in session so the hallways were silent, except for the clack of my heels on the cement floor.

My blood was boiling by the time I made it to the administration office. The woman behind the desk looked up when she saw me.

"May I help you?" she asked politely.

"I'm Willa Gravestone. My sister, Waverly—"

"She's in Principal Schneider's office." She pointed to the closed wooden door. "You can go right in."

"Thanks."

She nodded and then answered a ringing phone.

I knocked. A moment later, a balding man in a brown suit opened the door.

"Ms. Gravestone," he greeted. "Please come in."

I stepped into his office, my eyes passing over the polished bookshelves and registering the scent of lemon pledge. My gaze rested on my sister. She slouched in a chair, her expression surly.

She was all attitude.

I'd patched up Savage and Duke enough times to know the tell-tale signs of fighting, but from what I could see, she wasn't injured. No scratch marks or bruises. No split lip or swelling eyes.

"You okay?" I asked her quietly as I took the chair next to her.

She nodded but otherwise didn't say anything.

"Thank you for coming down so quickly," Principal Schneider said. "I'm sorry to interrupt your," he paused, his gaze sweeping over me in clear judgment, "work day."

I frowned. What the hell did this man think I did for work?

"What happened?" I asked, shoving aside my immediate dislike for the man.

"Waverly attacked a boy in the hallway between classes," Principal Schneider stated. "It took two teachers to separate them."

"Why did she attack him?" I asked.

"She won't tell us," Principal Schneider said. "But as I said on the phone, we have a zero-tolerance policy when it comes to violence, so the result will be suspension no matter what."

"I know my sister," I said. "And I know she wouldn't have attacked anyone unless they did something to warrant it."

"Ms. Gravestone," Principal Schneider droned. "This isn't the first time your sister has been in trouble—"

I looked at Waverly and interrupted Principal Schneider. "Did he touch you?"

"No," she said.

"Did he threaten you? What happened?" My eyes widened, pleading with Waverly to give me something.

"It's not like that." She looked at her nails. The red polish was already chipped and she picked at her cuticle, like she couldn't be bothered with this meeting.

"The boy's parents are calling for expulsion," Principal Schneider said. "Expulsion is a bit excessive, but I cannot let Waverly's transgression slide. She's suspended for a week and will receive zeros on all her homework assignments and tests. With her grades the way they currently are, your sister will fail her sophomore year unless she takes summer school to ensure she graduates on time."

"Fail? She's going to *fail*?" I felt lightheaded.

"Great," Waverly sassed, rising from her chair. "Can I go now?"

Principal Schneider's mouth pinched into a line and he nodded.

I rummaged in my purse for my keys and handed them to her. "Straight to the car. No detours."

Waverly took the keys from me and left the room, the door closing with finality.

"I had no idea she was doing so poorly in school," I said softly. "I know she has a tutor, but…"

"I've made a few calls to your mother that have gone unreturned. I wanted to discuss your sister's lack of motivation with her, but your mother hasn't made herself available." He paused. "Is everything all right at home?"

Fear drummed in my heart. "Yes. Everything's fine. My mother has been busy with work and now she's out of town."

Principal Schneider's eyes narrowed, and he looked like he was about to protest, but at the last moment changed his mind.

"If you need to discuss anything regarding my sister or her education, please call me."

"I will." He rose from his chair and came out from behind the desk. "I do want what's best for your sister, but there are only so many allowances I can make for her behavior. She didn't just attack any student. She attacked Cal Riskin."

"Cal Riskin," I repeated. "That name sounds familiar."

"He's the captain of the football team and the school's star quarterback."

Derision for the kid I'd never met completely enveloped me. I had my own history with a football player.

"You didn't speak to Cal and ask what he said to my sister to make her react the way she did?" I asked.

"I did ask him. He denied that he'd said anything and then his father..."

"His father what?" I demanded.

"His father—Cal Riskin Senior, is an attorney. A well-connected attorney."

I let out a huff. I knew how the world worked. There were those with money and power and those without. Those without lived by different rules and were punished constantly, while those with money and power did as they pleased. Even if my sister had been in the right, money and power could change the slant.

I was failing her.

She was sitting in the passenger side of the car, not even absorbed in her phone. Her backpack was by her feet.

"What happened?" I asked.

She looked at me. "Cal Riskin is an asshole."

"And that's why you attacked him?" I raised my brows.

Waverly shook her head. "He was one of the guys sitting on the wall when you dropped me off."

"Okay?"

"He saw you," she said, making it sound like an accusation. "And he said he'd pay good money to see you working it at the Crystal Palace—just like Mom."

I winced. Waverly's classmates knew our mom was a stripper. And teenagers had no problem circling the weak and bullying those that were different or below their social class.

"So, you attacked him for what he said?" I guessed.

She shook her head. "No. I was hell-bent on ignoring him, but then he said I wasn't going to amount to anything. That I'd be knocked up before graduation and I'd have to get on a pole just to support my trailer park brat—and that if I was nice to him, he'd throw a few twenties my way when he was home from college. That's when I attacked him. I got in one good punch before I was pulled off him."

Waverly was looking out the window, but when I didn't say anything for a good long minute, she finally glanced at me, worry constricting her face. "Say something. Yell, scream, tell me I'm an idiot for letting that guy rile me."

"You put some force behind it?"

She blinked and then rubbed her knuckles. "Yeah."

I nodded. "Good."

Chapter 10

"Do me a favor," I said to Waverly as I eased out of the parking spot.

"Sure, anything."

"Get your phone out and text Duke. Tell him to meet us at O'Reilly's."

"We're going to O'Reilly's?" she asked, her eyes lit with excitement.

"A champion fighter needs a meal fit for a champ, and I know how you love their corned beef and cabbage."

Her shoulders slumped and her lips quivered. "You're not mad at me?"

"For defending yourself against a horrible shit bag? No. I'm not mad at you for that." I sighed. "I wish your grades weren't in the shitter. I wish you weren't suspended."

"Tell me about it. Summer school is gonna blow."

"Call it your penance."

"I'll take it," she said quickly. "Just as long as we're okay."

"We're okay. Though I gotta admit, I feel like I'm failing you."

"You're the only one who isn't failing me. Well, you and Dylan. Jessica's parents are definitely going to make us stop hanging out."

"Can you blame them?" I asked. "Sneaking out. Parties. And now a second suspension. Actions have consequences."

"But you said you understood!"

"I do understand. Doesn't mean the systems already in place in the world care, though." I exhaled. "Look, Waverly, there's a lesson to be learned here."

"Violence isn't the answer?" she parroted.

"We don't live by the same rules as the Cal Riskins of the world."

I watched the light of understanding enter her eyes. "Oh."

"Yeah. I hate that it's that way, but it's true."

"So people like shitty Cal Riskin can say whatever they want? Why, because his daddy will protect him at all costs?"

"Cal is not better than you. But the world treats those of his echelon differently."

"That's *so* unfair."

"That's life. We were dealt a different hand."

"You're not even mad about what Cal said about you?" Waverly asked.

"No."

"Why not?"

"What do you think I heard all through high school, Waverly? This isn't new to me. This isn't the first time someone said something stupid just because of how we grew up or because our mom is *our mom*."

She noodled on that for a moment and then texted

Duke. A few seconds later, her phone chimed back. "He said he's with Savage and they'll meet us there. Do those two ever do anything separately?"

"Infrequently," I admitted.

"I don't think I've ever heard the story of how you guys met. I just remember them always being around. Like alley tomcats that won't go away."

I threw her a grin. "I'm glad they're hard to shake."

"Yeah," she said, suddenly serious. "Me too."

"I met them when they were fighting."

"Who were they fighting? A school yard bully?"

"Each other," I said with a laugh.

"No…" Waverly's mouth dropped open. "Seriously?"

"Seriously."

"What were they fighting about?"

"I don't even remember at this point. Boys fight all the time for no reason. Savage punched Duke in the eye. Duke busted Savage's lip. Then they made up and asked me if I wanted to climb a tree with them."

"All's well that ends well, huh?"

"Something like that. They came to see you, you know," I said.

"What do you mean?"

"The day you were born."

"No kidding."

I shook my head and turned down the street. "They scraped some money together, got on the bus, and came to meet you. The three of us stood at the nursery window and I pointed you out to them, and on that day, they vowed to protect you like big brothers. For life."

"Wow," she said quietly. "I had no idea."

The moment was imprinted forever in my mind. The three of us had stared at the new baby, who didn't yet know how hard life could be. We were three nine-year-olds honed by the hardships—and the miracles—of life.

"I can count on them in ways I've never been able to count on anyone," I said. "So, when Savage is being an overprotective dick, or Duke teases you, just know—"

"That I'm an ungrateful shit because they're gonna catch me if I fuck up?"

I didn't bother correcting her language, because what was the point?

"Yeah, exactly."

I pulled into O'Reilly's parking lot. Duke and Savage's motorcycles were parked underneath a big shady tree. It was spring, and the leaves were green and ripe. The heat of summer hadn't hit yet, but it was only a matter of time. That was the thing about Texas. One minute it was hot, the next minute it was...hotter.

Duke and Savage were sitting in a booth in the back. Four waters had already been ordered and were on the table. I slid into the seat next to Savage, across from Duke, who frowned.

Waverly plopped down next to Duke and reached for a straw.

"Wow, we're at O'Reilly's before 11 a.m., except this time it isn't because we were out all night binge drinking," Savage quipped.

I elbowed him in the ribs.

Waverly rolled her eyes. "Relax. I know you guys drink."

"Waverly got suspended," I announced. "Again."

"What did our Little Punk do this time?" Savage drawled.

"I punched the captain of the football team in his fat mouth for calling Willa a slut." Silence descended on the table. "Can I get a soda? I need some caffeine."

"He called Willa a slut?" Duke asked, his voice suddenly dangerously low.

Waverly nodded. "Among other things."

"What other things?" Savage asked, slipping into the same protective mode as Duke.

I looked at him, noting the feral glint in his eyes. That glint was a warning to anyone who knew him. He was in hair-trigger mode and could fire off at any moment.

I immediately took his hand and threaded his fingers through mine. He glanced at me and gave my hand a little squeeze, but his attention immediately focused back on Waverly.

Waverly tapped the rim of her water glass in thought. "He said I was going to be knocked up before graduation and that I'd have to work the stripper pole like Mom just so I could feed my brat. And he added that when he was home from college, he'd come by and throw me a few twenties. So, I slugged him as hard as I could and then launched myself at him and then hit him again. Teachers broke up the fight before I could finish kicking his ass."

"You told me it was only one punch," I remarked.

"I lied." Waverly grinned.

"He hit you back?" Savage asked.

"No. He never got a chance. Pussy."

Savage's lips twitched like he wanted to laugh, but he held it in.

"Give me your hands," Duke said to her.

She immediately held out her hands. Duke examined her knuckles and nodded. "You need ice."

"We need a server," Savage muttered. "What is it with you Gravestones and football players?"

"What does that mean?" Waverly asked.

I froze for a moment and then elbowed Savage in the ribs.

"Dude. What the fuck?"

"Will someone tell me what's going on?" Waverly demanded.

"When we were juniors, I had my own shitty experience with a football player," I stated.

Waverly's eyes widened. "Yeah?"

"Yeah," I said. I looked around. "Seriously, where is the server?"

"We don't come to O'Reilly's for the service, we come for the food that causes stomach pains after," Savage said.

"But so worth it," Waverly said. "So, what happened?"

"With what?" I asked.

"The football player."

"We were at a bonfire in a field," I said. "And Troy had been paying attention to me all night. Getting me beer and whatnot. And then he asked if I wanted to go for a walk." I stared at her. "Let that be a lesson to you."

She nodded.

I sighed. "He was getting handsy and saying I'd been teasing him all night, and that it was time to pay up. Just really gross stuff, you know? And when I told him I wanted to go back to the party, he grabbed me and shoved me to the ground."

"Willa," Waverly whispered.

Duke wrapped an arm around her shoulders. "It's okay, LP. Savage and I didn't like the prick from the moment we saw him, so we'd been watching out for her all night."

"Only I didn't know it," I admitted with a smile. "I didn't even have to scream before the both of them were there, pulling Troy off me."

"And then what?" Waverly asked, enraptured with the story.

"We wanted to kill him," Savage said lightly. "But Willa wouldn't let us."

"Right side of the tracks," I explained, and then pointed to the three of us. "Wrong side of the tracks."

"Rich daddy?" Waverly guessed, her expression turning glum.

"Very rich daddy," I said.

"Assholes," Waverly muttered.

"Why don't you go up to the bar and order for us," I suggested.

"Okay." Waverly climbed out of the booth.

"I'll help." Savage nudged me and I slid out to let him up.

The two of them headed for the bar, leaving me alone with Duke.

"You sat next to him," Duke said, his brows drawn together.

"Jealous?" I asked.

"Insanely."

"You have no reason to be," I said.

"No?"

"No."

"Why not?" he demanded.

"I sat next to Savage because I knew if I sat next to you, I'd be thinking about your texts from this morning." I leaned over the table and lowered my voice, "And I wouldn't be able to stop myself from touching you underneath the table. Happy?"

Duke smiled wide enough to make his dimples pop. "Insanely. But I'm still horny as fuck."

"You should do something about that," I teased.

"I tried. In the shower this morning. It didn't help at all, really. It was a warmup more than anything." He played with the discarded straw wrapper. "You told her about Troy."

"But not *everything* about Troy," I pointed out. "I don't want her to know about what you guys did to him *after* the party…"

"Were you ever going to tell her about Troy?"

"I was hoping I wouldn't have to."

"So, she's suspended," he said after a moment. "For how long?"

"A week. Just long enough to tank what's left of her grades. She'll fail her sophomore year and have to take summer school if she wants to graduate on time."

"Pull her out. Homeschool her. She's whip-smart. She can get her GED early."

"One little problem," I said. "I'm not her legal guardian and her legal guardian is missing in action."

"Fucking Angel," he muttered.

"I'm proud of her, Duke. Waverly, I mean. For standing up for herself."

"She stood up for you too," he reminded me.

I smiled. "Yeah. Pugnacious little thing. Thanks for teaching her how to land a punch."

He inclined his head. "That sounds a little bit like an apology."

"You were right and I was wrong," I quipped. "There. Memorize this moment, for it shall not happen again."

"Hmm. We'll see." His eyes surveyed me. "You look tired."

"Thanks. Might need to invest in a new concealer."

"That's not what I meant."

"Being responsible for a fifteen-year-old twenty-four seven is exhausting."

"You don't have to do it alone," he said slowly. "We can be around more. I can be around more."

"You're around all the time. Without you, without Savage, I'd…we'd…" I sighed.

"Family," he reminded me. "That's what we do."

"The girls offered the same," I said. "They said don't hesitate to ask."

"What do you need, Willa?"

"Some fucking stability," I said. "I've never had that. Waverly sure as hell hasn't had that. She's suspended this week, and then she'll be in summer school. But she needs more. She needs direction."

"She needs a summer job," Duke pointed out. "Something to focus on while she earns a little bit of money. She needs a reward in life, something real."

"I didn't want her to have to work so young. But she's already asked if she could work a summer job. She likes babysitting Darcy's kids, and they love her. She's shown an interest in baking, and Brooklyn's been teaching her. But she's at that age where I can no longer hide what we are."

"What are you?" Duke inquired.

"Poor," I blurted out. "Scraping by. I didn't want that for Waverly. I wanted new clothes and matching furniture. I wanted to take her to New York for her sixteenth birthday, but with the way things are going, I won't be able to afford it. Look, I'm not complaining, okay? I'll work as hard as I have to. I just want her to have all the opportunities I didn't get and right now that's not something I can provide for her."

"Maybe she doesn't want those opportunities," he said. "Maybe she wants your time and attention, and she wants to feel normal and have a boyfriend and get into trouble, but she doesn't care about matching furniture or new clothes. Hell, she prefers going to thrift stores instead of the mall anyway. She lives for that shit, you know? Are you sure this is even about Waverly?"

Waverly and Savage returned to the table. Savage carried all four sodas because Waverly was holding a bag of ice to her right knuckles.

"Gonna have to change your nickname to Rocky," Savage said as he set the glasses down. "Food's ordered."

"Thanks," I said, taking a glass.

"I don't like the name Rocky." Waverly settled in next to Duke, but the moment her phone chimed, she sat up and grabbed it. "It's Dylan."

"Fucking Dylan," Savage muttered.

"Be nice," Waverly said. "Or you don't get to meet him in a normal setting with real napkins." She looked at me. "Can I call him?"

I nodded.

She slid out of the booth again, phone and ice in hand, and went back to the bar area.

"Handful, that one," Duke stated with a smile.

"She's Willa 2.0," Savage quipped. "God, I love that kid."

Chapter 11

"What's the plan for Waverly while she's suspended?" Savage asked. "Ketchup."

Duke slid the glass Heinz bottle across the table and Savage caught it.

"Not sure," I admitted. "I talked to my boss before all this went down, and she said to take as much time as I need to figure family stuff out. So, I'm not worried about that, but I've only got one web design client and another potential in the wings. I need to make some extra cash. And I'd very much like not to prove Cal Riskin correct and get it by working the pole."

"Cal Riskin," Duke repeated. "Let me guess? Captain Dickwad?"

"Yep."

"He just *sounds* like a douche with that name alone."

I looked at him and grinned. "He's the second douche in line. Cal is Cal Junior."

"And unless we cut his balls off, he's going to procreate and make a Cal the Third." Savage took a huge bite of his burger.

"No," I said immediately.

"No, what?" Savage asked.

I grasped his chin and forced him to look at me. "Promise me, Savage."

"Promise you *what*?"

"You know what."

"I promise to leave his testicles intact."

I cocked my head to the side.

"I mean it." He batted my hand away from his chin. "Unhand me, woman, and let me eat my burger in peace."

"Duke?" I asked.

"Hmm?"

"I'm counting on you to keep Savage on the straight and narrow."

"Savage will do what Savage will do," Duke said, taking one of Savage's fries.

"Dude," Savage complained. "Get your own. Besides, no one can chain me. But I'll keep my promise. No ball squishing."

"I guess that's all I can ask for."

Waverly appeared at the table. "Thank God. Food. I'm starving."

"Violence brings out your appetite?" Savage asked with a roguish grin.

I elbowed him.

"Ouch." He rubbed his rib.

"Please, I barely touched you. How's Dylan?" I asked my sister.

"Fine." She sighed. "Well, not so much fine as ready to shove Cal into a locker, but I made him promise not to do it because the last thing I want is for Dylan to get suspended too. No reason for him to ruin his future. He's on the Ivy League track. I just had to have a boyfriend who's a brainiac."

She bent her head and focused on cutting her corned beef.

"This is where you say something encouraging," Savage stage whispered to me.

I elbowed him again.

"She's been nothing but encouraging," Waverly defended. "In fact, she's been so encouraging she's one step away from being a cheerleader."

"We still haven't figured out what we're going to do this week during your suspension," I said.

"Stay home and eat ice cream out of the carton?" she asked hopefully.

I raised my brows. "Let's save that for those really bad times in your life."

"This isn't bad?" she asked. Her blue eyes met mine.

I smiled slowly. "Not nearly as bad as a really bad haircut…"

Waverly mock shuddered.

"But don't think you're getting off easy," I warned. "I mean it. You're not going to get to sit around and use this as a vacation."

"I know." Waverly's phone danced across the table and she immediately grabbed it. "Hey, Jess." She scooted out of the booth and disappeared.

"Her phone rings more than mine does," I lamented.

"I could call you all the time," Savage said. "To make you feel better."

"You *do* call me all the time," I joked.

"I get bored easily."

"What a nice compliment." I rolled my eyes at him. "Call the brunette you rescued at Shelly's. Let her entertain you."

"That's already over," Savage said.

"Why?" I asked.

"She can work in the office at Charlie's," Duke said.

I blinked at the sudden change in conversation. "What? What are you talking about?"

"Waverly," Duke said. "Boxer can show her how to do spreadsheets, take orders, that kind of stuff. She'll be surrounded by Tarnished Angels so she'll be safe and watched over, and her time will be occupied."

"Oh, that's actually a great idea," I said with a sigh.

"Genius," Savage said. "She'll hate boring menial work so badly she'll be begging to go back to school."

"You sure Boxer won't mind?" I asked.

"Nah. He won't mind. He'd probably prefer it," Duke said. "The guy hates spreadsheets. You drop her off in the morning and I'll drop her back at your place when she's done for the day."

Waverly came back to the table, a huge smile across her face.

"What?" I asked. "Why are you smiling like a loon?"

"I'm a hero," Waverly said. "Everyone knows I punched Cal and I'm the most popular girl in school! I thought for sure I'd be ostracized! *This is so cool!*"

"Just don't forget those that knew you when," Savage said.

"Never." She grinned. "Just because I'm suddenly popular doesn't mean I'm going to ditch my best friend or my boyfriend. They're the best."

"So, if you get invited to sit at the cool kids table?" I pressed.

"Willa," she drawled. "Didn't you hear? I *am* the cool kid. Whatever table I'm at *is* the cool kid's table."

"My bad." I couldn't help the grin that spread across my face. "So, what you did turned out not to be social suicide. Good to know."

"It wouldn't have mattered if it had turned out like

that," Waverly said slowly. "I mean, I didn't hit Cal for any sense of clout. And if I'd thought before I reacted, I would've…"

"You would've what?" I queried.

She sighed. "Made the exact same decision."

"Atta girl!" Savage cheered.

I exited the restroom and came face to face with Duke.

"Hey," I said, head cocked.

"Hey." He grasped my hips and drove me back against the door.

"What are you—"

His lips covered mine and any protests I might've had flew out the window. My best friend was kissing me in a hallway in a restaurant where at any moment my sister or our other best friend might see us.

I placed my hands on his chest and closed my eyes as the sensation of his strong body pressed into me. "You're pure evil, Duke."

"Me? You're the one in the leather skirt."

I smiled against his lips and opened my eyes.

Ever since the night we fell into bed together, it had ripped the Band-Aid off the feelings we'd both suppressed for years.

Now there was no putting them away. They'd been unleashed, and the only thing to do would be to let them run their course. I just hoped we could still remain friends when it was over.

"When are you going to let me take you out on a date?" Duke asked as he took a step back.

"A date?" I sucked in a breath of surprise. "Why would you want to take me on a date?"

"Because that's what people do. They date. They go out to eat. They hold hands. They fight over the remote."

"Fight over the remote? That sounds like cohabitation."

He shrugged.

"What are you guys doing?" Waverly asked. "I thought you were going to the bathroom."

I jumped, not having heard her approach. My cheeks suffused with color. "I've used it. Duke was just…ah…he…"

"I told her if she has shit to do in the morning, I can take you to Charlie's," he said, not appearing at all flustered. "Savage told you about Charlie's, right?

He was so cool and calm, I wondered how he was able to think on his feet.

"Oh." Waverly bit her lip. "Yeah. He told me."

The three of us headed back into the main dining room. Savage was laying down some cash. Duke's phone chimed and he pulled it out of his pocket. He quickly scanned it and then said, "That was Crow. The desks and dresser are in the rental."

"Oh, that's great," I said.

"Can I drive home?" Waverly asked. "I need the practice."

I handed her the keys and she darted out of the restaurant. I shook my head and smiled.

"What?" Duke asked.

"I remember what it was like at her age. Always wanting to drive. The excitement, the taste of freedom."

"That's how I felt the first time I got on a Harley," Savage said.

"The first time you got on a Harley you crashed," Duke pointed out.

Savage grinned. "And a beautiful woman tended to my injuries. Good times."

I shook my head. "As much fun as it would be to go down memory lane, I've got to get going."

"There's a party at the clubhouse this Friday," Savage said.

"Family barbecue," Duke corrected. "The kids'll be there. You guys coming?"

"I don't know," I said. "Shouldn't I ground her from all fun things? Rules and all that?"

"You're letting her drive," Duke pointed out. "That's not a punishment."

"If she doesn't pass her driving test then that'll be *my* punishment." I sighed. "Not that it matters, I guess, since she won't have a car of her own."

I have to figure that out too.

"Well, think about it this way," Savage said. "By not letting her go, that means you're not going, and I'm gonna guess that by the end of the week, you're going to need a couple of beers to relax. So you'd be punishing yourself."

"You don't think I can handle Waverly's suspension week? Where's the vote of confidence?"

Savage grinned. "It's not so much my lack in confidence in you, but more like knowing she's a teenager with the biological tendency to fuck something up."

I sighed. "I'll think about the party."

Savage wrapped me in a bear hug and then went to his bike, leaving me with Duke. "You'll call me if you need anything, yeah?" he said.

"Sure," I said. "I always call you when I need help, don't I?"

"That was before."

"Before what?"

He tilted his head to one side and leveled me with a heated stare.

It sent goosebumps rushing up and down my neck. "You're still Duke and I'm still me. It's why I don't want—"

Waverly blared the car horn.

"If I didn't love that kid like my own sister, I'd kill her," Duke said lightly. He embraced me quickly like he usually did.

But damn if I didn't want to stand in his arms for just a little while longer, run my fingers along his cheek, and have his tongue in my mouth. I wanted to curl into his neck and breathe him in so the smell of him was in my head. I was drunk on Duke.

I climbed into the passenger side of the car and was immediately cold. I reached over and turned the air conditioner fan down and the temperature up.

"What are you doing? I'm hot," Waverly complained.

"Then take off your hoodie." I tugged on the sleeve as I said it. "I don't recognize this, by the way…"

"Dylan's," she informed me. "Buckle up."

Once I was clipped in, Waverly adjusted her mirrors and then gently reversed out of the parking spot.

How was it my fifteen-year-old sister had the boyfriend thing figured out and I was still acting like a dope?

Chapter 12

"Am I delusional, or was this furniture not that ugly in the store?" Waverly asked, skimming her hand across the top of the scuffed dresser.

"You're not delusional," I said, my mouth pinched. "This is hideous."

Waverly let out a giggle.

"I'm changing and then we're cleaning the dresser and moving it into the bedroom." I kicked off my heels and made a mental note to call Laura. I could work every shift she had available now that Waverly would be at Charlie's. But as much as I loved working at Leather and Ink, the truth was that I only did it for the employee discount. Now I needed something that brought in more cash until I had enough web design clients to sustain a business.

Mia was cutting me a deal on rent even though she said she wasn't. I didn't want people to have to cut me deals. I wanted to pay my own way. I wanted to pay Waverly's way.

As I was mulling over the idea of getting another job—or two—Waverly's phone rang.

"It's Mom," Waverly said. "Why is she calling me in the middle of the day? For all she knows I'm supposed to be in class."

"That's probably why she's calling. She expects to be able to talk to your voicemail."

Waverly's expression darkened and she pressed answer. "Hey, Mom. Hold on a second." She took the cell away from her ear and pressed another button. "Okay. I'm back."

"Hey, baby," my mother crooned through the speaker phone.

"Don't," she said, suddenly sounding far too adult. "You took off with all my books. You know that right? Not to mention my clothes? And Willa's clothes?"

"Don't be mad at me, sugar," Angel whined. "I'm a free spirit and go where the wind takes me."

She goes where the guy who shows her the slightest bit of attention goes.

"Listen, baby, Red and I are on a road trip and I don't know when I'm gonna be back."

I grasped Waverly's phone out of her hand, tapped the button to take her off speaker phone, and put the cell to my ear. "It's me," I said, walking toward the bathroom.

Angel paused. "Willa, I didn't know you were there."

I closed the bathroom door, ensuring I had some privacy.

"You're not gonna get on my case about taking off, are you? Look, I know it's a shit thing to do. I know I should've planned better, but I met Red and he's different—"

"They're always different," I interrupted.

"I want you to be happy for me. Why can't you do that?"

Anger gushed to the surface from the hole I'd buried it in. I bit my tongue. There was no use spewing accusations or hurtful words at her. It wasn't going to change her behavior. It wasn't going to bring her back. It wasn't going to turn her into the mother she was supposed to be.

"I'll take care of Waverly," I said, tears of rage filling my eyes. "I'll buy her clothes. I'll cook her meals. I'll make sure she graduates, all of it. But you owe me something, Angel... Do not come back here. You're free. You no longer have to be burdened with children. Live your life. I've got this."

I hung up on her. I took a moment and tried to get my shaking hands under control, and then I opened the door. Waverly stood just outside the bathroom, pretending to look nonchalant.

"How much of that did you hear?" I asked.

"Practically none of it," she said.

"So, all of it?"

"Yeah, pretty much."

With a sigh, I slung my arm around her shoulders. "Sorry you got a mom who doesn't know how to be a mom."

"Sorry you got one too," she said, bumping her hip against mine.

"At least we have each other."

"Right on," she agreed.

"You want to make a yellow cake straight from the box?"

"I thought you'd never ask."

"Willa."

I stretched my arms over my head and cracked an eye open, expecting the voice to belong to my sister.

But it wasn't Waverly. It was Duke, and he was sitting on the edge of the air mattress.

"What are you doing here?" I asked, shooting up quickly. I looked around. "Where's Waverly? What time is it?"

"Waverly turned off your alarm and let you sleep. She called me and asked me to pick her up and take her to Charlie's. I got you a blueberry muffin and a sugar coma coffee with so much caffeine it'll make your teeth rattle."

I rubbed a hand down my face. "I'm so confused."

"You're confused? I'm trying to figure out how to date my best friend. So I brought her snacks."

"Snacks are good." I couldn't help the smile that drew across my lips.

"You look cute first thing in the morning."

"You've seen me first thing in the morning," I pointed out. "Several times."

"Yeah, but it's never gonna get old."

A jolt rocketed through me and zinged to my core.

"I'll meet you in the kitchen, yeah?"

"Yeah."

I threw off the covers and his gaze was immediately drawn to my bare legs. I was wearing a T-shirt, but it had ridden up.

"Yeah, the kitchen," he said, his voice raspy. He got up and strode out of the bedroom.

Grinning, I watched him go.

After I brushed my teeth and splashed some cool water on my face, I went to meet him. Duke was sitting on the couch, holding a to-go cup of coffee. He was wearing his leather cut and heavy motorcycle boots, his eyes following me.

"Not that I'm not completely grateful for coffee and a

muffin," I said, picking up the pastry bag and coffee and bringing them to the couch, "but how did you get in?"

"Waverly gave me her keys," he said. "When I told her I wanted to bring you coffee and a muffin."

"You take such good care of me," I teased.

"I try." He took a sip of his drink. "Waverly said your mom called."

I sighed. "Yeah. She called."

"And?"

"What do you mean *and*? If Waverly told you Angel called, then didn't she tell you what I said to her?"

"We didn't have a chance to get into it," he said. "She mentioned the call in passing. But then Boxer handed her a donut, told her to sit at the desk, and she entered work mode."

"Cute," I said with a smile.

"So? What did Angel have to say for herself?"

"Same old bullshit. She's on a journey, and can't we be happy for her, blah blah blah. I told her not to come back this time." I looked at my lap. "I told her that we didn't need her anymore. That I would take care of Waverly and we'd be fine. Waverly heard. And we spent the rest of the day cleaning crummy furniture and baking a yellow cake."

I took a sip of coffee and hummed. "This is good. Taste's…wait." I lifted the cup away from my face and turned it around. The Pie in the Sky bakery logo was stamped on the cup. "You didn't."

"Didn't what?"

"Tell Jazz you were coming here?"

"Who do you think made you that coffee?" He gave it a chin nod. "That thing is a sugar coma waiting to happen."

"Duke," I snapped.

"What?"

"You can't—I mean—really?"

"That caffeine must not've kicked in yet because you're not making a lick of sense."

"You can't go to Pie and the Sky and buy me muffins and weird concoctions that my friend made up for me."

"Why not? I always buy you muffins." His brow furrowed. "Well, not always muffins. Sometimes a Danish. Cookies. Croissants."

"Stop," I said, my lips quivering.

"What's this about? You don't like muffins? Or other baked goods?"

"Duke." I nudged him with my foot, which he grasped and held onto. His thumb stroked across my arch and I nearly purred.

"Tell me, Willa."

"Jazz and Brielle are already giving me shit," I said.

"About?"

"About you and Savage. They don't believe that I'm just friends with you."

"Well, you and I *aren't* just friends."

"We're not?"

He pinched my big toe. "You don't have sex with your friends."

"What about friends with benefits?"

"Doesn't exist," he said.

"Fuck buddies?" I tried again.

"Jesus, woman, where's your sense of romance."

"I'm hoping I can deflect with humor."

"Try again."

"I wonder if kissing you that night was a mistake," I said quietly. "Because now we've crossed this line, a line we said we'd never cross again when we were sixteen, and now… There's so much at stake this time, Duke. Our friendship. Your friendship with Savage. My friendship with Savage. The three of us. What if we continue down this road, and it doesn't work? I couldn't bear to lose you. Either of you. There's a lot of stuff I can get over. Not having you guys in my life… God, Duke, I'd lose my shit."

"So, you're scared of digging deeper because you're worried about a future that hasn't played out?"

"Well, when you put it that way…"

I took a sip of my coffee and reached for the muffin.

"There's an Italian restaurant on the other side of town. A hole in the wall place. The husband cooks and the wife serves and they yell at each other in Italian."

"Ah, that's how you know it's authentic," I said with a laugh.

"Exactly. You have plans Wednesday night?"

"Hanging with my sister," I said. "I've got to keep a close eye on her right now. Who knows what she's liable to do, acting out her teenage rebellion in response to Angel ditching us. She's handling it well, but it's a lot to digest at that age."

He smiled slightly. "Okay." He let go of my foot and then stood up.

"Where are you going?" I asked.

"I got shit to do. Even though I'd rather stick around and see what fun we could get up to here, I think it'll keep."

"It'll keep," I repeated. "Duke?"

"Hmm?"

"We have the apartment to ourselves and you didn't try anything."

He leaned over and cradled the back of my head in his large hand, tilting my face up to meet his gaze. "I don't like how you're playing this, Willa."

"Playing? I'm not playing anything!"

"Good." He kissed me briefly and then let me go. "I'll call you later."

He strode to the door and left.

I stared after him, confused as hell.

Chapter 13

"I LOVE WORKING!" Waverly announced as she blew through the front door.

I closed my laptop and looked at her. "Yeah? You enjoyed yourself at Charlie's?"

"It was so cool," she exclaimed, shutting the door and locking it.

"Far be it from me to think spreadsheets and numbers are cool, but everyone's got a passion. Did Duke give you a ride?"

"No. Torque did."

"Torque? Seriously? On his bike?"

Waverly marched over to the fridge and pulled it open. "Not on his bike. He had the SUV because he had to go pick up Allison and baby Tank. Said it was no trouble. Torque's a cool dude."

"Torque is cool? The guy doesn't even talk."

"He talks."

"You know this how?"

"Because he let me help him rebuild an engine. I hardly spent any time in the office looking at spreadsheets."

"Wow. I still find it hard to believe that someone as surly as Torque spoke to you."

"Well, I wouldn't call it talking *exactly*. He grunted and pointed. He was really awesome about it though. He never got annoyed or anything."

"So, you rebuilt an engine?" I smiled.

Waverly pulled out a container of leftover cake. "I *helped* rebuild an engine," she corrected. "But it was fun and oddly cathartic. It helped me not to think about all this stuff going on, you know?"

"Mechanical meditation," I said. "And you're not seriously having cake for dinner."

"Why not?" she asked. "It's already cooked."

"Because we had cake for dinner last night, and that's not a healthy option. We did go to the grocery store and buy lettuce for a reason."

"I'm not a rabbit," she said with a grin. "The only vegetable I eat is in potato form. Preferably fried and smothered in ketchup."

"You'll die before thirty if you keep eating like that," I quipped.

"But I'll die happy." With a sigh, she reluctantly put the cake back into the fridge. "Salad it is."

I got up and stretched.

"How was your day?" she asked, her head back in the refrigerator.

"Good. Answered work emails. Called Laura and she's putting me back on the schedule this week."

I didn't tell her I also started calling around to restaurants to see if they were hiring.

"You dice," she said, tossing me an onion. "I'll tear the lettuce."

"Sounds good."

I was washing my hands when there was a knock on the door.

"Who's that?" she asked.

"It's not Dylan?" I inquired.

"No. What about you? Is it one of your boyfriends?"

I glared at her.

She grinned at me cheekily.

I dried my hands with a paper towel and went to answer the door. Brielle, Jazz, and Brooklyn stood at the threshold.

"Have you had dinner yet?" Brooklyn asked, holding a slow cooker in her hands.

"Uh, no. We were just about to make a salad. And Waverly's very happy about it. Aren't you, Waverly?"

"Ecstatic," Waverly called back.

I stepped away from the doorway and let the three of them in. "What are you guys doing here?"

"Just a little housewarming present," Brooklyn said. "I made chicken with green salsa in your brand-new slow cooker." She went immediately to the kitchen and set it down.

"And I made French bread this morning." Jazz lifted a brown bag toward me and showed the crusty loaf.

"I brought wine." Brielle held out a bottle of red to me. "I have no idea if its good, I just went by the label. It was pretty and it has flowers on it."

"I do the same thing," I said with a smile. "This was really sweet of you guys. Do you want to stay for dinner?"

"Can't," Brooklyn said. "Slash is taking me out."

"And Jazz and I are going to my parents' house for dinner." Brielle sighed. "We better go."

"Why? If we get there now, that gives Angie more time to ask you about your love life," Jazz pointed out.

"My pitiful, pitiful love life." Brielle said and then shook her head.

"Speaking of love life," Jazz said. "Waverly, I heard you have a cutie patootie of a boyfriend."

"Jazz," Brooklyn whispered.

"What?" Jazz shrugged her shoulders. "I want to see pictures."

"I've got some on my phone." Waverly pulled her cell from her back pocket and rushed to Jazz, ready to show off Dylan.

"He's got the eyes of a poet," Brooklyn commented when Waverly showed her the phone. "Are you going to bring him to the barbecue on Friday?"

"There's a barbecue on Friday?" Waverly asked.

"We might not go," I interjected.

"You have to go!" Brielle said. "I'm going. And I never get to go to these things because of my overprotective brothers."

"I'll beg," Jazz said.

"Don't punish your friends by trying to punish me for getting suspended," Waverly said.

I arched a brow. "Don't we have to at least pretend you're grounded?"

"Duke told me what that douche Cal Riskin said to you," Jazz said. "You deserve a medal. And at least three hot dogs at the barbecue."

"Duke told you?" Waverly asked. "When?"

Jazz nodded. "This morning. When he came into Pie and the Sky to get a muffin and coffee for Willa."

"Oh, yeah, that's right." Waverly nodded. "He asked me for my keys."

"How was the coffee?" Jazz asked. "I added more caramel this time."

"It almost made me violently ill it was so sweet," I said.

"So, a dollop more." Jazz nodded. "Got it."

The three of them left and I closed the door after them.

"Thanks, by the way," I said to Waverly. "For letting me sleep in."

"You needed it," she said.

"Well, it was thoughtful."

"You say that like I'm incapable of being considerate," she joked. "Thank God for them. I was really worried we were going to have to eat a salad."

"Son of a biscuit," I muttered as my eyes scanned the email on my phone.

"Everything okay?" Laura asked as she came around the counter at Leather and Ink.

"Hmm? Oh, yeah, fine thanks." I hoisted my purse onto my shoulder and fished around for my car keys. "It was a busy morning. Receipts are organized, I restocked what I could, and I made a list of the items and sizes we're out of."

"You're a doll." She smiled, her large brown doe eyes twinkling. "You're still good with the schedule this week?"

"Yeah, I'm good with it," I promised.

"And how's…everything else?" she pressed. "With Waverly, I mean?"

"She loves working at Charlie's," I stated. "I'm worried she's going to try and get suspended again because she's having so much fun. She has to do summer school, too. Otherwise she won't graduate on time."

"Not all kids are made for the classroom." She shrugged.

"Yeah, I know. I just want what's best for her, but if I'm

being honest I'm not sure I know what that looks like. Anyway," I smiled, "I'll see you later."

I had a few hours before Waverly was finished at Charlie's, and I wasn't ready to go home yet. I drove to Pie in the Sky for a little pick-me-up.

The bakery was busy and many of the tables were full. There were two young women behind the counter. One was on the register, the other the coffee bar.

"Hi," the brunette greeted. "What can I get for you?"

"A vanilla latte, please."

The girl working the coffee bar immediately began steaming the milk.

As I pulled out my wallet, I asked, "Is Brooklyn here?"

"She's in the back," she said. "Do you need to talk to her about catering an event?"

"No." Even if I was, there was no way I could afford her prices. Her business had boomed after she'd made a wedding cake for a wealthy Dallas socialite.

"I just wanted to say hi. I'm Willa."

"I'll tell her you're here." She handed me a few dollars back and I dropped them into the tip jar. She headed off the floor to the back area and a few moments later, Brooklyn came out, wiping her hands on her flour-dusted apron.

"I didn't know you were stopping by," Brooklyn said.

"Impromptu."

"You want to come back and talk while I finish piping?"

"Sure thing." I took my coffee from the barista. "Thank you."

"Enjoy it," the barista said.

I followed Brooklyn into the back. I sat on a stool at the huge island, marveling at her newest cake creation.

"Is that—" I peered closer.

"The Jolly Roger made out of chocolate." She nodded. "This is for a ten-year old's birthday."

"Wow. Impressive."

"Yeah." She smiled. "So, what do I owe the honor of your visit?"

"Just finished working and had some time to kill before I picked Waverly up at Charlie's."

"Ah." She cocked her head to the side. "Something more?"

"I'm going to have to get a second job," I admitted.

"You already have two jobs," she pointed out. "Working at Leather and Ink and your web design business."

"A third job, then. Leather and Ink is great, Laura's awesome, but let's face it, an hourly retail job won't cut it anymore."

"And the web design business?"

"I'm struggling to find clients. I was supposed to start working on a website for a small marketing firm, but she might cancel the project because of the budget."

"Might cancel?" Brooklyn frowned.

"Might, as in, if I come down in my pricing, I can still have the job," I said bitterly.

"Ah." Brooklyn nodded. "Doesn't want to pay you what you're worth."

"Yeah." I rubbed my temple.

"Take it from me, you're better off waiting for the clients that don't complain about your rate. Those that can afford you are the ones who also know your true value. They pay more and bother you less. It sounds counter-intuitive, but it's true."

"I know you're right. In the long run it's better. Short term though…which is why I need another job. I can wait tables or something. I don't care what it is. I just need a few shifts a week that bring in more cash. But then I worry about leaving Waverly at night."

"You can't keep her under lock and key. And you certainly can't be there every moment of every day," she said.

"I know, but right now, I need to be. I never thought my sister would be the troublemaker. But here we are."

"I'll bet she calms down," Brooklyn said.

"After she pranks the principal and gets expelled?" I asked morosely.

"No. I bet she calms down now that she has something to keep her busy. It's the first hint of stability you all have had in a while, right?"

"Yeah, but she's still living in a rental with her sister because her mom bailed on her."

"That might be the elevator pitch, but it's not the whole story. She needs attention in a way that she wasn't getting from the most important person in her life."

"Yeah, but Angel is gone now and—"

Brooklyn sighed. "I'm talking about *you*."

"Me?"

"Waverly adores you. You have to know that. All she's ever wanted was your time and attention."

"I gave it to her," I protested. "Any time she needed anything, I was there. Besides, if she really needs me, then why did she get a boyfriend and not tell me about him?"

"Because she was worried about what you'd think."

"This is complicated."

"Doesn't have to be. Look, Waverly learned early in life that her mom is a crappy mom. I can say that having had my own crappy mom. Let's face it, they're the type of women you have to survive. But this is a chance for you and Waverly to really bond. To lean on each other. She wants to be taken seriously."

"Then maybe she shouldn't sneak out to illegal parties like a child."

"Don't you get it," Brooklyn said with a sudden smile. "She's trying to be you."

"Me? But I don't go to illegal parties."

"No." She cocked her head to the side. "But you do call two bikers your best friends. Willa look…to her, you're the girl that runs with the bad boys. She thinks you're cool. Of course, she wants to emulate you. Why do you think she takes your clothes and wears them?"

"If Waverly wants to be like me so much, then why is her boyfriend seemingly a good guy? He didn't even want to go to the party, but he knew she was going with or without him, so he went to protect her."

She stared at me for a long moment.

"What? What did I say?"

"Duke and Savage do everything in their power to protect you. You don't think she sees that, too?"

I slowly lifted my vanilla latte to my lips. "Forget the bakery, Brooklyn. You should just charge three hundred an hour for therapy sessions. You'd make a killing."

Chapter 14

Waverly slid into the passenger seat and settled a Charlie's Motorcycle Repair shop plastic bag on her lap and closed the door.

"What do you have there?" I asked her.

"I got you a present," she said.

"Me? Really?"

She nodded and handed me the bag. I peeked into it and reached in to pull out a black tank top that had the Tarnished Angels skull logo stamped on the front.

"This is cool, thanks." I reached out to give her a one-armed hug.

"There's another tank in there for me. We'll have matching ones."

My conversation with Brooklyn flooded back to me. I heard Waverly's pronouncement with a new understanding.

"I was thinking we could wear them to the barbecue on Friday," she said feigning nonchalance. "Or not. Whatever."

"I think that would be fun. You sure you don't mind dressing like your annoying older sister?"

She grinned. "She is pretty annoying, but she's kind of cool too."

"Ingrate," I teased, tugging on the end of her red ponytail.

Waverly buckled herself in and then I put the car into gear.

"So, can I ask you something?" Waverly ventured.

"Uh oh. I'm not going to like this, am I?"

"No, I think you will." She bit her lip. "Dylan signed up to take a CPR class. He said there's still a spot open and that if I wanted to, we could take the class together."

"CPR class?" I repeated.

"Yeah. I had this thought, now hear me out. Darcy said her babysitter is going off to college next year and that they need a new one. Well, her kids like me and I like them, and I want to be prepared in case anything happens, you know? And I was thinking, I could become CPR certi-fied and I could start babysitting for people. I mean, Lily's six and takes ballet with a ton of other six-year-olds, so you know that's good word of mouth."

"You want to get CPR certified so you can start *babysitting*?"

"Well, yeah. I need to earn some money. I want to buy a car. And it's not cheap. Plus, I like working. I like feeling productive. I like working for what I want."

"Waverly…"

"I know what you're going to say," she said with a sigh. "You think I should stay a kid as long as possible. But I don't want to stay a kid. Don't you get it? It's not fair that you've had to shoulder all this."

"Shoulder all what?" I asked evasively.

"The financial burden of taking care of me. It

shouldn't be that way. We should take care of each other. I'm not a kid anymore. I see how hard you work, Willa. I want to help. It's in your best interest to just say yes now."

"It is?" I asked in amusement.

"Yeah, because if you say no, I'll just go behind your back and do it anyway. And then I'd be lying to you and then you'd find out and we'd get into a big fight. Let's just skip all that and get to the good part of you saying yes."

"Okay," I said, laughing. "You've worn me down."

"Yay! So I can text Dylan that I'll be taking the class?"

"Yeah, you can text him. Do I need to drive you?"

"No. He'll drive me."

"Straight there and back. No detours," I commanded.

"Yes, Warden. I got it."

"When's the class start?" I asked.

She pulled out her cell phone from her bag. "Tomorrow night is the first class. It's an hour and a half each class, four total days, every Wednesday for a month. I need six hours of training."

"So, for the next four Wednesday nights you'll be doing the course."

"Yep."

"Okay." I nodded. "Go for it. You have my full support."

"Thanks." She grinned and then buried herself in her phone.

As we pulled up to the house, her phone beeped. "Cool. Dylan's gonna swing by and get me at six thirty. The class starts at seven and ends at eight thirty. So I'll be home at a eleven."

"Eleven," I repeated. "Wait, *what?*"

She giggled. "Just kidding. I'll be home at nine. Or nine-ish depending on the traffic."

"Pure trouble, you are."

"Absolutely. But you love me for it."

"I need to make a call real fast," I said to her. "Why don't you head into the house."

"You can't do it inside?" she asked as she grabbed the plastic bag and her purse.

"Client thing," I lied. "I won't be long."

"Okay." She climbed out of the car and shut the door. I didn't pull out my phone until she was in the house.

I pressed dial and he answered on the first ring.

"Willa."

The way he said my name had my breath hitching and my belly fluttering.

"This Italian place you mentioned," I began. "Do you need a reservation?"

I checked my makeup one last time in the rearview mirror, ensuring that my red lipstick was perfect. My eyes were smokey and I was wearing a pair of jeans from Joni that felt like they'd been custom made for me.

It was strange, wearing clothes that belonged to someone else, but like anything, I put my own spin on it. I'd paired the jeans with a loose weave ruby red sweater that hung off the shoulders. Underneath was a silky white cami.

I hesitated to call this a date. We were meeting in secret, he hadn't picked me up at my house, and I wasn't able to dedicate the entire night to him.

A thrill went through me all the same. I wasn't sure if it was because what we were doing felt illicit, or if it was because this was a new adventure for us.

I got out of my car and locked it.

The scents of garlic and fresh pasta hit my nose the moment I entered the tiny restaurant. There were only eight tables in the entire place and a small bar that could seat six—if the six people decided to sit really close together, shoulder to shoulder.

Half the tables were full already. Duke was in the corner, tucked back, away from the door. Though it was dim in the restaurant, I'd found him easily.

He slowly rose from his chair as I approached, his gaze raking over me from head to toe. When I was close enough, his hand snaked out to grasp my waist and he pulled me close. I could smell his cologne and it made my head spin with giddiness.

"You look gorgeous," he said, his voice low. He grasped the back of my neck with his free hand and gave it a little squeeze.

I tilted my head up and received his kiss.

It was a brush of his mouth, unhurried, tender.

A low whimper escaped my lips.

Duke pulled back and I forced my eyes open.

We stared at one another and something began to shift between us. An understanding was developing; a kernel of desire budding into more.

He released me and then helped me with my chair. I raised my brow at him, but that only made him smile.

"What's good here?" I asked, moving the drippy white wax candle toward the wall.

He reached across the table and grasped my hand in his. "Everything."

"If I get the spaghetti and meat balls, will you *Lady and the Tramp* it with me?" I teased.

"You mean will you start at one end and I'll start at the other and our lips will meet in the middle?"

"Yeah."

His thumb skimmed over my knuckles. "Nope. Not gonna happen."

"You're no fun."

"Babe, if we do that, we're doing it in private because of what it'll lead to."

My cheeks flamed and I bit my lip yet it didn't stop me from smiling.

"I like this," he said gruffly. "You and me. Having dinner out in a restaurant."

While we were staring at each other, like we were trying to absorb every little detail, the kitchen door swung open. A rotund older woman with graying brown hair carrying two plates of pasta tromped across the tiny restaurant. She stopped in front of a table—another couple—and plunked the plates down, said something in rapid-fire Italian, and then headed to the bar.

She grabbed two wine glasses and a bottle of wine and marched toward our table. She set the glasses down in front of us and then quickly opened the bottle of wine. She poured a hefty amount into each glass and then placed her hand on her hip, looking from me to Duke.

Suddenly she smiled, leaned over and pinched Duke's cheek and then gave it a pat. She sailed away, disappearing into the kitchen.

"What just happened?" I asked in confusion as we dropped our linked hands.

"We just ordered."

"I don't remember getting a menu."

"You don't get a menu here." He grinned. "You get whatever Mama Leonardi wants to bring you."

"What if she brings me something I don't like?"

"Won't happen," he said.

"You seem really sure about that."

"This isn't my first time here."

I arched a brow. "Not your first time here?"

He smirked. "I've never brought a woman to this place. I've eaten here several times, always at the bar, and Mama Leonardi never disappoints. Trust me. Try the wine."

"What kind of wine is it?"

"Red."

"No shit, Sherlock," I said with a laugh. I reached for the glass of wine and brought it to my lips. I took a sip and then sighed. "Yeah, okay."

"Good?"

"Massive understatement."

There was yelling from the direction of the kitchen, but no one seemed to mind. A moment later, the door swung open again and Mama Leonardi was suddenly back at our table, carrying a small tray. She set down two plates, a basket of bread, Balsamic vinegar, and olive oil.

Her hands were a flurry of action as she salted, peppered, oiled, and vinegared each plate. Then she held out the basket of bread to me.

I took a piece, but I was unsure of what to do with it.

Mama Leonardi mimed breaking the bread and dunking it into the concoction on the plate.

I did as she mimed and stuck a piece in my mouth. My eyes widened in delight, causing Mama Leonardi to cackle. Instead of pinching my face like she'd done to Duke, she pinched my side and said something in rapid Italian before scurrying away.

"What did that mean?" I asked.

Duke grinned. "I think that was her way of saying you need to eat more."

I smiled back at him. "I kind of love this place. Can it be our place?"

His eyes softened. "Yeah, babe. It can be our place."

"Do me a favor," I said.

"What?"

"Don't call me babe." I bit my lip. "It feels…"

"Feels what?"

"Impersonal," I blurted out. "Like that's what you call all your hook ups. Because I *know* that's what you call your hook ups."

He paused as he stared at me. "And you don't want to be a hook up?"

"No, I don't want to be a hook up."

"Then what do you want this to be?"

"I don't know yet."

"I think you do," he said, reaching for his glass of wine. "I think you know *exactly* what you want, but you're afraid."

"How would this work?" I demanded.

"The way it's always worked."

"It'll change everything."

"Damn right it'll change everything," he said, and then leaned forward. "I've wanted you since I was sixteen-years-old. I thought you wanted me too, but when you didn't, I buried all that shit. Buried it down deep so it didn't ruin our friendship or change anything between us. But God damn it, Willa, burying it wasn't the same as killing it. Do you know how many nights I've lain awake wondering what it would've been like if you'd made a different decision. If you'd decided that summer that you wanted me?"

"We were too young," I protested. "We didn't know what we wanted."

"How easy that lie just rolled off your tongue," he said bitterly. "You want to know why no other relationship in your life ever worked out?"

"Why don't you tell me," I said. "Since you claim to know me so well."

"Babe," he drawled with an infuriating smile. "I know you better than you know yourself. Which is why I played the long game."

"What the hell are you even talking about?"

"That night we hooked up…you admit that it was you who came on to me?"

"You didn't stop me…"

"Damn right I didn't. You needed a man to show you what it was like to feel like a real woman. That fucker you were dating sure as hell didn't know what to do with a woman like you. Well, I showed you, didn't I? I showed you what you needed."

I suddenly didn't care that we were in a restaurant. And that other people could hear our dirty laundry. This was a storm that had been brewing for years, and now it was time for lightning.

"I didn't stop you that night," he repeated. "But you don't get to go down this road with me if you're not prepared for what it really means."

"What's it really mean?" I asked, my voice breathy.

"It means you and I are going to belong to each other, Willa. It means when it happens, you're choosing to be with me. And even if you wanna keep it secret a while longer, you gotta know that when I look at you from across whatever room we're in, I'm going to be thinking about the fact that you're *my* woman and I've claimed you."

I swallowed.

"I chose you a long time ago. And I think, if you really dig deep, you've always known that. And it scares the hell out of you."

"It does," I whispered. "You know it does."

"It's why I haven't pushed harder than I have."

"You're pushing now."

"It's the right time. Again, *you* came to me that night."

"You wanted it," I pointed out. "You admit that every time we talk about it. All you asked me that night was, '*are you sure?*'"

"And the moment you said yes it was done." He smiled slightly. "What's the problem now? Is it me you're unsure about? What's stopping you from letting yourself be happy?"

"No. No, it's not you. It's me."

"Yeah, I knew that, I just wanted you to admit it out loud."

"Jerk," I huffed a laugh.

"I get it. Your life is insane. Your mom bailed, you've got Waverly to take care of, you're in the beginning stages of getting your business off the ground. You've got a lot on your plate. But you're allowed to have something just for yourself."

"You mean, I'm allowed to have you?" I asked with humor.

"Just say the word and I'm yours. I'm ready for this. I want you. I wanted you then. I want you now. I'm not going to stop wanting you. Ever."

His eyes were intense and his words made warmth bloom in my belly.

"You've always been the one thing I could count on." I bit my lip. "You and Savage."

"You and I getting together isn't going to change that."

"It will."

"It *won't*."

"You sound pretty sure of it. Nothing is absolute. Nothing is for sure."

Our conversation was interrupted by the arrival of Mama Leonardi. She placed three plates in front of us, pointed to each one and explained what they were in Italian. I caught the words *calamari* and *caprese* but didn't catch the third.

She poured more wine into our glasses and then left.

"Smells good," I said.

"Yep."

I took my napkin and placed it in my lap. And then I loaded up my plate with a little bit of everything.

Duke did the same. He took a piece of *calamari*, dunked it into the marinara sauce, and then plopped it into his mouth.

"Fuck, that's good."

His voice came out a growl, reminding me of the first night we'd spent together. My nipples pebbled underneath my sweater at the memory.

"What's this?" I asked, pointing to the ball of fried dough.

"Fried mozzarella," he said with a grin.

"Oh, hell yes."

"See? I knew you'd love this place."

"You were right."

"Because I know you."

"Back to that, are we?"

"You know me, too," he pointed out. "The other stuff? The relationship stuff? The sex stuff? We get to find that out together. It could've been bad, you know? That night we spent together. We could've had sex and realized there was no chemistry there."

"Yeah," I snorted. "That *so* didn't happen."

"Why do you think that is?" He cocked his head to the side. "This isn't me fishing or being arrogant. I really want to know why you think we were so good together."

I stared at my plate as I ventured to answer. "Because you *do* know me so well. And because we have a history. I felt like…like I could really be vulnerable. In a way that I couldn't be with other men in my past."

"Say it, Willa. Say what you really mean."

"Safe. You make me feel safe. Safe enough to let go." I met his gaze. "Safe enough to fall."

He reached out to cup my cheek. "Because you know I'll be there to catch you."

Chapter 15

"So, you never did tell me why you were suddenly able to meet me tonight," he said, obviously shifting the conversation to lighter topics.

"Waverly's taking a CPR class with Dylan. Every Wednesday for the next four Wednesdays." I let that settle between us, letting him do with it what he would.

"So that means I get to take you on a date every Wednesday for the next four Wednesdays."

"I was hoping you'd say that."

He smiled.

"The class is only for an hour and a half. And I'd rather—that is—I'm not ready to share it with her, what we're doing."

He ran his napkin across his lips, trying to hide his grin.

"What?" I demanded.

His grin turned into a laugh.

"I don't get it! What's so funny?"

"Willa," he said after his laughter subsided. "She knows."

"What? How! I didn't tell her."

"No, you didn't tell her," he agreed. "But Dylan saw us kissing outside Boots. He told her. She confronted me when I dropped her off at Charlie's."

"She didn't," I said, my mouth gaping.

"Oh, yes, she did."

"What did she say?"

"She wanted to know what my intentions with you are." His grin slid across his face. "So, I thought it only fair to level with her and tell her the truth."

"The truth."

"Yep."

"So, she knows." I leaned back in my chair. "Wow. And she didn't let on that she knew. I mean, she hasn't busted my chops or anything. No more than usual, I mean."

"She probably will tonight when she gets home."

"You think?"

"Yeah. Because I texted her that I was taking you out on a date. She said to have you home by eleven." He winked. "Oh, and to also bring home a tiramisu for her."

"That Little Punk," I said with a laugh.

"That nickname sure does fit, doesn't it?"

"Yeah, it totally does." I shook my head and felt a great sense of relief unfurling inside of me. "I'm glad she knows, actually."

"So, you're not pissed."

"No. I hate keeping stuff from her. And she's proven she can keep a secret."

"You know what else this means?"

"What?"

"I can pick you up at your house on my motorcycle and drive you home."

I smiled. "Like a real boyfriend."

"Boyfriend. Is that what I am?" he asked, his smile softening.

"Yeah, Duke. You're my boyfriend."

Mama Leonardi descended on us and gestured at the table. She patted my shoulder and nodded happily before scooping up the empty plates and carting them away.

"You guys coming to the clubhouse barbecue?" he asked.

"Yeah, I think so."

"You know, if we tell people we're together, you can sit on my lap at the bonfire." He grinned. "And then you can sleep over in my room."

"That sounds like a perfect night. It really does, but I just—I'm not ready for everyone to know. I'm not ready for us to be on display. That's so much pressure."

"Pressure? What kind of pressure?"

"The kind of pressure to make stuff official. The Old Ladies are all awesome. I love them. They've been so good to me and to Waverly. But they'll ask questions and want to know."

"Want to know what?"

"When you'll make me your Old Lady. When I'm getting inked. When we're having little Dukes."

He raised his brows. "You want to make little Dukes with me?"

I blushed. "No, that's not what I meant."

"So, you don't want little Dukes with me?"

"Little Dukes? I can hardly handle one big Duke."

His smile stretched slowly across his face. "I don't know, Willa. You handle big Duke just fine."

"This is getting out of control," I snapped, my face flushing even more. "Mia and Allison have babies. Joni and Brooklyn are pregnant. I just know I'll get asked about what's in store for our future."

"Doc and Boxer don't have kids," he pointed out.

"No. Not yet. But she's feeling the pressure."

He shrugged.

"Don't shrug at me," I demanded. "You just got me to put a label of boyfriend girlfriend on this. But when it's out in the open, everyone will be watching, speculating, and encouraging. You know how they are. We'd be like the newest episode of Animal Planet. Biker mating rituals and how they impress the female of their choice."

Duke's shoulders lurched as a boisterous laugh escaped his mouth.

Mama Leonardi returned to the table with three plates of different pastas. One of which was spaghetti and meatballs. She peppered the dishes, added a heavy sprinkle of Parmesan to them, and then left.

"You're not wrong," he said. "About the Old Ladies voicing their opinions. But it's only because they mean well and already think of you as one of them."

"They don't."

"Of course they do. Why else would Mia and Joni have bought you and Waverly brand new clothes."

"I knew it!" I yelled. Realizing how loud I'd been, I looked around the restaurant and said, "The pasta. I knew it would be good."

Duke chuckled.

"I knew some of the clothes were new. They totally lied about it."

"They didn't want you to feel like a charity case. They're aware of the insane pride you have."

"Insane pride? About what?"

"Getting you to take any kind of help. Jesus, it took you years to ask Savage and I for shit without feeling bad."

I thought about what he said and then nodded. "Yeah, okay." I served myself some pasta.

"So, getting back to these little Dukes you mentioned…"

"Forget I said anything."

"Not likely. You mentioned kids."

"Not really. I mean, I mentioned them in the generic sense. Not the actual sense. I'm not ready."

"Ready for the actual kids or this conversation?"

"Duke," I sighed. "Please."

"Fine. I'll let it go. For now. But just think of a little Duke with your hair and my dimples. Tell me that doesn't do things to you."

"It does nothing to me," I lied.

"Okay."

"Don't say *okay* like that!"

"Like what?"

"Like you think I'm lying."

"You *are* lying." He grinned. "I know your tells because I *know* you. And you're thinking about it."

"Am not."

"Are too."

"You're ridiculous," I said, but I couldn't stop the laugh.

"I am."

I was about to take a bite when my phone rang. "Sorry," I said around my fork.

"Like you have to apologize."

"Right." He was a biker and constantly getting calls. I looked at my phone. "It's Savage."

"Answer it," he said.

"And say what?"

"Whatever you want." His eyes bored into mine.

I pressed the answer button. "Hey."

"Where are you?" he asked.

"I'm out to dinner with a client," I lied, wincing when

Duke's jaw clenched.

"Damn, sorry. I wanted to see what you were up to."

"Why? Are you bored?"

"Yep."

"Contrary to popular belief, I was not put on this earth to entertain you."

"Uh, yeah you were."

"Call the brunette," I said.

"I told you we're done."

"Then you have to wait to see me. I'll be at the barbecue on Friday."

"Awesome. Later."

I hung up and shoved my phone back into my purse.

"So, I'm a client?" Duke asked.

"What was I supposed to say? That I was on a date but not drop your name? He would've bugged me about it. You know how he gets."

"I know how he gets," he said quietly.

"I'm still not convinced he'll be okay with this. With us."

"He loves you, and wants you to be happy. And he's my best friend and Tarnished Angels brother. He'd want me to be happy too."

"I should be the one to tell him. When it's time to tell him."

"You want to tell him without me there? Like hell you will. He deserves the truth from both of us."

"When I'm ready?" I pressed.

He sighed. "When you're ready."

"Good. Because frankly, I'm not sure I have the bandwidth for Savage's chaos right now."

"I'm not sure anyone can handle his chaos," he said with a laugh.

Savage was the quintessential Dr. Jekyll and Mr. Hyde.

He could flip from easy-going to insane in an instant. He wasn't called Savage for no reason. He wasn't unstable or unwell, just capable of extremes with the ability to back up his name.

We finished our dinner and I was pleasantly full. There was a little wine left in the bottle and I poured it into Duke's glass.

Mama Leonardi brought us a tiramisu with two forks and then scooped up our dinner plates. "The food was delicious," I said to her.

She smiled at me. "*Grazie.*"

"Can I have another tiramisu to go? For my sister?" I wasn't sure why I added the last part, but I thought Mama Leonardi would appreciate that little tidbit.

She nodded, said something else, and headed back into the kitchen. Mama Leonardi returned in a bit with the takeout bag and set it on the table and then she set the bill in front of Duke. With a wink and a touch to his shoulder, she was gone again.

Duke quickly laid down some bills, and then rose from his seat. He took the bag and then waited for me to stand. He held out his hand to me and I grasped it. He tugged me toward him and we headed out of the restaurant.

"I've got something for you," he said as he led me toward his motorcycle.

"A night ride on the back of your bike?" I asked.

"Next Wednesday," he said with a smile. "When your sister isn't at home waiting for her tiramisu."

He riffled through his saddle bag and pulled out a plastic bag with a pink ribbon tied at the neck.

"You brought me lemon drops?" I asked with a smile.

"I couldn't bring you flowers, could I?" he teased.

I lifted the bag of lemon drops to my nose and sniffed. "Hmm. Lemony, sugary deliciousness." I plopped them in the to-go bag with the tiramisu and then placed my hand on his chest. I leaned in close, my lips near his mouth. "Thank you for dinner."

He grasped my hips and hauled me into the hard wall of his body. "Anytime, babe. Anytime."

"What did I tell you about calling me *babe*?"

His grin was lopsided. "You're my only *babe*, babe. Now shut up and kiss me."

Chapter 16

WAVERLY WAS on the couch when I got home. As I walked in, I was completely unable to wipe the dopey grin off my face. I set the to-go bag next to her.

"Your tiramisu, my lady," I quipped.

She grinned. "Your lipstick is smeared."

"Shit, really?"

"Really, really." She set her phone down.

"Okay, I know you know," I said. "About Duke and I."

"There's a Duke and you? Officially?" Her eyes widened and they looked extremely hopeful.

"I guess, officially…yeah." I rubbed the back of my neck. "But we're not telling anyone. It's kind of a secret."

"Why is it a secret?"

"Because we want to explore our relationship without all the outside pressure."

"Oh. Okay." She frowned.

"You can't tell *anyone*. Not even Jessica…"

"Dylan already knows. He's the one who told me."

"I'm not worried about Dylan."

"Are you worried about me?"

"No. I know you're oddly good at keeping secrets."

She bit her lip. "Savage doesn't know?"

"Not yet. We're not ready to tell him."

Waverly scrunched her nose. "Okay. I'll keep my lips sealed. But I think you should tell him sooner, rather than later."

"Relationship advice? Really?"

She grinned and I couldn't help but laugh.

"He makes you happy," she said.

"Yeah. He does."

Waverly reached into the bag and pulled out the lemon drops. "He bought you your favorite candy."

"Yep."

She sighed, all dreamy. "You want to sit and gush about our boyfriends?"

"You'll gush with me?" I asked in surprise.

"Well, yeah, I've wanted to gush for a while, but there really hasn't been a lot of time. What with everything falling apart."

"Well, it's not falling apart now," I said. "I think we've rounded a corner."

"God, I hope so. It's exhausting being a delinquent." She grinned and I burst out laughing.

"You, kid, are my absolute favorite."

"Come on!" Waverly moaned. "You're taking forever to get ready!"

"Hold your horses, punk," I called back. I swiped my lips with clear gloss, fingered my hair-sprayed waves, and then left the bathroom.

Waverly was tapping her Doc Marten clad foot impatiently, her hands on her hips. But when she saw me, she grinned. "You look hot."

"Thanks."

"Trying to impress Duke?"

I pointed a finger at her. "Remember what I said."

"My lips are sealed." She mimed zipping her mouth shut and throwing away the key.

"Well, we survived this week. Let's go eat our weight in hot dogs."

"You said it," she quipped. "Though, honestly, it went by pretty fast, didn't it?"

"For you, maybe." I locked up the house and then tossed her the keys. "You're driving."

"Am I designated driver tonight?" she asked. "I can be if you want."

"There's being a bad influence, and then there's being a bad influence," I said. "Though I guess I should be the one worried about *your* influence on me."

"Never gonna let me live it down, are you?" she asked as she opened the driver's side door.

"Probably not." I buckled myself in. "How do Dylan's parents feel about you?"

"It's just his mom," she said. "And she works all the time."

"Ergo she has no idea that you're corrupting her son."

"There's no corrupting going on. More like, he's my clean-up crew when I mess up." She pulled away from the curb. "Jessica's parents won't let her hang out with me, even when my suspension is over. Not that I blame them, but still."

"Give it time," I suggested. "And show them you're not going to drag their daughter into trouble anymore."

"No promises." She threw me a grin, but it was forced.

Though she was teasing and trying for levity, I could

tell being separated from her best friend weighed heavily on her.

It was good we were going to the clubhouse where she could be distracted by food and conversation.

"You're not going to be bored?" I asked.

"Why would I be bored?"

"Because there won't be anyone there your age," I said.

"There's no one my age at Charlie's, and I'm never bored there."

"Good point."

"I'll be fine."

She spoke with an assurance that was new. She'd always been closed off, and rarely did she like being around people she didn't know well.

"Speaking of fine," she said, "make sure you act completely normal around Duke."

"Completely normal? What does that even mean?"

"I mean, if you want to keep this a secret, you can't stare at him with that look you had when you came home, even when you think no one is watching. Someone's always watching."

"You speak from experience, do you?" I asked with a laugh.

"Yep." She grinned. "Jessica told me how Dylan watched me when he thought no one was looking."

"So what you're really saying is the best friend is the one who's watching."

"Yep. And even though Savage is kind of oblivious, he's not stupid. So just… act normal."

"Thanks for the tip," I drawled.

"It's what I'm here for." She grinned.

Crow and South Paw were guarding the gate of the clubhouse and waved us through. Waverly turned into the gravel parking lot and her breath hitched.

"You okay?" I asked her as she cut the engine.

"Um. That's Dylan's bike," she said, pointing to a motorcycle.

"Really?"

She nodded. "Did they—oh God, Savage wasn't kidding."

"Wasn't kidding about what?" I demanded.

"The other day, he said he was going to invite Dylan to the barbecue so he and the other guys could grill him."

I sniggered. "Ha, no pun intended."

"Shut up."

"Maybe they just want to roast him?"

"Willa!" she snapped.

"Sorry, doll," I said with a wide grin. "This is just the way they are."

"Great," she muttered.

"He didn't tell you he was coming?"

She shook her head. "No, and I'm going to give him hell about it."

"Maybe he thought you'd bail if you knew he was invited."

"Yeah, maybe."

"Besides, I think you should cut him some slack. Dylan is clearly in love with you if he's willing to brave a night with bikers who are insanely protective of you."

A smile blossomed across her face. "You think he's in love with me?"

I tugged on the end of her ponytail. "You idiot."

She laughed. "Come on, let's go save my boyfriend from Savage being Savage."

"What about Duke?" I asked. "You don't think he's going to give Dylan hell?"

"Nah, Duke will be too busy staring at your ass to give Dylan hell."

We climbed out of the car and headed up to the clubhouse steps. When we stepped inside, we saw a cluster of people busy in the kitchen. Darcy was covering a plate of hamburger patties while Mia cut open packages of bratwurst and hot dogs.

"Yes! You guys are here!" Mia exclaimed. "Do me a huge favor. Grab something from the kitchen and take it outside. The guys have already fired up the grill, the coolers are full of drinks, and for the love of God, whatever you do, don't let the dogs inside. Monk got into a plate of raw burgers already."

"Hello," Darcy said, her eyes twinkling. "Welcome to crazy town. Hope you enjoy your stay."

"I didn't bring my passport," Waverly quipped.

Darcy laughed. "Will you check on Lily? If I know her, she's already lied to Boxer, Zip, *and* her father about how many cookies she's had. I don't want her spoiling her dinner."

"Will do." She saluted as she grabbed a condiment carrier in one hand and a fruit platter in another.

"There's also a very cute boy here who claims to be your boyfriend," Mia said, her smile widening.

"I better get out there then," Waverly stated. "Dylan needs reinforcements." She headed off in the direction of the back yard.

"Your sister is a life saver," Darcy said. "I swear she's the only one who can wrangle Lily."

"Waverly told me you're losing your babysitter to college next year."

"Yep." Darcy nodded. "Here, Mia. Throw them on this cookie sheet."

Mia dumped the bratwurst onto the cookie sheet and then arranged them so they fit neatly side by side. "There's always so much leftover food that we don't have to cook for a few days," she said. "It makes life easy for a while."

"Waverly's taking a CPR class," I said. "So when she sits for Cam and Lily, she's fully prepared for anything that may happen."

"God, what a good kid," Darcy said. "A true gem. As far as I'm concerned, the minute Waverly has her license, we'll phase out Audrey."

"You think my sister's a good kid?" I asked in surprise.

"Well, yeah." Darcy cocked her head to the side. "Oh, you mean because of the suspension."

I shrugged. "It's the second suspension."

"We heard about why she got suspended," Darcy said. "As far as I'm concerned, that principal is a shit bag extra-ordinaire."

"Not so much the suspension as the lying to her older sister about going to a party," I said.

"She's a teenager. That's what they do," Darcy said.

"Let's get out there," Mia said. "I'm dying to see Waverly around her boyfriend."

The three of us grabbed the trays of food and headed to the back yard. Silas and Cam were kicking a soccer ball back and forth as two dogs lounged in the grass away from the commotion. Lily was sitting on Boxer's shoulders, munching on what looked like the remains of a cookie.

The Old Ladies sat in a cluster with the babies in front of them on a blanket on the grass, and the Tarnished Angels were chatting in smaller groups; some around the grill, others on the lawn.

We dropped the food at the grill and Darcy gave her husband a kiss on the lips. He pinched the tongs at her and then went back to manning the fire.

Savage and Duke stood with Colt. Mia went to him

and he automatically reached out and pulled her into his side.

"You," Savage said, pointing a finger at me.

"Me, what?" I demanded.

"You little liar."

"Liar? I'm not a liar."

Savage grinned, a dangerous glint in his eye. "I know what you've been up to."

"I haven't been up to anything," I said calmly. I saw Duke out of the corner of my eye, staring at me while he took a sip of his beer.

"This past Wednesday," he drawled. "You said you were out with a client."

"I was."

"I don't think so."

I glared at him.

He grinned cheekily. "You were on a date with someone, weren't you?"

"No, I was out to dinner with a client," I insisted.

"You're a web designer," he pointed out. "Your meetings are through email and Zoom. I think you're seeing someone in secret."

I crossed my arms over my chest. "Hate to disappoint you, but you're wrong. I really was out to dinner with a client."

"Beer?" Duke asked.

"Please," I muttered. I placed my hand in the center of Savage's chest, leaned in close and asked, "How much have you had to drink?"

"Boxer broke open the new batch of moonshine," Colt said. The Tarnished Angels president couldn't suppress his grin. "Savage took it upon himself to be the unofficial taste tester."

"Where did you eat?" Savage asked.

"What?"

"Dinner on Wednesday night? With your *client*? What restaurant?"

"An Italian wine bar. Now shove off and let me enjoy myself. It's been a long week." Duke returned and handed me a beer. "Thanks," I said to him.

"You know I love you." Savage roped his arm around my shoulders and pulled me against him. "And if you were dating someone, it's my right as your best friend to make sure he's not a dickbag. Just like I did with Dylan."

He gestured with his chin.

I turned my head and saw Waverly and Dylan talking to Torque.

"No way," I said with a laugh. "Is Torque *actually* talking?"

"It appears that way," Mia quipped.

"What did you find out about Dylan, by the way?" I asked him.

"Kid's fucking smart," Savage said. "Volunteers as a tutor and keeps his grades up. No record of trouble."

"The exact kind of guy you want Waverly with," Duke added.

I looked at my sister and her boyfriend. He gazed down at her with amusement and adoration, and she stared up at him with the same look.

"Mia!" Allison called. "Scarlett needs a diaper change!"

"On it," Mia yelled back.

Colt let her go, but not without a steamy kiss. They didn't care about the audience around them. They were publicly affectionate and deeply in love.

I glanced at Duke to find him still staring at me.

"I'm gonna go chill with the Old Ladies," I said to him. "I'll talk to you boys later."

I followed Mia to the group of women. Mia leaned down and scooped up her infant daughter and then went inside.

Joni took a sip of her drink and then grimaced. "Baby's foot is underneath my ribs. I'm so ready to be done with the pregnancy thing."

Allison smiled. "That's usually how it works. You get so annoyed about being pregnant, you no longer worry about a baby coming out of you."

"Nature's design," Darcy agreed.

"Where's Doc?" I asked.

"She's still at the clinic," Joni said. "She'll be here in about an hour."

The back door opened and Brooklyn exited, holding a pastry box. "Jesus, woman," Slash growled from behind her, holding his own pastry box. "You didn't have to bring the entire bakery."

"Do you love me?" Brooklyn asked her man.

"Yeah."

"Does baking make me happy?"

"Yeah."

"Then why are you griping?" she grinned up at him.

"Foreplay," Darcy said with a laugh.

Allison giggled. "No doubt."

I shook my head. I was surrounded by happy couples, several of whom had babies or were pregnant. It made me think about the conversation I'd had with Duke on our date.

"What is this?" Brooklyn demanded, pointing to a platter on the table.

"It looks like cookies," Boxer quipped. "Doesn't it, Lily Burger?"

Lily nodded.

"This is an insult. A travesty!" Brooklyn stated. "You

got *store bought* cookies? Knowing *I* was coming to this shindig?"

"Did she just say shindig?" Joni asked in amusement.

"Uh oh," Darcy muttered.

"Uh oh what?"

"Three, two, one," Darcy chanted.

The moment Darcy said *one*, Brooklyn burst into tears, brushed past Slash, and went into the clubhouse.

"What the hell was that about?" I asked in confusion.

"New batch of second trimester hormones," Joni said with a sigh. "I know it well."

Slash set his pastry box next to the one Brooklyn had left and then went inside after his wife.

"They'll be back in like—" Joni looked at Darcy and then Allison "—what? Twenty minutes?"

"I'd say closer to thirty," Allison projected.

"Care to make it interesting?" Darcy asked.

"Fifty bucks," Joni said. "I think it'll be twenty minutes."

"I guess thirty," Allison said.

"Twenty-eight minutes." Darcy looked at her watch. "And the time starts now."

"Twenty-eight minutes?" I repeated. "That's oddly specific."

"What's your bet?" Joni asked me.

"I don't have fifty bucks to lose," I said wryly. "But I'm going with twenty-two minutes."

Mia returned to the party, carting a newly diapered baby. She took a seat next to Joni on the patio couch and got comfortable.

"Damn, I forgot to get a drink." Mia made a motion to get up.

I waved her down. "I'll get it for you."

Mia smiled. "Angel. Sparkling water, please."

"Sure. Anyone else need anything?"

Allison looked up from her spot on the blanket next to her son who'd fallen asleep with his bottom in the air. "Same for me, please."

Joni and Darcy shook their heads and then I went off to get drinks. I was bent over at a cooler when I heard, "You had to wear those jeans, didn't you?"

I slowly stood up and looked at Duke over my shoulder. "It's possible that I might've thought a minute or two about what they'd do to you if I wore them…"

His dark eyes scanned my face. "You're not wearing lipstick."

"No, I'm not. Lipstick smears."

"Jesus," he muttered. "You're lethal."

I grinned. "So, do you have a plan for how the hell we can sneak away for a few minutes and not get caught?"

"When the sun sets, and we light the bonfire." He took a step toward me and dipped his head. His voice quieted when he said, "Watch for me. You'll know when I can't wait any longer."

Desire flickered in my belly.

"Willa!" Waverly called.

I reluctantly pulled my gaze away from Duke to peer at my sister. "Yeah?"

"Come hang out with us," she said, gesturing toward her and Dylan.

"I'll be right there." I shot Duke a look and then went and dropped off the drinks before heading to my sister and her boyfriend. They were still standing with Torque. I didn't know Torque well, but I knew he was taciturn and gruff.

"Hi, Torque," I said.

"'Lo," Torque greeted. He took a sip of his beer.

Waverly rolled her eyes. "Oh my God. Dude, open your mouth and say *hello* like a normal person."

My jaw gaped as I heard my sister chastise a six-foot giant of a biker.

But Torque cracked a smile and said, "Hi, Willa."

"Uh, hi." I blinked.

Waverly elbowed Torque in the side. "See? Wasn't that hard."

"You're pushing your luck, Little Punk," Torque growled. With that pronouncement, he took his beer and left.

"How the hell did you get away with that?" I demanded. "I've never even heard him say more than a few words at a time."

"She likes playing with fire." Dylan grinned at her and opened the can of soda in his hand.

"Speaking of fire," I quipped. "How is it you have the balls to come to a barbecue full of bikers you've never met?"

"They're her family," Dylan said with a shrug. "They just want to make sure I'm not a creep."

"Okay, but what if *I* think you're a creep?" I asked. "I'm the big sister after all. It's me you have to make an impression on."

"So do you like him?" Waverly asked.

"Too soon to tell," I teased. "You kids have fun. I'm gonna go hang out with the adults."

"Adults," Waverly said. "Yuck."

Just as I sat back down with the Old Ladies, Brooklyn and Slash came out of the clubhouse, drawing my attention. I watched as Slash brought their linked hands together and kissed the back of her palm. Brooklyn smiled and stole a hand across her baby bump.

I glanced at Darcy. "Time?"

Darcy looked at her watch. "Twenty-seven minutes! I'm the closest! Pay up, scoundrels!"

"Pay up for what?" Slash demanded.

"We made a bet to see how long it took you to comfort Brooklyn," Joni said. "And by comfort, I mean *comfort.*"

Brooklyn's face suffused with color and then she buried her head in her husband's shoulder in obvious embarrassment.

Slash, on the other hand, looked pleased with himself. He let go of his wife and she ambled over to us and took a seat.

"So, you guys are using my hormones against me to make money?" Brooklyn asked. "That's like a new level of hustling."

"It's a rite of passage. You're one of us now," Allison said.

Brooklyn snorted. Slash appeared by her side and handed her a cup. He bent over, whispered something in her ear that made her blush, and then went to talk to Zip.

Boxer sauntered over to the group of us and hoisted Lily off his shoulders. He set her down and then reached into the pocket of his jeans and nudged the phone in Lily's direction. "You're calling Doc for me, okay?"

Lily took the phone. "Why am I calling her?"

"Because you're cute, and she'll feel guilty for not being here if she hears your voice. I want her at the party. You're up."

Lily nodded. "You're right. I am cute."

"You have no idea. Now, let's see what you can do," Boxer said, pointing to the phone.

Lily touched the screen and then put the cell to her ear. "Aunt Doc, its Lily Burger. Listen, Uncle Boxer misses you and he wants you to come to the party, so you should come to the party." She paused a second and nodded. "K, see you soon."

She hung up the phone and handed it back to Boxer. "Here ya go."

"That was fast," Boxer said.

"She had to go." She grabbed Boxer's fingers and dragged him toward the table of food. "You owe me another cookie."

Darcy hastily looked at Brooklyn.

Brooklyn raised her brows. "I've made my peace with the fact that Lily shows no allegiance when it comes to baked goods."

"She called Linden Aunt Doc," Joni said. Her lip started to wobble and then she burst into tears. "So damn cute!"

"Zip!" Darcy called out. "Your wife needs you." She looked at her watch. "Ladies, place your bets."

Chapter 17

"Silas found his new idol," Mia said, looking fondly at her son as he kicked the soccer ball around with Cam and Dylan.

"I think it's safe to say that Dylan has the Tarnished Angels stamp of approval," Darcy said.

"Don't tell Waverly that," I quipped. "I think she likes to be a rebel. She might break up with him just to prove a point. And he's a good influence on her. We need that."

"Finally!" Boxer yelled.

A slender blonde with a pixie cut strode up to him and placed a hand on his chest. "You have no patience."

Monk—Doc and Boxer's dog—ran up to greet her. After Doc kissed Boxer, she bent down and gave her yellow lab a vigorous rub. The fur baby rolled over onto his back and showed off his belly.

"Hey, girl," Mia called out to her.

"Hey." Doc smiled and took Boxer's hand, bringing him with her toward us.

"You ready to tell them?" Boxer asked her.

She peered up at him with blue eyes. "Might want to cover your ears. They're going to squeal."

"Oh my God," Joni breathed. "You're pregnant!"

Doc snorted. "No."

"Rats," Joni muttered.

"We've set a wedding date," Doc said, tugging on Joni's ponytail.

"Yeah, yeah, you've been talking about it for months. I'll believe it when I see it," Joni teased.

"Two weeks from today," Doc said. "Believe it."

"No." Joni frowned. "You're not serious."

"As a heart attack," Doc said.

"Hey, Lily Burger! Come here a second," Boxer called out.

Lily ran over to us and hastily brushed her blonde curls and a cookie crumb from her face.

"What are you doing two weeks from Friday?" Doc asked.

"Dunno. Why?"

Boxer looked down at her and smiled. "You want to be my best Lily Burger? I'm marrying your Aunt Doc, and I need someone to stand next to me and hold the wedding rings."

"*Really?* You mean it?" The little girl's grin was so wide it nearly split her face.

"I mean it," Boxer said.

"Can I wear pink?"

"Yep."

"Can I wear purple?"

"Yep."

"Can I wear black like Waverly wears black?"

Boxer grinned. "You can wear whatever color you want, Lily Burger."

"Yay! Cam! Guess what! I get to be a Lily Burger and

hold rings!" She ran off to talk to her brother, but her statement pulled the attention of all the Tarnished Angels.

"Hold rings?" Zip frowned. "What's she talking about?"

"I finally convinced Boxer to set a wedding date," Doc joked to the Tarnished Angels VP.

Zip sniggered.

"He's been really hard to pin down, right?" Brooklyn teased.

"She pinned me last night," Boxer stated.

Doc elbowed him in the ribs, causing him to wince and then chuckle. "Consider this our engagement party."

"You can't call this your engagement party," Joni protested. "There aren't any adorable decorations."

"There's no fruity drinks in champagne flutes," Mia added.

"I didn't bake anything for you!" Brooklyn panicked.

Doc touched her shoulder. "I really didn't want to make a fuss, okay? Which is why we're doing it this way."

"Well, can I at least make your wedding cake?" Brooklyn sniffed.

"Absolutely." Doc smiled.

"This calls for moonshine," Savage said, setting a glass liquor bottle full of clear liquid down on the patio coffee table.

"What about for the rest of us who can't drink?" Allison asked.

"I'll get you a soda," Torque said.

"Thanks." She stared up at her husband and the heat between them scorched the air.

I turned away and met Duke's eyes.

"Well, give me that bottle," Doc teased. "I'm marrying Boxer. I'm gonna need some liquid courage."

"Hey, you're stuck with me now, woman." Boxer wrapped his arm around Doc and pulled her into his side.

"Happy to be stuck," Doc said, looking up at him. "Promise."

Boxer brushed his lips against Doc's temple and hugged her tighter.

"What are you doing about a dress?" Darcy asked her.

"Oh man, they're about to talk wedding semantics," Zip said. "Come on, men. Let's char some animal flesh over a fire."

"You're vile," Joni threw out. "But I'll take two burgers when they're done."

Zip leaned down and whispered something in her ear and then pressed a kiss to her cheek.

The Tarnished Angels were overtly affectionate with their women and loved their children like mini-van driving suburban fathers. It was an unusual sight; one I found I enjoyed a lot.

I wondered how they'd react if Duke and I announced we were together.

No doubt they'd laugh and tease and say they knew something was between us all along.

The men wandered away, not at all interested in listening to wedding details. Colt slapped Boxer on the back and the others congratulated him. Boxer looked happy about the news. Doc, on the other hand...

"Are you okay?" I asked her.

"Yeah, I'm okay."

"Then why don't you look happier? I thought weddings were happy occasions," I teased.

She smiled, but it slipped. "I am happy. It's just strange knowing both my parents won't be at my wedding. Not that I want them there," she hastened to add. "They're not the best people in the world and my mother especially doesn't understand what I have with Boxer. But..."

"But?" Darcy prodded.

"But if I don't invite them, then this is the line in the sand. There's no coming back from that. So, I kind of have to choose, you know? Do I want my wedding day to be easy and fun without the baggage of my parents, knowing that it's going to be the nail in the coffin of our relationship? Or do I invite them, even though they haven't been in the same room as each other since they divorced?"

"Your wedding should be about you and Boxer. No one else," Mia said. "Not even us."

"Well, if I had it my way, we'd go away for the weekend and come back married," she said. "I don't want the fuss. But this is a nice compromise. Small party, just close friends. Nothing too fancy."

"Hence two weeks from today without time for it to spin out of control," Darcy said. "Got it."

"You and I need to have a discussion about your cake," Brooklyn said. "So, then I can talk to Brielle about decorating it."

"Speaking of Brielle," Mia said. "Weren't she and Jazz supposed to come tonight?"

"Yeah, they were. But they were literally on their way here and they found a stray dog on the side of the road and brought it back to Brielle's. They're trying to find the owner," Brooklyn explained.

"Are we going wedding dress shopping?" Mia asked Doc.

"Hmm, I don't think so. The idea gives me hives," Doc said. "I love Boxer. I love all of you. I don't need a big wedding, or a dress with a long train to make the day special."

Joni and Mia looked at each other and then Mia asked, "Can we throw you an engagement brunch?"

"Do we have to have champagne?" Doc asked. "I'm kind of anti-champagne."

"No," Mia snorted.

"You've forgotten champagne's rival for best early morning beverage," Darcy said. "Bloody Marys."

"You should've led with that." Doc grinned. Her cell phone rang and she pulled it out of her back pocket to look at the screen. "It's my mother."

"Did you tell her you're getting married?" Brooklyn asked.

"Yeah. I sent her a text."

"You didn't," I said with a laugh.

"If you knew my mother, you'd get it," Doc said. "I should've sent her an email." She sighed. "I better answer it. How much more do you think I can piss her off?"

"Tell her your wedding is being catered by The Crab Shack," Darcy suggested.

"Stellar!" Doc said. "Hello, Mother. Hey, guess what…"

The sun set and we were all full of food. The guys had been imbibing on moonshine, but the rest of us were pacing ourselves.

Gray and Colt lit the bonfire and we sat on logs and camp chairs. Dylan perched next to Waverly, their legs touching.

My eyes met Duke's across the blaze. His gaze said everything in that moment.

"I meant to tell you," Mia said, addressing Waverly, "I dig the shirt."

Waverly grinned. "Thanks."

"Want me to show you how to make it cooler?" Mia asked.

"What did you have in mind?" Waverly asked.

"T-Shirt cutting," Mia explained. "I have to put Scarlett down. You want to come with me and then I'll show you?"

Waverly looked at Dylan. "You mind if I leave you alone?"

"Go for it." Dylan ran a hand through his tousled brown hair. "I can handle myself."

Zip pounded him on the back. "We'll keep him entertained."

"I feel like I should be worried. Should I be worried?" Waverly asked, but she hopped up anyway and followed Mia into the clubhouse.

"She's completely come out of her shell," Brooklyn said, adjusting her body in her chair.

"She's even managed to get Torque to talk," Slash said. He sat next to his wife and took her hand in his. "How the hell did she accomplish that?"

"I have a younger sister about Waverly's age. She's at boarding school on the East Coast—she's into horses. Torque pays her tuition—loves her like his own sister. Anyway, I think Waverly reminds him of her. They should meet," Allison said. "When my sister's back for the summer."

"That would be great," I said.

My eyes wandered across the fire and fixated on Duke. He was listening to Savage talk, but when Duke's gaze met mine again, he ever so slightly inclined his head.

I took a sip of beer and then stood up. "I'm going to hit the restroom." I stretched my arms over my head and then sauntered into the house, making sure to put an extra little sway into my hips because I knew Duke was watching.

The screen door slammed shut and I headed to the second-floor bathroom. I sent Duke a text telling him where I'd gone.

Nerves of anticipation swirled in my belly as I waited for him to make his appearance.

A slight knock sounded on the door and I quickly unlocked it and opened it. He entered and then closed the door.

Electricity crackled between us and when his hands reached out to grasp my hips, my knees went weak. He guided me back against the sink and slid one of his thighs between my legs and pressed against my cleft.

The rough denim grazed me in all the right places.

He rocked against me for a few moments until I was gasping.

Duke backed away, but only so he could turn me, our faces reflected in the mirror. His eyes were dark with intense desire and mine were wild. My skin was already flushed.

His fingers went to the button of my jeans and he lowered my zipper. Then he glided his fingers into my panties.

"Jesus, you're fucking wet," he growled against my neck.

He swirled the tip of his finger between my folds and pressed against the most sensitive, aching part of me.

I backed up against him as he held me with one hand, pleasuring me with the other. Our gazes remained locked on one another in the mirror, my cheeks flushing with need.

The hours of stolen looks and days of postponed lust

culminated between my legs. Just as I was on the verge of coming, Duke withdrew his finger.

"You fucker," I ground out.

He chuckled as he shoved my jeans down around my ankles, taking my black lace thong with them.

I heard the clanging of his belt as he undid his buckle.

"Grip the counter," he rasped. "And bend over. I'm going to fuck you raw."

"Duke," I pleaded.

"I haven't been with anyone since you, Willa. I don't want anyone else. Fuck."

"Yes," I begged. "Fuck me raw."

The head of his shaft teased my entrance and then he thrust into me.

It burned as he stretched me from this angle and I hissed.

"Sorry, baby," he growled.

"Don't stop."

"Wouldn't dream of it," he gritted.

He slammed into me from behind, again and again. I watched in the mirror, not believing this was us.

I took one of my hands off the counter and was about to slide it between my legs when Duke growled, "No. That's for me to do."

I put my hand back on the counter and arched my back, wanting him to hit the perfect spot that would make me detonate around him.

One of his hands reached around me to tease me. The other went to my neck where he gave my throat a slight squeeze as he pulled me toward him.

The power he had over my body was unimaginable. I didn't have to worry about my pleasure. Duke would take care of me.

He always took care of me.

"Come for me, baby. Let me feel you," he whispered against my ear.

Duke ground his fingers against me at the same time he squeezed my neck. It was the perfect cocktail my body needed and I came with a soft moan.

With his hand still around my neck, his fingers playing with me, and him buried inside me, he came with his own shuddering release.

He dropped his hand from around my throat but made no move to leave.

"Damn," he whispered.

"Yeah," I said.

We were still connected when our eyes met in the mirror.

"You okay?" he asked, kissing my hair.

"Better than okay."

He touched my neck. "Even this?"

I smiled. "*Definitely* that."

He chuckled slightly and then eased himself out of my body.

I quickly moved to grab a few pieces of toilet paper and dabbed between my legs. I turned around and saw Duke sliding his boxers and jeans up his legs.

"You don't want to clean up?" I asked, gesturing to the remains of my release at the base of his shaft.

"Hell no," he said. "I want the reminder of you there."

"Weirdo," I huffed a laugh.

He leaned in and kissed me, his tongue sliding into my mouth. "You go first. I'll follow."

I nodded and hastily pulled up my pants. I looked in the mirror, ensuring my hair was in place and that I didn't look like anything out of the ordinary had happened. Aside from my flushed cheeks, I appeared the same.

I was glad I hadn't worn lipstick. Nothing to fix.

EMMA SLATE

I looked at my phone as I walked down the stairs. I'd only been gone ten minutes.

Dirty, secret quickie sex with my best friend was my new favorite thing.

Mia and Waverly came out of Colt's room just as I got to the bottom of the stairs.

"What do you think?" Waverly asked, turning and showing me the back of the Charlie's Motorcycle Repair shop tank.

"Oh, I like this a lot," I said, touching a cut out.

"I'll show you how to do yours," Waverly said. "Mia taught me."

"You're too cool for school," I quipped.

"I know, that's why I got suspended." She grinned. "Twice."

Chapter 18

"MAKE GOOD CHOICES," I said to Waverly as she climbed out of the car.

She peered down. "I'll try."

"Waverly," I warned.

"I'll make good choices. I will not choose violence," she said. "Scout's honor."

Nodding, I said, "You'll call me? If there's a problem with the administration?"

"There won't be."

She shut the passenger side door and then walked to Dylan, who was waiting for her at the other edge of the parking lot. He waved at me and I waved back.

The rest of the weekend had been quiet. Waverly and I had stayed in, setting up the last bit of our new space. It felt strange to live there—neither one of us admitted it, but we both refused to get completely comfortable and settled in. Even though the house belonged to Mia and it was stable, we didn't truly believe in stability.

Duke sporadically texted but he was busy with the club and Savage was AWOL.

I went to Leather and Ink and opened the store. It was a slow shift and I was in the middle of surfing the internet when Mia came in.

"Hey," she said, looking rosy, a smile across her face.

"Oh, thank God," I said with a grin. "You're going to save me from boredom, aren't you?"

She grinned in commiseration. "It was the same when I was bartending. The slow shifts make you want to die."

"Preach."

Mia chuckled.

"So, what brings you in today? Another lingerie body suit?" I teased.

"Not for me," she said. "For Doc. The engagement brunch gift."

"Great gift idea," I said.

"You're coming, right? To the engagement brunch?"

"Oh." My brow furrowed. "I hadn't thought, I mean, I didn't assume—"

"What? That you were invited? Of course, you're invited. You might not be an Old Lady, but you're Duke and Savage's best friend. That means something."

Though it was the truth—that I wasn't an Old Lady—I didn't expect it to sting the way it did. The only way to officially become an Old Lady was to come clean about what Duke and I were doing. But I wasn't ready to tell Savage, and I definitely wasn't ready to slap the label of Old Lady onto myself. That meant Duke would be my man, officially.

But wasn't he already?

After what we'd done on Friday night...

"Thanks," I said, clearing my throat. "I'd love to come. Let me show you to some of the new things we got in. I think they're definitely Doc's style."

Forty-five minutes later, I was handing Mia back her credit card. "When's your shift over?" she asked.

"Two."

"You're picking Waverly up from school?"

I nodded.

"Do you have time to stop off at Shelly's in between the end of your shift and picking her up?"

I frowned. "Sure. Everything okay?"

"Yeah. I just wanted a chance to talk to you in private, without a bunch of distractions going on. Nothing bad," she assured me.

"You're so cryptic."

"I prefer mysterious. But I'll take cryptic." She smiled and took her brown bag. "I'll see you at two thirty at Shelly's, yeah?"

"Okay."

With a wink and a wave, she left. A few more customers came in before the end of my shift, but by the time the clock rolled around for me to leave, I was itching to go.

Shelly's wasn't technically open, but the front door was unlocked. The barback was setting a case of liquor onto the bar and said, "Hey, sorry we're not open yet."

"I'm Willa. I'm meeting Mia here."

"Oh, sorry. Boss is in the office." He hitched his thumb over his shoulder.

"Thanks."

I headed in the direction of the office and even though the door was open, I knocked.

Mia was behind the desk and she lifted her head. "Awesome, you're here. Come in."

"I feel like I'm about to get a lecture," I said, sitting in the chair in front of her desk.

She set her pen aside and closed a three-ring binder.

"Not at all. I wanted to discuss the redesign of Shelly's website with you."

"You're not serious," I said.

She frowned. "Of course, I'm serious. Why wouldn't I be serious?"

"Because you know I'm all but flat broke," I said baldly. "Look, I appreciate what you're trying to do, but you've done enough. Really. The rental was more than generous. You don't have to offer to hire me."

"I don't know what you think, but I'm not offering to hire you out of charity," she admitted pointedly. "You're a damned good web designer. I love what you've done with Brooklyn's website. It's fresh and easy to navigate, and it handles the insane traffic from all the custom orders and inquiries she gets."

I stared at her. "Duke didn't ask you for this?"

"No."

"Savage?"

"Nope. I swear. This is something I've put off for a while. It needs to get done. I know you; I like you and I respect your work. This is one of those moments where I'm saying *Shut up and take my money*. So Willa, shut up and take my money."

"I'm sort of afraid not to," I quipped. "You're small but mighty."

"Good, glad that's sorted."

"You want me to do what I did for Brooklyn? Create a few homepage templates so you can choose one and tell me what you want built out?"

"Sounds perfect to me."

"I'll charge you exactly what I charged Brooklyn. I'm sure she already told you my rate."

"She did, but from one business owner to another, it's time for you to increase your rate."

"I'll do that," I said. "But I don't feel right about charging you more than I charged her. It would feel like gouging."

"You deserve to be paid for the work you do. It's not gouging. It's about knowing your worth. But it's your choice. There is another lesson here; I'll pay you what you're worth if you ask, but if you don't listen to me, I won't throw more money at you just to be nice. A deal is a deal," she said with a laugh.

I laughed along with her and then stood up and headed for the door.

"You might want to consider getting business cards made," she said. "I have a feeling your business is going to boom."

"From your lips," I stated. "Add it to the list of things I need to do."

As I headed out into the parking lot, I couldn't help the smile that stretched across my face. My savings account had been sorely depleted by Angel's abandonment, and I'd had to wait on purchasing a monitor to design on. Now, it looked like I'd be able to afford it.

I drove to Waverly's school and sat in the parking lot. While I waited for the final bell to ring, I texted Duke, telling him that Wednesday I was taking him to dinner to celebrate my turn of fortune.

I could do this. I could get my sister to graduation, I could grow my business, I could have Duke. My life didn't have to fall apart just because circumstances had been hard in the past. The tides were turning.

The front doors of the high school blew open and students poured out, ready to be free for the day. I looked for Waverly but didn't see her flaming locks in the sea of kids. I was just about to text her when she appeared.

Jessica and Dylan were with her. She hugged Jessica

and then jumped into Dylan's arms. He swirled her around. The two of them were the epitome of high school puppy love.

Dylan set her down and she immediately ran to the car, calling something out over her shoulder to him.

She wrenched the passenger door open and threw her bag in the back before climbing in.

"Hi!" she chirped.

"You're in a good mood," I noted.

"The *best* mood. I had a great day today."

"Yeah? I'm so glad to hear that. I had a great day today, too."

"Yeah? Look at us. All happy and stuff." Waverly grinned. "You go first, why's your day so good?"

"Mia hired me to redesign her bar's website." I smirked.

"Yes!" She gave me a high five.

"Okay, what's your good news?" I asked.

"There's a lot. Jessica's parents are going to let her take the CPR course I'm taking with Dylan. The instructor already said she can make up the class she missed. This is the start of the friendship embargo being over."

"Hurray. What other good news?"

"No one gave me hell at all today. Not the admin, not the students. Oh, and Cal wasn't at school."

"He wasn't?" I frowned. "That's weird."

"Apparently he broke his fingers over the weekend and his dad said he could stay home for a few days."

"He broke his fingers?" I repeated. "How?"

"He was at a gas station and some guys mugged him and slammed his hand in the car door."

My pulse drummed hard in my neck. "Which hand?"

"His throwing hand," she said distractedly. "He might

lose his scholarship if it doesn't heal right. I mean, I know the guy sucks and he's a raging asshole, but still…"

"Yeah," I murmured. "That sucks for him."

"So, what are we doing to celebrate this good news of ours?" Waverly asked.

"Burgers and fries?" I asked. "And strawberry malts?"

"You know who has the best strawberry malts, don't you?"

"Boots."

"Yup."

I grinned. "Text Dylan to meet us there."

"You're the coolest sister ever."

"I've got to run out," I said to Waverly.

She looked up from her books and set down her pencil. "It's eight o'clock."

"Yeah."

A smile dawned across her face. "Oh. I get it."

"What do you get?"

"You're about to go have sex with Duke, aren't you?"

"Okay, whoa." I held up my hand. "Please don't talk like that ever again."

"Ever?"

"Well, at least wait until you're eighteen."

"Noted." She snorted. "Is that where you're going?"

"No. I'm not going to have sex with Duke," I promised.

"Then where are you going?"

"I left something at the clubhouse the night of the party," I lied. "And I haven't seen Duke or Savage since that night."

"What did you leave at the clubhouse?" she pressed.

I paused. "I really should've thought this lie through

better."

"Yeah, you should've." She grinned. "Tell Duke I said hi."

"I'll be back before ten," I promised. "You'll be okay?"

"Yep. I'm going to finish my homework, take a shower, and then cut up some of my T-shirts."

"Your new ones?"

"Yeah. The way Mia showed me. I want to wear them to school and show them off."

"Okay. Call if you need me."

"I won't need you." She dove back into her homework.

"Sometimes, your words; they hurt," I teased.

I drove to the clubhouse where I knew Savage and Duke would be. They lived there full time, not having any need or reason to rent a place. At the clubhouse, they had private rooms and a cleaning service that came twice a week. The Old Ladies cooked in batches and they never went without. It was a cheap, easy life where they could stay close to their brothers and the club.

Crow and South Paw saw my car and immediately opened the gates. I waved to them as I drove through. I parked, locked my car, and marched up the clubhouse steps.

The living room was empty, but I saw the liquor bottles open on the counter, so I knew they were here. I headed to the back yard.

There was a fire going, and Savage, Duke, Acid, and a few others I didn't know were sitting around, passing liquor bottles back and forth. Savage had a woman on his lap and so did the silver fox who wore a Tarnished Angels cut but was definitely not a member of the Waco chapter.

Nomad, probably.

"Willa," Savage called out. "Grab a beer, sit with us."

"I need to have a word with you," I said, my voice low.

My gaze darted to Duke. "Both of you."

"Bitch's got attitude. I like it."

I looked at the man who had spoken. He wore a leather cut, but I didn't recognize him.

He grinned and patted his knee. "Why don't you come over and sit your pretty little ass right here."

"Dude," I snapped. "I'm not in the mood."

He just chuckled. "You've got sass. I like that. I like that a lot."

"Joker," Duke rumbled. "This is Willa."

"Your Old Lady?" Joker asked, his eyes darting from Duke to me.

"Best friend," Duke clarified as his jaw clenched. "And not a club whore."

Joker rubbed his chin. "So she's not off limits?"

"She's off limits," I stated.

Savage whispered something in the woman's ear. She hopped off his lap but made sure to bend over far enough so that I could see her red thong peeking out from underneath her denim skirt.

He smacked her ass before she walked away, sashaying past me without a look.

"Let's make this quick, yeah?" Savage asked.

I rolled my eyes. "Is that all you care about? Getting your dick wet?"

"I like you more and more, babe," Joker piped up.

"Okay, who *are* you?" I demanded.

"I'm the Sergeant at Arms in the Coeur D'Alene chapter," Joker explained.

"Well, I understand the road name," I drawled.

"Don't let the name fool you, sugar tits." He took a sip of his beer.

"You call me sugar tits one more time and you'll be feasting on your balls."

There was a collective silence and tension swelled. Joker slowly lowered the bottle from his lips. "I think I just fell in love with you."

Without another word, I turned and went into the clubhouse. Duke and Savage were on my heels.

"What's up, Willa?" Savage asked when I stopped in the living room.

"Waverly told me what happened to Cal."

"What happened to Cal?" Savage asked, widening his eyes.

"Don't," I snapped. "I know it was you." I looked at Duke. "You let him do this, didn't you?"

"There's no *letting* Savage do anything. He just does," Duke said, his tone quiet. "But you need to explain to us what it is you're talking about, because honestly we have no idea."

"You didn't break Cal's fingers?" I asked, confused.

"Oh, full stop," Savage said, his tone darkening. "We don't fuck with minors. Cal is a dick, but he's just a high school kid, not some grown ass man. We don't use violence unless it's serious. Although whoever did it, way to go."

"Then who—" I cut myself off, feeling sheepish. I blew out a breath of air. "I'm sorry, I just thought, with our history—"

"It *wasn't* us," Duke reinforced.

Savage was clearly done with the conversation and left without saying a word, leaving me alone with Duke.

"I thought your head was going to explode out there," I said, gesturing with my chin toward Joker.

"You handled it," he said. "In a very Old Lady type of way."

"He has such a punchable face."

Duke rubbed his jaw and cracked a grin. "I would've paid good money to see that."

"It would've caused more problems than it was worth."

"You know how we resolve this? So it doesn't happen again?" Duke asked.

"I have a feeling I know what you're going to say," I drawled. "Now is not the time or place to talk about it. People are watching us."

"You never want to talk about it," he pointed out. "And it's starting to piss me off."

"I'm yours, Duke. In all the ways that really matter."

"Then why won't you take this public? I think you're running out of good reasons to keep our relationship under wraps. What are you scared of?"

I took a deep breath. "We can explore that more on our date. Don't bail on dinner with me. Please?"

"Dinner," he repeated. He stared at me and sighed. "Wednesday? Same place?"

"Different place. I want to sit in a booth."

He grinned. "Mama Leonardi will be mad if you don't come back."

"I'll come back. But…"

"But what?"

"I don't want us to fall into some boring routine just because we already know everything about each other. You know?"

"What makes you think you know everything about me?"

I raised my brows. "Don't I?"

"The important shit, yeah."

"What don't I know?" I demanded.

He took a step closer. "You don't know about some of my morally corrupt sexual fantasies that I have involving you."

A smile bloomed across my face. "Well, well, well. Guess you can still surprise me, after all these years."

Chapter 19

"Do you think Savage is going to call again like he did last time we were on a date?" I asked Duke as we slid into the same side of the booth at La Creperie.

"Doubtful," Duke said with a rueful chuckle.

I snorted. "Was he with a woman when you left?"

"Yep."

"Good, maybe she can keep him occupied."

Duke stared into my eyes. "I didn't tell you when you walked in, but you look dynamite tonight."

I grinned. "Thanks."

"Red suits you. You should wear it more often."

I'd splurged on a provocative red dress from Leather and Ink that was expensive even with my employee discount. It crossed over my breasts to form a halter and was tight all the way to my waist, where it flared out. It fit me as though it was made for me, and I reasoned that since it hadn't sold in the store for a few weeks it was meant to be mine.

And now Duke was looking at me like he wanted to forgo dinner and eat me instead.

Goosebumps prickled along my neck.

"You look good too," I said. "You clean up nice."

He'd worn a white button-down shirt with the sleeves rolled up showing his arms. And though he still had on his leather cut, his jeans were new. It was about as dressed up as a biker was ever going to be. He'd never be a suit-and-tie kind of man. And more importantly, he never tried to be something he wasn't.

"Good evening." A server interrupted, appearing at the table seemingly out of nowhere. "May I start you off with something to drink?"

"Do you have champagne?" I asked him.

"We do."

"I'll have a glass, please."

"For you, sir?"

"Glass of rye. A few rocks. Thanks."

The server nodded and then left us alone.

Duke looked at me. "I didn't know you liked champagne."

"Don't know if I do," I said with a laugh. "But remember when I asked you to dinner, I told you there was something I wanted to celebrate?"

"And what *are* we celebrating?" he asked. "You never did say."

"I'll tell you when we have our drinks so we can toast. Let's look at the menu," I said.

After a few minutes our server returned with our drinks and set them down in front of us. "Have you decided what you'd like?"

"Sorry, not yet. We need a few more minutes please," I said.

"No worries, take your time." He left us alone again.

I raised my glass toward Duke. He did the same with his drink.

"To success," I stated. "Mia hired me to re-design Shelly's website."

"To success."

We clinked glasses and I took a sip.

"How is it?" he asked.

"Not worth the hype," I said with a laugh. "But I'll enjoy it. Have you decided what you want?"

"Not yet. I don't know what anything on the menu even is. What the hell is *cassoulet*?" Duke asked.

"No idea," I said. "Let me flag our server down."

The server returned to the table and explained, "A *cassoulet* is a French stew made with beans. Our *cassoulet* is made with duck, and the beans are stewed with pork to give them a richer flavor."

"So, pork and beans?" Duke raised his brows.

"Yes, sir. And duck."

Duke looked at me. "It's the French version of beanie weanies."

"No doubt," I said with a smile.

"We'll have one of those," Duke said.

"Excellent." The server smiled. "What else can I get for you?"

I looked at Duke. "We've gotta do it."

"Do what?"

"Snails. We've got to get the snails."

"Seriously?" he asked.

I grinned. "Where's your sense of adventure?"

Duke looked at the server. "And an order of snails, please."

The server nodded and took away our menus. Duke turned to me, angling his body so that he blocked the rest of the restaurant.

"Speaking of adventure," Duke said, his voice low.

"I know that tone," I said, arching a brow.

He settled one arm on the top of the booth, and the other, he moved underneath the table to rest on my thigh. His fingers crept over my dress, playing with the material until he inched it up my thighs.

"You're not serious," I hissed.

He shot me a devious grin. "I'm serious."

His hand continued to wander, until he grasped my thigh and slowly eased my legs open.

"The question is," he breathed, his head tilting so he was whispering in my ear, "will I be able to make you come before the food gets here? And will you be quiet?"

"You're playing a dangerous game," I stated, my heart thundering in my ears.

"And you love every second of it." His finger teased the edge of my thong before sliding under it from the side. He settled the pad of his finger against my cleft and then refused to move. I had no choice but to wiggle against him.

"Easy," he said. "This is my game."

"You're all about the games," I gasped.

After a few beats, his finger stroked me, dipping in and out of my body, but not far. Just a bit, every so often. Teasing me, setting my nerves on fire.

Though Duke's body was blocking me from sight, I knew that any moment, our server could appear at our table.

Duke thrust his finger deep into me, our eyes meeting.

My skin prickled and sweat broke out along my brow. Duke looked cool and collected.

"I'm disappointed in you," he whispered, biting my earlobe. "You're usually a hair trigger."

I gritted my teeth. "It's your fault this is taking as long as it is."

"I own my part in this," he said, just as he added

another finger. Then his thumb pressed against the bundle of nerves between my thighs.

I bit my lip to stop my moan as I spasmed around him.

"Another round for you both?" the server asked, startling me.

I was in no shape to say anything.

Duke raised an eyebrow at me and then turned his head to glance at the server, all the while still blocking my body from sight.

"Yeah, that'd be great, thanks for keeping an eye on us." Duke smiled.

"My pleasure." The server beamed before sailing away.

"You're evil," I hissed at him.

Duke slowly removed his fingers from my body and then tugged down my skirt. Then he stuck those two fingers into his mouth, his dark eyes glistening with need.

"And you taste perfect."

"Who would've thought snails would be so damn delicious?" I asked as I dunked a piece of French bread into the remaining butter and garlic.

"Who would've thought I still want to kiss you despite the garlic?" Duke teased.

I chuckled. "Admit it. They were good."

"They were. Not as good as the *cassoulet* though. What can I say? French beanie weanies speak to my foster-kid heart."

Duke rarely talked about his time in the system. While growing up, he'd done everything possible to avoid going home. His foster parents didn't even care where he was. So he spent most of his time with me and Savage, hanging at whatever place I lived in.

I turned my left wrist over, my eyes scanning the small shamrock tattoo at the base of my thumb. Savage and Duke had matching ones in the same place.

Duke saw me looking at the tattoo and suddenly he took my hand, his thumb skimming across the ink.

He had been the one to come up with the doodle. We'd been sitting in the back corner of the school library, Savage and I taking turns reading Mary Shelley's *Frankenstein* out loud to Duke.

"Pay attention," I'd snapped in exasperation. "Or you won't pass this next test."

"Won't pass it anyway," Duke muttered, continuing to sketch something on a piece of paper I couldn't see.

"Not with that attitude," I said with a sigh.

"I'm not like you," Duke said. "It doesn't matter how hard I study, or where I study or how I study, I won't pass the test. You're done with the first page by the time I've figured out the first question."

"Mrs. Sanderson said you can take the test orally," I said. "So no more excuses. Pay attention."

"I want to see it," Savage said.

Duke lifted the piece of paper and showed us the three-leaf clover. Two of the leaves were tattered and had tiny holes, like insects had eaten away at them. But there was one leaf that was intact.

"We're this three-leaf clover," Duke explained. "Savage and I are these two leaves here. And you're this one. The one without any marks or anything."

"I like it," Savage stated. "I want a tattoo of it."

"Yeah, that would be cool," Duke agreed.

The two of them began discussing the best placement for it. But all I could think about was what Duke had said.

There was one leaf that hadn't been destroyed by the elements. That leaf was me.

And in that moment, I knew, in Duke's eyes, I was perfect.

That was the summer that changed everything.

I shook off the memories and focused on the present.

"So, what are we getting for dessert?" I asked Duke.

His eyes darkened.

I grinned cheekily. "I meant actual dessert, Duke. Sheesh, you maniac."

"What can I say? I have years to make up for. Think about if we'd actually stayed together back then. Think of all the years of sex we could've had."

We got so lost in staring at one another that I didn't see the server approach.

"In the mood for something sweet?" he asked.

Duke looked at him and smiled. "Read my mind."

The server cocked his head. "Fantastic. My favorites are the chocolate eclairs and the lemon and sugar crepe."

"Both of those, please," I said.

"Great. Any coffees?"

"None for me, thanks," I said.

"I'll have a coffee," Duke said. "Thanks."

I cuddled into his side and rested my head against his chest. Duke's fingers teased the bare skin of my upper arm.

"I hate this part of the date," Duke muttered.

"What? Why?" I demanded.

"Because I know in about half an hour we'll be paying the check and leaving. Which means you go home without me."

I placed my hand on his thigh. "This is called *dating*, Duke."

"Yeah, I know. And you deserve it. You deserve to be treated well. And you deserve the anticipation of getting ready for a date. You deserve the courting."

I snorted. "Courting."

"That's what this is, Willa. I'm courting you. But I would like to get to the place in our relationship where I get to go home with you and stay the night."

"I currently share a bedroom with my sister," I pointed out.

"It's a two-bedroom rental," he said. "You could easily move your desks into the living room. Let Waverly have her own space."

"I could."

"You don't want to," he stated.

"No, it's not that, it's just…she's going to be in summer school, you know? She's going to need a quiet place to study. That second bedroom is better off as a shared office space."

"You could move to a three-bedroom."

"In my price range? Forget it."

"I meant the three of us could move into a three-bedroom," Duke said. "Bedroom for us. Bedroom for Waverly—with enough space that she could put a desk in her room and study there. Third bedroom is your home office."

I blinked. "You're serious."

"Yeah. Of course I'm serious. Why wouldn't I be?"

"Because we've only just—"

"Only just what?" he interrupted. "Started dating? Officially maybe. Unofficially, I think we've been together almost a decade."

"No. You don't get to say that. You don't get to use years of history when we were just friends to make this go at warp-fucking-speed."

He was about to say something when the server set down our desserts and Duke's coffee. He discreetly left the check at the end of the table and then left us alone again.

Duke splashed some cream into his cup and gave it a

quick stir.

"You're already pissed at me, so maybe now is a good time to talk about taking our relationship out into the open," Duke said. "You said we could talk about it over dinner. Well, we're at dinner."

"Yeah, I did promise you we could talk about it, didn't I?" I muttered.

"I don't get it. Why the fuck are we still keeping this under wraps? Your sister knows and she's happy about it. And for the love of God, please do not use Savage as a reason for us not taking this public. I need a real reason from you. Something that makes sense."

"What if it's not all it's cracked up to be," I blurted.

"What? Dating me?"

"No," I whispered. "What if—Duke—what if I suck at this? What if we go down this road and you realize I'm no good in relationships? What if I'm not the girlfriend you want me to be?"

He didn't say anything for a moment. "Look at me."

"No." Tears gathered in the corners of my eyes.

"Coward."

With a gasp, my gaze whipped to his.

He was smiling slightly. "I'm gonna say something that you might not want to hear, but I'm gonna say it anyway."

"Okay."

"I *know* you suck at relationships."

"Hey!" I protested.

"Let me finish. You suck at relationships because you were with the wrong guys. I'm not the wrong guy. I'm *your* guy, and we're perfect for each other."

"What if I hurt you just by being me?"

"You hurt me more by not claiming our relationship out in the open. You do more damage to us and to our future by hiding."

"Future?" I asked softly. "We have a future?"

He cradled my jaw in his hand and stared into my eyes. "Yeah, we have a future. I'm not going anywhere. I've seen you at your worst and I still want you. I want you more than anything in the world. Okay?"

I sighed and my insides went gooey. "Okay."

"I'll keep this under wraps until you're ready to announce it, but in private we gotta get something straight."

"What's that?"

"I'm not going anywhere, and I'm not letting you run from this. We've already crossed the line from friendship to something more, and I'm never going back. It's too late for that. You hear me?"

"I hear you."

"Say it," he said.

"We're together."

"Try again."

"You're my boyfriend," I said softly.

"Nope. Not good enough."

I rolled my eyes. "You love me and I love you, and one day I'll be your Old Lady and I'll get your name branded onto my body so everyone in the whole world knows that I belong to Wylder 'Duke' Cavanaugh."

"If we weren't at a fancy restaurant, I'd find another use for that sassy mouth right now."

"I just told you I loved you and you're talking about blow jobs? And besides, being in a fancy restaurant didn't stop you from putting your hand up my skirt."

Duke reached for his coffee but then said sternly, "Promise me that you don't have unresolved feelings for Savage, and that it's not the reason you don't want to tell him."

"You're joking, right? Tell me you're not actually thinking that."

"It's crossed my mind a time or two…"

It was my turn to place my hand on his thigh. "I'm sorry, Duke. I didn't know that was even a thought in your head. No, I've never wanted Savage. Not back then, and not now. He still doesn't know, does he?"

"About the summer you and I lost our virginities to each other? No. He has no idea. And if I'm wrong and he does, then he's a damned good liar."

I closed my eyes briefly and smiled. "That was a good summer." I opened my eyes to find Duke scrutinizing me.

"Yeah, it was a good summer," he agreed, something intense moving between us.

"Tell you what," I said, reaching for my purse. "You slow our relationship down a touch on your end, and I'll speed it up on mine. We'll meet somewhere in the middle. Yeah?"

"Yeah."

I riffled through my purse and found my wallet. I slapped down a credit card onto the top of the check presenter without even looking at the bill.

"It's just a receipt. I already paid," Duke said, reaching to the presenter and handing me back my credit card. "I gave the server my card on my way to the bathroom."

"This was supposed to be my treat," I said. "I can afford to take you to dinner, Duke."

"I know you can."

"Then why did you do it?"

"Because I wanted to. I'm done arguing, Willa. Let me take care of you."

"Okay, Duke." I cradled his cheek and brushed my thumb across his stubble. "I'll let you take care of me."

Chapter 20

We walked across the parking lot of the restaurant toward Duke's bike which was parked right next to my car.

He opened his saddle bag and pulled out a bag of candy.

I held it up toward the streetlamp. "Root beer barrels."

"I'm trying to win your affection. How am I doing so far?"

"So far so good. What will it be next week, I wonder?"

"You'll have to wait and find out." He gently grasped my hip and pulled me toward him. His free hand sank into my hair, cupping the back of my head to angle my lips toward his. His mouth devoured mine. He tasted like chocolate and lemon from the dessert we had shared, and I sank into him.

When we'd said a proper good night, he finally lifted his head from mine.

I sighed.

"What cuisine are we doing next week?" Duke asked.

"How about we adventure with chopsticks," I suggested. "Sushi?"

"Raw fish?"

"You just ate snails. I think you'll like raw fish."

"I'm game." He grinned. "Savage and I are going to Odessa for a few days."

"I won't see you?"

"You won't see me. I'll try and check in, but no promises."

"I get it."

"You do?"

"Well, yeah. I mean, that's never changed, right? Ever since you and Savage got in with the club, time hasn't been your own. I get it." I frowned. "Did you think because we'd taken our relationship to the next level, I'd all of sudden stop understanding the needs of the club?"

He rubbed the back of his neck. "Would it kill you to be more needy and demanding and wanting to talk to me?"

"I don't care if you're in Odessa. You *will* check in with me, Duke." A smirk appeared on my lips. "Ignore me at your own peril. Or I'll have an epic meltdown the moment I see you again."

"That's more like it." He smacked my ass. "Text me when you get home safe."

"Why don't you text *me* when *you* get home safe?" I sassed.

"I'll text you the moment I'm home—something that's gonna make you blush."

"I look forward to it." I kissed him one last time and then climbed into the car, setting the root beer barrels on the seat next to me.

When I turned down the rental's street, I saw a motorcycle parked in front of the house. I pulled up behind it and cut the engine. It was Savage's Harley.

I shot off a quick text to Waverly asking why Savage

was here. I waited a few seconds to see if she'd reply, but my phone remained dark.

With a deep breath, I got out of the car and went inside. Savage was sitting on the couch, a pizza box open on the coffee table, along with a few empty beer bottles.

"Hello person who doesn't live here," I quipped.

He didn't take his eyes off the TV. "Is that any way to greet your best friend, who bought you a new TV since you didn't have one?"

I sighed and set my purse and phone down on the small table by the door.

"I didn't ask you to buy the TV," I said.

"You never ask for luxuries. Which makes it all the more fun to give them to you." He finally muted the television and looked at me. "You're dressed up."

"Yeah." I plopped down on the couch.

"Were you on a date?" he asked.

"I was not on a date," I lied.

"No? Then where were you?"

The front door opened and Waverly blew in.

"A TV!" she said in way of greeting. Her top bun was disheveled, and she was wearing jeans and her newly cut T-shirt.

"Say goodbye to it because it's going back to the store," I said.

"What? Why?" Waverly demanded. "Oooh, pizza." She reached for a slice and shoved it into her mouth.

"Because *we* didn't buy this TV," I explained.

"Consider it a housewarming gift," Savage said. "Just accept it, it's not a big deal."

Waverly swallowed a bite of pizza quickly and said, "Yeah, please don't send it back. The TV needs a nice home. I'll take good care of it, I promise!"

"Oh great, the next thing I know you'll be asking for a puppy," I quipped.

"Ooooh, *can* we get a—"

"*No*," I interrupted. "Absolutely not. Let's start small. Like a goldfish or plankton or something."

"What about a hamster?" Waverly asked as she finished off her slice of pizza.

"No. No rodents," I said. "I don't do rodents. How was your class?"

"Good. Jessica's got a crush on the instructor, and she's already volunteered to be his CPR dummy three times," Waverly said.

"That girl is boy crazy," I said. "Glad you had a good night."

"Sounds like Jessica is the one having a good night," Savage joked.

"And how was *your* night," Waverly asked suggestively.

"Yeah, how was your night?" Savage asked with a raised brow.

"My night was good," I said.

Out of the corner of my eye, I saw Waverly wince. She knew she'd tripped up.

"How good?" Savage pressed. "This is the part where you finally tell me you're dating someone."

"Fine, I'm dating someone," I admitted.

Savage grinned. "I knew it! Who is the lucky fucker?"

"A guy," I said evasively.

"You're not going to tell me who it is?" he asked.

"Nope."

"Why not?" he demanded.

"Because I really like this guy and I want to keep him to myself a while longer."

"Because you know Duke and I will put him through

the wringer," Savage said. "To make sure he's good enough for you."

"Yeah, and like all my other boyfriends, you'll scare this one away too."

"What can I say? You have shitty taste in men," Savage teased. "Even Waverly has chosen better than you. Dylan came to a barbecue with the boys and held his own. What, you don't think your man can handle us? You know, at some point we're going to have to meet him."

"And when that time comes, he will be prepared." I stood up and turned, Savage's eyes immediately dropping to my skirt.

"Well, well, well." Savage rubbed his jaw, but it didn't hide his smirk. "Someone had a *really* good night."

Waverly frowned in confusion, but I knew what he was referring to immediately. I hastily grabbed a couch pillow and put it behind me to conceal the residue of my release on my dress.

"Bye, Savage," I said pointedly. "Thanks for dropping by."

"Thanks for the pizza," Waverly said, reaching for another slice. "And the TV."

"Sure thing," Savage said, rising from his seat. "Duke and I are headed out to Odessa tomorrow so I won't be dropping by randomly with pizza. At least not this week."

He kissed my cheek and then grabbed Waverly's messy bun before pulling her into a hug. "Stay out of trouble," he said to her.

"*You* stay out of trouble," Waverly sassed back.

"No promises." He grinned, and then left.

∽

"But why do I have to go to school?" Waverly demanded the next morning. "It doesn't make sense. I already have to go to summer school, so why not blow off school now?"

"Because we can't do anything that lets them know anything is amiss. As far as the school system knows you're at home every night with a loving mother who cooks dinner, not hanging out with bikers, pizza boxes, and your older sister."

"This isn't going to work long term," Waverly muttered as she grabbed her book bag. "We need another plan. I won't make it through two more years of high school where you're forging Mom's signature and making excuses for her."

"Yes, you will make it. And the way you do that is to go to school and pretend everything is okay. If anyone from the administration asks about paperwork that didn't make it to us or anything like that, you tell them we moved. Give them this address."

"What do I say if one of them wants to call Mom?"

"Tell them she lost her phone and got a new number. Tell them they can talk to me at any time while Angel gets her phone sorted. Come on, you kept Dylan a secret for weeks. You can figure out how to lie to the admin. I have faith in you."

She grinned. "So you're saying you want me to be sneaky and underhanded?"

"Waverly, this is really important. Do you understand what happens if the school system finds out Angel is gone?"

"I feel like we need a secret handshake," she said.

"Most definitely." I urged her out the front door. "We better go or we'll be late."

"You know, Dylan's offered to drive me to school, so

you don't have to leave this early on days you don't have to be at work."

"But that would mean you'd be on the back of his bike," I pointed out. "And you know how I feel about that."

"You get on the back of Duke's bike. And Savage's. And I've ridden on the back of *their* bikes. Several times."

"Get in the car, Waverly. And stop being a teenager."

"I've got a few more years of that."

"Saints preserve us. I'll never make it." I went to the driver's side door.

"Ouch, what am I sitting on?" Waverly asked, reaching beneath her to pull out the bag of candy.

"Ah, Duke's version of a flower bouquet." I took the bag from her and tossed it in the back.

"I love this for you." She grinned. "I love this for me, too. Because when you get candy, I get candy."

"I shared the lemon drops with you," I said. "But if you touch those root beer barrels, I will end you. Sister or not."

She blinked. "You need more coffee."

"That is true." I buckled my seat belt and started the engine. "Doc's engagement brunch is on Saturday."

"Mkay."

"So, I'll be at Brooklyn's house from one to four. So you're free to see whoever you want to see, hang out with whoever you want to hang out with. Just not alone at the house."

"Heard loud and clear, chief." Waverly saluted.

I pulled into the parking lot of the school. She hopped out quickly and with a wave, she was gone—striding toward the brick wall where Dylan waited for her.

My phone buzzed.

It was a text from Duke.

DUKE

> About to hit the road. Don't eat all those root beer barrels in one sitting.

Grinning, I typed out:

ME

> Miss you too. Drive safe. And act surprised when Savage mentions the mark on my dress from last night...

My phone rang immediately.

"Yes?" I answered.

"What the fuck," he growled.

"He didn't tell you about last night?" I asked. "He was at my house when I got home. He bought us a TV and was eating pizza on the couch. He saw the stain on my dress—thanks, by the way, I had no idea I walked through the restaurant with that—"

"I didn't notice," he muttered. "How did you explain that to Savage?"

"I finally came clean about dating someone but told him I wasn't ready for you guys to meet him."

"That won't fend him off for long."

"No," I said with a sigh. "It won't."

"There's a solution to this."

"Telling him. Yeah. I know that."

He was silent for a moment and then he said, "We could show up together at Doc and Boxer's wedding." There was some shuffling on the other end of the phone and Duke murmured something to the other person. "Think about it. Gotta go. Talk later."

Duke hung up and I was left staring at my phone. Finally, I shook myself out of my daze at his words and put the car into reverse.

Before I exited the parking lot, I saw a trio of girls heading for the school. They were all wearing cut up T-shirts.

Cool kid, indeed.

As I drove home, I thought about what Duke had said to me about attending Boxer and Doc's wedding. It would be a declaration. An announcement.

The weirdest thing about taking my friendship with Duke to a sexual level was that it hadn't been weird at all.

Why hadn't we been doing this the entire time?

"Oh, right, because we were sixteen, and life was hard enough," I muttered.

I was driving on autopilot and instead of going straight home, I made a detour to Pie in the Sky.

"Hey," Jazz greeted with a smile. "You just missed the rush."

"Perfect. It's gonna be a long workday, so I'll need one of your special concoctions."

"You got it." Jazz grabbed a cup and then pointed to the chalk board that listed the drinks. "We made the drink official, by the way. You can now order Witch's Brew in three different sizes. I've already had a large. The baby kept me up all night."

I frowned. "Baby? What baby? You don't have a baby."

"I have a fur baby," Jazz clarified. "Brielle and I found a puppy the night we were supposed to go the Tarnished Angels barbecue. That's why we didn't make it."

"Oh, right. Brooklyn mentioned that."

"We took the dog to the vet. He's not chipped, and we called all the shelters to see if someone put out a lost and found for him. No dice. So, I decided to keep him."

Jazz grabbed a pitcher and dumped milk into it. She adjusted the steamer wand on the espresso machine and then began to foam the milk.

Her phone trilled in her apron pocket. She reached into it and pulled her cell out. Jazz pressed a button and put it to her ear. "Hello? Stop grumbling at me. It's not his fault."

She turned off the steamer and set the milk aside. Then she got to pulling espresso shots.

"Don't take that tone with me! You were the one who decided to bring him to the tattoo parlor. If he's such a problem, take him back to the apartment." She listened for a few more moments and then said, "Homer, you big softie. I'm off at two. I'll be by to pick him up. Yes. I promise."

She hung up.

"What was that about?" I queried.

"I asked Homer to look in on Fluffernutter."

"You named the dog Fluffernutter?" I asked in amusement.

"Damn right I did." Jazz looked at me over her shoulder and smiled. "Since Homer lives in the same building as us, I asked him to do me a favor. All he has to do is walk one floor down. Well, the big grump didn't like hearing that the dog was going to be alone for more than a few hours, so he brought him to the tattoo parlor. Apparently, he's an escape artist, and managed to get outside. So Homer just spent the last hour running around looking for him. You know where he was?"

"Where?"

"He made friends with the guys who own the taco truck. He was eating a soft taco when Homer got there."

I laughed. "I think you should change his name to Houdini. Or Hell Hound."

"Or Helldini? Anyway, he's all bark and no bite—Homer, that is." She swirled whipped cream on top of my drink and then added the caramel drizzle before putting on the lid.

"How's living with Brielle?" I asked.

"It's a blast. Even if her grumpy brother decided he just *had* to move into the same building."

"So you punished him by making him watch your dog?"

"He *volunteered* to watch my dog. I just asked him to take him for a walk. He went above and beyond. That's on him." She sighed. "Still, I should probably do something nice for him."

Her phone rang again. She rolled her eyes. "Jesus. He's calling again. Hang on." She answered it. "Yes?" she snapped. Her expression softened almost immediately. "Three. Yeah. Thanks."

She hung up and shoved her phone into her apron.

"What was that?"

"He wanted to know how many tacos I wanted," she said. "It was sweet and...weird." She looked me up and down. "You're not dressed like you usually are. Are you working at Leather and Ink today?"

"No. I'm working on Mia's website."

"You're working on Mia's website?"

"She hired me." I cocked my head to the side. "When was the last time we hung out? I feel like it's been forever and we need to catch up."

"We definitely need a catch-up session. I'll see you at Doc's engagement brunch, though. If three hours isn't enough time to drink and gab, then we'll just have to take it to Shelly's another day."

"Good plan."

Brooklyn came onto the floor, wiping her hands on a towel. "Hey! I didn't know you were coming by."

"Detour for caffeine and sugar so I can get cracking on Mia's website. Thanks, by the way."

"What did I do?" Brooklyn asked.

"Didn't you have something to do with Mia hiring me?"

"Not really. She asked how I liked the website and how you handled changes that needed to be made. Aside from that, you sold yourself with the excellent work you did. Hey, you want to see what I'm making for Doc's engagement brunch?"

"Yeah."

I followed her into the kitchen. The door chime jangled and a moment later Jazz said, "Good morning!"

There were six cookie sheets on the wooden island, all full of pastries.

"They're cooling, but then I'll decorate them with chocolate frosting," Brooklyn said.

I peered closer. "Are those—wait—is that a penis shaped pastry?"

Brooklyn chuckled. "They'll be penis shaped chocolate eclairs filled with white cream because...yeah."

"Oh my God!" I squealed with laughter. "That's hilarious."

Brooklyn grinned. "Dirty pasta and penis shaped cakes are so passé. I thought this would be a little different. And way more fun."

"Well, you nailed it."

"Speaking of nailed...how's the sex with Duke?"

The to-go coffee cup slipped from my hand and spilled all over the island. Hot coffee splattered onto a few rows of pastry penises.

"Shit." I made a grab for the coffee. "Fuck. I'm sorry."

"Why are you sorry? It's my fault. I sprung that question on you." She grasped a kitchen towel and went about mopping up the mess I'd made. But it was no use—a few of the penis pastries were lost in the line of duty.

"I guess there's no point in attempting to lie to you about it." I hastily glanced in the direction of Jazz, but she was interacting with customers up front and hadn't heard my exchange with Brooklyn. "How'd you know?"

"I put it together the night of the barbecue. You both came back smelling like sex." She touched her nose. "Pregnancy, man. It's like I have all these weird superpowers. Super smell is one of them."

I swallowed. "Does anyone else—I mean, were you the only one who—"

"As far as I know, I'm the only one who knows your dirty little secret." She grinned. "I haven't shared it with anyone, and I wanted to confront you about it because *oh my God, it's true!*"

"Yeah." I nodded. "It's true. Only…it's not just sex. It's more. He wants more. And I want more too. But I'm not ready for everyone to know."

"I knew there was something between you guys," Brooklyn said. "I can't tell you how vindicated I feel right now."

I chuckled, but I was suddenly dying to talk to someone about it who wasn't Waverly. "My sister knows, but I've sworn her to secrecy."

"So, I'm guessing you haven't told Savage yet."

"No. Not yet."

"Why not?"

"Because it's been the three of us as a tightly knit friend group for so long that I'm afraid everything will change."

"But it *will* change. You can't stop that. As someone who actively attempted not to change my life, this—" she pointed to her belly "—kind of made me understand that when things change you just have to roll with it."

"Falling in love with Slash changed things too," I stated.

"*Definitely*," she laughed.

"Duke, Savage and I...we work, you know? The three of us work as friends. They're my chosen family. I love them. But now I'm in love with one of them and I just... don't know how it's going to change our dynamic."

"The relationship is serious..."

I sighed. "Yeah. It's serious. There are real feelings here. And I didn't want to deal with it—in the beginning. But here we are, and I can't...*unfeel* them, you know? And I don't want to."

"Your world is shifting. Your relationship with Duke will become the center of your universe. I don't mean that in a bad way, or even to suggest that the rest of your life will get shoved to the side because of it. But when you build a life with someone, when you make that decision, it becomes the most important thing."

"I have Waverly."

"Yes. Who's currently the grand old age of fifteen."

"Who's at the height of her rebellion," I admitted. "Though we have found a sort of rhythm. I asked her not to lie to me anymore. We'll see if that sticks."

"Are you using your sister and your concern about how Savage will react to keep your relationship under wraps?"

"Maybe," I admitted.

"Well, I'll keep your confidence, and if you ever need to talk about it..."

"Thanks," I said with a smile.

Chapter 21

"Brooklyn knows," I said the moment I answered Duke's call.

"Brooklyn knows what?"

"About us."

"Did you tell her?"

"No. She smelled it."

"Smelled what?"

I looked toward the bedroom even though the door was closed and Waverly was asleep. I pitched my voice lower anyway. "The sex, Duke. She smelled the sex we had the night at the clubhouse with her pregnancy nose, and now she *knows*."

He let out a low chuckle.

"It's not funny!"

"You're right. It's fucking hilarious."

"You can't see me right now, but I'm glaring at you."

"I know you are."

I sighed. "You might get your way after all."

"What's my way?"

"The way where everyone knows about us."

"There will be hell to pay if Savage is the last one to find out. We should probably tell him before any more people find out, don't you think?"

"Yeah." I sighed. "Where are you now?"

"In Odessa. In a dank motel room where the air can't keep up with the humidity so everything is damp and musty smelling. The air, my clothes, my skin."

"You sharing a room with Savage?"

"Yeah. He went out to grab us food from the local diner and it gave me time to call. Ah, key in the door, he's back. Hey, asshole, say hi to Willa and tell her you made it here in one piece."

"I made it here in one piece," Savage called.

I smiled. "Glad to hear you guys are good. Well, I'll let you enjoy your dinner."

"Thanks, I will."

He hung up and I set my phone aside.

At some point, Savage would find out. It was the law of cascading failures. First one person, then another, then before you knew it, your entire secret wasn't a secret anymore. He deserved to know, and he deserved to hear it from Duke and me, not anyone else.

The bedroom door opened and Waverly came out into the living room, rubbing her eyes.

"Did I wake you?" I asked her.

She shook her head. "Couldn't really sleep. Tossed and turned for a while."

"We should return that mattress. Wasn't it a money back guarantee if you didn't fall asleep in five minutes?"

"Oh, I fell asleep, I just didn't stay asleep. Why are you still up?"

"I wanted to talk to Duke. And Savage," I added.

She went to the faucet and filled up a glass of water. "They make it to Odessa okay?"

"Yeah. They're fine."

"You miss him, don't you?"

"Would you tease me if I said yes?"

"Yeah, I'll tease you." She grinned and then drank her water.

I did miss him. And it wasn't like he hadn't gone out of town for a few days for club business before. But it was different now.

"Damn it," I muttered.

"What?" Waverly asked.

"Everything's changing."

"Buck up, kiddo. That's life," she quipped.

"No kidding." I cocked my head to the side. "You going back to sleep? Or you want to find an old re-run of something to watch?"

"Re-run." She plopped down onto the couch next to me. "I'm glad Savage bought the TV. And I'm glad you caved and decided to keep it."

"Yeah, otherwise we'd have to talk to each other."

"Or play cards."

"Or backgammon."

She smiled. "Doesn't sound so bad."

"Nah, it doesn't sound so bad," I agreed. I flicked on the TV and started surfing.

We landed on the *Gilmore Girls* episode where Rory skipped school to visit Jess in New York.

"I kind of hate this episode," Waverly said.

"Yeah? Why?"

"Because Rory is like, insanely selfish. Missing Lorelai's graduation to visit a guy who bailed the first moment shit got hard."

"You're not supposed to have this much emotion about a TV show."

"Um, that's *exactly* what you're supposed to have about

a TV show. Come on, you totally agree with me."

"I stand behind my statement that Jess, the second time around, was her soul mate."

"She should've married Logan."

I wrapped my arm around her shoulders and tugged her toward me. "You're the best. You know that?"

"How am I the best?" she asked with a smile.

I paused, pensive for a moment. "I didn't know if we'd get here, you know?"

"Here, where? Watching *Gilmore Girls* re-runs on a school night?"

"No. *Happy*."

"Happy," she repeated. "Yeah. Like really, really happy, right?"

"Really, really happy."

We fell into silence, our eyes glued to the screen. When the episode was over, I looked at Waverly. "You should probably go to bed."

"Yeah, I probably should…"

I bit my lip. "One more episode?"

She grinned. "One more."

~

"I finally understand wedding registries," I said to Mia. "What the hell am I supposed to get Doc? I'm flying blind here."

"Why don't you buy her some ridiculous kitchen contraption she'll never use, but every time she sees it, she'll be plagued with intense guilt?"

"What ridiculous kitchen contraption do you never use?" I inquired.

"Take your pick," she said with a grin.

We were at a department store, currently in the kitchen

section, and I was severely overwhelmed by all the beautiful things. I wanted to be able to shop without looking at price tags. One day.

One day...

"If you were getting married, what would you want?" Mia asked.

"Matching glasses that aren't chipped. The ones that come from a real store in a real box," I said automatically.

"Boom. That's what you should get Doc. Although, might I suggest a nice set of cocktail glasses?"

"Done."

Twenty minutes later, we were headed out of the store. Scarlett was strapped to Mia's chest and she was blissfully content in her carrier.

"Thanks for suggesting the outing," Mia said. "I've been going a little bit stir crazy. Scarlett hasn't been sleeping much at night, so my sleep is super erratic. I nap in the middle of the day and I'm up late at night with her."

She stole a hand down her daughter's back and leaned her head down to brush her cheek against Scarlett's head.

"She's so cute though," I said. "And I swear she's bigger every time I see her."

"That's not all in your head."

"You have to get back, or do you have a few minutes?" I asked her, loading my purchase into the trunk.

"I'm good for a bit."

"There's a park not far from here. We could go for a short walk?"

"Perfect."

The sun was shining and thankfully the humidity wasn't completely out of control. It was still before the heat of the day, though, so we only had about an hour before all that changed.

"I have to admit, I sort of had an ulterior motive in asking you to shop with me," I said to her.

"Oh?" Mia nestled Scarlett into her stroller and put up the sunshade. Scarlett didn't even make a squawk.

I took a deep breath. "I want to start the process of legally adopting Waverly. But in order to do that, I need an attorney."

"The club has a great attorney," she said.

"Yeah. I know." I rubbed the back of my neck. "I was hoping I'd be able to…I mean…I want to keep this private. I don't even want Waverly to know until I have something to tell her."

"Why wouldn't you tell her before you begin the process?"

"Because in order to legally adopt her, my mother has to sign her parental rights away. And I just…she doesn't need to deal with that shit right now. I've been mulling this idea over since she got suspended—the second time, I mean. We can't go on like this. Right now, I'm kind of terrified that the school is going to find out that Angel bailed on us and they'll call CPS. They'll take her away. She's way too old to be put in foster care, and I'm perfectly capable of taking care of her financially. But you know how it is…"

"Yeah, I do know how it is," she said quietly. Suddenly she smiled. "I'll call Vance and ask him to give you a buzz."

"Thanks, Mia. I really appreciate it."

We walked a few loops around the pond, discussing Doc and Boxer's upcoming wedding, the website I was redesigning for her, and how Waverly was feeling about life and everything that had been thrown at her.

"You're Wonder Woman," Mia said. "Juggling everything that you are."

"You're juggling a lot too, you know," I said with a laugh.

She grinned. "I forget I'm only a few years older than you."

"Sometimes I forget I'm twenty-four. There are days I feel ancient." I shook my head. "Life changes a lot in a short amount of time, doesn't it?"

"It does. It really does," Mia agreed.

The next morning, Waverly was out of the house by ten. Jessica came by to pick her up and then they were off to get Dylan. They were going to see a movie and get some food. The day was supposed to be easy and I shouldn't have been worried.

So why was I?

At one o'clock on the dot, I showed up at Brooklyn's house. Not only had she catered Doc's engagement brunch, but she was hosting it. A long table had been set up so we could dine alfresco. There were twinkle fairy lights in the trees, and votives in mason jars on the table.

"Is that—did you hire a bartender?" I asked Brooklyn.

"Where's the fun in making your own cocktails," she said with a grin. "We've got Bloody Marys, Blackberry Mojitos, Bellinis, and Espresso martinis. Virgin options for the several of us who can't imbibe."

"I'm imbibing," Allison announced. "Well, I'll have one and then switch to virgins. Tank hates the bottle. He prefers my nipples."

Darcy sniggered. "I'm pretty sure he's not the only one."

The two of them stepped up to the bar and ordered their drinks.

"The place is gorgeous. You guys outdid yourselves," Mia said to Brooklyn, Brielle, and Jazz.

"We're the magic musketeers of catering," Jazz said. "I've earned my cocktails today though."

"Same," Brielle moaned, rubbing her head.

"It's hair of the dog for you," Jazz teased her friend.

"Rough night last night?" I asked her.

"My mother set me up on a date," she recounted. "I needed three tequila shots before appetizers just to find him interesting."

"Where does your mother find these guys to set you up with?" I asked.

"Let's see. The hardware store, the plant nursery, the vet… Last night's winner-winner-chicken-dinner was from the grocery store."

"Grocery stores aren't a terrible place to meet men," Joni said.

"When I pinned my mother down and asked her what section of the store he was in, she said the frozen food aisle. After meeting him, I'm guessing his cart was full of Hot Pockets."

"Ew." Mia winced.

"You need a decoy," I said to her.

"A decoy?" Brielle frowned. "I'm not following."

The three of us stepped up to the bar. "I'll have a Bloody Mary, please."

"Make that two," Jazz said.

"Make it three," Brielle added.

"You got it." The bartender flipped his shaker and scooped ice.

"A decoy," I said. "A fake boyfriend. Your mom will think it's real and then she won't bug you anymore and keep trying to fix you up with duds."

She smacked her head. "Genius. Except the only guys I know are friends of my brothers and none of them will fake date me…or real date me."

"There's just one tiny problem." Jazz smiled and picked up the Bloody Mary. She took a sip. "Oh, that's spicy. I like it."

The bartender grinned. "You seem a little spicy yourself."

"I'm a hot tamale," Jazz said. "Like the candy."

"You're cute," he said.

"So are you."

"Hold on a second," Brielle interrupted. "Can you guys do this another time? We're in the middle of figuring out a solution to *my* problem. I'm *literally* standing here telling you I can't find a man."

"From the sound of it, we did figure out the solution to your problem," I said. "But there was something else Jazz wanted to add."

"Sex," she blurted out and then shot the bartender a wink.

With a roll of her eyes, Brielle grabbed Jazz and dragged her away from the bartender onto the lawn. I followed.

"What about sex?" Brielle asked.

"Well, you need it," Jazz said.

"What, like right now?" Brielle asked with a grin.

"It wouldn't hurt. You've been uptight lately. No offense. If you get a fake boyfriend, you won't be having real sex."

"I don't need to have sex with my fake boyfriend. I've got one of those in my underwear drawer."

"I know, his name is Big Boy and I hear it almost every night," Jazz said.

Brielle's eyes widened. "Wait—do you *hear* me?"

"The walls are thin, and like I said, you've been pretty hard up lately."

"Me hard up? What about you? You're not getting

any."

Jazz sobered. "Right, I'm not getting any."

I watched them verbally spar with each other as I drank my cocktail. "You guys sound like me and Waverly. I mean, not about the Big Boy part, but the sisterly fighting you're doing."

Jazz wrapped her arm around Brielle's neck. "We're basically sisters. It's why I can tease her about her dildo."

"Oh my God, can you please stop?" Brielle demanded, her cheeks nearly as red as her hair. "You're impossible."

Jazz looked over her shoulder at the cute bartender. She waved at him. He waved back.

"Go," Brielle said with a sigh. "I know you want to."

"Thanks!" Jazz said as she began to head back to the bar.

I looped my arm through Brielle's and we headed toward the Old Ladies who were sitting on Brooklyn's brand-new patio furniture. She and Slash had only recently moved into the house, but she'd already made it a home.

"Where's Doc?" I asked.

"Late." Mia shook her head and set her phone aside. "Emergency at the clinic. She'll be here in about twenty minutes."

"She can be late to her own brunch," Joni said. "But we have to draw the line at her being late to her own wedding."

"Boxer and I are already on it," Mia said. "We've got a plan."

"What's the plan?" Darcy asked.

"The plan…is…that we won't let her be late to her own wedding," Mia said.

"Oh, yeah, sure. Sounds foolproof." Joni laughed.

"We'll call the clinic," Darcy said. "And tell them under

no circumstances are they allowed to page Doc or call her or anything."

"Good. That's good," Mia said.

"We should probably take her phone the night before, too," Joni said.

"Yes, definitely."

"And someone should sleep over and make sure she's not going to make a run for it," Allison said.

"She's not going to make a run for it," Mia said with an eye roll. "Well, probably not."

"I'll stay over with her," Darcy said. "My kids don't need breast milk or diaper changes."

"I like this plan," Mia said. "Good job, team."

"We're getting her down that aisle," Joni said. "She deserves her happy ending."

"A wedding isn't the end," I pointed out.

"No. But it's the symbol of the happy beginning of the next chapter," Joni said.

"Ugh, you guys are all so happy and well sexed it makes me insane," Brielle grumbled.

"We're well sexed?" Darcy said with a laugh. "How can you tell?"

Brielle pointed at Joni and then across the way to Brooklyn who was still at the table adjusting place settings. "Pregnant." Then she pointed to Mia and Allison. "New babies."

"What about me? I don't have new babies," Darcy said.

"No, but the way Gray looks at you after your years together speaks volumes."

"Well, what about Willa?" Mia asked. "She doesn't have babies. Is she well sexed?"

Brielle looked me over. "I don't know, but there's something different about her."

I raised my brows. "Something different about me?"

"Yeah." Brielle nodded. "Your skin is glowing." Her eyes widened. "Are you pregnant?"

"*No.*" I snorted. "I'm most definitely not pregnant."

"She's right though." Allison leaned closer to me. "You do look different."

"Don't know why," I said. "I'm not doing anything different."

Could they hear the rapid pulse of my heartbeat as I spit up the lies? My eyes roved over the group as they scrutinized me.

But Joni…

Joni lifted her glass to her lips and winked at me.

"Oh my God!" Doc cried as she stepped out onto the terrace. "This is almost as beautiful as your wedding." She reached for Brooklyn and gave her a hug.

We collectively scrambled up and went to greet the bride.

"I'm sorry, I'm sorry," Doc cried out with a smile. "I know I'm late and that's really bad form, but I—"

"It doesn't matter." Darcy shoved a Bloody Mary at her.

With a chuckle, she took a drink. "Oh, that's spicy!"

"You should see the bartender," Jazz called from the bar.

Chapter 22

An hour later, I was finally able to corner Joni as she was coming out of the bathroom. She opened the door and I pushed my way inside, closing the door behind me.

"I know girls like to go to the bathroom together, but this one's a little small and I'm the size of a mammoth, what with child," Joni quipped.

"*You know*," I accused.

"I know what?" She blinked her blue eyes and twirled a strand of sorrel colored hair around her finger as if to feign innocence.

I crossed my arms over my chest and waited.

"Zip was picking up a to-go order at La Creperie last week and saw you guys cozy in a booth," she said. "That's my spot for when I get a craving. And boy did I have a craving. He brought home fifteen lemon and sugar crepes. I ate about half of them."

"Joni…"

"Okay, fine." She glared. "I ate all of them. You happy? You got me to admit it."

"This bathroom meeting isn't really about you and

your eating habits. And for the record, the lemon and sugar crepes are to die for, so no judgment on my end."

"I haven't told anyone," Joni said. "If that's what you're worried about. I assumed because you didn't tell us, you didn't want us to know."

I took a deep breath. "What about Zip?"

"What about Zip?"

"Did he tell anyone?"

"Why would he?"

"Because men gossip," I pointed out.

She nibbled her lip. "I don't think he's told anyone. If he was going to tell anyone though, it would be Colt."

"Would Colt tell Mia?"

"I don't know." Joni frowned. "And like I said, I don't think he's told anyone yet. Are you like, gonna become his Old Lady?"

"Doesn't becoming an Old Lady mean an official public announcement?"

"Yes."

"Then no, not yet."

"So what is this?" She crossed her arms over her chest. "Are you guys just sleeping together? Is that why you're keeping it a secret? You guys think this will fizzle out and you don't want anyone to get hurt?"

"It's none of your fucking business what I'm doing with Duke," I shouted. "He's *my* best friend! He's belonged to me longer than he's belonged to the club!"

My chest heaved with emotion as I stared daggers at her. "How dare you insinuate that I'd use him for sex. It cheapens our relationship."

Joni stared at me for a long moment and then smiled. "That's totally what I thought."

"What?" I asked in confusion as I began to calm down.

"You *love* him." She sniggered, unfazed by my outburst. "Darcy owes me five bucks."

"You've been betting on my love life?" I asked, mouth agape.

"Yup. About half the Old Ladies thought you'd pick Savage. But I knew. I've seen the way you and Duke look at each other when you think no one is watching. You're never as sneaky as you think you are. Trust me. I know."

There was a knock on the bathroom door that made me freeze. "Guys?" Mia called. "The door isn't soundproof."

"Crap," I muttered, rubbing my head.

"Looks like you could use another drink," Joni said, reaching around me to open the bathroom door.

The entire group of Old Ladies was crowded into the hallway. No one said anything for a long moment, and then a hand appeared out of nowhere with a full Bloody Mary.

"Drink this," Jazz said.

I took the cocktail from her. "Thanks. Okay, minions, can you back up so we can get out of here?"

They dispersed, and by tacit agreement we all moved to the living room.

"I think I speak for everyone when I say this party just got a lot more interesting," Doc said, fiddling with the straw in her mojito and smiling ear to ear.

"Was it boring before?" Brooklyn asked.

"No. Not boring. Tame," Doc said. "But now we have some really interesting things to discuss!"

"Not that talking about breast pumps isn't fun," Jazz interjected. "It's just that some of us can't really add our two cents on that topic yet."

"So," Allison said. "You and Duke..."

"Damn it," Darcy muttered.

"Pay up, wench," Joni said with a laugh.

"Well, don't just sit there," Mia said. "Tell us how this happened and what it all means."

And then for the next hour, I spilled the beans.

⁓

"It's just so romantic," Brielle said dreamily. She was several cocktails in and her cheeks were flushed.

"So does this mean that Savage is available?" Jazz asked.

Everyone looked at her.

"What? He's *hot*. And from what I gather, ever so slightly unhinged," she expounded. "That's a turn on, by the way…"

"Yeah, it comes from a place of loyalty," I said. "That's the kicker. Sometimes he's a tad overprotective."

"So, Waverly knows about you guys?" Mia asked.

I nodded.

"And how does she feel about it?" Brooklyn added.

"She loves the idea." It felt strange baring my soul to so many people, but these women *were* my people. "Duke's been there for her as much as he's been there for me."

"What does this mean for your future together?" Joni asked.

I pointed at her. "That, right there, is why I wanted to keep it under wraps."

"You're not ready to think about it. Got it," Darcy said with a nod.

"Of course I've thought about it," I admitted. "It's impossible not to. But with Duke…we were together long before we were *together*. That doesn't make sense, does it?"

"I think it does," Brooklyn said slowly. "You guys were

kids when you met. Now you're adults and you're exploring what that means."

"What does it mean?" Mia wondered. "Does he want kids? Do *you* want kids?"

I laughed. "On our first date—which was officially two weeks ago—he literally mentioned the idea of Little Dukes running around."

"These men…" Allison shook her head and shot me a rueful smile. "They can't wait to have families. It's like a bunch of bikers obsessed with reproduction. It's hot."

"I could wait. I'm only twenty-four," I said.

"I'm thirty-one," Doc said. "And I'd still like to wait. Well, my brain is telling me to wait, but my body… That clock that everyone talks about? Yeah, it's finally ticking."

"I've got Waverly to watch out for. I've got my business that's just starting to do something. What's the rush?" I demanded.

"There's no rush," Mia assured me. "Hell, I didn't even know if I wanted kids when I got with Colt."

"And look how that turned out for you," Joni ribbed.

"Yeah, it turned out exactly how it was supposed to," Mia admitted. "But it's okay to enjoy what you've got now without all that other stuff."

"So how hot is the sex with Duke?" Jazz asked.

I arched a brow. "You know I love you, but do you really think I'm going to kiss and tell?"

"Whoa." Jazz blinked brown eyes. "This is serious with Duke."

"Yeah, serious." I nodded.

"Well, cheers," Brielle said, lifting her glass. "To hot sex and happiness."

"I'll drink to that!" Doc grinned.

Brielle's phone was on the floor in front of her and it lit

up with an incoming call. She silenced it. "It's Roman. I'll call him later."

The screen went dark and then lit up again with an incoming text.

"He will not be ignored," Jazz said with a grin.

Brielle sighed. "Not a moment of peace with three older brothers. He's probably checking to see how much I've had to drink."

"He needs a girlfriend," Jazz quipped. "Then he'd be occupied and wouldn't bother you as much."

With a roll of her eyes, Brielle pressed a button and got up from the living room floor and headed toward the kitchen.

"Can we cut into the cake now?" Doc asked.

"It's your party," Brooklyn said, rising.

Mia hopped up from her seat. Joni held out a hand and Mia helped her. Joni sighed. "I wonder what my ankles look like. It's been so long since I've seen them."

Jazz crawled over to her, lifted her pant leg and said, "Furry. They're furry."

"You're so not helpful," Joni said with a laugh.

Jazz stood up. "It wasn't a judgment, it was fact."

Brielle came back into the room, her phone clutched in her hand. "Two things. One," she looked at Jazz, "your dog peed on a customer."

Jazz grinned. "That's my boy. What's the other thing?"

Brielle turned and looked directly at me. "Two, your sister and her friends are at Three Kings."

I groaned. "She promised me."

"Promised you what?" Brooklyn asked.

"That she wouldn't get into trouble."

"She's not in trouble," Brielle said.

"She's underage and she's at a tattoo parlor," I said. "Damn it."

Darcy raised her glass to me. "Welcome to motherhood."

"The bartender has a heavy hand," I muttered. "I'm sorry to pull you away from the party."

Brooklyn put on her blinker and looked in the rearview mirror. "I was the only one entirely sober aside from Joni. I don't mind. Plus, I kind of want to find out about all this drama with Waverly while we're on the way to get her."

"You're terrible," I said with a laugh. "My life amuses you?"

"Kinda. My life is nothing if not serene now. Smooth sailing with my super-sexy biker husband."

"Slash is still on you about pulling back?"

"Yeah. He'd be happy if I sat around at home, knitting little booties for the baby. But that's Allison's territory."

"I think he'd prefer that even if you weren't pregnant."

"Too true." She smiled. "It's nice having someone worrying about me all the time."

"It's not smothering?"

"Oh. It's completely smothering." She laughed. "But it's still sweet. There's something so comforting about a man like Slash protecting me."

Brooklyn pulled into the parking lot of Three Kings Tattoo Parlor.

I reached for the car door. "I'll be a few minutes."

"No rush," she assured me.

I got out of the car and walked into the tattoo parlor. The reception area was stuffed with leather couches and smelled like sandalwood. I could hear the buzz of a tattoo gun working in back, but otherwise the place was quiet.

Dylan and Waverly were sitting on one of the couches.

Jessica perched in a chair and was flipping through an art magazine.

I put my hands on my hips. "Seriously?"

"It's not what you think," Waverly said immediately "I swear."

"So you weren't trying to get a tattoo?"

"No," Waverly assured me.

"Wouldn't have worked anyway. You have to be eighteen," Jessica said without looking up. "I already asked."

"So, *you're* the reason why the three of you are here?" I asked.

"No," Waverly said. "I'm the reason why we're here. I swear I wasn't trying to do anything sketchy."

"Ha, get it? Sketchy? Tattoo parlor?" Jessica said with a grin, causing both girls to crack up. She stood up. "Come on, Dylan. I'll drop you off at home."

"Bye, Willa," Dylan said with a wave.

"Bye." I turned to my sister and plunked my hands on my hips.

Waverly nodded. "Are you—are we going home?"

"No. I haven't had a chance to try the cake Brooklyn made for the engagement brunch yet. I came to get you, and then I'm going back."

"Are you going to yell at me in front of everyone?"

"No, I won't yell at you in front of everyone. But they were all there when Roman called Brielle, so they all know what you're up to."

With a sigh, Waverly grabbed her bag and headed out into the parking lot.

Brielle's eldest brother strode out from the back. Roman was tall with brown hair, wearing an army green T-shirt that showed off his heavily inked arms. "Hey, sorry to drag you away from the engagement brunch. Just thought you'd want to know what your sister and her friends are up to."

"Yeah, they're making a habit of going places they shouldn't," I said with a sigh. "Thanks for letting us know."

"For the record, she didn't try to get inked. Her friend on the other hand…"

"Jessica used to be so sweet. Now she's becoming a rebel?" I shook my head.

"And that guy…is he your sister's boyfriend?"

"Yep. What was she here for if she wasn't trying to get a tattoo?"

"Not sure," he admitted. "They were looking around. When I got done with my last customer I came to walk him out, and there they were."

"There they were."

He shook his head. "Is it me, or do kids start looking younger and younger as you get older?"

"I wouldn't know yet. Maybe *you're* just getting older and older," I pointed out. I leaned forward and kissed his cheek. "Thanks for looking out for my sister. I appreciate it."

"It takes a village." He shrugged. "And I'm no stranger to teenage theatrics and antics of a teenage girl. I'm pretty sure my mother had to dye her gray hair because of Brielle."

I rolled my eyes. "Something to look forward to."

Chapter 23

"Take two pieces," Brooklyn said, handing me the aluminum to-go tin. "Then you guys can get out of here."

Waverly was talking with Brielle and Jazz. About what, I had no idea.

"Is it that obvious?" I asked.

"You're killing my buzz," Doc teased.

"Sorry."

"I'm kidding. Nothing can kill my buzz. Those mojitos are *strong*."

"Take a few penis pastries for the road," Brooklyn said. "I baked far too many."

"Waverly!" I called. "Let's go!"

I tossed her my keys and then carried out the hoard of baked goods Brooklyn insisted I take.

"See you guys later," Mia called out.

The Old Ladies blew a bunch of kisses and waved in our direction as we left. Waverly and I hadn't discussed what had happened—there was no privacy and I hadn't wanted to get into it with her until we were alone. So, it had to wait until I was ready to leave the party.

"Were you and Dylan thinking about getting matching tattoos?" I demanded as I climbed into the passenger side.

Waverly waited to answer until she was buckled in and the car was started. "No. It had nothing to do with Dylan."

"Then what?"

"It was two-fold," Waverly explained. "One, I wanted a Three Kings Tattoo T-shirt for T-shirt cutting purposes."

"Right, you're the trend-setter now."

"Yeah." She agreed. "But I wanted to talk to Roman about a tattoo design for you and me."

"You did?" I asked, glancing at her.

She nodded. "I mean, you have the clover tattoo with Duke and Savage. But we're sisters. I wanted to share something with you. It was stupid. Never mind."

"Not never mind. I think it's—God, Waverly. Are you trying to make me cry?" I suddenly blubbered.

"I think that would be the vodka. I can smell it from over here," she said with a laugh. "I just wanted it to be a surprise, you know? If I'd known Roman was going to call you about it, I would've waited. I know I've got a few more years before I can get a tattoo, I just thought it could be something cool to share with you."

"You sweet little idiot," I said, wiping my eyes. "You're impossible to stay mad at."

"It's because my motives were pure of heart."

"Yeah. Okay." I snorted.

When we got home, I immediately kicked off my heels. Waverly took the pastries from me and set them on the coffee table.

"Forks, immediately," she commanded.

"I'm working on it," I said with a laugh, unbuttoning my pants. "I need sweats first."

"Oh, yeah. Better plan."

"Let's change, chill, and devour."

"And nap."

"Wow, we sound old. When did we get old?"

After we changed and were sitting with the pastries, I handed her a fork and said, "While we're being honest about stuff, I think it's only fair to tell you something."

"Okay," she said, turning to look at me.

I took a deep breath. "Here goes. I'm meeting with a lawyer in a few days so I can start the process of becoming your legal guardian. It means having Angel relinquish her parental rights, and I don't know how that'll go...but I want to be your legal guardian."

Waverly didn't say anything, her face devoid of expression.

"You hate the idea," I said quietly. "I just thought it would be better for you, for us in the long run. So if there's a problem with the school, I can deal with it head on. Among other reasons, but yeah...crap, I—"

"Stop talking," she said.

I immediately closed my mouth.

"You've been the only person in my entire life who's been there for me. You've put me first. Always. Now you want to become my legal guardian?"

My throat tightened. "Yeah. I do. Because I don't want anyone to be able to take you away from me."

She lifted her head. Her blue eyes were shiny with tears. "I want that more than anything, Willa. More than anything."

Waverly was sprawled out on the couch in a sugar coma, her legs thrown across my lap. Her black toenail polish was chipped.

"Do you resent me?" she asked quietly, not opening her eyes.

"Not even a little bit," I assured her.

"You could've left a long time ago. Why didn't you bail? Things have been bad for a long time, but you're still here."

"You know I love you, but you weren't the only reason I stuck around," I admitted.

"Duke and Savage?"

"Yeah."

"I still have a hard time calling them by those names."

I smiled. "Yeah. Sometimes I forget they weren't always bikers."

She opened her eyes and slowly sat up. "My teeth feel fuzzy. I'm gonna brush the sugar off them." Waverly lowered her feet to the floor.

"I was nine when you were born," I said.

"Yeah. So you tell me all the time."

"Hush, Little Punk."

She grinned.

"What I'm trying to say is this; I was nine and it was already hard with Angel. Then you came along—"

"And made it harder?"

"Shut up, will you?" I laughed. "Yeah, it was hard with you being a newborn and all, but you gave me something to look forward to. You made the really sad and difficult moments better. You didn't know how hard life was yet. Smiling came so easy to you. So did laughter. You were this bright spot in a really dark childhood. And it wasn't just me, you know? It was the three of us. It was hard for us. But you gave us something to protect. You gave us a reason for wanting to get out of that shit hole of a life. You're the reason we all wanted better. We wanted it for *you*."

Waverly swallowed, but she didn't say anything. After a moment, she nodded, and then went toward the bathroom.

My phone rang.

I hoisted myself up from the couch to peer at my ringing cell.

"Hello," I greeted.

"How many drinks have you had?" Duke asked.

"I stopped at two—they were strong. I'm already home with Waverly."

"I thought engagement brunches were supposed to get rowdy."

"I've had two penises."

"So Joni totally called for male strippers, huh?"

I laughed. "Nah. I'm talking about pastries in the shape of penises that Brooklyn baked."

"I knew you girls were going to get wild."

"It was tame. You're thinking about bachelorette parties, and Doc didn't want one of those. It was all the Old Ladies could do to convince her to have a brunch. By the way, is Boxer having a bachelor party?"

"Hell yeah, he's having one. We're going to pull an all-nighter. Strippers, snorting coke off of said strippers, and then some other things that I'm not allowed to talk about."

"So, bourbon and an all-night poker game with just the guys and a few cigars?"

Duke laughed. "Yeah, exactly."

"You guys aren't like normal bikers," I said.

"You mean we're insanely loyal to our women and have no wish for different pussy?"

"Charming, Duke. Really charming."

"They call me Duke Charming."

"Who's *they*?" I quipped, but didn't give him a chance to respond. "How are things in Odessa?"

"Getting sorted," Duke said. "There was some fuckery going on, but Savage handled it."

"If I was allowed to know, would I even *want* to know?"

"No."

"Figured. Where are you?" I asked.

"Right now? Outside a shitty dive bar on the outskirts of town. Savage is inside, chasing a skirt."

"Ah, so you had time to call *your* skirt, huh?"

"Something like that. I'll be back Tuesday," he said.

"All right."

"We're still good for Wednesday?"

"Yeah, we're good for Wednesday. Hey, let's try something different this time, okay?"

"Sushi is different. We talked about this, remember?" he asked.

"No, I mean, why don't you come over here. Pick me up for our date and drive me there instead of meeting me like we usually do."

"That means you're getting on the back of my bike…"

"So it does."

He paused. "You've worked out the shit about us?"

"Yeah."

"You'll tell me more on Wednesday?"

"Yeah."

"Good."

"Good," I agreed.

"Later," he said gruffly.

He hung up and I set my phone aside.

"Willa and Duke, sitting in a tree," Waverly teased.

"Gah!" I put my hand to my heart. "I didn't even hear you come back."

"How could you hear anything over the flirting. You guys are gross, by the way. Like *seriously* gross."

"Thanks." I snorted.

She beamed. "I'm really happy for you guys."

I opened the door and cocked my hip.

Duke's gaze lowered. "I'm a fan of the outfit, but I'm not sure it's restaurant appropriate."

I grasped the lapels of his leather cut. "We're not going to a restaurant."

He entered the foyer and quickly closed the front door.

It had been a bold move, answering the door wearing a beet red negligee, but it had been days since I'd seen him, and we had the house to ourselves. There was no fear of Waverly walking in since she was at her CPR class and Savage was occupied.

I urged Duke to the couch and made him sit. And then I straddled him, the negligee riding up my thighs.

His hands settled underneath the slip to grasp my legs.

"I missed you," I said.

"Yeah?" He grinned. "Prove it."

I ground against him, my cleft rubbing against the fly of his jeans. He was already rock hard. I lowered my head and brushed my lips against his.

His tongue slid into my mouth as he hauled me even closer.

Sparks flared between my legs as Duke made love to my mouth. His hands wandered from the back of my thighs to my hips. They settled there for only a moment until he glided them up to caress my breasts.

His thumbs teased my nipples through the lace cups, turning them into hard points. He stopped kissing me.

"Come here," he rasped, urging me to sit up higher so my breasts were level with his mouth. He flicked his tongue and dragged it across the lace. He was toying with me, sucking my nipples between his lips.

I moaned, pressing into him more.

"Undo my fly," he commanded.

With trembling fingers, I reached between us. I popped the button of his jeans and lowered the zipper. I got off him so that he could raise his hips.

He shoved his jeans down, along with his boxers.

I grasped his firm erection in my hand, giving it a little squeeze. He threw his head back and closed his eyes.

My thumb swiped across the head of him, causing him to shudder. I leaned over and took him into my mouth, as far back as he would go. He tasted like man and musk. He tasted like Duke.

I was heady with need, delirious with want. I sucked him greedily, taking as much of him as I could, so much so that I nearly choked.

"Come here, baby," he whispered. "I need to be inside you."

I released him with a pop and then I climbed onto his lap. I gripped him again, angling him toward my body. I gently slid down until he was nestled inside me.

He grabbed my hips. "Ride me."

I gyrated against him, pleasure cresting in tiny waves that grew with each movement. He kept one hand on my hip, but the other went to my breast. He released it from the lace and pinched my nipple between his fingers.

A heavy, dull pulse throbbed between my legs with each twist of my nipple.

Somewhere, a cell phone rang.

It wasn't mine.

Duke's hand left my hip to reach into his leather cut.

"Are you fucking kidding me right now?" I growled.

"Let's play a game of control." He grinned and answered the call. "Hey, Prez. No, I'm not busy."

With renewed determination, I clamped around him, watching as his eyes shot to mine.

Stop that, he mouthed.

I did it again.

Leaning back, I took off my lingerie and tossed it aside. I swirled my hips as I caressed my breasts, painting my fingers around my nipples.

"Uh huh," Duke said and then he clenched his jaw.

I ceased moving and slid my hand down between us to play with myself.

"Sure, I've got it. Later." Duke hung up and threw his phone to the side. It hit the floor with a crash.

"Not without me," he gritted out. "Don't you dare come without me."

He gripped my hips and speared up into me. I screamed and all the pressure released inside of me.

"Fuck yes," he moaned. "Fuck, Willa."

Duke closed his eyes as he continued to rock up into me, eventually stilling.

I collapsed against him, burying my flushed face in the crook of his neck. "If you ever answer another call while you're inside me, I'm going to take your phone and throw it against the wall."

Chapter 24

I PULLED AWAY JUST ENOUGH to lower my head and kiss him. "Welcome back."

"It's good to be here." He cradled my head and slammed his lips against mine.

"I'd get off you, but I need, ah…"

With one hand holding me, he sat up and took the shirt off his back. "Take this."

"Thanks." I climbed off him and stuck his shirt between my legs and awkwardly waddled toward the bathroom. I looked at him over my shoulder. "You want to shower?"

"Depends. You gonna be in it with me?"

"Of course."

Duke rose from the couch and hoisted his jeans and boxers up but didn't button his pants. "Yeah. I've been wanting to…"

"What?" I asked when he stopped.

"Been wanting to shower with you," he rasped.

He followed me into the bathroom and stripped out of

his clothes. I added mine to the pile. I got the water hot, and soon steam filled the small room.

I grabbed us two fresh towels and hung them on the towel rack on the wall. I pulled back the curtain and stepped inside. Duke was quick to follow.

We were both tall and the shower wasn't very large to begin with. It was hard maneuvering around each other for the hot water. I nearly slipped, but he quickly steadied me.

"This was a bad idea," I said with a sigh.

"Not a bad idea. The shower's too small. You need a larger bathroom."

"Hmm. Yeah, but this is all I've got."

Water sluiced down his inked body. The Tarnished Angels club tattoo was over his heart and I traced it with my fingers. "You want to hear more about the bachelorette brunch?"

"Not really."

"Let me tell you the best part at least," I suggested.

"What was the best part?"

I told him about the showdown with Joni in the bathroom and how everyone else heard me yelling at her from the hallway.

He let out a booming laugh and I couldn't help it, I laughed with him.

"Did you know they were all betting on who I'd wind up with? It was a fifty-fifty split that it would be you."

"It's like they were betting on horses," Duke said with a shake of his head.

I brushed my hand along his jaw. "I want to go to the wedding with you. As your date."

He'd been reaching for the bar of soap but stopped. "Yeah?"

I nodded.

"You know that means we've gotta tell Savage."

"Yes."

"Soon…"

"Yes."

"Like, *tomorrow.*"

"Yes," I agreed.

"You ready for whatever that brings?"

"I'm not sure," I admitted.

"At least you're honest. Maybe a black eye will look good with my leather cut."

"You think he's gonna punch you?"

"It's Savage. And we didn't tell him first, you know? He's gonna take that personally."

"Yeah. He will," I sighed.

"Won't be the first time I've taken a shot from him," Duke said and then grimaced. "God damn he's strong…"

"If it comes to that I'll comfort you in a very special way…"

I got out of the shower first and then handed him a towel.

"You know," he said, tying the towel around his waist. "If we lived together, we could make sure to have our own bathroom. And then we'd have space."

"I'm not opposed to living together," I admitted slowly. "But we literally just moved in, and you and I aren't even officially public yet…even though the girls know."

"So what? You don't have to stay here because you just got here. Everyone that moves in winds up leaving shortly after, anyway."

I left the bathroom with Duke trailing behind me. I went into the bedroom I shared with Waverly, trying not to be seduced by Duke's words. I'd love more space. I'd love to wake up with Duke next to me and not worry about one of us needing to sneak out.

Not to mention…daily sex with Duke? Yeah. I could *totally* get on board with that.

"Tell you what, let's get through telling Savage and see how that goes, and then let's get through Doc and Boxer's wedding and after that we'll revisit this conversation."

"I'll hold you to it," he stated.

I opened the bottom drawer of the dresser, and it caught. I worked it out slowly. I picked up a T-shirt and a pair of leggings.

He raised his brows. "You're not getting back into the lingerie?"

"It served its purpose," I teased.

"Speaking of serving its purpose, you got my shirt all dirty."

"Washer," I explained. "You can hang out in your jeans and I can ogle your chest at my leisure. Though it might be a good idea to bring over a change of clothes or two for future use."

"Where will I keep them?" he asked.

"I'll make room for you in a drawer."

"You barely have enough room as it is," he pointed out.

"Do you want part of my drawer or not?" I asked, refusing to continue down this argumentative path.

"I do," he admitted.

I gathered his shirt and a few other things and walked to the washing machine. He followed me.

"I know you, Duke," I said, turning around to face him after I started the wash cycle. "This is more than just wanting us to live together. So, what is it?"

He went to the couch and grabbed his jeans, pulling them up and fastening them. Then he took a seat on the couch. Leaning forward, he rested his forearms on his thighs. "I don't want to live at the clubhouse anymore. It's fine for when you want to crash after a party. It's fine if you're not a family man…" He looked at me, his eyes dark and intense. "But I want to come home to you, Willa."

"It won't just be me," I said slowly. "Waverly, too. We're a package deal."

"I know that. I've watched her grow up. She's basically my kid sister. Of course I know that when I ask you to live with me, it means her too. That's a given. And I'm happy about it."

"You want stability? You want routine? You want normal?"

"Nah, I'll never be normal. I'm a biker. But happy? Yeah. I could be happy. And I think if you let yourself, you could be happy too."

"Happy," I said. "What a novelty."

"I think we've earned it. After all our years of hardship."

"Most definitely," I agreed. "I gotta ask…"

"Yeah?"

I tapped my finger against my lips. "You weren't serious about Little Dukes, were you?"

He shrugged.

"No, I need a real answer here."

"Eventually, I'd like a couple of Little Dukes or Little Willas." He grinned.

I let out a sigh. "We tell Savage, we go to the wedding together, and then we re-evaluate."

"Whatever you want."

"Don't say it like that."

"Say what like what?" he demanded.

"Like you're placating me, but also like you're already planning things in your head for our future."

He shrugged again. "Can we order food? I'm starving. You can lecture me some more after that, if you want."

I floated awake, coming slowly into consciousness, but I refused to open my eyes. After dinner, Duke and I had lain down on the couch, with me nestled between the couch cushions and him. My head was on his chest, his arm was around me, and a blanket was covering us both.

"You guys look cozy," Waverly whispered.

"There's leftovers on the counter," Duke whispered back.

"What did you order?" she asked.

"Sushi."

"Ew."

"Try it before you say that," I said, finally opening my eyes.

"Crap, did I wake you?" Waverly asked.

"Yeah, the door shutting did. Don't worry about it. And seriously, the sushi is *amazing*."

"Raw fish on rice? Not sure I can get behind that," Waverly said.

"We got steamed dumplings, too," I said, struggling to sit up, but it was challenging trying to move against Duke's bulk.

"Is this how it's going to be when Duke moves in here?" Waverly asked as she tromped toward the kitchen. "I come home to you guys spooning on the couch and leftovers on the counter?"

"He's not moving in here," I said immediately.

"It would be cramped if he did," Waverly said. She reached for a dumpling and bit into it. "Okay, that's amazing."

"Amazing enough to attempt a dragon roll?" I asked.

"Why not, I'm suddenly feeling adventurous. Which one is it?"

I angled my leg over Duke and slid off the couch. "Let me make you a plate of the best stuff."

"Did you guys order the entire menu?" she asked.

"Duke is big and he eats a lot," I teased.

"Hey, you were keeping up with me," Duke said, sitting up and scratching his chin. The dryer had beeped after we finished dinner and Duke was fully clothed by the time Waverly came home.

As I made her a plate, Duke asked her, "Would it bother you?"

"Would what bother me?" Waverly asked.

"Wasabi," I explained, pointing to the mound of green. "It's spicy, so be careful. And pickled ginger. It'll change your life, I swear."

She nodded, took the plate from me, and went to sit on the floor. She set the plate onto the coffee table and looked at Duke. "Would what bother me?" she asked again.

"If I lived here," Duke said, eyeing me out of the corner of his eye.

I shot him a glare.

Waverly shook her head. "Aside from the space thing, nah. Just as long as I don't hear you going at it with my sister, I think it'd be okay."

Duke looked at me. "I wouldn't move in here. There really isn't enough space. Not with you needing a place to do your homework and Willa's need for an office."

"Homework," Waverly said glumly. "School blows. It really does."

"I didn't care for school much either," Duke said.

"Try your rolls," I said.

"In a sec," Waverly said. "How'd you stick it out? I mean, I've got two more years, plus summer school. Summer school, Duke. The best part about school is the freedom during the summer."

"I stuck it out because I had Willa breathing down my neck. She's the reason I graduated. She and Savage." He leaned back against the couch. "Have you asked yourself why school is hard for you?"

"They just don't get me," Waverly said miserably.

"Is it a social thing?" I asked.

She shook her head. "No. I mean, the teachers. They gave me a tutor because I was failing some of my classes."

"That's usually what happens when you're failing. You get a tutor," I said.

"Yeah, okay, but did any of them ask *why* I was failing biology?"

"Why *were* you failing bio?" I asked.

"Because they care more about homework than they do the tests. They give out a bunch of busy work and it's boring. I ace the tests. Every time," she said. "But they don't care about that. It took Dylan five seconds to realize I'd already read the entire bio book cover to cover. I didn't need a tutor. I still don't. I just don't *care*."

"You needed a challenge," I said in sudden realization.

Waverly shoved a piece of sushi roll in her mouth, her cheeks puffing out. She chewed slowly and then finally swallowed. "Okay. I'm a convert."

Chapter 25

WAVERLY POLISHED OFF THE last of the leftovers and then leaned back. "Whew, can you be fish drunk? Because that's what I feel like right now."

I laughed. "How can you be fish drunk?"

"No idea, but I'm it." She got up and took her plate to the sink. She rinsed it quickly and then loaded it in the dishwasher. "I'm gonna take a shower and do some laundry. You have anything you need me to throw in?"

I shook my head.

"Thanks for dinner," she said, traipsing toward the bedroom.

I waited until the shower was running before speaking. "Not cool."

"What?" he asked, getting up off the couch.

I dogged his heels. "Asking Waverly how she'd feel if you lived here."

"I was trying to prove a point. And I think I've proven it." He scooped up the empty containers and dropped them into the garbage. "I'll take this out for you so it doesn't smell like fish, and then I'm gonna head out."

"Leaving so we don't fight?"

"There's nothing to fight about," he said with a grin. "You can be annoyed if you want, but there's not really a reason to be."

I sighed.

Duke grabbed the bag of trash and set it by the door. He quickly laced up his boots, made sure he had his belongings, and then picked up the garbage again.

"So tomorrow we tell Savage, yeah?"

I nodded. "Yeah. Where do you want to do it? Shelly's?"

"Might as well," he said. "It won't matter where we tell him, I still expect a punch to the face."

He leaned in to kiss my lips, but I covered my mouth to protect him. "Fish breath."

"I'll risk it."

I slowly lowered my hand. He pecked my lips and then pulled back. "It's gonna be okay. However he reacts, we'll deal. Okay?"

I nodded.

"I'll see you tomorrow."

I locked up after he left and then went to the bathroom and waited for Waverly to tell me to come in.

"Can I brush my teeth?" I asked her.

"Sure."

"So you like sushi," I said lamely.

"Apparently. Did you guys have fun tonight? It looked like you had fun. Cuddling all cute and stuff."

I thought about earlier, our sex on the couch, how easy it was with him. How he knew my body in ways I needed a man to know.

"Yeah, we had fun." I squirted toothpaste onto my toothbrush. "We're telling Savage tomorrow."

"Oh yeah?"

"Yeah."

"You sound nervous."

"I am nervous."

"Why?"

"Because it's Savage," I said. "And he could go all…*Savage*."

"He loves you guys. He'll want you both to be happy."

"I'm not sure it's that easy."

"Why do you make everything hard, Willa?"

"Excuse me?" I squeaked.

The water turned off and Waverly's hand shot out of the curtain to grab her towel from the rack. "In the words of my really smart boyfriend, you need to get out of your own way."

"What the hell does that mean?" I demanded.

She drew back the shower curtain. The gray towel was wrapped around her body and her red hair was slicked away from her face, her skin flushed from the heat of the water.

"It means, you're a self-sabotager, and every time something is going well for you in your life you look for reasons to detonate it, not believing it can be real or lasting. Duke's loved you forever and Savage is your best friend. He might be snippy because you guys didn't tell him right away, but you're not giving him the credit he deserves. He loves you both and wants you to be happy."

My mouth dropped open. "You didn't by any chance read Psychology for Dummies, did you?"

She grinned and stepped out of the tub. I was forced to back up to give her space—which there wasn't much of in the tiny bathroom.

"I tried to push Dylan away and he called me out on it. You and me, we're kind of the same. Mom fucked us up. Our dads…well, they're not in the picture. What if for once in our lives you and I just cut out all the drama and decide to be happy?"

I stared at her for a long moment and then I said, "I can't wait until you're twenty-one. We're going to have some damned good wine and emoting sessions."

"You only have to be eighteen in Europe to drink," she pointed out with a smile. "We could just pretend to be European…"

"We'll wait until you're twenty-one," I quipped. "Besides, that gives us several more years to accumulate emotional baggage to dissect."

"You don't need any more emotional baggage. You're pretty bogged down as it is."

"Um. Rude."

"Um. *Right.*" She smiled. "Now brush your teeth. I can smell your fish breath from here, and even though he loves you, fish breath will not keep a fella."

"Oh, so you're an expert at keeping fellas now?"

She shrugged. "I do okay."

"Can I have three shots of tequila, please," I said to the bartender at Shelly's.

"Sure thing," she said.

"You're not going for bourbon, huh?" Duke asked from his spot next to me. "He likes bourbon better."

"You know how he gets when he does bourbon shots. Let's not make this harder on ourselves."

We were perched on two stools waiting for Savage to join us. I'd texted him earlier in the day and asked if he wanted to grab a drink at Shelly's.

Savage strode in, his eyes wandering around the room until he found us at the bar.

"Good timing," Duke said to Savage. "Willa just ordered us tequila shots."

I handed Savage a saltshaker.

The three of us quickly did our shots and sucked on limes.

"Oh, that was horrible," I said with a shudder.

"Another round?" Savage asked.

"Definitely not," I said. "Why don't you guys grab us a booth and I'll get the first round of beers."

The guys wandered off to the corner booth while I ordered three pints. I brought them to the table and set them down. Before I could sit by Duke, Savage grabbed me and pulled me into the booth next to him.

He slung an arm around me and said, "Slide your fingers through my hair."

"*What?*" I demanded.

"Quick, pretend you're my newest piece of ass," he growled.

"You're a pig," I muttered, shooting Duke a look.

Duke clenched his jaw and reached for his pint of beer, just as the brunette Savage had hooked up with a few weeks ago approached the table.

"Hey Savage," she greeted.

"Hi Elizabeth," he said. The hand he had around me wandered down toward my breast. I smacked his hand away and glared at him.

His innocence was completely phony.

"How ya been?" she fished.

"Busy," Savage said. He nuzzled against my hair and pulled me closer.

I didn't have time for this.

I stared at the young woman standing at our table who looked hurt, but clearly didn't have enough pride to walk away from the situation.

Sighing, I said, "Look, I'm not his girlfriend, or his newest piece of ass. Savage is Savage. He doesn't do relationships and if he promised you a repeat performance, he's a liar and an asshole. Sorry to disappoint you."

"A *raging* asshole," Duke added.

"Definitely," Savage agreed with a smile.

I elbowed Savage hard enough to make him grunt.

"You're a pretty woman," I said to Elizabeth. "You don't need to hang around this table hoping Savage has a come-to-Jesus moment about you. Besides, there's a really cute guy sitting at the bar checking you out as we speak."

Her expression brightened. "Really?"

I nodded. "Really. Polo shirt. Corner."

Elizabeth looked over her shoulder at the guy, who quickly turned his head, having been caught staring.

"Go ask him if he'll buy you a drink," I suggested. "And forget Savage. He probably wasn't even that good in bed, anyway."

"Hey," Savage protested.

I shot him a look.

"Thanks," Elizabeth said. She tossed her brown hair over her shoulder. "See ya around, Savage." And then she sauntered over to the guy at the end of the bar and I watched as a smile bloomed across his face.

"Get off me, you dog." I flung Savage's arm away from me and then immediately stood up. Duke scooted over and I took a seat next to him.

"You're a true best friend," Savage said to me. "Thanks for that."

"Maybe when you sleep with women you could tell them up front that there won't be any repeats," I said.

"I do. They must not hear me."

"Do you do it when you're inside them?" Duke demanded.

Savage grinned and shrugged.

"You dick," I muttered.

"You love me." Savage said and then took a drink. "How's your week been?"

"Good. Busy," I said. "Actually, I have some news to share."

"Yeah?" Savage asked, leaning back against the booth.

I nodded. "Yeah. You know how you wanted to meet the guy I've been dating?"

"Yeah. I need to meet him and make sure he's not a complete douche."

"He's not a complete douche," I said. "He's here. Right now, actually."

Savage looked around the bar for a moment. "Where? Please tell me he's not part of the group that looks like casting for Accountants Gone Wild."

"No." I turned to face Duke. "He's not part of that group."

Out of the corner of my eye, I saw Savage focus back on us. Suddenly, it seemed very quiet despite the noise of the bar.

Duke's arm came around me and he pulled me into the wall of his body. Savage took in the gesture.

I waited for the explosion.

"You guys sure you don't want another shot?" Savage drawled.

"I'm-I'm sure," I stuttered. "Well?"

"Well, what?" Savage asked.

"What do you think?"

"About?"

"*Us*," I snapped. "Duke and me. We're together now."

"You want me to say something?" Savage asked.

"Yes, please," I begged. He was being far too calm, far too controlled. This wasn't like him at all.

"Well, I'll tell you what I think."

I took a deep breath.

"I think it's about fucking time," Savage said. And then he grinned. A big joker sized grin. "He's been in love with you for years. And you've been wasting your time with douche canoes who are more comfortable with blow up dolls than a real woman."

Duke let out a low chuckle.

"Way to go, dude." Savage held out his fist to Duke who bumped it with his own. "Bout damn time you sealed the deal. Locked that shit down."

"She took long enough to come around, didn't she?" Duke asked.

"Yeah, she did."

"Hey, *I'm right here*," I snapped.

"Quiet, Willa," Savage said, a twinkle in his eye. "This here is man talk."

"I should've elbowed you in the junk when I had the chance," I muttered.

"I just have one stipulation about this new development," Savage said.

"What's that?" I demanded.

"You name your first born after me," he said. "Cooper works for a boy or a girl."

"How about we name the dog we get after you?" I joked. "Cooper is a good dog name."

"Once a savage always a Savage." Savage lifted his beer. "To you guys. Fucking, finally."

We clinked our glasses against his.

"Fucking, finally," Duke repeated.

~

Duke's phone rang. "I'm gonna take this outside so I can hear."

I nodded.

He leaned over and gently brushed his lips against mine and then left.

"That's gonna be a little weird getting used to," Savage said, hand around his second pint.

"Yeah, for me too," I admitted.

"I'm not lying. I really am happy for you guys."

"I'm glad," I said with relief. "I was worried about how you'd react. In fact, you've been the source of a crazy amount of my stress recently…"

"Why? Did you think I was going to lose my shit?"

"Well, yeah," I admitted with a sheepish grin. "I'm glad you didn't though."

"Why the secrecy?"

"I wanted to make sure that he and I were…that we were…"

"Not just fucking."

I winced and nodded.

"Because you weren't going to potentially blow up our friendship and it wasn't going to be worth it if all you were doing was fucking?"

"Right again," I said. "Damn, you're insightful, aren't you?"

"I can, on occasion, be insightful."

"Don't worry. I won't tell anybody," I jested.

He smiled. "Nothing's changing. Well, I'll start knocking before I enter rooms. God forbid I see you riding his dick. There's close, then there's *let's not even go there*."

"You mean it?" I asked quietly.

"About knocking? Absolutely."

"No. About how nothing is going to change. How it's

still the three of us. Now and forever. Even if it's also me and him?"

"It'll always be the three of us. I still think you should name your first squirt Cooper."

"First?" I raised my brows.

"Oh come on. I see the way Duke looks at you. You'll have many squirts."

"Savage," I warned.

"I need a bunch of godchildren to corrupt. Get crackin', woman. Time's a wastin'."

Chapter 26

WE STEPPED out of the bar, the air warm as our skin adjusted to the outside world. Duke held my hand, his fingers laced with mine. Savage was still inside, flirting up a storm with a blonde he'd met when he'd asked her to play pool with us and be on his team.

"You were worried for nothing, weren't you?" Duke asked.

"Don't lie, you were a little worried too," I prodded.

"Worried is too strong a word. I'd say *concerned*."

"You think he'll ever find someone and be happy?"

"He finds plenty of someones, and he's regularly happy," Duke quipped.

"You know what I mean. One woman for an extended period of time that could turn serious."

"He's not ready. He might never be ready."

"Hmm. You're paired off," I reminded him. "You're no longer out there on the prowl…hunting."

"Ah, so you think he'll wake up one day in the near future, his life suddenly meaningless and empty because he has no one to share it with?"

"Yes," I said.

"Men don't work that way."

"I'm not talking about *men*, I'm talking about Savage. I think I know him pretty well."

"Not as well as me."

"Fancy a wager?" I asked.

"What kind of wager?"

"The kind of wager like the Old Ladies made. About if I'd wind up with you or Savage?"

"Yeah, only, this time we'll make a bet on if Savage will get serious with someone."

"In what time frame?"

"Within the next six months," Duke said. "I vote no."

"I vote yes. What are we betting? Money?"

"Nothing so trivial as money," Duke said. He backed me up until he had me pinned to the side of my car. "The winner gets to have his or her sexual fantasy completely fulfilled."

"A sex bet?" I snorted. "Of course, you want a sex bet."

"To make it more interesting, we don't share our fantasies until the winner has been declared."

"One stipulation," I said.

"Name it."

"No degradation."

He held out his hand. "Deal."

I shook on it. "Deal."

Duke angled his body against mine, our locked hands nestled between us. "You know there are no losers in this game."

"I'm aware. That's why I had no qualms about making the bet."

He kissed my jaw and then my lips. "So, Doc and Boxer's wedding…"

"Yeah?"

"You and Waverly want to meet me there? Or you want me to ride my bike over and the three of us go together in your car?"

"It's probably easier if I meet you there," I said.

"Right," he said quietly.

"Plus, I kind of want you to see me when I walk in. I'm gonna look hot."

"You always look hot."

"But this time, I'm gonna look really, *really* hot."

"You don't get it, do you?"

"Get what?"

"You could wear sweats and have your hair in a messy ponytail, and I'd find you hot."

"Basically, you want to have sex with me all the time."

"Pretty much, yeah."

I grinned. "That's nice."

"Nice?"

"Yeah. The perks of a relationship are nice."

"That's the only thing that's really changed, you know. The sex part."

"I like that," I admitted. "I like that it was just easy and natural with us."

"It was a good night," he said. "The night we hooked up, I mean. But I like where we are now."

I snuggled against him. "Me too."

"It smells like sawdust in here," I said, closing the front door.

Waverly didn't look up from the book she was reading. "Does it?"

"Yes."

"Huh." She turned the page, stuck a bookmark in it, and then closed it. "So? How did it go?"

I grinned. "It was great."

"Yeah? So did Savage freak?"

"Nope."

"Dang."

"You wanted Savage to fight Duke?" I asked with a snort.

"Not really. But you were so convinced it was going to happen."

"I was wrong."

She put her hand to her ear. "I'm sorry. I didn't quite hear you. What was that?"

"Hey, it's a school night. Why aren't you in bed?" I demanded.

"Seriously? We're doing that now?"

"Nah. Just getting you off my back. What are you doing tomorrow after school?" I asked, plopping down on the couch next to her.

"My schedule is wide open, actually. Why?"

"I have nothing to wear to Doc and Boxer's wedding. And I don't think you have anything either—since Angel took off with all of your fancy outfits."

"She probably sold my clothes for cigarette money," she said glumly.

"It's a safe bet. She probably sold mine for scratch-off money. Anyway. I was thinking we could go to Folson's."

"Folson's is a department store."

"Yep."

"With full prices."

"Also yep."

"Meaning I won't have to piece together an ensemble from thrift stores."

"Waverly?"

"I like my thrift stores," she defended. "I get to be off beat and eclectic. The moment I start shopping at department stores, my whole reputation goes out the window."

"What reputation would that be?"

"The reputation that I'm the badass girl from the wrong side of the tracks that pulls herself up by her bootstraps."

"Yeah, I guess you can't be that girl if you shop at a snooty department store. But what about me? I have nothing to prove and I want to wear something new that'll make Duke follow me around like a puppy."

"He'd do that even if you wore sweats."

I stared at her in surprise.

She frowned. "What?"

"You sure it's okay that I wore my boots?" Waverly asked, the silver wrapped wedding present sitting on her lap.

"You wore them to Brooklyn and Slash's wedding," I pointed out. "Why are you worried about them now?"

"I wear them *everywhere*. I was wrong, okay?" she blurted out.

"Wrong about what?"

"I thought I wanted to dress how I normally dress, but I feel underdressed now."

"You mean angry-teen-meets-angry-punk-meets-angry-goth isn't doing it for you today?"

She glared at me.

After Folson's, I'd taken Waverly around to some of the best thrift stores in Dallas. She'd found an 80s prom dress with a full skirt. She'd paired it with a denim vest that had been bedazzled, added stockings and her heavy Doc Martens and a black lace choker.

"I love how you're dressed," I said. "It's classically your style."

"But what if it doesn't reflect how I feel about the world anymore?" she asked. "What if I'm dressing how I've always dressed because I was trying to prove a point, and now I don't care if I'm proving anything anymore?"

"Translation?"

"I want a pair of heels."

"Take my phone," I said. "And call Mia. You guys are the same size."

"What if she's already at Brooklyn's helping Doc get ready?"

"That's a risk you're going to have to take. I'd trade shoes with you in a heartbeat, but I wear size behemoth."

Brooklyn and Slash were hosting Doc and Boxer's wedding. They had the space and Brooklyn loved to entertain. With the help of Jazz and Brielle, the decorations and cake would be impeccable. Doc hadn't given a lot of time to prepare for the wedding, but Brooklyn had become an expert at pulling off last minute events.

"Damn," Waverly muttered, setting my phone down. "Mia's already there."

"Guess you'll have to party in your trademark boots."

"Guess so."

I turned down the road that led to Brooklyn and Slash's property. After I parked the car and turned off the engine, Waverly unlatched her seat belt.

"You go on in," I said to her, reaching for my phone.

"Gonna text your boyfriend to come out and meet you?" she teased.

"Yep." I grinned.

With a mock salute, she headed up the pathway. She pushed open the front door and stepped inside. I shot off a text to Duke and waited.

For some reason, nerves swirled in my belly.

That feeling quickly turned to appreciation when he came out of the house. He'd cleaned up for the wedding. His jeans were new and he wore a blue button-down shirt, along with his heavy motorcycle boots, and of course, his Tarnished Angels leather cut. But he was rocking the stubble.

I climbed out of the car and stopped to look at him.

He smiled, appearing boyish. His dimples popped, and it reminded me of when he was a teenager.

Without a word, we moved toward one another. He reached his hand out to grasp my waist while the other cupped the back of my neck.

He tilted my head back to receive his kiss. There, on the sidewalk, he plundered my mouth with his tongue, tasting me.

"You look incredible," he growled against my lips.

"You haven't seen the best part." I pulled away from him and turned so he could see that the formal blue dress had a short skirt and almost no back.

He trailed a finger down my spine and I shivered.

I turned around again and placed my hand on his chest, just over his heart. I felt the heavy drumming of its beat.

"You don't look so bad yourself," I quipped.

"You and your compliments," he teased, bringing my hand to his lips. "You spoil me."

His tongue grazed my knuckles, making me shiver.

The front door opened. "Hey, Duke, stop pawing your woman and get your asses in here!" Savage yelled.

Duke clasped my hand in his and we headed for the house. Every available space in the living room and foyer were graced with blooming white flowers and lit candles in glasses. There were photos in silver frames atop the mantle of the engaged couple. Nothing as formal as engagement photos, but pictures of them from other Tarnished Angels events and some where they weren't even in the frame together. Pictures of them as children.

I pointed to a photo of Boxer when he couldn't have been more than seven-years-old, his face covered in mud. "Trouble even then, right?"

Duke grinned. "No doubt."

There was a small table in the corner of the living room stacked with wrapped presents of all shapes and sizes.

Darcy came down the stairs and stopped halfway. She wore a tight black dress that showed off her amazing body.

I hoped I looked half as good as her after I had kids.

That thought entered my head before I even had a chance to stop it.

"Well, that's new," I muttered.

"Hmm?" Duke asked, turning toward me.

"Nothing. Hey, Darcy," I called.

"Hey." She beamed. "You want to come upstairs and chill with us and the bride before the ceremony?"

"Love to." I squeezed Duke's fingers before letting go.

I followed Darcy up the stairs but looked back for a moment to find Duke watching me with a devious little smirk on his lips.

That smirk set a spark of pleasure between my legs.

Darcy opened the bedroom door and I followed her inside. The room was all Brooklyn. Sage green walls, heavy oak furniture built to last, and photos of her and Slash from their wedding. Joni and Allison were perched on the king-sized bed, talking in low tones.

"Where's the blushing bride?" I asked.

"More like fuming bride." Joni grinned.

I raised my brows. "Why is she fuming? And why are you laughing at her?"

"Because she's a dirty rotten friend," Doc shouted as she came out of the ensuite bathroom. She wore a dainty rhinestone head piece in lieu of a veil, and a bathrobe to keep her dress from getting dirty before the ceremony. She looked like a fairy queen with her pixie haircut.

"And why is she a dirty rotten friend?" I asked.

Mia stood by the dresser which she was using as a makeshift table. She popped open a bottle of champagne, poured a flute and then crossed the room to hand it to me. "Because Joni told her she wasn't allowed to drink before the ceremony."

"Just one glass to take the edge off," Doc pleaded.

"You have even one glass on a near empty stomach and it's gonna go straight to your eye sockets and you're gonna blubber your vows," Joni said, still on the bed. "You told me to remind you of that when we got to this point. So, here we are."

"I can't even pee in peace." Doc glowered.

"Lift your skirt," Joni demanded. "Prove to me you didn't strap a flask to your thigh."

"I will do no such thing," Doc said. "I'm offended you'd even—"

Joni held out her hand.

Doc stared at her for a long moment and then with a sigh, she reached under her robe and extracted a flask. "It's just Bailey's. It doesn't even count."

She marched over to Joni and placed it in her palm, but then Darcy immediately filched it.

"It would just go to waste if you had it," Darcy said. "I'll take care of it. Willa will help." She winked at me. "Right, Willa?"

"Definitely," I agreed.

Darcy took a sip from the flask. "Damn, this is perfect." She handed it to me and I did the same.

"Double fisting at a wedding," I quipped. "I'm classy."

The bedroom door opened and a beautiful brunette of average height strode inside. "I never thought in a million years that when I became a mother, I would talk about bodily fluids so much."

I handed her the flask.

"What's this?" she asked, taking it from me.

"Bailey's."

"Ah, perfect." She took a sip.

"Willa, you know Rachel, right?" Mia asked.

"Yeah, we've met," I said with a smile. "You left town around the time Duke and Savage got patched in."

Rachel nodded. "Oh, that's right. Hi, again."

"She's been living with her mom in Laramie, but she's moving back to town," Mia explained.

"Welcome back," I said.

"Thanks," Rachel said. "You, Duke and Savage are the inseparable trio, right?"

I nodded.

"She's Duke's Old Lady now," Mia informed her.

"Girlfriend," I interjected. "Not an official Old Lady yet."

"Semantics." Joni waved her hand.

"Ah, Duke." Rachel nodded. "I like him a lot. And Savage too."

"Your mom's moving back with you, isn't she?" Allison asked.

"Yeah. She's done with the winters in Wyoming." Rachel grinned.

"I'm just glad Cash is close in age to Tank," Allison said. "They'll grow up together."

Joni placed a hand on her belly. "And this one, too."

"A group of hellions, mark my words," Darcy said.

"Oh, of course," Joni said. "A son of Zip? Hellion for sure." She winced. "Little bastard just kicked me in the ribs."

"He heard you talking smack," Rachel said with a laugh. She looked at Doc. "Boxer's getting a bit antsy down there."

Doc rolled her eyes. "He's probably worried I climbed out the window and I'm on the lam. He hasn't seen me since last night. I should put him out of his misery and marry him."

"Should I go tell everyone to take their seats?" Mia asked.

Doc nodded.

Mia went to the bedroom door, but it flew open before she got to it. Lily entered first, followed by Brooklyn.

"Aunt Doc, Uncle Boxer said to stop…" She frowned and looked up to Brooklyn. "I forgot the word he said."

"Primping," Brooklyn supplied with a smile.

Lily nodded, her blonde curls bouncing. "Yeah, he said to stop primping, and to get your ass down there and make an honest man out of him. Also, what does that mean?"

"She doesn't remember the word *primp*, but she remembers the word ass," Darcy muttered.

"Good timing, Lily Burger," Doc said. "Go tell Uncle Boxer that we're ready to move and groove."

The little girl ran out of the room, the clatter of her shoes hitting the wooden stairs as she went.

"Colt's not put out that Boxer asked Lily to be his best man, is he?" Darcy asked Mia.

Mia grinned. "Nah. He was perfectly happy to relinquish the job."

"We should go take our seats," Darcy said. "But first, another nip of that Bailey's."

Rachel and Brooklyn stayed behind with Doc, but the rest of us left the room. We took the stairs and headed toward the back yard.

"They really do have the perfect space for weddings," Darcy commented.

"The really do," I agreed.

Slash and Brooklyn had a few acres—enough room for a large wedding tent and for people to park and roam freely on the property. Jazz and Brielle were attempting to get people into the chairs that had been set up for the event. A jazz trio was near the back of the aisle that Doc would walk down.

Savage sat on the aisle seat, with Waverly next to him. There was an empty chair in between them and Duke.

"You look hot, babe," Savage said by way of greeting.

I flicked his ear as I passed him.

"What?" he asked, rubbing his ear. "I gotta behave now that you and Duke are swapping spit?"

"Uh, ew." Waverly wrinkled her nose.

I took a seat next to her and immediately Duke put his hand on my thigh.

"You don't swap spit with Dylan?" Savage asked her.

"Can we please stop talking about spit?" I demanded.

"Hi, Waverly!" Lily screamed and waved from her spot at the altar next to Boxer.

Waverly waved back.

The Old Ladies took their seats next to their men.

Before Allison could even sit down, Torque was handing baby Tank to her. "He's hungry," Torque said.

"I don't want to miss the ceremony," Allison said, but Tank was beginning to fuss.

"Just stick a nipple in his mouth," Darcy suggested. "It shuts up men of all ages."

"The woman is not wrong," Gray added.

"I don't have a shawl," Allison said. "I'd prefer not to flash anyone while they're saying their vows."

"I have an idea. Hold on," I said, quickly getting up and going to where Brielle and Jazz were sitting.

"Hey, girl," Jazz greeted. "Stellar dress."

"Thanks. Did you guys get tablecloths and linens for the wedding?"

"Yeah." Brielle nodded. "Why?"

"Is there an extra one, by chance?"

"There's a few." Brielle got up and I followed her into the house. She opened Brooklyn's pantry, stepped inside, and came back out holding a white tablecloth. "Why do you need it?"

"Not for me. For Allison. I'll explain later. Thanks!"

I rushed out of the house and headed to Allison and handed her the linen.

"Ah, genius." Allison smiled and took it. "Thanks!"

With the movements of a pro, she had the tablecloth across her body and was undoing her outfit to free a breast and begin feeding baby Tank.

The jazz pianist played a few notes and everyone fell silent. Heads turned to watch the bride come down the aisle.

I was surprised that Rachel came first, holding a bouquet of flowers.

"Who's that?" Waverly whispered.

"Rachel," Duke answered for me. "She's an Old Lady."

"Whose Old Lady?" Waverly asked.

I placed a finger to my lips and she fell silent.

Brooklyn followed Rachel. As she walked, she kept her eyes on Slash, who tracked her every move.

Waverly's gasp pulled my attention from the couple so

obviously in love it hurt to look at them—and they weren't even the bride and groom.

Doc stood at the back of the aisle, a satisfied smirk on her lips. I quickly looked at Boxer, wanting to gauge his reaction. He looked dumbstruck and then a slow grin pulled across his face.

"That's the best wedding dress I've ever seen," Waverly said.

Instead of traditional white, Doc wore red. It was a strapless sweetheart neckline and the full skirt was calf-length. It was a mix of modern and vintage and the color emphasized her strawberries and cream complexion, making her skin seem to glow.

The trio began to play a slow jazz number, and Doc all but glided toward Boxer. When she came to a stop in front of him, he took her hand and brought it to his lips.

They shared a look only they were privy to, and my throat thickened with an onslaught of emotion.

The justice of the peace began to speak and asked them to recite their traditional vows.

"Interesting choice," I whispered to Duke. "Not going for writing their own."

"You write your own, but you say that shit to each other in private. This is all just ceremony."

I met Duke's gaze and then smiled softly and leaned in to kiss him.

"Who has the rings?" the justice of the peace asked.

Boxer let go of Doc's hand, but only so he could turn and lean down toward Lily. "Ring please, Lily Burger."

She looked up at him. "I don't have Aunt Doc's ring."

"I gave it to you for safe keeping. That's why you're my best Lily Burger. Your job is to make sure the ring is safe."

"Oh, it's safe." Lily nodded. "But I don't have it."

"Where is it?" Boxer demanded gently.

"I buried it."

"I'm sorry, you *what*? You *buried* it?" he asked, his jaw dropping open. "Like a dog buries a bone?"

"Not like a dog." She frowned. "Like a dragon with its gold and jewels and stuff."

"Where did you bury it?" Boxer asked.

Lily pointed to the other side of the property.

"I'm guessing he wishes he'd asked Colt to be best man," Joni said with a rueful laugh. "Ow!"

"Ow what?" Zip asked from next to her.

Joni went on, "That was a strong one."

"Strong what?" Zip asked, placing his hand on her belly.

"Strong contraction," Joni said calmly.

Zip's eyes widened. "Contraction? Are you having my baby?"

"Relax," she said with a wide smile. "They're far apart. I've got a ton of time before my uterus is ready to shove a turkey through a keyhole."

"Ugh. Seriously?" Waverly asked. "Gross."

"Uh, Joni?" Rachel said.

"Yeah?"

"I don't think you have that much time," she said. "Your dress is wet."

"I'm a nurse. I'm pretty familiar with—" She suddenly stopped talking and she let out a small grunt. "Okay, that's kind of strange."

"What? What? What's strange?" Zip demanded.

"I kinda feel like I have to push," she said, struggling to stand.

"Push? Push what?" Zip yelled.

"The baby." Joni took Zip's hand and stood. "My water definitely broke."

"You can't give birth to the baby here," Zip said. "We

need to get you to a hospital."

"Not gonna make it," Joni said.

Doc shoved her flowers at Brooklyn. "Here's what we're going to do. Acid, run to my car and get my med bag."

"On it," Acid said. "Where are your keys?"

"No idea. Break a window if you have to," Doc said. "Okay. Zip, get on Joni's other side. We need to get her into the house."

"Wait," the justice of the peace said. "I haven't announced you man and wife yet."

"Then hurry up," Boxer said. "I've got a ring to find."

"And I've got a baby to deliver," Doc said.

The justice of the peace sighed. "I now pronounce you man and wife. You may now kiss the bride."

Doc arched a brow at Boxer. "Make it snappy."

Chapter 27

Joni stopped mid step, clamping down on Zip's hand. Her face contorted and her skin flushed. After a few breaths, she nodded and began walking again.

"I'll call an ambulance," Darcy said.

"Lily Burger and I are going to find Doc's wedding ring," Boxer drawled, letting go of the back of Doc's neck.

"Do you think you can make it up the stairs?" Brooklyn asked.

"I think so," Joni wheezed.

"Good," Brooklyn said. "You can use our bed." She looked over her shoulder at Slash. "We're going to need a new mattress protector when this is over."

Her husband shrugged.

"I'm ruining your wedding," Joni huffed as she ambled up the aisle.

"Are you kidding? You just gave us a good story," Doc said. "Easy, watch your step."

"But your wedding dress!" Joni moaned. "I'm gonna get placenta all over it."

"Ugh," Waverly muttered. "That's it." She looked at

me. "This wedding just got weird and gross. Can I please go hang out with Dylan?"

I smiled. "Yeah. You can go hang out with Dylan."

"Save me a slice of cake," Waverly said as she leaned over to grab her purse from underneath the chair. "I'm gonna chill out front and wait for him."

"Okay, but please don't do anything where I'm going to get a phone call," I quipped.

"I wore the wrong shoes for a bank job," she teased. "Bye, Duke. Don't let my sister drink too much."

"Roger that," Duke said.

"Later, Punk," Savage said to her.

The rest of us remained outside while Doc and Zip got Joni inside and upstairs.

"This is really exciting," Brielle said.

"Very exciting," Jazz agreed. "I'm kind of hungry. And we *did* cater this thing."

"Thank God," Mia said. "I'm starving."

"Doc won't care if we eat, will she?" Jazz asked.

"I think she'd be offended if we didn't," Savage said.

Jazz looked at him. "I'm going to choose to believe you."

Darcy hung up the phone. "The ambulance is on its way."

"I don't think they'll make it in time," Colt said, his expression filled with concern.

"It'll be fine," Mia said, squeezing her husband's hand. "She's got Doc."

Colt blew out a breath of air. "Yeah, okay."

"Found it!" Lily screamed from the other side of the property.

"As far as weddings go, I'm pretty sure this is the craziest one I've been to," I said, rising from my chair.

"Ha." Jazz snorted.

Brielle giggled.

"What?" I demanded. "What's that about?"

"We catered a wedding a few weeks ago," Brielle explained. "The bride walked in on the groom having sex."

"With a bridesmaid? How cliche," I said.

"No. With his future mother-in-law," Jazz said.

"Oh my God. No way," I said.

"Yeah." Brielle nodded. "Oh man, the yelling and the screaming—"

"And the crystal smashing," Jazz added.

"Well, let's start on the food," Mia said. "And we'll wait to toast until we have ourselves a new baby Tarnished Angel."

Twenty minutes later, Zip ran out of the house, his face full of elation. "We've got a baby boy!"

Cheers resounded throughout the back yard.

Colt slapped Zip on the back and offered his congratulations.

"How's Joni?" Mia asked.

"Perfect. A fucking champ. How she did that without drugs, I'll never know." Zip beamed.

"Well, Dad," Darcy quipped. "We got a name yet?"

Zip looked at Colt when he said, "Everett James. Everett because Joni likes the name. James after you."

Colt's expression turned grave. "I'm honored, brother."

A siren wailed in the distance, the sound of it getting louder as an ambulance approached, and Zip headed back inside.

"Time to pop that champagne to celebrate the new baby," Mia said.

"And Doc deserves it," Darcy said. "For delivering a baby at her own wedding."

"Joni made this day perfect for Doc," Boxer said.

"Getting married wasn't perfect enough?" Allison asked.

Boxer grinned. "My woman is never happier than when she's being a doctor. So, on the day she married me, she also got to do what she loves to do. Couldn't have planned it better."

Doc and Brooklyn came out into the back yard. Doc was still in her wedding dress, which was completely pristine.

"How are you still clean?" Jazz asked in shock.

"Brooklyn gave me an apron," Doc said with a grin. "Joni and baby are in the ambulance on their way to the hospital, but everything went smoothly."

Boxer strode to her, wrapped an arm around her shoulder, and pulled her to him. "We know how to throw a party, don't we?"

"We sure do," she agreed, beaming up at him.

"Found your ring," he said.

She held out her hand and he slid it onto her finger. She caressed his cheek. "I need a drink."

He kissed the top of her head. "You've earned it."

"I earned it too," Brooklyn said with a grin. "I lost an apron—and a mattress cover—to the cause. Guess I'll have to settle for sparkling water, though."

"I'll put it in a champagne flute for you," Brielle said. "Then you can be all fancy pants."

We ate great food and drank cocktails. The jazz trio played and the sun trekked across the sky as the day turned to evening. The bugs came out, but citronella torches had been set up around the back yard and helped to keep them at bay.

I was sitting at a table by myself, enjoying a slice of wedding cake when Mia came over and sat down next to me, Scarlett asleep in her arms.

"She's zonked out," I said.

"Milk drunk. Combined with the jazz music, it's like the ultimate soporific effect."

"There is something soothing about the music," I agreed. "I like that I can hear people talk over it, not struggle through some overly-loud heavy metal band."

"Hmm. There is that." Mia looked in the direction of Boxer and Doc, who were currently swaying against one another. Doc was nestled in Boxer's arms, her eyes closed.

"It's like they've forgotten we're here," Mia said with a soft smile.

"They look so happy," I noted. "Like, *really* happy."

Duke and Savage were across the lawn, talking to Rachel. She said something and then Savage embraced her. I caught Duke's eye and gave a little finger wave. He waved back.

"They're not the only ones who are happy," Mia teased.

"I'm happy. Things are good. Really, really good." I grinned. "So good I'm not sure I even trust it."

"Been there," Mia drawled. "Been there."

"Where have you been?" Darcy asked as she approached.

"At that place where things are so good in your life that you don't trust it," Mia said.

"Ah." Darcy took a seat. "Rach looks good."

Mia nodded. "She does."

"You think she's ready to move back to town?" Darcy asked.

"Not for me to say," Mia said, looking down at her sleeping daughter. "But I'd rather have her here than in Wyoming."

"She's going to take over in the office," Darcy said. "Help Boxer with the spreadsheets."

"Yeah, Boxer hates that shit," Mia said with a laugh. "When Waverly was helping out the week that she was suspended he was happier than a pig in shit."

I snorted out a laugh. "She actually liked working. Can you believe that?"

"Speaking of work," Darcy said. "Lily's ballet teacher is starting her own ballet school, and as it turns out, she needs a website. I gave her your contact information."

"Thanks," I said with a huge grin.

"Excuse me, ladies," Duke said as he approached the table. "Willa, you want to dance?"

I raised my brows. "Sure."

He took my hand and helped me up and then led me toward the dance floor. Duke pulled me close and we just fit together like matching puzzle pieces.

"I was watching you," he said, his lips pressed to my ear. "During the vows."

"Yeah?" I shivered from his warm breath across my skin.

"You looked a little emotional."

"I was," I admitted. "I didn't expect to be. But they're…she…"

"Boxer and Doc have been through a lot," he finished for me. "Can you keep a secret?"

"Debatable," I teased.

He chuckled. "He's surprising her with a trip to Scotland."

"I think that's called a honeymoon," I quipped. "Why's he making it a surprise?"

"Because she won't take off from the clinic otherwise. Everyone in the clinic is in on it."

"Poor Doc. Workaholic extraordinaire. She deserves a vacation. Why Scotland? Why not some place warm and tropical where you can sit topless on a beach?"

"Is that what you want? For your honeymoon?"

"Duke."

"Willa."

He dipped his head and lowered his voice even more. "I'd take you to a beach. One with white sand and water so clear you can see the bottom. You'd fall asleep underneath an umbrella. And as the afternoon turned into evening, with the sun dipping into the ocean, I'd peel your swimsuit off you and I'd slide into you from behind, the smell of the sun and sand on your skin."

I shivered and buried my face into his neck. I suddenly wanted to be alone with him, anywhere else but here.

"Let's go for a ride," he said, his voice hoarse.

Nodding, I let him pull me off the dance floor. We passed the table I'd been sitting at with Darcy and Mia, both of whom looked at me like they knew what was happening.

"Hey, where are you guys going?" Savage called out, drawing everyone's attention to us.

"I left something in my car," I lied.

"What did you leave in your car?" Savage asked, a smile drifting across his face.

"Savage?" Duke asked.

"Yeah?"

"Shut the fuck up," Duke growled. He clasped my hand tighter and hauled me toward the house, nearly plowing into Brooklyn and Slash, who definitely looked disheveled, no doubt from a quick tryst.

"Do weddings make people frisky?" I asked once Duke

and I were out front. "Brooklyn and Slash clearly had the same idea we did."

Duke chuckled. "I wonder how many babies are drunkenly conceived at weddings."

"Enough, that's for sure. Ah, there's no way I'm getting on a bike in this dress and in heels. I didn't bring Spanx and I'm wearing a thong."

"Damn it," he muttered. "We'll take your car."

"And go where?" I asked.

"I don't give a fuck. Anywhere. Keys."

I grabbed my keys from my purse and tossed them to him. He caught them and immediately unlocked the passenger door. He opened it for me and I slid inside before he closed it.

He jumped into the driver's side and shoved the key into the ignition.

My heart beat in anticipation, sending a throb between my thighs.

"There," I said, pointing ahead. "The street loops around and there's a hanger of trees."

Without a word, he put the car into drive and a few moments later he parked again. He lowered the driver's seat until it was nearly flat. "Come here."

I awkwardly climbed over him, bumping my knee against the gear shifter and my head on the ceiling.

"This is something we should've done when we were sixteen, before the growth spurts," I quipped.

"We'll make it work," he said, his voice husky. He grasped the back of my head and guided my mouth toward his.

His other hand skated up the skirt of my dress and grasped the meaty part of my leg, his fingers dipping into my thong. He teased my entrance for a few moments and then slipped a finger inside me, causing me to shudder. He pleasured me until I was wet and aching.

After he removed his finger, he growled, "Unzip me."

I reached between us and undid his zipper. I gently took him out of his boxers and gave him a few squeezes before angling myself on top of him.

I sank down onto his erection, taking him fully.

"Fuck, Willa," he groaned.

My skirt bunched around my hips and I rocked against him, the tight quarters constraining my movements. But being on top with my knees out near his sides, he was hitting the spot inside me that made my eyes roll back in my head.

Duke gripped my hips, urging me harder and faster, until I was screaming my release. I leaned down and buried my face in the crook of his neck as I continued to grind on top of him. Finally, his body went taut underneath me and he came.

When he finally recovered his breath, Duke said, "It's safe to say, car sex is all it's cracked up to be."

Chapter 28

I CLIMBED off him and rolled over into the passenger seat.

"Meet me at the clubhouse," Duke commanded.

"What? Now?" I asked.

"Yeah, now." He grasped my chin and pulled me to him for a deep kiss. "We're not done."

"We're not?" I asked breathlessly.

"Fuck no. That was just a warmup. I've got you for a few hours to myself. You don't have to be anywhere. I don't have to be anywhere. And your sister is off doing her thing. Come back to the clubhouse with me and I'll make you come with my tongue."

"Jesus," I laughed. "Were you always this crass, or do I just bring it out of you?"

"Were you always this sexually charged, or do I bring it out of you?" he taunted.

"Touché." I paused. "I like this. You and me."

He turned his head and grinned. "Yeah?"

"Yeah." I nodded. "I think it's going well. Do you think it's going well?"

"I think it's going well. Except for when I talk about the future. Then you get all weird."

"I'm trying not to be weird about it." I sighed. "But nothing good in my life lasts. And right now, everything is so fucking good, Duke. I don't want to jinx it."

"But that's the thing, Willa. When things are bad, I'll be there. When things are good, I'll be there. I'll *always* be there."

I reached out and touched his cheek. He turned his face to kiss my palm. We stared at each other for a long moment and then climbed out of the car.

"You're good to drive?" he asked.

I nodded.

"So, you'll meet me at the clubhouse?"

"On one condition," I said.

He raised his brows and waited for me to speak.

"Go back into Brooklyn and Slash's house and get some wedding cake to go. I'll wait here."

"You don't want to face them after we just had sex in the car, but you want me to?"

"No wedding cake, no repeat performance."

"Oh, I see. We're resorting to sexual blackmail here?"

I took a step forward and pressed a hand to his chest. "I'll make it worth your while."

"You do have something I want," he admitted.

"What is it?"

"I don't think I'm going to tell you," he said. "I think I'll let it be a surprise."

He wrapped his hand around my throat and leaned forward to brush his lips against mine. Then, with a gentle squeeze he released me.

"I'll get you your cake," he said, and then sauntered past me.

"Don't forget a slice for Waverly, too. I promised her."

He turned to look at me over his shoulder and winked. "It'll cost extra."

"Can I afford it?" I asked. "What with this surprise you're not going to tell me about?"

"You can afford it," he assured me.

I stood outside Duke's clubhouse bedroom, suddenly filled with nerves.

"What's wrong?" Duke asked as he pushed the door open, gesturing for me to go in first.

"I don't know. I just have this anxiety all of a sudden," I admitted.

"About what?" He strode inside and closed the door.

"About…you."

"Me?"

"Well, not *really* about you. Just about what you want." I cleared my throat. "Sexually. I don't think I like the idea of surprises. In the bedroom, I mean."

I turned away so he wouldn't see the embarrassment washing over my cheeks.

"Hey," he said quietly. "Look at me."

With a deep breath, I faced him.

"This is part of it, yeah? Exploring each other this way. Whatever you're comfortable with, okay? If you don't like something, you tell me."

"I'm not afraid I won't like it, I'm afraid I *will*," I blurted out.

"Sit," he commanded.

I sat.

He came over and kneeled in front of me. Duke took one of my heels off, setting it aside. He did the same with the other.

"We have to be honest with each other. In and out of the bedroom," he said. "I won't ever shame you. Or make fun of you. I'll do anything to make you feel good. You just gotta tell me what it is you want and you get it."

I nibbled my lip as Duke grasped one of my feet in his hands and began to massage the arch of it. "What is it you want? You were pretty evasive earlier."

"I wasn't evasive," he said. "I was seducing you. I wanted you curious enough to ask, but I also wanted to be in private when I told you."

I was nearly purring as I said, "That feels good."

"Too hard?"

"Harder."

He dug his thumb into the soft flesh of my foot and I gasped in pain, but then it quickly bloomed into pleasure as he released the pressure and then focused on another area.

"Oh," I said softly.

"I've got a feeling you like a little pain with your pleasure," he said.

"I might..." My cheeks flamed in embarrassment again.

He continued massaging my foot and I slowly relaxed.

"I want to blindfold you," he announced.

"That would be okay."

Duke lifted his head to look at me. "I want to fuck your ass, Willa. And I want to do it while you're blindfolded."

My breath hitched. "I've never... ah... I mean no one's..." I closed my eyes, thinking about my vision being impaired by a blindfold while Duke ran his hands all over me...in me.

I shivered and opened my eyes to find him intently watching me. I licked my lips and nodded.

He didn't react like he'd heard me. All he did was

switch which one of my feet he was massaging. I leaned back on my elbows, staring at him.

When he was finished massaging my foot, he released it. And then his hands slowly glided up my legs, underneath my dress.

He slid his palms beneath my thighs and yanked me forward so I hung off the bed. With glittering eyes still on me, he lifted my skirt.

I wriggled and reached for my thong.

"What are you doing?" he asked bluntly.

I stilled at his forceful inquiry. "Removing my panties."

"Did I tell you to remove them?"

Goosebumps erupted along my skin. "No," I said hoarsely.

"Stay exactly where you are, unless I say otherwise. Understand?"

I opened my mouth to reply, but no sound came out.

"Willa, do you understand?" he asked again.

"I understand," I whispered.

He studied me for a moment and then he demanded, "Spread your legs. Wider. Yes, just like that."

Duke's eyes slid from mine to focus on my body. The lights were on and there was no hiding anything from him. Not the way I began to quiver, not the way my hands clenched in anticipation of his touch.

I thought I was going to go mad waiting as he took his sweet time to move.

He made me wait so long I had to bite my lip to stop from calling out for him to do something.

And then finally—*finally*—he bent his head and gave me a long, slow lick over the lace. I was sensitive, and the fabric teased my aching, needy flesh.

He grasped my hips to hold me in place and then his tongue licked me again. It drove me mad, not having his tongue on me. The barrier of lace teased and provoked me.

He didn't kiss the sensitive skin of my inner thighs or use his fingers, all he used was his tongue, focusing on the spot between my legs. Duke sucked the damp fabric into his mouth for a moment and then released me. He reached into his pocket and extracted a knife.

"Hold still." He flicked his blade open and shredded my panties with it.

Duke set the knife down and then bent his head again. He blew on my mound and then with his voracious, greedy mouth, began to suck me.

Pressure built and built until I was on the verge of coming, and just as I was about to topple over the edge, he pulled back.

"What the fuck," I demanded.

"Not yet," he growled. He rose from the floor and moved the blade safely to the nightstand. He opened the drawer and pulled out a black scarf.

"Stand," he commanded.

I awkwardly slid off the bed, my thighs wet with pleasure.

"Turn."

I turned and he immediately slid the scarf over my eyes and tied it behind my head. It was firm enough to squeeze lightly so it wouldn't fall, but not so tight that it was uncomfortable. He brushed the hair away from my nape and placed a kiss at the curve of my neck where it met my shoulder. I felt him tug on the zipper at the side of my dress and he slid the straps off my shoulders. He pushed the dress down so that it pooled at my feet.

"Lift your foot," he said.

I did as he bid and stepped out of the dress.

He stood at my back, close enough that I could feel the

abrasive leather cut against my skin. His hands cradled my hips and then skated up my chest to caress my breasts. His thumbs swiped over my nipples, causing them to harden.

He pulled me back against him. One hand teased my breast, while the other moved down to play between my legs.

"You're ready to come, aren't you?"

His low voice tormented my heightened senses.

I nodded.

"You want me inside you," he rasped.

I nodded again.

He sank his finger into the seam of my body and I shuddered around him, but still didn't come. I clenched, silently demanding more.

Duke removed his finger.

"On the bed, Willa," he said. "On your stomach."

He gently pushed between my shoulder blades, forcing me down.

The comforter was soft and warm, the air was cool, and I was primed for pleasure.

I listened intently as Duke was undressing and realized he was taking his time, seemingly drawing this out for his own amusement.

He'd left me aching and unfulfilled, reducing me to a quivering, frustrated mess.

The bed sank beneath me and then his hands were on the back of my calves. He massaged them as he trekked higher, spreading me as he went.

"I wish I had a headboard to tie you to," he growled against my ear. "Then you'd truly be at my mercy."

"I'm at your mercy now," I gasped when I felt the hard length of him press against me.

"I like you this way. Splayed out, all but begging me for it."

"Is that what it'll take?" I gritted out. "Begging you?"
Smack!

"Ow!" I yelled.

He smacked my ass again. "Hush, Willa."

Duke rubbed the sting away with his strong hands until my skin was warm with pleasure. Desire bloomed in my belly and I widened my legs in anticipation of what was coming.

"You love this," he rumbled, dipping his fingers between my thighs. "You're soaking wet."

He worked a finger in and out of me until I was slippery and shaking. I bit my lip to stifle my cry when he removed his finger.

But then he glided his finger between the cheeks of my ass. I gasped at the new, invasive feeling, but I trusted Duke and I wanted him more than any man I'd ever been with. He went slow and not very deep, letting me adjust to the new sensation. I let out a low moan.

He pushed a little farther.

I gripped the comforter, sweat from need breaking out all along my skin.

He bit my ass cheek hard enough to leave a flash of pain.

Duke slowly eased his finger out of me and then he was urging me onto all fours. I heard the unscrewing of a jar and then the dribble of liquid on the small of my back. He set the jar aside and glided his fingers in the oil, smearing it lower between my creases. The crown of his shaft teased my back entrance until he slowly inched forward.

I gasped. It was so much larger than his finger.

"I've got you," he whispered, placing his hand on my mound. His fingers were slick with oil as he toyed my folds open.

"Oh God, Duke," I moaned.

His finger swirled around the nub between my thighs and that was all it took for me to detonate. I screamed as shockwave after shockwave ripped through my core, all the more powerful because I'd been forced to wait for him.

And while I was in the middle of coming, Duke slid all the way inside me.

I felt him everywhere. He was heat and lust, and it was all consuming. He thrust his fingers inside me while he fucked me and it wasn't long before I was clenching around him again, coming hard and fast.

"Fuck," Duke groaned as he orgasmed, pumping himself inside me as he released.

He gently eased out of me and then we both collapsed onto the comforter. My breathing was labored and erratic, and when I inhaled, I smelled the heady mixture of the intoxicating scent we'd made together.

Duke removed the blindfold and tossed it to the ground and then he wrapped his arms around me and dragged me into his embrace. He tangled his legs with mine and he brushed his lips along my shoulder.

"You okay?" he asked.

"Okay?" I turned my head to look at him. "That was…yeah. Better than okay."

"I didn't take things too far?"

"No."

Our lips met in a drugging kiss.

I sighed in his arms, wishing I never had to move again.

Chapter 29

After a shower, and wearing a pair of Duke's basketball shorts, a rogue Tarnished Angels tank, and my high heels, Duke walked me to my car.

He opened the driver's side door for me and leaned in to kiss me.

I placed my hand on his bare chest—he hadn't bothered with a shirt, just a pair of jeans.

God, he looked good. Inked and muscled, and all *mine*.

"What's that dopey grin for?" he asked, handing me the slices of wedding cake that were in the aluminum to-go container.

"It's not a dopey grin," I protested.

"Trust me. It was dopey."

"I was just thinking how good you look without a shirt on."

"Then you should be looking at me with lust-filled eyes, not giving me a dopey grin." He smiled, obviously teasing me. "I think I know what that dopey grin was all about."

"What was it about?"

"You think I'm cute."

I chuckled.

"And you're happy. Like really happy, aren't you?"

I sighed. "Yeah. No denying that."

He clasped my chin and brought my lips to his for another kiss. "Wish you could stay the night."

"Me too."

"I think we're ready to take our relationship to the next level," Duke said.

"We just took it to the next level when you, ya know…"

"What?" He blinked. "What did I do?"

I blushed.

"You're hilarious, you know that, right? When have you ever been shy? Furthermore, you've got a dirtier mouth than a trucker and you can't even say *anal sex*?"

"Oh my God, stop." I blushed harder. "I just didn't expect to like it so much, okay?"

"Baby, you're gonna like everything we do together." He grasped my hips and hauled me toward him.

"You make me feel safe enough to explore everything," I admitted. "Thank you for that."

I kissed his lips.

"As for taking our relationship to the next level, I was referring to something else…" he said.

"What?"

"I think it's time we take Waverly to Mama Leonardi's."

"You think we're ready for that kind of commitment?" I teased. "Taking my sister to our place?"

"Our place," he said gruffly. "I like that. And yeah, I'm ready for that kind of commitment if you are."

"I am."

He raised his brows.

"Don't look so surprised. You grew on me. It only took the better part of a decade, but there it is."

Duke tucked a strand of hair behind my ear. "You were worth the wait."

I leaned forward and kissed him again. "I'll text when I get home." I tossed my dress into the passenger seat, along with my purse and the cake.

Waverly wasn't back by the time I made it home. I shot her a text to let her know there was piece of cake for her in the fridge. The house was too quiet without her in it.

I went into the bathroom and looked at myself in the mirror. I had whisker burns on my cheeks and neck, and my eyes were bright and my face was flushed.

Smirking, I reached for the small bottle of moisturizer on the edge of the sink. I fumbled with the bottle and it clattered to the floor. I bent over to retrieve it when something sticking out from behind the toilet caught my eye.

With a frown, I touched it. It was a piece of paper taped to the back of the tank. I grabbed it—realizing quickly that it wasn't a piece of paper, but an envelope.

I flipped it open and gasped at the crisp bills. There were hundreds, fifties, and twenties. Some tens. I took it out and counted it. It was nearly four thousand dollars.

Four thousand dollars hidden in an envelope behind the toilet.

Four thousand dollars that didn't belong to me.

Four thousand dollars that I couldn't account for.

I shoved the money into the envelope and marched out into the living room. I tossed it down onto the coffee table and then riffled through my purse for my phone.

"You're home?" Duke asked after answering on the first ring.

"I'm home."

"You sound weird. Shit, I knew it. I knew I took it too far. I—"

"No," I interrupted. "This isn't about you and me. I…

277

Duke, I found an envelope of money taped to the back of the toilet."

He paused for a moment. "Waverly's?"

"Yes. I assume so. I have no idea why the hell she'd have that kind of mone—oh God, what if it's Dylan's and he's into something illegal?"

"How much is in the envelope?"

"Four grand."

He whistled.

"I know." I rubbed my temple. "This is bad, right? I mean, where the fuck is a fifteen-year-old getting that kind of cash?"

"You're thinking the worst. You've got to calm down."

"How do you know I'm thinking the worst?"

"Because *I'm* thinking the worst. And if it is the worst, I'll kill someone to protect her—"

The sound of a key in the lock in the front door turned my attention from the conversation.

"She's home. I'll call you later."

I hung up and tossed my phone aside.

And then I waited.

Waverly came inside, her face blooming in happiness when she saw me. "Did you wait to eat your slice of cake so we could eat it together?"

"I didn't eat my cake."

She frowned and closed the door. "You're not in your wedding clothes."

"Don't change the subject."

"We were talking about wedding cake. Ergo, wedding clothes, wedding cake, by transitive property—"

I held up the envelope.

Her face slackened and then went white. "You found my money."

"It's yours, then?"

She nodded. "But it's not what you think."

"What do I think?"

"I don't know, but it's not that."

"Look, I don't know what to think," I admitted. "So you're going to tell me why the fuck you have four grand in an envelope taped to the back of our toilet."

She crossed her arms over her chest in silence.

"Waverly, where did it come from?"

Waverly bit her lip.

I knew that look. It was the look she always had right before she spilled the beans about a long-term lie she'd been telling.

"Let's go for a drive, and I'll show you."

I let Waverly drive. I was too angry to get behind the wheel, and my sister was eerily calm. Calm and confident in a way I'd never seen before.

We drove into the industrial part of town where all the old brick and cement warehouses were. We passed shirtless men working on muscle cars, punks spray painting graffiti on brick walls, and homeless in groups from one block to the next. A couple of skater kids were doing tricks on their boards, one of them with a blunt hanging from his mouth.

Waverly turned down an alley of sorts and parked the car.

"Please tell me what the hell is going on here," I said, climbing out of the car.

She held her keys in her hand as we walked down the alley to a small warehouse. There was an old, rusted steel door to get into the building, but there was also a rolling gate large enough for a car to drive through. Waverly looked at her keyring, found the one she wanted, and unlocked the door. She stepped inside ahead of me and flipped the light on.

The smell of sawdust and varnish hit me immediately. It was the scent that had been on her clothes, I realized.

There were a few pieces of furniture scattered about the warehouse floor, along with sanders of different types, tools I didn't recognize, and paint brushes.

"I must be slow on the uptake here because this almost looks like a furniture warehouse," I said.

"That's exactly what it is."

I blinked stupidly. "You're making furniture? Waverly, what the—"

She snorted a laugh, interrupting me. "No. I'm not that skilled. We don't make the furniture, we furniture flip."

"Come again?"

"We furniture flip. Jess, Dylan and I find old furniture, either for free that's about to be picked up for trash, or we get it online. We get it into Jess's Mom's SUV and we haul it here. Then we wood putty any holes and make repairs, sand it, paint it or stain it and then sell it. We pay for the warehouse—but it belongs to Dylan's uncle so he's cut us a deal."

"And you've done enough of this in the last few weeks to make four thousand dollars?" I asked in shock.

"No. Not in the last few weeks. The last few months."

"The tutoring sessions," I said in realization.

She nodded. "I had to convince Dylan it was a better use of our time, but yeah. Mom had no idea what I was really doing, of course. I knew I wouldn't be able to keep this a secret once you were home more. It was only a matter of time before you found out."

"How did you ever get the idea for this?" I asked.

"Saw it on YouTube."

"Of course," I said dryly.

"And it didn't look that hard. And you know what? It's fun. The hunting for furniture is fun, then turning an old piece of junk into something beautiful is fun, and making money is the funnest."

"No doubt. Whose tools are these?"

"Mine."

"*Yours?* How did you buy them?"

"With money…"

"Where did you get the money?" I pinned.

"Dylan's uncle. He's what you'd call a *cash investor.* We've already paid him back. That's how well we're doing."

"Jesus, if not for the secrecy, I'd be fucking impressed. Scratch that, I *am* impressed. But you can't keep coming to this part of town. It's not safe."

She sighed. "Yeah, I knew when you found out about the workshop, you'd put a stop to it."

"Not a stop. We'll find you another space, I swear. This is…wow, I'm really blown away."

"Can I show you my favorite piece?" she asked.

"Sure."

She led me to the back corner of the workshop to a large solid wooden desk that had been painted dark green with a semi-gloss clear finish; the ornate drawer handles sprayed gold against the stunning green.

"This is gorgeous," I admitted. "You'll sell this one right away, I'm sure."

"No, I won't. Because it's yours."

"Mine?" I asked in confusion. "I don't get it."

"I refinished it for you. So when you finally get your dual monitor, you have enough space to use it."

"You did this…for me?" I asked, emotion coating my throat.

"Well, yeah." She smiled. "You've done so much for

me. I wanted to return the favor. And this'll help you run your business."

I grabbed hold of my sister and dragged her into an embrace. "Jesus, kid. You know how to shock the hell out of me."

She laughed and hastily pulled away, but only so she could swipe at the tears gathering in her eyes.

"It's perfect," I said. "And I'm completely in love with it."

"Thought you would be."

"I swear we'll find you another space to work out of, okay?" I said. "I'm really proud of you."

"Ditto, sis. Ditto."

"Just one question. Why tape the money to the back of the toilet?" I asked.

"I learned from the best, didn't I?" she smirked. "I knew you wouldn't be like Mom and take it, but I wasn't ready to answer questions about it either. The sock drawer was out because we share a sock drawer."

"You've got the making of a criminal mastermind."

"I know, right?"

Chapter 30

I STRODE INTO O'REILLY'S, greeting the bartender as I surveyed the entirety of the room.

An attractive, dark-haired man in his thirties, dressed in a black suit sat in my usual booth. I immediately approached him, a friendly smile on my face.

"Mr. Prescott?"

He looked up and slid from the booth, his hand held out to me. "Please, call me Ansel. Ms. Gravestone, right?"

"Call me Willa."

We shook hands and then he gestured to the seat across from him.

"Thank you so much for taking the time to meet with me," I said, reaching for the glass of water already on the table. "Have you been here long?"

"Only just arrived," he assured me with a smile. "And I'll be happy to help you."

I let out a breath of relief.

"Vance didn't give me much detail about your case," Ansel said. "Only that you wanted to acquire legal guardianship of your fifteen-year-old sister."

"Waverly," I clarified. "Yes, that's the gist of it."

Mia had put me into contact with Vance Raider, the club's attorney. He didn't practice the type of law I needed to gain guardianship of Waverly, but he'd referred me to a colleague of his, and within twenty-four hours Ansel had called me personally, requesting a lunch meeting.

"You hungry?" he asked suddenly.

I blinked. "Yeah. I'm hungry."

"You picked this place. Tell me what's good."

His conversation about something as normal as food immediately put me at ease.

"Can't go wrong with corned beef and cabbage," I said.

"Done. If it wasn't a working lunch, I'd order a Guinness."

"Good man," I said with a chuckle.

After we ordered, we got back to the matter at hand.

"So, tell me about your situation," he said, leaning back in the booth and peering at me with intelligent blue eyes.

"You don't want to take notes?" I asked.

"Not right now. I learn better by listening." He inclined his head. "So, tell me everything. And don't leave *anything* out."

"My mom is a flake," I said dryly. "And she bailed several weeks ago with some random guy she's with for the time being. Took the RV—which we were living in—our clothes and all our personal belongings…everything. Didn't even call to say goodbye."

"You and your sister were living in an RV?" he asked.

"Mom was behind on rent in the last shit hole we were living in," I said slowly. "And instead of telling me, she went out and bought a used RV and said she wanted to take us on a road trip this summer. *So we could all bond.* Her words, not mine."

Even though I'd proverbially shut the door on the relationship with my mother, it was still bitter. I was getting emotional and I needed to take a deep breath.

"She's all talk. That's how she is. Anyway, she'd had the RV for only a few weeks. It was just long enough for us to move all of our things into it when Waverly and I came home one day to find out we didn't *have* a home at all. Mom—and the RV—were just gone."

"And the guy she ran off with?"

"No idea who he is."

He mulled my words over for a moment. "Then what happened?"

"My boyfriend's club got involved. He's a member of the Tarnished Angels."

"Ah, okay." He nodded. "Vance called me. I've heard some local attorneys have an affiliation with the club, but that's hearsay. The details of any such relationship, if it even existed, would be attorney-client privilege so let's leave that alone and move on."

I waited for some sort of derision or perhaps even an outright rejection or refusal to take my case, but it never came. He just sat there, waiting for me to proceed.

"Waverly and I moved into a house owned by the wife of the club president. I pay rent, utilities, everything. I work part-time at Leather and Ink, a retail boutique, but I've recently started my own web design business. I'm in the middle of one project, but I have another lined up. The fact is, I've been financially responsible for my sister for years. Now I'd like to make it legal."

"I see."

"Her school has no idea," I said. "It's nearing the end of the school year and I was hoping to make it to summer break without them knowing. I don't want CPS called. Waverly and I can't be separated. She can't be moved to another home. I can take care of her. I *have* taken care of her. And she wants this."

"You've spoken to her about the situation?"

I nodded. "She's on board. Eager, even."

"The courts don't usually take the feelings of a minor into account," Ansel said. "Despite the fact that Waverly wants you to become her legal guardian, there's going to be more to it than that. We have to prove to the court that you're financially stable enough to support your sister, and that your mother has abandoned any and all parental responsibility."

"How do we do that?" I asked.

"A letter from your boss at the boutique, bank statements, financial records. However, because you haven't been in business long, being a small business owner will not be counted favorably."

I frowned. "What does that mean?"

"It means because you're self-employed, the courts will scrutinize your finances in a way that wouldn't happen if you had a full-time job with benefits and retirement plan, for example. The courts see known career paths as stable, but business owners as a liability. For example, if you worked for a Fortune 500 company as a graphic designer, you'd be good…but own your own business? That's a different story."

"Well, what can I do?" I demanded. "I can't all of a sudden muster loads of clients or change time and say I've been successful for years."

"Stability is the key," Ansel said. "The courts will want to see that you'll be able to provide stability for your sister until she's of legal age. Part of it is financial, but there is another aspect to it you may not have considered. The courts also want to see that Waverly will have a stable home life."

"I'm missing something here, aren't I?" I asked.

"Are you married, Willa?"

I shoved the key into the lock and twisted. I pushed open the door and let out a yelp.

Savage was lying on the couch, his head on the armrest, facing the door.

A scowl bloomed across his face.

"Oh, sorry," I sassed. "Did I wake you from a nap? A nap on *my* couch in *my* house? A courtesy text that you were coming over would've been nice, by the way."

He swiveled his body so he was sitting upright and his feet hit the floor.

"Close the door, Willa," he said, his tone ominous.

I stared at him. "What's going on?"

"Close. The. Door."

There were times I could tease Savage about being *Savage*.

This wasn't one of them.

He was pissed about something.

I had to tread carefully.

He wouldn't hurt me, ever, but when he was mad there was usually a good reason and I wanted to figure out what was going on. So, I closed the door and set my purse down.

"Come here."

"No," I said. "I'm staying over here. Because I'm not sure I trust your mood right now."

He rose from the couch. "I thought I knew you. I thought you wouldn't hurt him. I thought—"

"Wait—what's going on here?" I demanded. "What the fuck are you talking about?"

"I saw you," he gritted out. "Having lunch with that fucking *suit*. In our booth. In our restaurant."

"You were at O'Reilly's," I said and then immediately relaxed. "Got it. And you saw what you saw. Which was, what, exactly?"

"I saw him pay. And then I watched you hug him. Fuck, Willa, you were crawling all over him. I can't believe —Duke's stupidly in love with you. You know that. He's been in love with you since we were kids. This is going to destroy him."

"You want a beer?"

He blinked. "Huh?"

"That took the wind out of your sails," I quipped. "Go on, keep accusing me of cheating on Duke. But while you do, I'm gonna have a beer. Because, Lord, it's been a day. My own best friend thinks I'm a cheating hussy because he saw me hug someone at a restaurant. Wonderful."

"Not *someone*. A man. A man I don't recognize." He squared his shoulders. "Well, explain it to me then."

"I don't owe you an explanation," I snapped. "And I certainly won't defend myself when you've already decided I've cheated."

I marched over to the refrigerator and pulled out a beer—one of Savage's favorites—and yanked open the drawer to find a bottle opener.

After I took a long sip, I turned to face him. His jaw was clenched and judging by his countenance, I knew he was trying to rein in his emotions.

"Where's the loyalty?" I asked quietly.

"I saw what I saw."

"You don't know what you saw, you idiot," I said. "If I was cheating on Duke, do you really think I'd be that dumb to do it at our place? Where I know you eat at least twice a week?"

He rubbed the back of his neck and had the grace to look sheepish. "So you weren't—aren't—cheating on Duke?"

"No, doofus. I'm not cheating on Duke." I took another sip of beer and finally kicked off my heels. "Oh, that's better."

"Well, are you going to tell me what it was?"

"Tell you before I tell Duke? I don't think so."

"So, it is about Duke?"

"No, jerk. It's about Waverly." I sighed. "The suit is Ansel Prescott, and he's a colleague of Vance Raider."

"Raider," he repeated. "The club lawyer?"

"Yup."

"Why are you seeing a lawyer?"

"Because I want legal guardianship of Waverly," I said. "And I met with Ansel today to discuss it."

His face fell. "Oh."

"Yeah. *Oh.*"

"And?"

"And what?"

"What did he say?"

"He's taking the case," I said. "But he laid out some ideas that I've been mulling over."

"What kind of ideas?"

I offered him my beer. He came over and took it.

"He said the courts need to see stability. Financial stability, as well as a stable home life."

"Okay," he said, brow furrowing in confusion. "You've basically been raising Waverly this entire time anyway."

"True. However, the courts are going to give me a hard time because I'm newly self-employed, and the easiest way to prove I have the means of taking care of Waverly is to get married."

"Wait, like *married*, married?"

I swiped the beer and took another drink. "Yep. Married."

Savage burst out laughing.

"What's so funny?" I demanded.

"You just got to the point where you didn't break out in hives admitting you were in a relationship. Now you've got to get married. Have you had a panic attack about any of this yet?"

"You're fucking hilarious, you know that?" I growled. "Like full on fucking hilarious."

"You're not going to do something stupid, are you?"

"Is that a rhetorical question?"

"I mean, you *are* going to ask him to marry you. He'll say yes, you know."

"I know," I said softly. "I just…damn it."

"What?"

"He's waited so long for me," I said. "And now this moment—this thing that I need—isn't about *us*. It's about my sister."

"You love him."

"Yes," I admitted. "Of course, I love him. I *love* him. And it's not fair. It's not fair that he hasn't gotten to have anything normal."

"Neither have you," he pointed out. "Neither have I. Neither has Waverly. It's why you're going to ask Duke to marry you, so you can be sure that Waverly has something none of us had. A true family. A true home, even if it's just a few years until she flies the nest."

"Don't tell him," I said. "I want to be the one. Please?"

He nodded. "Okay."

"Savage, I mean it."

"Heard you loud and clear. You'll tell Duke when you're ready, which I'm guessing will be as soon as possible."

"The sooner the better," I agreed. I rubbed my forehead. "I need to shower off this day."

"Day isn't over," he pointed out.

"It is for me. Jess is driving Waverly home and I'm contemplating eating an early dinner of ice cream and hot fudge."

"Most women would be happy to get married to their boyfriend that they love."

"I was kind of hoping Duke would propose when he was ready. When *I* was ready. Not because of…"

"Yeah." He nodded. "Okay." Savage roped me into a hug and then kissed the top of my head. "Sorry I thought you were a cheating slut."

I chuckled. "Apology accepted."

"You mean it?"

"Yeah. I love that you have Duke's back."

"I shouldn't have doubted you though. That wasn't okay. Even if I was trying to protect my boy."

I gave him another squeeze and then let him go. "It's fine. Really. I'm not mad."

"You're a good sport," he said.

"I have to be. To put up with you," I teased.

Chapter 31

"WHERE THE FUCK IS MY PHONE?" I muttered. I crouched down to riffle through my purse but came up empty handed. I dumped everything out of it, wondering if my cell had gotten lost in the abyss, but no luck.

I grabbed my keys and went to look in the car, pondering if my phone had fallen out of my bag and slid underneath the seat.

It wasn't there.

Had I left it at O'Reilly's?

I thought back, wondering when the last time I had it was. But the afternoon had been kind of hazy.

With a sigh, I went back inside and closed the door. At least I had my keys and wallet.

I twirled up my damp hair, got onto my laptop and googled *best ways for a woman to propose.*

I felt like an idiot.

How was I supposed to propose to a dude?

Flowers? No.

Candles? Not a chance.

Lingerie? *Definitely.*

Duke loved barbecue and riding his motorcycle. He loved the outdoors and getting his hands dirty. He was a self-made man who was fiercely loyal to his club and those he considered family.

And I loved him so much it hurt, and all I wanted to do was make him feel special. Instead, I was about to come to him and ask him for something I needed, making it more about me than him.

But it was more than that.

I loved him, and we were already heading down the path of spending our lives together. I wasn't only coming to him with something I needed, I was coming to him with real love.

He would be there for me no matter what, that much I knew.

I lost track of time as I thought about the kind of man he was and what he was willing to do for me, and I was startled when I heard the sound of a key in the lock. Waverly came in, her red hair in a messy bun. She slung her bag onto the couch and held a to-go container in the other.

"You didn't answer your phone," she said in way of greeting.

"I lost it," I said.

"Oh, that sucks." She lifted the to-go container and handed it to me. "You have to settle for mud pie because I wasn't sure what to bring you."

"Thanks," I said with a smile.

"It's from Boots—with Uncle Bill's compliments."

"Uncle Bill, huh?"

"Yeah, I think he has a thing for you."

I snorted. "I've never met the man. How could he possibly have a thing for me?"

"The night you tracked me down and found out

about me and Dylan," she said with a wry grin. "He was in the kitchen. So he definitely saw you in action. He said, and I quote, 'Your sister sure is a spitfire. I like that.' So, if you ever get sick of Duke, just know you have prospects."

"Good to know. Fork?"

"I'll get you one." She headed into the kitchen and opened a drawer. "You look kind of down in the dumps."

"The mud pie will do a lot to cheer me up," I said. "Thanks for thinking of me."

Waverly came over to the couch and plopped down, handing me the fork. "I'm a good listener."

"I met with Ansel Prescott today," I said.

"Oh yeah, that was today. What did he say?"

I sighed. "I've got to ask Duke to marry me."

"Really? Why?"

I explained to her what Ansel had said.

"Wow," she said when I was done.

"Yeah."

"I guess that means he's moving in here," she said thoughtfully.

I shook my head.

"If you get married, you live together. That's kinda how it goes," she said.

"No. I mean, there's not enough room in here for the three of us. What about that beautiful desk you redid for me? Not to mention the fact that you need a workshop. Remember?"

"I remember. So, we're moving?"

"I think so."

"We like, *just* moved in here."

"Duke's shoes are huge."

"Not to mention you guys are gonna be doing it at night. Better we have a few more walls between us. Oh, that reminds me, I need to invest in noise cancelling head-phones because *gross*."

"You're rotten, you know that?"

She grinned. "You love me."

"I do love you."

"So how are you going to propose to him?"

"No idea," I said. "Got any ideas?"

"I'm inclined to say something to do with moonshine."

I raised my brows. "How do you know about moonshine?"

"Not because I've tasted it."

"Uh huh."

"Okay, I've tasted it," she admitted. "But it singed my nose hairs and I vowed never to touch the stuff ever again."

"It's okay, Waverly. I was fifteen once."

"Yeah, like, a garillion years ago. And I'll be fifteen-and-a-half in a few months."

"Oh, we're adding a half now to your age? You're defi-nitely getting old," I teased.

"Can I have a party? For my sixteenth birthday?"

"You want a party?" I asked in surprise.

"Less *party*, more of a cake-made-by-Brooklyn. Uncle Bill said I could have the gathering at Boots."

"That's nice of him."

"Yeah." She nodded. "Can I invite some people from the WID?"

"What the hell is the WID?"

"Seriously?"

"Yeah, seriously. I'm lost."

"WID stands for Wrought Iron District. It's where my workshop is. That's what they used to make in that area way back in the dinosaur days of the 40s."

"You actually know people from the area?"

"Yeah."

"Okay," I said in bemusement. "It's kind of official. You're cooler than I am."

"Now that," she plucked my fork from my hand, "is a fact."

∼

"I've got a fresh pot of coffee brewing for you, I took your favorite red lipstick from your purse, and Jessica is giving me a ride this morning," Waverly said as she stood over my bed.

I peered up at her through the crack of my lids. "Huh?"

A horn honked. "Gotta go. That's Jess."

I sat up and rubbed my face. The front door closed and my sluggish brain finally put together what she said. "She took my favorite lipstick!"

By the time I got up and scrambled to the front door and wrenched it open, Jess's car was peeling down the street.

I didn't have a phone to text yell at her, so I had to settle for a grumble. With a yawn, I ambled my way into the bathroom. I stood under the hot water, hoping that would help me wake up, but I had a long day ahead of me and I couldn't do it without sugar and caffeine. I was prepared to caffeinate myself to high heaven by driving to Pie in the Sky and ordering a Witch's Brew if need be.

I got out of the shower and threw my wet hair up into a knot. As I poured a cup of coffee, there was a knock on the front door.

It was too early to be a delivery. With a frown, I took my coffee and went to see who was at the door.

I peered through the peephole and saw Duke at the threshold, holding a few brown paper shopping bags.

"Hey," I said as I opened the door. "What are you doing here? I thought I was supposed to see you later."

"I came to return this." He held out my missing cell phone.

"Where did you get that?" I demanded, taking it from him and stepping back so he could come inside.

He didn't reply. Instead, he walked over to the couch and set the bags down. "Check out what's in there."

"Okay," I said in confusion. I came over to the couch and stared into one of the bags. "Are those—no! They're not."

"They are," he said with a grin, making his dimples pop.

"The leather pants I had my eye on from Leather and Ink?" Even with my employee discount, the pants would have been a stretch since money was tight.

"Yep."

"You bought them for me? This morning?"

"Yesterday," he said. "Before Laura closed up shop. That's not the only thing…"

"You got me the matching leather jacket and—*oh, hell no*, you didn't—"

"I did. I so fucking did."

"The boots?" I breathed. "Duke, the mother-fucking-fuck-me motorcycle boots!"

"Like them?"

"Like them? *I love them*! I mean, I love them like I'll get on my knees and thank you later kind of love them."

He chuckled. "You forgot something."

"Did I?"

"Yeah, this." He gently leaned over and kissed my lips,

slipping his tongue into my mouth. It was so deep and so good, I spilled my coffee.

"Damn it," I muttered against him.

He chuckled again and pulled away. "I'll clean up while you go change. We're going for a ride."

"Okay." I handed him my coffee cup and then grabbed the bags of clothes. "Are you going to tell me how you came to be in possession of my cell phone?"

"I'll tell you after we get to our destination."

"Where are we going?" I called out over my shoulder as I headed into the bedroom to change.

"You'll see."

I was still caffeine deficient, but the excitement of the new clothes and Duke's surprise worked like magic. I quickly donned the leather pants, laced up the boots and threw on a loose tank underneath the leather jacket. I pulled my hair back into a ponytail and went out into the living room.

"Am I a ten or what?" I teased, cocking my hip and throwing my hands wide for his inspection.

His gaze slowly dipped down my body and his smile was heated. "Nah, babe. There isn't even a number for that level of hot."

"Flattery and showing up unannounced with new clothes will totally get you laid."

"Ah, then my plan is working," he said lightly. "Take your keys but leave everything else. You won't need it."

I turned off the coffee maker and then locked up the house. Duke was already straddling his bike when I came down the walkway. He held out a helmet to me which I immediately put on.

"You're really not going to tell me where we're going or how you have my phone—which I totally thought I lost, by the way."

"Patience, darlin'. Patience. Hop on."

I climbed on the back of his motorcycle and immediately scooted as close as I could to him, wrapping my arms around his massive body. He cranked the engine, dropped the bike into gear and then torqued the throttle and we sped off.

Nestled close to him, with the warm air on my cheeks, I sighed and breathed in the moment. He drove through town, winding through the streets with expert precision. On the back of his bike, I felt free. My breaths were deeper, and any burdens I carried from the outside world lifted off my shoulders and my mind cleared.

I understood why Duke and Savage spent so much time on their bikes. It was a way for them to work out whatever troubled them.

We rode out of city limits and for a moment, I wondered if he was taking us to Brooklyn and Slash's. But he turned in the opposite direction of their house and we continued on our way.

It was another ten minutes or so before Duke pulled up to a house and parked. He turned off the engine and held the bike upright while I climbed off. I removed the helmet and set it on the seat behind him as he kicked out the stand and eased the bike to rest on its perch.

"Where are we?" I asked in confusion.

He swung his leg over the bike and stood. He grasped my hand, linking his fingers through mine, and we headed up the sidewalk to the wrap around front porch of the house.

The steps squeaked, which made me smile.

Duke didn't knock on the front door—he twisted the knob and pushed it open, gesturing for me to enter first.

I shot him a frown of confusion, and then went inside.

I came to a stop not two steps into the foyer. Candles in

tall, clear glass votives rested on the stairs, lined the hall-way, and even the room off the hallway which looked to be the living room. The fireplace mantle had candles, too.

But that wasn't what was shocking.

It was the three leaf clovers that covered the entire floor of the house.

"What is this?" I asked, crouching down to pick a clover up and examine it.

"You didn't really think I'd let you get away with proposing to me, did you?"

My jaw dropped open. "You know? How do you know?"

"Savage," he said. "He took your phone to prevent you from making any sort of arrangements."

"Duke, I…you can't…I have to be the one to—"

He placed a finger against my lips, silencing me. "Let me show you the house."

I nodded.

He dropped his finger and then took my hand. "Upstairs first."

My hand tracked the wooden banister as I followed him up the stairs. "It was built in 1915, but it's been completely renovated. All the charm and original build quality is preserved, but it's fully up to date with modern plumbing, wiring, and AC."

I saw at once what he meant. It still had all the beauty and craftsmanship of an old home, but it had been modernized, made even more apparent by the giant bath-room connected to the biggest bedroom.

There were three other bedrooms upstairs, along with another full bathroom.

Duke took me back downstairs. I peeked into the living room with the fireplace mantle. "Does the fireplace work?" I asked.

"Yep."

"Oh. Oh, wow." I nodded.

"There's another room down here," he said, walking ahead of me to a closed door. He opened it and allowed me to peek inside.

It had custom designed shelves and immense windows that exhibited the grassy plains of horse country beyond the panes of glass. He took my hand and led me to the spacious kitchen with an island in the center and a dining nook.

"You want to see the best part?" he asked.

"There's more?"

He nodded.

We went out the back door and headed toward a metal building. He opened the door and we stepped inside.

It was rustic, made of steel, wood and concrete. It had a small kitchen, a full bathroom, and a bedroom.

"Is this like a mother-in-law suite?" I asked.

"Not quite." He winked, grasped my hand, and pulled me toward the other end of the room to another door. "It's a workshop and one-room apartment combo."

I tilted my head back to look up at the roof. There was so much space here.

"For Waverly," I said in realization. "You're thinking of this for Waverly."

He nodded. "She needs her own space. You said she needed a new workshop since you didn't want her in that neighborhood."

"And the house?" I murmured.

"For us." He turned me toward him. "For our family."

Chapter 32

D᷉UKE TOOK a step toward me and grasped my hips. "I've loved you since we were kids, Willa. I don't want to wait anymore. Marry me. Be my wife. I'll protect you, love you, do *anything* for you."

Tears gathered in my eyes as I cradled his cheeks in my hands. "I was supposed to be the one to make the passionate speech."

"You can if you want. But you don't need to convince me to do anything. I was already yours. From the moment you wiped the blood from my lip after my first school yard fight I was in love with you. I was in love with you before I even knew what it meant. I don't know who I am without you, Willa."

"Duke," I whispered, my hands dropping from his face.

He leaned forward and pressed his lips to mine.

"I know you didn't want it this way. I know you wanted time," he went on. "But Waverly needs this. So, let's make it official. Let's get married. Let's move into this house; let's have a bunch of kids who will get the lives we never had. Let's give them a home, a real family, and let them never once worry about where their next meal will come from or whether or not they have parents to protect them."

He released me and took a step back. He reached into the pocket of his leather cut and pulled out a jewelry box. He flipped open the lid and presented me with a diamond ring that made me catch my breath. It wasn't gaudy or extravagant. It was simple and classic, but stunning.

It was the kind of ring I dreamed about having one day, offered to me by a man who thought I was the world.

"What do I give you, Duke?" I asked softly. "I bring you my problems and you just…"

"Fix them?" He grinned.

"Yeah. You fix them. You've always fixed them." I took a deep breath. "You've never asked me for anything. What do you get out of all this, Duke?"

"I get you."

I shook my head slowly. "It's not enough."

"You're not enough?" He raised his brows. "You're all I've ever wanted."

I plopped down on the cement floor of the shop and crossed my legs.

"What are you doing?" he demanded.

"We're negotiating."

"What? What do you mean negotiating? You're ruining my marriage proposal. You get that, right? Do you know how much work went into making sure this didn't look like a slapped together, last minute proposal?"

"Sit." I patted the spot in front of me.

With a grumble, Duke sat. We faced each other, our legs crossed. His emotions were running higher than mine.

"Tell me how you managed all this." I waved my hand around, gesturing to the shop and beyond.

"Savage called me the minute he left your place yesterday."

"Lying bastard," I said lightly. "He promised he wouldn't tell you."

"Yeah, well, Savage is Savage. He told me the situation, and he told me you were planning on proposing to me."

"So naturally, you had to beat me to it."

"Naturally."

"Go on," I urged.

He set his hands on my upper thighs. "I called Slash's realtor weeks ago to get her working on something for us. She called last night, actually, said she had something that might work. She brought me here, and I knew. I knew it was perfect for what we needed. What Waverly needed. So, I put it in an offer."

"You put in an offer—Duke, are you saying you're already in the process of *buying* this place?"

"Yeah."

I took a deep breath. "Continue."

"Offer was accepted almost immediately. As you can tell, no one's living here. I asked if I could use it to stage a proposal. You should've heard the realtor sigh. I swear she almost swooned." He grinned.

I smiled back.

His hands inched up my thighs. "I went ring shopping while Savage, Jessica and Waverly set this up."

"Set up. You mean the candles and the clovers?"

"Yeah."

"But, how did you come up with an idea so fast?" I asked. "When I thought I was going to be the one to ask you, I was in a panic because I couldn't think of anything so perfect for you."

His eyes met mine, staring into me, like he was seeing me all the way down to my marrow. "I've known how I was going to propose to you since we were sixteen-years-old."

Duke clasped my thighs and urged me to scoot closer. I unfolded my legs and inched my way toward him.

"You asked what I wanted," he said, his voice suddenly low and intense.

I nodded, my heart rapidly thumping in my chest.

"I want you pregnant, Willa. I want you pregnant with my baby and I want it soon."

I swallowed, a dull throb suddenly pulsating between my legs.

He took a hand off my thigh and grazed his thumb along the seam of my leather pants, pushing gently. My breath caught and my back bowed.

"I want to walk into the kitchen and see you standing there, round with my child. I want to come up behind you, slip one hand underneath your nightgown and another in your panties, and I want to make you come so hard with just my fingers you have to grip the counter to catch yourself. I want to be in that large tub, and I want you to climb on top of me, take me into your body and use me for your pleasure. I want you so happy and thoroughly fucked and sated you don't ever remember when we didn't have this."

"Duke," I whispered.

He pressed the heel of his hand against my cleft and rubbed me quickly into a consummate orgasm.

"Say yes, Willa."

"*Yes.*"

Duke slid the ring onto my finger and then brought it to his lips. He kissed my knuckles, his gaze heated.

His phone buzzed in his pocket.

"Interrupted so soon," I said with a mock frown.

"It's Savage," he replied with a grin. He pressed a button. "You're on speaker phone."

"You seal the deal?" Savage demanded.

"Damn right I did," Duke said, looking like the cat that got the canary…and the cream.

"Good. We're at O'Reilly's. Come meet us so we can celebrate."

"Us?" I asked.

"Me and Waverly," Savage said. "Hurry up."

He hung up. I looked at Duke. "That little sneak." I shook my head and grinned. "She pretended not to know where my phone was."

"She knew all. I even sent her pictures of rings while I was shopping so she could help me choose the right one for you."

"You didn't."

"I did."

He closed up the workshop, and we headed back into the house.

"What do we do about the candles and clovers?" I asked.

"We blow out the candles, and then I text Crow to get over here with South Paw and clean it all up."

"Prospects. Poor suckers."

"They're about to become brothers," he said. "They've put in the time and hard work. Proven their loyalty and put up with some bullshit so we could make sure they were in it for the long haul. They're good guys, and they won't be doing bitch work for much longer."

"They are good guys," I agreed.

After blowing out the candles, we left the house and stood at his bike. I took a moment to really admire my ring.

"Do you like it? If you don't, I'll get you something else."

I placed my hand to his cheek and stared into his eyes. "I love it."

"Yeah?"

"Yeah."

"I worried it might be too traditional."

"This traditional, I like." I gently brushed my lips against his, my body still hungry for more of him. "Did you really have to promise to celebrate at O'Reilly's just now?"

"You don't want to celebrate with Savage and Waverly?" he asked in surprise.

"I wanted to celebrate with you first. Naked."

"Oh, you did." He gripped my hips and hauled me toward him.

I wrapped my arms around his neck and pressed against him, rubbing ever so slightly. "Someone wants a family... We better get busy."

He cradled my cheeks and stared into my eyes. "I can wait. If you're not ready, I'll wait, just say the word and we'll wait."

I bit my lip. "I'm not sure I'll ever be ready, Duke. So, I think it's one of those things where you just have to decide what kind of life you want. And I want you happy. I want *us* happy." I peppered his jaw with kisses. "I'll go off birth control. And we'll see what happens."

Duke parked his motorcycle under a cluster of trees and we headed into O'Reilly's, hand in hand. Waverly chucked a fry at Savage's head and he responded in kind.

"Looks about right," I said with a grin at Duke.

Savage climbed out of the booth, shoved Duke away from me, and embraced me hard. "Happy for you guys. So fucking happy," he whispered.

I squeezed him and pulled back so I could look at him. "You mean it?"

"Never meant anything more," he assured me.

"My turn," Waverly said, elbowing Savage out of the way. She launched herself at me. "I want to hear about your proposal!"

"Why?" I laughed. "I heard you were in on the whole deal."

She grinned at me. "Yep, but I still want you to tell me all the things." She grabbed my hand and stared at the ring. "Wow, the jewelry coming out of Cracker Jack boxes these days is next level."

"Didn't you approve this ring?" I demanded, tweaking her nose.

"Yeah, I did. It looks beautiful on you."

Savage and Duke were speaking a few feet away and then Savage slapped Duke on the back.

"I'm starving," I said.

"You can have some of my fries, but they're cold," Waverly said.

"They were my fries, punk," Savage said, coming over to Waverly and wrapping his arm around her neck. "I shared them with you."

"Fries for breakfast," I said. "That's healthy."

"We eat hashbrowns in the morning, why not fries?" Waverly asked.

"Valid," I admitted. "Oddly valid."

"Is it too early for a celebratory Guinness?" Savage wondered.

"Nope," Duke said. "I'm getting one. You want one?"

I shook my head. "Just a Doctor Brown's soda."

"Soda for breakfast, Willa? For shame," Waverly tsked.

Savage ruffled Waverly's hair and then released her. "Let's go order the drinks."

"What do you want to eat?" Duke asked me.

"Surprise me," I said, with a wink.

His gaze heated.

"Yuck. I'm standing *right here*," Waverly muttered.

"Seriously. They're nauseating," Savage agreed.

Savage and Duke went to the bar and Waverly and I plopped down into the booth.

"So, you're supposed to be in school. You're not in school. Where does school think you are?"

"I called the school pretending to be Mom and said I was sick."

"If only you used your superpowers for good," I quipped.

"But I want to be a super*villain*, not a superhero," she replied.

I leaned back against the booth. "It's looking like we're moving…"

"Yeah, I know." She nodded. "The house is beautiful, and I can't believe I get my own workshop. When I saw it I burst into tears. I can't believe it's real."

"You, burst into tears?" I asked.

She opened her eyes wide. "I'm getting sentimental in my old age."

Chapter 33

"I DON'T WANT a wedding like Doc and Boxer's," I said. "Or even a wedding like Brooklyn and Slash's."

"Okay," Duke said with a shrug. He shoveled in another bite of corned beef and cabbage like I hadn't said anything.

I looked at Waverly and frowned.

She shrugged.

"We could have a party," I suggested. "After we're all moved in. If you want…"

"Okay." Duke set his fork down and reached for his pint of Guinness.

"*Duke*," I whined.

"What?" he demanded.

"You don't want a wedding?" I asked in exasperation.

He looked at me, then at Savage, who was grinning in amusement, to Waverly who was watching the play with interest.

"Do I want a wedding," Duke repeated. "Does any man actually *want* a wedding?"

"Does any man actually *want* to get married?" Savage quipped.

"Hush you," I stated to Savage, and then returned my attention to Duke. "You really don't want a wedding?"

"Nope. Don't care either way. If you'd wanted one, I'd have gone along with it to make you happy, but I don't give a flying fuck about it."

I glared at him.

"What?" he asked. "What's that glare for?"

"I don't know. I'm just annoyed." I sighed.

"We have to get married quickly, right?" Duke asked.

I glanced at Waverly and then back to him. "Yeah."

"You want the stress of throwing a wedding together quickly? It's not like a proposal."

"There's flowers, the food, the music," Savage listed.

I raised my brows at him.

"I helped Boxer with some shit," Savage said. "Believe me. You're better off signing some papers, getting it done, and getting on with life. Besides, it should be about the *marriage*, not about a wedding. That's not the same thing."

"I'm pretty sure that was your best man speech," I said.

"If he's the best man and that was his speech, then let me give mine. As maid of honor and all." Waverly lifted her glass. "To Willa and Duke. It's about damn time."

"Waverly," I snapped.

Savage raised his glass. "It's about damn time," he repeated.

With a sigh, I lifted my glass. "It's about damn time."

Duke shot me a look.

I shrugged. "If you can't beat 'em, join 'em."

We finished our food and then Savage paid. "Call it your wedding gift."

"Call it, try again," I said, elbowing him in the ribs as we walked out of the restaurant.

"What do you want?" he asked. "I mean, it's not like there's a registry."

"No, I guess there isn't," I said with a grin.

"How about a nice vase?"

"Why do I need a vase?" I asked.

"For the flowers that Duke is gonna bring you when he fucks up," Savage said.

"Always thinking ahead," Duke stated. "Nice."

Waverly looked at Savage. "Take me to the mall."

"Why do you need to go to the mall?" Savage asked.

"Because I need to buy a gift, too," she said.

"You don't," I said. "You refurbished the desk, remember? That's enough."

She rolled her eyes. "No dingus, that's a gift for your business. I want to get you a gift for *you*."

"What about me?" Duke asked. "You gonna get me something, too?"

"Obviously," Waverly sassed. "So, will you take me to the mall?"

"Can't your boyfriend take you?" Savage asked.

"He's in school. Please?"

Savage sighed at her shift in tone from bossy to begging. "Fucking malls. Okay, Little Punk. Let's go. It'll give the lovebirds some alone time."

Waverly followed Savage to his bike, but made sure to call over her shoulder, "Use protection! I'm too young to be an aunt!"

Duke wrapped an arm around my shoulder and pulled me into his side. He whispered in my ear, "Who's gonna tell her?"

"The pregnancy test," I quipped.

"You said that without flinching," he commented.

"I did, didn't I?" I suddenly smiled at him.

"What?"

"Nothing. Everything."

He covered my lips with his, but he didn't deepen the kiss. He pulled back but didn't release me. I settled my face in the crook of his neck and sighed.

"One year."

"You want to wait a year to start a family?"

I shook my head and looked at him. "Let's have a party on our one-year wedding anniversary. After we've moved in. After I'm legally Waverly's guardian. After we," I swallowed, "start our family."

His eyes heated and he cradled my cheek. "Whatever you want, babe. Whatever you want."

"Savage is going to keep Waverly occupied all afternoon," I said quietly. "Take me home and make me scream your name."

He grinned. "Your wish is my command."

~

We were on each other the moment we entered the house. He quickly stripped me of my leather jacket and pants, leaving me in my lacy bra and panties set.

He cupped my breasts and teased my nipples with his thumbs until they sharpened into points.

I ached between my legs and wanted him there immediately.

"You're beautiful," he whispered gruffly.

"You always made me feel beautiful," I said quietly. "Even when I was taller than all the guys in school."

He bent his head and sucked a nipple through the lace. I arched into him, my fingers digging into his hair.

Duke's large hand settled at the curve of my waist and pulled me into him. He sucked my nipples until my knees were weak and I nearly collapsed onto the floor.

His free hand slid between my legs, teasing my needy body.

"So wet," he murmured against my breast. "So perfect."

He worked his finger into me, gliding it in and out until I was panting with want.

It wasn't enough.

I wanted more.

"Give me another finger," I commanded.

"No." He removed his finger and then traced my lips with my own desire. And then he stuck his entire finger into his mouth and licked it clean.

"Go to the wall," he commanded, his voice suddenly deeper, darker.

With a shiver, I went.

"Turn around."

I turned.

"Place your hands on the wall and don't move."

I settled my palms flat. There was the clanking of a belt buckle being undone and I swiveled my head to watch him get undressed.

"Eyes forward," he demanded, stilling his movement. "If you turn around again, I'll stop right now and leave you wet and unsatisfied."

"You bast—"

He stalked toward me and quickly spanked the curve of my ass, causing me to inhale a sharp breath.

I'd been unprepared for his edicts, but his every word caused me to listen intently to his commands and do as he said.

He gently rubbed the sting away, and my skin was warm from the attention.

I closed my eyes and pushed into his hand.

He removed it and then I heard his boots hitting the

floor, followed by the rustling of his jeans as he took them off.

I felt him at my back, the warmth of him, the strength of his body.

He was in the prime of his life—and I was going to be the recipient of his stamina, and of his desire.

"Spread your legs. Wider. Good. Just like that."

He took a finger and drew a nonsensical shape on the small of my back and then dragged it lower, between my cheeks, but not stopping. He continued until he was at my slit. He pressed just the tip into me again and it took every ounce of my being not to push against him. He paused for a moment and then rewarded me and went in farther.

"So, you *can* listen."

"Shut up, Duke."

He withdrew his finger and then quickly slapped the curve of one cheek.

I moaned and pressed my forehead to the cool, smooth wall.

"You like that, don't you?"

He slapped me again, causing me to wriggle in pleasure and pain.

I heard him drop to his knees and then his thumbs were spreading my cheeks. He tongued my wet slit, darting in and out until I was a panting, writhing mess.

"Mmm," he murmured. "Fucking delicious."

I was just on the verge of coming when he pulled away —yet again.

Biting my lip so I wouldn't curse him out, I quickly forgot his torture because I felt the head of his shaft tease my entrance, smearing my desire all over my skin.

He pressed at the small of my back, signaling he wanted me to bend and arch.

"If only you could see yourself right now," he growled.

"You're bent over like a fucking offering. God damn, Willa."

"Please, Duke," I begged.

"Please what?"

"Please make me come."

The head of his shaft was pressed against me again, and then he thrust inside me.

I screamed in rapture.

I was so full; impossibly full. I wanted more. I wanted him seated all the way inside me, despite the discomfort, despite the pain of him being just a bit too big for my body at this angle.

"I'm going to fuck you every day," he growled, his chest touching my back. "Fuck you every day so I can hear you scream my name. Fuck you every day so you're so god damn full of me you don't remember a time when I wasn't inside you. Fuck you every day, giving you so many orgasms you beg me to stop. And then I'll fuck you until you're pregnant. You'll wake up with my head between your legs. You'll go to sleep with my dick still inside you. And still you'll beg for more. Won't you?"

"Yes," I gasped.

His hands reached around to play with my nipples. A shot of desire sparked between my legs and then one of his hands left my breast to stroke me between my thighs. He quickly found the engorged nub and paid homage to it.

I slapped my hand against the wall as my orgasm washed over me, but still Duke didn't stop thrusting. If anything, his pace quickened. He grew harder, longer inside me. We were messy and sweaty, and he slipped out of me.

Duke turned me around and grasped my elbows, backing us up until we hit the couch. He gently pushed me down, grabbed my legs, and opened me up to him. He gripped his erection and guided it back inside my body. He settled my legs onto his shoulders and then he began to rut.

His skin flushed with heat and pleasure; he took me with a mindless determination. My second orgasm was shorter than the first, an intense burst.

Duke rammed into me, clenched his jaw, and came with a raspy growl.

For a long moment, the only sounds I heard were our heavy breaths, nearly drowned out by the beating of my own heart.

He slid out of me, his seed pouring down my leg. Duke bent over, and with a finger, he pushed some of it back inside me.

Exactly where it belonged.

We were naked and lying side by side, long ways, on the couch. "We gotta shampoo these couch cushions," I murmured, snuggling against him, brushing my lips across his pectoral.

"Or we could throw the thing out," he said.

"Yeah. That's probably easier," I agreed. "But what do we do in the future?"

"We buy our own couch to go in our own house."

"No, I realize that," I said with a chuckle. "I just meant, if we're going to have repeat performances, we need to figure out a game plan."

"Cover it in plastic?" he suggested wryly. "You can just spray and wipe up the jizz."

"Classy. Real fucking classy," I muttered.

"You got a better idea? We can't throw out a couch every time I fuck you on it. We'll go broke."

I grinned and looked up at him.

He smiled down at me. Duke stroked my hair and then kissed my forehead. "Leather couch for the win."

I closed my eyes and sighed. "I like this."

"Sex with me?"

"Yeah, but also the cuddling."

"Cuddling is nice," he agreed. "It'll be hard to cuddle in the kitchen though."

"Huh? What do you mean?"

"Oh, you didn't realize that I plan on fucking you in every room of the house we bought?"

"I hadn't thought that far in advance," I admitted. "And *we* didn't buy anything. You did."

"Same difference. What's mine is yours."

"You have more than I do."

"So?"

"I don't want to feel like, well, like I *owe* you for anything."

"You don't owe me for anything. Everything I've ever had has been yours. Even when I had almost nothing."

"But now you have *something*."

"Willa, are you trying to tell me that you're not a gold digger marrying me for my money?"

"It sounds that way, doesn't it?" I said with a huff. I wriggled out of his embrace and sat up to face him.

I was still in my bra, and I'd put on my panties again, but I was exposed.

"Look," I said with a sigh. "Waverly is my responsibility—"

"Stop."

"Huh?"

"Stop. Just stop." He put a finger to my lips and forced me to be silent. He dropped his finger. "Did you think that when I asked you to marry me, I wasn't going to take financial responsibility for your sister, too? I found a house, specifically with her needs in mind."

"Yeah, but—"

He placed his finger against my lips again. "No *buts*. I'm happy to do it. Honored. Okay?"

I gently grasped his finger and brought it away from my mouth. "Yeah, but we're rushing to getting married because I *need* to get married. To gain guardianship of her. I love you, you know I do."

"So *we* can gain guardianship of her. And so what? I'll tell you something right now, Willa. If this is the reason I get to marry you sooner rather than later, than I'm happier than a pig in shit."

I wrinkled my nose. "There's an image."

"It doesn't matter, okay? That's what I'm trying to tell you. I love you. I've always loved you. I've always wanted to marry you. Now I get to."

"But the money—"

"Doesn't matter. We need money? I'll make more. Or you will from your business. I was never going to let either of you do without. You've got to know that."

"I do. I just…damn, Duke."

"You don't have to do it alone to prove a point. You get that, right?"

"Yeah. I guess." I frowned. "I'm so used to figuring it all out on my own."

"And now you don't have to."

"Now I don't have to." I paused. "It'll take some getting used to."

"How long you think it'll take?" he asked with a grin.

"I dunno? Forty years?"

He snorted. "My bet is on fifty."

Chapter 34

Duke's cell phone rested on the coffee table and it lit up with an incoming call. "Do me a favor," he said. "Grab that for me. You're sitting up and I'm comfortable."

"You just want me to climb over you and give you the money shot," I teased, but I was already going for his phone, even as I joked with him.

I saw Savage's name across the screen and handed it to Duke. "It's Savage."

"Bastard has impeccable timing," he drawled.

"Not really. We were already finished."

He raised his brows. "Babe, that was just round one." He pushed a button and set the phone to his ear. "Yeah?" Duke glanced at me. "Hang on." He held the phone to me.

With a frown, I took his cell from him. "Hello?"

"Hey," he said. "Waverly tried to call you and said your phone went to voicemail. She wants to talk to you."

"Oh. Yeah, sure."

"Hey," Waverly said. "Your phone went to voicemail."

"I turned it on silent," I said. "What's up?"

"I found this really cool dresser on marketplace. Can Jess, Dylan, and I grab it this afternoon?"

"Where is it?"

"Dallas."

"Who's driving?"

"Dylan."

"You'll be home for dinner?"

"Ummm…"

"Let me rephrase. *You'll be home for dinner.*"

"Willa," she whined.

"School night, Waverly. Come on, just do me a favor and be on your best behavior for the next few months while we sort out this legal stuff."

"So, once you're my legal guardian, you'll let me be the rebel punk that I am?"

"Sure," I said with a laugh.

"Fine. I can play nice. Maybe. Turn your phone on. You gotta be responsible too, you know."

I hung up his phone and set it aside.

"I'm disgusting," I announced. "And I need a shower."

Duke looked at me with hooded bedroom eyes. "I think you look perfect."

I wrinkled my nose. "I need to clean up before Waverly gets home."

"Why didn't you let her stay out later? Why did you insist she be home for dinner?"

"Because it's a school night." I cocked my head to the side. "You would've let her stay out later?"

He shrugged. "Knowing what we did when we were her age, yeah I probably would've let her stay out past dinner. She's with her friends. Kids I like, actually. I don't see the harm in that."

I'd been straddling Duke, and I awkwardly maneuvered myself off him so that I didn't knee him in the chest when I moved.

"I have a feeling I'm going to be the hard ass parent, and you're going to be the softie," I said as I retrieved my cell phone.

"What makes you say that?" Duke demanded. "I'm a biker. I'm the hard ass."

"Yeah, right! Have you seen Boxer with Lily? She's got him wrapped around her finger."

"Yeah, but that's Lily. You can't say no to Lily. No one can."

"Thus, proving my point." I glanced at my phone and saw several missed messages. "Someone blew up my phone. I've got like forty missed texts."

"Who from?"

I quickly scanned through them, a smile creeping across my face. "The Old Ladies offering their congratulations on our engagement, along with your boys. I'm guessing you told them you were proposing?"

He shook his head. "Nope. I just told Savage." He paused. "I guess that means he told them."

I grinned.

"You're not mad?" he asked.

"Why would I be mad?"

"Didn't you want to be the one to share the news?"

I shrugged. "This is fine too." I looked back through my phone. "Oh, this is fun. I've been put on an Old Lady group text. Joni wants everyone to come over tomorrow morning to see the baby—and to celebrate our engagement."

"Nice."

"Very." I set my phone down. "Now, are you going to get your ass up and shower with me?"

"Yeah, I'm moving. You kinda wore me out though. I need a nap."

"I wore *you* out? Seriously? I was kind of hoping for soapy shower sex."

"Damn, you really know how to celebrate an engagement." He hopped up from the couch. "I'll follow you, sweet cheeks. I like the view."

"If you call me sweet cheeks ever again, you'll be sticking nothing between those sweet cheeks. Got it?"

"Got it…vixen."

~

Duke and I were huddled around my laptop when Waverly came in. "What are you guys doing?" she asked.

"Filling out our marriage license," I said. "Romantic, isn't it? You get to fill out paperwork before you can devote yourself to the one you love."

"Sounds about right, actually. You need a license to drive. Of course you need a license to get married."

I frowned. "Stop it."

"Stop what?"

"Stop sounding like an adult. I don't like it."

"Sorry, let me try again. Willa," she pleaded. "Why did I have to come home for dinner?"

"Better," I remarked.

"Much better," Duke agreed. "Let me try on my parenting voice. Go to your room! You're grounded!"

Waverly and I looked at each other and then burst into laughter.

"What?" Duke demanded.

"You're *so* not the hard ass," Waverly said.

"Right? I was trying to tell him that, but he didn't believe me. Where's the dresser?" I asked.

"Storing it in Jess's garage. Where's the couch?"

"I accidentally set it on fire," I lied.

She peered at me. "Methinks you're lying."

"Methinks you don't get to ask any more questions about it," I said.

"Fine."

"Didn't Savage take you to the mall?" Duke asked.

"Yes."

"Where are your shopping bags?"

"I gave them to Savage. Willa would snoop if I brought her present into the house."

I gasped. "I do not snoop."

"No? You're a first-class snooper! Remember the envelope behind the toilet?"

"I wasn't snooping. I dropped something and I saw it out the corner of my eye," I protested.

"If it looks like a snoop…" Waverly shrugged.

"I think this household is suffering from low blood sugar. I'm calling for a pizza," Duke said, picking up his phone from the kitchen table.

"We really should get in the habit of cooking," I announced.

Waverly and Duke looked at each other and then burst into laughter.

I sighed. "This parenting thing. I'm pretty sure you have to cook to be a parent."

"Mom didn't cook," Waverly pointed out, taking a seat at the kitchen table.

"Well, I'd like to be the antithesis of Angel in every way. Is it too late to put in a request for a wedding present?"

"Brooklyn already gave us a slow cooker. It even had food in it. Those were the days, huh?"

"Not a slow cooker. Cookbooks."

Waverly blinked. "Cookbooks? I don't understand. We have the internet."

Duke angled my laptop toward him and opened a new browser. His fingers clacked against the keys and then he said, "Mastering the Art of French Cooking by Julia Child. French cooking? You think she has a recipe for that French version of beanie weanies?"

"You're kidding, right?" Waverly asked. "The French don't eat beanie weanies."

"Instead of a pizza tonight," I said. "Why don't we take her to La Creperie?"

"Works for me," Duke said.

"Okay, but I'm not eating snails. Snails belong in flowerbeds, not on your plate," she quipped.

"Eating out twice in one day," I said to Duke, wrapping my arms around his neck. "You spoil us."

"That's the plan." He grinned and brushed his lips across mine.

I wished for more than anything that he could come in and stay the night, but Waverly and I shared a bedroom.

"I'll be here tomorrow morning before you have to drive Waverly to school," he said, settling his hands on my hips. "We'll drop her off and then go to the courthouse and get our shit straight with the marriage license. We've got to wait three days, but then we can get it done."

"Get it done," I teased. "How romantic."

"My proposal was pretty damn romantic, wasn't it?"

"It was romantic and perfect, and I appreciate every thoughtful gesture you do for me. For us."

He kissed me one last time and then sauntered down

the walk toward his bike. I waited until he'd zoomed away before heading inside.

Waverly was at the kitchen table, devouring a crème brûlée we'd ordered to go.

"I'm not going to get any of that, am I?" I asked.

"Better hurry up and find a spoon."

"So, it's safe to say you actually like French food," I said, heading to a kitchen drawer.

"Better than like. I rescind my snails comment."

"Thought you might."

I pulled out the chair next to her and dug my spoon into the container.

"We need to talk," she said.

"Sounds serious." I stuck the spoon in my mouth and nearly moaned over the custard and caramelized sugar hitting my tongue.

"It is serious," she said, blue eyes wide as she peered at me.

I faced her and set my spoon down. "You don't approve of me marrying Duke."

"I do." She nodded. "You know I do. I love him like my own brother. And he makes you happy. This is about what happens after you get married. After we move into the big house. Just, after…"

She paused and I didn't push, knowing she was going to speak when she was ready.

"I've been thinking a lot about this, and I'd really like something from you."

"What do you need?" I asked. "If it's within my power, you know I'll give it to you."

She nodded and cleared her throat. "I want to drop out of school."

"*What?*"

She held up her hand. "I want to withdraw from

326

school. I don't want to go to summer school. I want to get my GED and then I'd really like to take classes at the community college that will help me focus on growing this furniture flipping business. I don't love school. I'm bored. I want to spend more of my time focusing on what I love to do. And the furniture thing...it's different each time. Each piece is unique in its own way, and I love every aspect of it. I love hunting for a piece. I love the creative reinvention of it, and I love actually selling the pieces. I love being able to provide for myself. And I don't want to have to wait until I'm eighteen to do it."

"Yes," I said immediately.

She blinked. "Really?"

I nodded. "I think you've really got something here. And I've never seen you so excited to get up in the morning. We're not all cut out for school. Hell, Duke nearly failed high school because of his dyslexia. You don't have to follow the same path as everyone else and I can't tell you...how *proud* I am, that you've figured it out so early in life. A lot of people don't."

"Mom didn't," she murmured.

"No. Angel didn't. She looked outward for satisfaction. That never works. You found something that makes you light up on the *inside*. And I'll do anything I can to help you."

She took my hand and gave it a squeeze. "You're going to be an awesome mother. Which, judging by how Duke looks at you, it'll be sooner rather than later..."

I laughed. "What are you even saying right now?"

"It's okay, you know." She grinned. "To want all that. To want a family. To want kids. You'll be good at it."

"You think so? How do you know?" I asked, suddenly feeling vulnerable enough to ask my sister to weigh in.

"How do I know?" she demanded. "Seriously? You've

all but raised me, Willa. And I think you've done a pretty damn good job."

"Except for the sailor mouth," I pointed out.

"Nobody's perfect. But I'm pretty fucking close."

"Waverly," I said, laughing.

"It's true, though. Dylan tells me I'm perfect."

With my free hand, I reached out and touched her jaw. "He's right."

She let out a long exhale. "I'm going to marry him."

"Are you?" I asked.

Waverly nodded. "Yes. One day, I'm going to marry Dylan." She peered at me. "You don't think I'm crazy for saying that, do you?"

I smiled. "No, I don't. I met my soul mate when I was younger than you. I'm happy you found each other. I mean that."

We stood up and hugged, and I held onto her for a moment.

"Because he's my soul mate and all—"

"No sleepovers," I interrupted. "When you turn eighteen, we'll talk."

Chapter 35

WAVERLY CROSSED THE PARKING LOT, heading toward Dylan. From a distance, I watched him survey her. When they were close enough, she jumped into his arms and he held her like he never wanted to let her go.

"Kid's a goner," Duke commented from the driver's side of my car.

I nodded. "Yeah, he loves my sister. And I couldn't be happier about that."

I didn't share with him what she'd confided about Dylan. Sisters needed to have secrets.

"Yeah, he's pretty cool." Duke put the car in reverse and drove out of the parking lot.

"Last night, she asked if she could drop out of school and get her GED."

He paused for a moment and then asked, "What did you say?"

"I said yes. Not all of us thrive in the classroom."

"No. We don't," he agreed. He glanced at me quickly. "I think that was smart on your part, Willa."

"Yeah?"

"Yeah. So many parents want their kids to do something, not understanding that they don't all fit into the same mold, and that sometimes *something* doesn't look like what they were taught."

"You don't fit the mold." I smiled.

"Neither do you."

"I'm glad we found each other," I said, reaching for his hand.

He gave it to me and squeezed my fingers before letting go.

It only took us half an hour at the courthouse to get everything signed and ready for our marriage. It was weird to think that I'd be marrying my best friend in a few days. It felt like we'd been together for years, and the truth was, we had been. Not romantically, but in all the ways that tell you whether a long-term relationship is going to work out or not.

"I'm sorry I'm an idiot," I said when we had finished in the courthouse and stepped back out into the sunshine.

"Okay, I'm gonna need a bit more." He pulled his sunglasses down over his eyes and grasped my hand.

"I had no idea what I was missing," I said.

"Ah, you mean sexually," he teased. "Yeah, to think we could've been boning for years."

"Charming." I snorted. "But no, that's not what I meant. I mean the entire package. The sex is great, don't get me wrong, but it's such a novelty for me to be in a relationship where I can truly be myself. Does that make sense?"

"Yeah. It makes sense." He unlocked the passenger door and opened it for me. "I still think it would've been nice if we'd been fucking all these years."

"Duke," I hissed. "Seriously? Watch your mouth."

"Or what? You'll wash it out with soap?"

I scooted past him, but stopped close enough to whisper, "No. I'll punish you by making you put that mouth to better use."

"What time are you meeting the Old Ladies?"

"In an hour."

"Then I'm driving like a bat out of hell to your house and I'll be cursing up a storm, just so you can punish me the way I deserve."

I grinned. "I was hoping you'd say that."

I arrived at Joni's late—and flushed.

After he'd made me come on his tongue, I thought for sure he'd satisfy me again with his cock, but the bastard had stood, looked down at me while my skin glistened with my release, and then decided he just had to be somewhere else.

So now I was turned on, ready for more, and I had to wait.

I was going to make him pay.

Slowly. Completely. Until it was *his* turn to beg.

There was a sign hanging on the front doorknob that read *Don't Use the Doorbell - Sleeping baby, please knock softly.*

I knocked gently.

A few moments later, the door opened.

"You're late," Darcy said, holding a drink in her hand.

"I got tied up." I leaned forward and sniffed the drink.

"It's a virgin." She stepped back and I came inside to the foyer. Her eyes took me in, slowly, and then she grinned. "Tied up, you say? Please tell me you actually mean you were literally tied up."

"Ah, no." I blushed.

"But you wouldn't mind, would you?"

"You sure that's a virgin?" I pointed to her drink. "Because if you're going to pester me about my sex life, I deserve something to grease the wheels before I spill, no?"

Mia and Allison were sitting on the living room carpet, their babies on a shared blanket in front of them. Brooklyn sat in a plush chair, while Doc perched at the end of the couch. Joni sat at the other end with her newborn asleep in her arms.

"He just fell asleep," Joni stage whispered. "And I'm not ready to let go of him to put him in his crib."

I crouched down next to her to peer at the sleeping baby. He was pink and squishy all over.

"His brow is furrowed like a little Yoda baby," she said with a soft laugh. "Zip looked the same when he was born."

"Maybe it means he'll be wise," I suggested, touching her shoulder and rising.

"We can hope," Joni said. "Grab a drink and then come back and tell us all the things."

"What about all the things?" I asked.

"Show us the ring, then tell us all about the proposal, and then *after* the proposal," Brooklyn said with a wink.

"I want to know about the dirty stuff," Darcy said.

"Same," Mia announced.

I looked around the room. "Rachel isn't here."

"Cash had a pediatrician's appointment," Mia said. "She'll try and make it later."

"Got it." I nodded. "I need a drink."

"I'll get you sorted," Brooklyn said, holding out her hand to Doc who helped her stand. "Thanks. I'm just big enough, and that chair is just comfortable enough that I never would've gotten up without help."

I followed Brooklyn into the kitchen and she opened

the refrigerator. "Sparkling water, cranberry juice, regular water, orange juice…"

"Sparkling water with cranberry, please," I said.

She pulled out the bottles and set them on the counter. "Listen, I know you just got engaged and the wedding is in a few days because of Waverly's situation, but Jazz, Brielle and I want to do something for you. Something small. Something girly. Something that will make it more like a wedding and less…"

"Transactional?"

"Yeah, that."

"What did you have in mind?"

"A spa day."

I laughed softly. "I'm in. I'm *so* in."

"Great. I'll book it. You don't have to do a thing." She handed me my drink.

"You're the best."

"Let's get back out there. They'll kill me if they think I know any juicy details before them."

"They don't *really* think I'm going to spill the beans about my sex life, do they?"

"What else do we talk about at brunches and parties?" she teased.

I laughed again and followed her back into the living room. I took a seat on the floor and set my drink on a coaster on the coffee table.

"Joni finally decided to put Everett in his crib for a nap," Mia explained. "She'll be back in just a minute."

"And she told us you weren't allowed to divulge anything until she's back," Darcy added. "Or there would be hell to pay."

The women were all staring at me with amusement splayed across their faces, and I suddenly felt like I was in the hot seat. But I was finally about to become one of them, an Old Lady.

"Are you crying?" Mia asked.

"No, I—yes! I'm crying." I suddenly burst into tears.

"Are you pregnant?" Joni demanded as she strode back into the living room.

I shook my head. "No. I swear, I'm just…fuck. I'm so happy."

"Yeah," Mia said dryly. "You look *really* happy…"

The room erupted into laughter, including me.

"Uh, Joni," Darcy said, pointing to Joni's chest.

Joni looked down. "Damn it. I'm lactating. Did you have to cry?"

"Welcome to my life story," Mia muttered.

"The joys of motherhood. It's like I can perform a magic trick or something." Joni sighed and sat down.

I dried my cheeks. "Sorry. I'll try not to cry anymore."

"I'll try not to lactate, but no promises," Joni remarked.

"You just gave birth. I'm pretty sure you get a pass," Doc said.

"So why the tears?" Mia asked. "I mean, I know you're happy, but…"

"Everything is so perfect. I was just overwhelmed by it all."

"You sure you're not knocked up?" Darcy asked.

"I'm sure." I bit my lip. "I did just go off my birth control, though…"

"No shit." Mia's eyes widened. "You and Duke are trying already?"

"We're not trying outright, but also not staying on birth control," I explained. "Just a, let's-see-what-happens sort of thing. Let nature take its course and be happy if it happens."

"Wow," Doc murmured.

"What about you?" Mia asked, throwing a look at Doc.

"What about me?" Doc demanded.

"You're about to leave on your non-honeymoon honeymoon to Scotland," Darcy said. "Scotch is potent, that's all I'm saying."

"So, show us the ring," Doc said, leaning forward, holding out her hand.

I could take a hint. Doc didn't want to talk about babies or about her starting a family with Boxer, and I'd gladly oblige and take the focus off her.

"That's gorgeous," Darcy said as she peered over the couch to get a better look.

"Tell us about the proposal," Brooklyn said.

"Screw that." Darcy riffled through her purse and pulled out a mini bottle of vodka. "Let's get her drunk and make her tell all about the sex."

"When did you get booze?" Mia asked in exasperation.

"Stopped off at the liquor store on my way over." Darcy shrugged.

"It's not even ten o'clock in the morning," Joni said with a laugh.

"Relax, it's a girls' brunch. It's not like I just opened a bottle of tequila. Okay?" Darcy said.

"Thank God," Mia muttered. "Dangerous things happen at girls' hang outs when tequila is involved."

"Like what?" I asked, intrigued.

"We get drunk, demand our men service us, and then *boom!* Pregnant," Joni explained.

Darcy unscrewed the lid and poured a splash into my drink, hardly enough to be considered an actual cocktail. I stirred it with my finger and took a drink. I couldn't even taste it, which either meant I had to be careful, or there really wasn't that much in there.

Mia turned her attention to me. "So, the proposal?"

"Right," I said with a dreamy sigh. And then I told them the entire story, including the house Duke had put an offer on. "He thought of everything. It was…incredible."

"I can't believe he found something so perfect so quickly," Allison said.

"He was house hunting for a while, apparently," I admitted. "I think probably as soon as we got together."

"It took Torque and I months," Allison said.

"That's because Torque had very specific ideas about what he wanted, whereas you didn't care as much," Darcy said.

Allison shrugged. "I gave him this one. He's given into me on other things. It works for us that way."

"What is it with Tarnished Angels men?" Doc asked. "They're like…I don't know. A different breed of men. Committed, like immediately. They want families and babies."

"I never thought Boxer was going to meet a woman he'd want to be with forever," Joni said. "But you're right. They meet the one and then it's like, insta-bondage." She paused. "That came out wrong. You know what I meant."

"Speaking of bondage," Darcy said.

"Okay, what's up with you?" Joni demanded.

"What do you mean?" Darcy asked.

"I mean, you're like sex obsessed and it's the weirdest thing ever," Joni said.

She sighed. "Sorry. Sex is all I can think about lately. I think it's my body's last-ditch effort to get me to squeeze out another human before my eggs dry up. I'm fighting for all it's worth, but y'all are not helping with the cute babies you're popping out."

"Sorry, we'll stop," Joni said with a wink at Mia.

Mia laughed. "Yeah, we'll stop."

"No. Don't stop," Darcy begged. "Keep having babies so I don't have to have another one."

"You could have one more," Brooklyn said, rubbing her rounded belly.

Darcy shook her head. "Rationally, I'm done. Hormonally, I keep trying to suck the seed out of Gray."

I was mid-sip, and her comment effectively made me spit my drink out all over the coffee table, causing another round of laughter.

"I doubt he's complaining," Doc teased.

"He said his dick is sore." Darcy sniggered. "Like my hoo-ha is a clamp of steel or something."

"If you guys keep talking this way, I'm gonna need more than a splash of vodka," I said.

Darcy rummaged in her bag again and pulled out another mini bottle. She tossed it to me and I caught it. "Have at it, champ. We're not going anywhere for a while."

Chapter 36

"When are you guys getting your tattoos?" Darcy asked as she took a bite of her Philly cheese steak.

"Tattoos?" I asked in confusion. "Oh, because I'm his Old Lady. Weird. I never thought I'd say that."

"Never?" Joni pressed. "Really? Or were you lying to yourself this entire time?"

"Maybe a little bit of both," I admitted, finishing off the pickle that had come with my French dip sandwich. We'd ordered lunch to make it easy on all of us. The babies had been fed, changed, and were now napping.

A nap sounded like a fabulous idea, but I still had errands to run before I picked Waverly up from school.

"Willa?" Mia pressed.

"Hmm?"

"The tattoos," she reminded me. "When are y'all getting branded?"

I sniggered. "We kind of already did." I held up my wrist.

"Yeah, but that's not really about you and Duke," Darcy said. "I mean it is, but it's about Savage too."

"So as Mia puts it, I've got to get Duke's brand on me somewhere?" I asked.

"Yep. That's the way it works," Doc said. "I definitely didn't think I'd like it, but it gives me a sense of security. One I didn't realize I wanted. You can remove a ring; you can't remove a tattoo so easily."

"I can't wait to get my tattoo," Brooklyn said. "After the baby's born, I mean. Slash already got his, of course. It feels kinda lopsided on my end right now."

"Here," I brushed the spot underneath my right ear. "I think I'd like his name right here, with a little heart."

"Well, I think that's perfect," Joni said.

I finished off my lunch and then helped clean up.

"So, you're really not having a wedding? Like at all? Not even a party?" Mia asked.

I shook my head and grabbed my purse. "I'm really not. I told Duke we can do something for our one-year anniversary, but right now, everything needs to be simple and easy. Life has been too crazy to complicate it any further."

"Don't I know it," Doc said. "I have a lot of anxiety about leaving the clinic for ten days, but Boxer thinks a vacation will be good for me."

"It's not a vacation, it's a honeymoon," Mia said with a laugh. "But he's right. You need time away from the clinic."

"Naked time," Joni added.

"I have to go," I said.

"You're leaving?" Joni pouted.

"I have to," I said. "I need to get some stuff done before I pick Waverly up from school." I made the rounds, hugging everyone goodbye.

"In case we haven't said it enough already," Mia said,

embracing me, "we're really happy you're one of us now. Officially, that is."

I pulled back, tears in my eyes. "Damn, you guys. You have me all up in my feelings."

With a final wave, I left Joni's house, careful not to slam the front door so as not to wake the sleeping babies.

After talking with the Old Ladies, I realized that even though my wedding was going to take a grand total of about five minutes, and that it was merely a formality, it didn't seem right that I didn't at least dress the part of a bride.

Once I was in my car, I shot off a text to Waverly.

ME

> We're going wedding dress shopping after I pick you up from school.

After a few minutes, my phone buzzed with her reply.

WAVERLY

> Marathon or sprint? You know what, it doesn't matter. We need caffeine for fuel.

I set my phone in the drink console and then put the car into gear. My vehicle was caked with pollen so I went through an automatic car wash and then drove to an electronics store. I'd done a little bit of research about purchasing a second monitor for a dual monitor setup, but I picked the sales guy's brain before making the final purchase. It was a business investment that would make my life a hell of a lot easier, even if I did flinch when I signed the sales receipt.

I wheeled the cart with the monitor out into the parking lot toward my car. I unlocked the trunk and put the monitor inside and then returned the cart and glanced at my phone, noting the time.

"Shit," I muttered. I was going to be late getting to Waverly.

I quickly got into my car and started the engine. I slowly backed out of the lot and headed in the direction of her school.

As I turned into the street, I heard a loud crunching. I briefly wondered if I'd rolled over something, but the noise continued until I stopped at the light.

With I sigh, I pulled into a vacant parking lot of an empty strip mall with signs for storefronts available for rent in all the windows. I put the car into park and got out to investigate. I walked around the vehicle but saw nothing, until I returned to the front driver's side wheel. A large plastic container of some sort had been rammed between the body of the car and the wheel.

"What the hell?" I muttered, removing the refuse and tossing it aside.

Just as I stood up to get back in my car, tires screeched to a halt. I turned and saw the sliding door of a van open, and two men wearing black masks jumped out. I reached for my door handle and fumbled with it in a panic, but my clammy fingers slipped off.

The men were too fast anyway, and before I could even react, they were on me. A brutal hand grasped my neck, and another covered my mouth to stifle my scream. I instinctively reached up to try to pry the man's hand away from my throat. Something sharp pinched the skin of my arm and out of the corner of my eye I saw the other man —he'd stuck me with a needle. I struggled for a moment, determined to get free, but I wasn't strong enough.

Before I had a chance to try anything else, the man holding my neck pushed me to the ground and his accomplice pulled a fabric bag over my head.

My limbs weakened as I sank into darkness…

I was completely at their mercy.

And then I passed out.

The smell of urine jolted me awake. I shifted my body, my drugged mind coming to the realization that my pants weren't wet and I hadn't soiled myself.

The urine wasn't mine.

My brain made the connection that I probably wasn't alone.

It was dark and I couldn't see anything in front of me. I turned my head and realized the bag was still covering my face. My wrists were cinched together and bound to my ankles, which were also tied.

I tried to stretch out my legs, but they immediately hit a blockade.

I'm trapped.

My heart began to pound, and I started to sweat in panic. I arched forward and leaned over while also bringing my knees up toward my chest to try and get my hands near my face. Everything was a struggle because of how I was tied up. My hamstrings screamed in pain as I attempted to grasp the edges of the bag with my fingers. I fumbled for a moment, but I was finally able to bend my head down far enough and pinch the end of the fabric, and I gripped it tightly and wrestled the hood off.

It was still pitch black and I couldn't see, but the air outside the veil was immediately cooler and I took a few deep breaths. My throat was dry and I swallowed several times. I licked my lips, grateful that my mouth hadn't been taped.

"Is—" I cleared my throat "—anyone else here?"

I heard the rustling of what sounded like denim followed by a whimper.

"My name's Willa," I said. "Who's there?"

"Sailor," came a raspy reply. After a moment she said, "I peed myself. I couldn't hold it anymore."

I had no idea how old she was, but from the sound of her voice I guessed she was younger than me. Without light, I had to rely on sound and touch.

Bile churned in my belly as I realized how dire our situation was. Flashes of my abduction came to the forefront of my mind, and I immediately tried to stifle the images.

"How old are you, Sailor?"

"Sixteen. How old are you?"

"Twenty-four."

"Do you—do you know where they're taking us?" she asked, her voice trembling.

"No." I had no idea, but I'd been plucked right off the streets in broad daylight. I might not know where we were being taken, but I had a pretty good idea of *why* we'd been taken. "Sailor, is there anyone else in here with us? Do you know?"

"There's someone else. A leg is touching mine, but the person's not awake. I can hear breathing, though," Sailor said. "I think it's another girl, but I don't know for sure."

"Good. That's good."

"That's *good*? That there's someone in here with us?"

Her voice was rising in fear, and the last thing I needed was for her to have an anxiety attack. If I had to calm her down, then I wouldn't be able to focus on figuring out where we were and how to get out.

"It's good that she's breathing," I clarified. "Okay, Sailor. I need your help."

"My help? With what?"

"With getting out of here."

"We don't even know where we are, how are we going to—"

"*Be quiet for a second*," I hissed.

She immediately shut up. I listened intently for a moment. I heard the distinct rumble of road noise, but it was muted. We went over a bump, and it jostled me into Sailor.

"Sorry," I said as I righted myself.

"It's fine," she assured me.

"Well, we're in a truck or a cargo van, that much I know."

"Why isn't the other girl awake yet?" she asked, her voice shaky and filled with trepidation.

"Don't worry about that right now. She's breathing, so she's going to be okay." I leaned away from Sailor to press against the wall. There was no give to it. Even if I was able to maneuver my body around in the tight space, I doubted I'd be able to kick a hole into it. And even if could, then what?

As scary as it had been being kidnapped off the streets, I knew it was going to be far worse once we stopped and were unloaded.

Unloaded, because we were human cargo.

My heart battered the walls of my chest.

This is life or death.

I shoved away my anxiety and terror, just like I had every time Angel got involved with some creep who got drunk and smacked her around. Walls were thin in cheap motel rooms and dingey apartments. I'd slapped a smile on my face many times and distracted Waverly from the sounds of crying and pain. I'd protected my younger sister the best I could—and I'd do that now.

For Sailor.

And then, for myself.

"How did you get here?" Sailor asked.

"I was in a parking lot—" I said "—when a van pulled up."

"Yeah?"

"Yeah. There was a plastic thing in between my wheel and the car so it was making this weird crunching noise. I got out to see what it was, and they grabbed me before I could get back in the car... Sailor, these are evil men. They—"

"I know," she interrupted. "I've seen videos about human trafficking. Oh my God, we're going to die, aren't we?"

"Don't think like that. How long has it been? When did they take you?"

"I work at a fast-food joint. I was dumping the trash out back. That's when they snatched me. They drugged me. I've been in and out of it...I think it was a day or two ago. I'm so tired..."

"Your parents must be worried sick about you," I said, trying to get her to at least think of the people she loved.

She let out a laugh that sounded far too sardonic for a sixteen-year-old. "My dad's a drunk. He spends more time in a bar than he does at home. I doubt he'll even notice I'm gone."

"And your mom?"

"Died when I was a baby."

I didn't offer my condolences. It would just come off as pity. The drone of the truck's engine continued as we bumped up and down the road.

"Any siblings?" I asked.

"No." She paused for a moment. "You're trying to distract me, aren't you?"

"Yeah... Is it working?"

"Kind of. What about you? What about your family?"

"I have a sister your age. I was on my way to pick her up from school." I sighed. "And I just got engaged."

"No…"

"Yeah." I swallowed hard.

"What about your parents?" she asked.

I thought about what Sailor had confided in me and admitted, "My mother is a stripper. She ran off with some random guy. She's somewhere in Alabama. Or Arkansas. I have no idea really. My dad bailed when I was young."

"So, you take care of your sister?"

"Yes."

Oh God, Waverly.

Duke and Savage would protect her. They'd figure out a way to make it so that she didn't get pulled into the system.

They'll protect her.

They'd have to because I wasn't going to be there to…

"Willa?"

"Hmm?"

"Can I…do you mind if lean against you? Would that be okay?"

I scooted my body closer to hers and we pressed against one another. "Yeah, Sailor. That would be okay."

Chapter 37

Sailor dozed off after a few minutes of leaning up against me. I heard her breaths even out and knew her body was trying to work the drugs out of her system. I was glad she could sleep through what was going on.

I couldn't.

I cried silent tears, trying not to wake the young woman trapped next to me.

I was so stupid. I hadn't been paying attention to my surroundings while I'd gotten out to examine my car…

My car.

Where was my car now?

My phone?

I felt for my engagement ring. It was gone. No doubt my kidnappers had taken it, thinking they could make an easy buck by selling it.

After they sold *me.*

I was under no illusions about what was taking place.

You think it's not going to happen to you.

You think you're safe.

You think you're special.

You think the world gives a damn about you.

Why? I wanted to shout. *Why now? Why give me everything I've ever wanted only to rip it away from me?*

My life would be truncated, ending before it had truly begun.

My abduction would destroy the people I loved. They'd wonder what happened to me. They'd never find closure.

A muffled gunshot rang out and suddenly the truck lurched hard to one side, causing me to crash into Sailor. There was a loud screech and then a forceful bang as the truck came to a stop at a sharp angle, like we were suddenly no longer on level ground.

"What happened? Where are we?" Sailor demanded, suddenly awake.

"I don't know, but something's wrong."

"What's going on?" she pleaded.

"I heard a gunshot. Be quiet for a minute."

Sailor huddled close to me and I heard the muted sounds of shouting, followed by doors being wrenched open and then slammed shut outside.

I instinctively scooted lower, hunching my body over Sailor, trying to shield her. In that moment, Sailor was my sister and I would do whatever I needed to in order to protect her. Even if it was futile.

The other woman in the space with us was still unconscious, and I assumed that the drugs were too strong for her to wake up.

Suddenly, everything was quiet.

Sailor was shaking against me. I tried to remain still, my senses on high alert at impending danger.

A metal rolling door screeched open, but I didn't hear any voices or footsteps. In a split-second decision, I decided to trust that whoever was out there was a better option for us than the shit bags that had abducted us.

"We're in here!" I yelled. "Help!"

I kicked out my legs and hit a wall. When I did, it made a resounding thud. A few moments later I heard heavy footsteps and then suddenly a door opened, and flash of light shone directly into my eyes.

I burrowed my head into Sailor to hide against the brightness.

"*Willa!*"

I peered up at the sound of his voice. "Duke?"

"Fuck, *lower the light*," Duke snapped.

The beam dropped, and as my eyes began to adjust to my surroundings, I saw Acid holding the flashlight.

My panic immediately cleared when I realized we'd been rescued.

We wouldn't be sold.

We wouldn't have things done to us that made us wish for death.

I glanced at Sailor, who was still shaking and huddled up next to me. In the light, I realized she'd found a way to remove her own hood at some point. Her blonde hair was a tangled mess, but she didn't look injured.

"How did you know we were here?" I croaked, looking at Duke.

Duke's face was grim as he pulled out his knife. Sailor smushed herself deeper into me.

"It's okay," Duke said. "We're here to help."

"Sailor," I said. "This is Duke. My fiancé."

Sailor lifted her head and whatever she saw on Duke's face made her nod and wriggle away from me. Duke slashed the ties at her ankles and at her wrists, setting her free. Then he quickly did the same to me.

He stuck the knife back in its sheath and immediately cradled my cheeks in his hands, his eyes swimming with emotion.

"Duke," Acid said, pulling our attention away from one another.

Acid had shined the light to the far side of the tiny compartment where we'd been held. It was the other woman.

She wasn't moving.

Acid crouched down next to her, gently tugged off her hood, and felt for a pulse. He shook his head. "She's gone."

"No, no, no, no—" I murmured in shock.

"I'm going to be sick," Sailor said, and then vomited next to the corpse.

I thought for sure the other girl with us would wake up…that the drugs would run through her system the way they had through mine, but I hadn't been able to protect her.

A surge of emotion hit me hard and fast.

"Acid, take Sailor outside. Let her get some air. We'll be out in a minute," Duke commanded.

Sailor looked at me.

"They're Tarnished Angels. You've heard of them?" I asked.

She shook her head in negation.

"You'll be safe with them. I promise."

"Okay," she whispered.

Acid handed the flashlight to Duke and then held out a hand to Sailor. She took it, and he ushered her out of the compartment toward the back rolling door of the truck.

Duke stood up and reached for me.

"Where are we?" I asked.

"Just outside Laredo."

"Laredo," I murmured. "They were taking us to Mexico, weren't they?"

"Yes."

He turned around and led me through a small doorway in the truck, past large furniture, and rolled up carpets in clear plastic wrapping.

"This looks professional," I stated.

Duke paused for a moment and then said, "It is. This isn't the first truck we've found."

Bile churned in my stomach. "There have been more?"

"Yes."

"A lot more?"

"Just…more."

We stepped out into the night. It was evening and the sky was full of stars. The air was stagnant but not overly hot. I thought about being in the truck during the height of summer. How many people died in trucks like these? No ventilation, no air-conditioning…

Duke pulled me into his arms and I felt him shudder. He squeezed me so tight it felt like he was going to break me.

"Thought I lost you."

My body began to shake, as if there was no longer any capacity for adrenaline to power me. "How did you find us?"

He pulled back and stared at me like something was wrong.

"What is it?" I asked.

"You might not like the answer."

"You rescued me," I reminded him. "I don't care what you did."

"I put a tracker in your car," he said with a slight smile. "Waverly called me just a few minutes after you failed to show up at her school. She knew something was wrong because you're always on time or early, and if you're not going to be, you call. You didn't call this time. I checked the tracker and saw where your car was. Junk yard outside of town. Savage and I drove there and found the guys who'd taken you. It took a bit of convincing for them to give us the details of the route the truck was on, but they finally came around."

I raised my brows. "They *came around*?"

Duke scratched his jaw. "One of them is dead. It got ugly as soon as they saw us. Savage got hold of the other one. He's still with him now."

"Oh." I pressed my hand to his chest directly over his heart. He covered my hand with his.

"Give me a second." He took out his cell. "Gotta call Savage and let him know we found you. I'd hate to be the asshole he's with right now." He dialed Savage. "Hey. Yeah, we've got her. Okay, hang on…" Duke handed me the phone.

"Hey," I said.

"You're okay?" Savage asked, his voice sounding raspy.

"Yeah, I'm okay."

He let out a huge sigh of relief. "Put Duke back on."

I gave the cell to Duke.

Savage said something on the other end and Duke replied, "Yeah, give me a minute to talk to Prez."

He took my hand and we walked over to the other side of the truck. Illuminated by the headlights were two men face down in the ditch next to the road. The truck was angled sharply and had a blown tire, and I realized one of the guys had shot the tire out. We were on a long, remote stretch of Texas highway, and all was quiet.

I looked at the men, their hands bound behind their backs.

Acid had a pistol trained on one of them and Boxer had a shotgun in hand.

"Where's Sailor?" I asked.

"In the cab of our van on the other side of the truck,"

Colt said, not taking his eyes off the men. "Why don't you join her."

"Are they going to—"

"No more questions," Colt said, glancing away from the men on the ground and striding toward me. "We'll talk later. Go. *Now.*"

I did as he commanded. As I walked to the van, I heard Duke say, "I have Savage on the phone."

I looked over my shoulder and watched as Duke handed his cell to Colt.

Colt took it and put it to his ear. "Yeah." He paused. "Take care of it."

The president of the Tarnished Angels hung up the phone and handed it back to Duke. Colt turned his attention to me, scrutinizing me as I walked away, unable to take my eyes off him.

The look on his face told me more than a thousand words could have.

There wouldn't be any mercy. Not tonight.

Boxer had yet to say a word. The normally good-humored biker looked untamed, an all-consuming rage brewing within him, like it was taking all his willpower not to pull the trigger on the massive shotgun he held.

I finally looked away and rounded the corner of the truck and then climbed into the front seat of the van next to Sailor. No sooner had I slammed the door shut than two gunshots rang out through the night.

It was done.

Sailor's eyes were wide and her lips were pinched with exhaustion and terror. Her pants were still wet. She tried to tug down her shirt to cover it, but it was no use.

"It's okay," I said and looked her straight in the eyes. "You're safe now, but I need something from you—"

Sailor leaned her head against my shoulder. "I won't

say a word. I swear on my life I won't say a word. I just wanna go home."

"You understand how big a deal this—"

"I get it. I swear to you, not a word." She paused and then said, "You're lucky to have Duke. He saved our lives tonight."

"Yeah, he did."

Sailor was quiet for a moment and then said, "I wish I had someone who loved me enough to come save me."

Chapter 38

DUKE OPENED the driver's side door of the van and climbed in. "Last chance to use the bathroom. We're going to be on the road for a while."

"I don't have to go," Sailor said.

"No?" Duke raised his brows. "You're not going to make me pull over in ten minutes? Acid said he gave you a bottle of water and you downed the entire thing."

"I don't have to...crap. I totally have to go. Power of suggestion I guess," Sailor announced.

I unlatched my seat belt and got out of the van so Sailor could use the side of the highway as a bathroom. She hopped down and ambled off toward the ditch behind the furniture truck.

"Sit in the middle," Duke said.

"But my legs. I'm twice as long as her."

"Please, Willa." His tone darkened. "It's taking all my willpower not to lose my shit. Just...be close to me."

"Okay," I said. I settled in the middle seat and took the bottle of water he offered me. I drank a few sips. It was tepid but soothed my dry throat immediately.

Sailor climbed back into the van, said nothing about the new seating arrangement, and buckled herself in.

"Everyone good?" Duke asked.

We nodded.

"Are you hungry?" I asked Sailor.

"No." She looked out the window. Her stomach rumbled.

"Liar," I said with a laugh.

Sailor shot me a sheepish smile.

"There are some protein bars in the glove box. Sorry, we can't stop for food."

Acid trekked over to the van and climbed into the seat behind us before shutting the sliding door. "We can take off. Prez and Boxer will take care of the truck."

"What about the girl?" I asked, turning my head to look at Acid.

"Girl's dead," he said flatly. "They're going to pull her out of the truck, set the two men and the truck on fire, and let the authorities handle it."

Sailor made a small noise of distress. I patted her thigh in comfort. As Duke started the van, I looked out the window to the side of the road, watching Boxer and Colt get to work.

"Where's Waverly?" I asked once we were on the road.

"With Darcy and Gray at their house." He handed me his cell. "Call her."

It was just after eleven, but I knew she wouldn't be asleep with what was going on.

I quickly dialed her.

"Duke! Is she—did you find her?"

"Hey, Little Punk," I said, feeling tears prick my eyes at the sound of her voice.

"Willa…" She burst into tears in a way that was completely unlike her.

I waited for her to cry it out for a minute, and when she started sniffling, I said, "I'm okay."

"You're not hurt?"

"No."

She let out a sigh of relief. "I'm so glad. So, so glad. When you didn't show up at school, I called Duke. You're *never* late."

"You're the reason they found me," I said.

"Where were you? What happened?"

"I'll tell you about it later," I said.

"Will you—are you going to come over to Darcy's and get me?"

"I don't know what time we'll be getting back to Waco," I said evasively.

"Probably around four in the morning," Duke supplied.

I nodded to let him know I'd heard him. "We won't be getting back until early tomorrow morning, like four in the morning, or later."

"Where are you?"

"Laredo."

"Laredo! What the hell?"

"Get some sleep," I said. "I'll see you in the morning, okay?"

"Okay," she said quietly. "I—I love you, Willa."

"Love you, too."

I hung up with her and handed Duke his cell phone. He slipped it into his pocket.

"When we get back to Waco, you can just drop me off at the bus station," Sailor said. "I can walk home from there."

"You really think we're going to drop you off at a bus station so you can walk home alone—after we just rescued you from being sold as property in Mexico?" Acid demanded from the back seat.

"Acid," I warned.

"When we get back to Waco, you're going to see Doc," Acid explained. "She's the club doctor."

"They didn't touch me," Sailor announced. "I mean they didn't…you know. They just drugged me."

Duke's knuckles loosened on the steering wheel ever so slightly. "Acid's right. You're getting checked out by Doc."

"Okay," Sailor said. "So, who were they? The men that took us?"

"Cartel," Acid said.

"Acid, *enough*," I snapped. "She's only sixteen."

"*Enough?*" he snapped back. "The girl was just fucking rescued from being trafficked. She has a right to know why we did what we did."

"Duke, back me up here. Sailor's the same age as Waverly," I stated. "Would you tell Waverly any of this?"

"Yes," Duke said immediately. "I'm with Acid on this. And I'll be telling Waverly the truth about what happened, because girls her age are going missing and she needs to be aware so she can protect herself."

I sucked in a breath. "Can we just get back to Waco, please?"

"Yeah, we can get back to Waco."

It was two in the morning and Sailor was asleep. She was small enough that she'd been able to bend her body in half and was using my lap as a pillow. My fingers sifted through her blonde hair.

Acid had stretched out in the middle seat in the row

behind us. His breathing was heavy so I knew he was asleep, too.

Duke and I hadn't spoken in an hour.

Anger radiated off him and I didn't have the energy to be combative.

"I thought I was going to die," I said quietly.

He flinched like I'd punched him in the jaw.

"It happened so fast, you know? One minute I was in a parking lot removing a piece of plastic from the wheel well...the next minute a van was screeching into the lot behind me and—"

It was hard to finish the sentence without emotion boiling up from within me, but I fought through it and went on, "And then when I woke up in the truck, I spent all my time making sure Sailor didn't panic." I looked down at her. "She's got a shit home life, Duke. She reminds me so much of me and Waverly."

"Parents?"

"Alcoholic father. Mom's dead. She was working at a fast-food joint taking out the garbage when they snatched her." I swallowed. "How many others have there been, Duke? How many others weren't found in time? How many others were left to die?"

"Too many, Willa. Too many."

"Willa," Duke murmured.

"Hmm?"

"We're here."

I opened my gritty eyes and stared ahead at the club-house. "Sailor," I said gently, shaking her awake.

With a groan, she sat up and rubbed her eyes. "Where are we?"

"The Tarnished Angels clubhouse."

"What time is it?"

"A little after four," Duke said.

She rubbed her eyes. "Okay."

"How does a shower and a real bed sound to you?" I asked her.

"It sounds great."

We climbed out of the van.

As Sailor, Acid, Duke, and I headed toward the clubhouse, Savage barreled out the front door.

He stalked toward me and didn't stop until he'd wrapped his arms around me and hauled me into his chest, squeezing me tight.

"You smell like fear," he muttered.

"Good to see you too." I squeezed him back, despite his insensitivity.

He let his arms drop and he pulled back just enough to stare into my eyes.

"The guys you and Duke…" I took a deep breath. "You showed them no mercy, right?"

"None," he assured me. He turned his attention to Duke and walked to him, exchanged a few words I couldn't hear and then Savage slapped Duke on the back. Savage went to the van and climbed into the passenger side.

The front door of the clubhouse opened and Slash came down the stairs. "Willa," he said, his tone grave.

"Hi, Slash."

He paused for a moment and then said, "Ah, fuck it." Slash hugged me. It wasn't long, but it was tight and appreciated. Slash wasn't one for showing emotion unless it was for his wife, so the gesture was unusual.

"Take our room," he said, pulling back. "Sheets have been changed, the room has been cleaned, and it's got a private bathroom."

"You sure?" I asked him.

"Yes. Brooklyn would want it that way."

"Okay, thanks."

Slash gave Duke a chin nod and then went to the truck.

I glanced at Sailor, whose face was slack with shock. "You okay?"

"Yeah." She nodded. "Yeah, I'm okay. Just…"

"What?" I prodded.

"All these bikers are really hot."

Despite the situation, I let out a laugh. "Yeah, they are."

Sailor realized that Duke was still standing next to us. She ducked her head in embarrassment. "Sorry, I'm so tired my filter is completely gone."

"That's okay," Duke assured her. "We like hearing that we're hot."

We walked inside and Doc was sitting on the couch. She immediately stood up as we entered.

"Hey, Doc," I greeted in exhaustion.

"*That's* Doc?" Sailor asked, her mouth agape.

"You must be Sailor," Doc said with a smile.

Sailor nodded.

"Doc is the best Doc there is," I said. "She delivered a baby at her own wedding."

"You did that?" Sailor asked.

"I did," Doc said with a winsome smile.

"In her wedding dress," I added.

"I can tell you the story if you want, while I check you out. Is that okay?" Doc asked her.

Sailor instantly moved closer to me.

Doc's expression softened. "I know you've been through a lot, but all I want to do is make sure you're okay. In order to do that, I need to take a little blood and see if the drug they gave you is still in your system. That's all."

EMMA SLATE

"Take mine first," I said, sitting on the couch. "Duke, why don't you find Sailor a clean towel and a change of clothes, so after we're done here she can shower?"

Duke nodded. "Good idea." He leaned in close to brush his lips against my cheek and then left, heading up the stairs.

Doc opened her bag. "I came prepared." She pulled out everything she needed to draw blood.

"You're married to a biker?" Sailor asked Doc.

"Yep."

"Which one?"

"He was one of the guys who rescued us," I said.

"Acid?" she asked.

"No. Boxer," I said. "One of the guys who…"

"Shot the bastards that took us," Sailor said, skin paling. "He's scary."

Doc patted her shoulder and gave her a smile. "I'll tell him you think so."

Chapter 39

"Sailor's showering. Doc said she'll stay with Sailor so you can get some sleep." Duke closed the door of Slash and Brooklyn's clubhouse room.

I nodded but didn't move from the edge of the bed.

Duke came further into the room and set some clothes next to me. "I brought you some of my stuff to change into."

I didn't reply. I didn't even act as though I'd heard him.

He took my hands and gently helped me stand, and then he was leading me to the bathroom. Duke released me and then turned on the shower.

"Hot," I said. "Make it really hot."

"Okay."

"*Scalding.*"

"Willa—"

"I have to scrub every last inch of my skin. I have to remove any trace of this night…of this horror."

With a nod, he turned back to the shower and fiddled with knobs until the water was so hot it began to steam up the room. I stripped out of my clothes, never wanting to see them again, and got into the shower.

Gritting my teeth, I let the water pour over me. I grabbed the soap and made a lather. I washed away the terror. I washed away the hopelessness. I washed away my inability to save all the women who were kidnapped daily, all over the world.

I washed away the tragedy of not knowing the name of the girl who'd died in the truck with us.

And when I finally felt like I'd tortured myself enough, I turned off the water. I slid back the curtain to find that Duke hadn't left the bathroom but was instead holding up a towel for me to dry off with.

I stepped out of the shower onto the fuzzy blue bath-mat, and he draped the towel around me. And then he hugged me to him.

"I'm getting you all wet," I murmured, even as I snuggled deeper into his arms.

"Doesn't matter," he rasped. "What matters is that you're safe."

"None of us are safe."

He sighed. "That's not true—"

"It's an illusion. They took me—"

"Yeah, but I rescued you. I'll *always* rescue you."

"What do we do now?" I asked.

"Right now, you let me take care of it and you try to let tonight go as best you can. Let's get some sleep."

"Sleep," I repeated. "Oh God, you haven't slept yet. You've been awake for—"

"Don't worry about it. I wouldn't have slept until I knew you were safe." He took my hand and led me to the bedroom. "And you *are* safe, Willa. I'll be back in a few minutes. I need to shower before I can crash."

"You could've showered with me."

"No. You needed that time for yourself," he said. He handed me a clean T-shirt and then I slipped into a pair of his sweats. I crawled beneath the covers and drifted off, only waking just a bit when he took me into his arms.

In his embrace, I slept.

The smell of coffee roused me from a sound sleep. Duke was sitting on the edge of the bed, watching me with bloodshot eyes, a mug in his hands.

"What time is it?" I asked, my voice hoarse.

"A little after nine," he said.

I stretched my legs out and groaned. My entire body felt like one massive bruise. I sat up and twisted my torso. "Why are you awake?"

"Prez called church."

"Now?"

He nodded and handed me the cup of coffee. "He asked that you come."

I raised my brows. "To *church*?"

"Yeah."

"But I thought only brothers attended church," I said, perplexed.

"Yeah, that's usually how it's done."

My gaze narrowed. "What's going on?"

"I'm not entirely sure," he admitted. "Waverly's here. You want to see her for a few minutes before we go?"

I nodded.

"All right. I'll send her to you."

He got off the bed and headed to the door. I tracked him with my eyes, my brow furrowed.

Why was I getting the feeling he could barely stand to look at me?

I set the coffee cup onto the nightstand and then climbed out of bed and went to the bathroom. I did my business and then brushed my teeth and washed my face in a hasty attempt to clean up.

"Willa?" Waverly called out.

"Be out in a second." I dabbed my mouth with a white hand towel and then went into the bedroom. I'd barely made it out of the bathroom before Waverly launched herself at me.

I hugged her, dipping my head and settling my cheek against her coconut smelling hair.

"Hey," I murmured.

"Hey," she mumbled.

I was about to make some snarky quip about her latching onto me, but she trembled in my arms and I bit my tongue.

After a few moments, she finally released me and stepped back. She plopped down onto the edge of the bed.

I reached for my cup of coffee, took a small sip to test the warmth, and then swallowed a gulp of the strong brew.

"Your engagement ring is missing," she said, biting her lower lip.

I nodded.

"I brought you a change of clothes." She picked up the blue duffel bag and set it on the bed.

"Thanks," I said, relieved. I wouldn't have to parade around in Duke's massive clothes for long. I wasn't sure where the clothes I'd worn yesterday had gone, but it didn't matter, because I was never going to wear them again.

"Duke told me a little bit of what happened."

"Told you *what* exactly?" I set my mug aside and then unzipped the bag.

"No specifics, just that they rescued you from a furniture truck that was taking you over the border."

I pulled out a pair of clean underwear and took off Duke's sweats. "Yeah, those are the broad strokes of it. Have you met Sailor yet?"

"Sailor? Who's Sailor?"

I had to sit down to pull on the yoga pants because I was so sore.

"Sailor's the girl who was in the truck with me," I explained. "She crashed here last night."

"No, I haven't met her yet."

"She's probably still sleeping," I said. "We didn't roll in until around four in the morning."

"Why are you even awake right now?"

"Colt called a meeting," I said slowly.

"Oh."

"Thanks for bringing me the clothes. That was thoughtful of you."

She nodded. "I didn't know if you had clothes here yet or not. Why aren't you in Duke's room? You're his Old Lady now…"

"Slash gave us his and Brooklyn's room for the night because of the private bathroom."

"Oh." She rubbed her forehead.

"I'm okay," I said quietly.

"Are you? I'm not sure I believe you."

"I'm still processing," I admitted. "But because of our mother, I'm pretty sure this'll just be another bad memory in a long line of bad memories I've had to put away and patch over."

"Do you ever wonder if one day you'll uncover something so dark that you won't be able to patch over it again?"

"No." My tone was firm. "Because I refuse to give the bad memories legs. They can't follow you around without legs."

"Maybe we should metaphorically douse them in kerosene and light them on fire."

"There's an idea." The air-conditioning was cranking to get ahead of the impeding heat and I was cold, so I grabbed the sweater Waverly had brought for me.

I picked up my coffee and the two of us headed into the main area of the clubhouse—which was full of people.

All the Old Ladies were there, including Joni, who sat in the recliner with Everett asleep in a sling.

"Willa," Mia greeted when she saw me. Conversation ceased and the room went quiet.

"You guys know," I said flatly. "About what happened?"

Darcy nodded and moved to embrace me. "So glad you're okay, doll."

"Thanks. And thank you so much for taking care of Waverly while I was…"

"Hey, that's what we do. We're family," Darcy said.

"You guys didn't have to come," I mumbled, feeling embarrassment coat my cheeks.

"Of course, we had to come," Rachel said.

"We didn't just come for you," Mia said. "Though, you're reason enough."

I frowned. "I don't understand—"

"Colt called church," Joni stated. "And asked all the Old Ladies to come."

"Everyone? What's going on?"

"Guess we'll find out soon, won't we," Allison said. Tank fisted his mother's blonde hair into his chubby hand and attempted to eat it. With a distracted smile, she gently removed her hair from her young son's clutch.

Doc came into the living room, not appearing as though she'd been awake late into the night. "Hey." She wrapped an arm around me and embraced me in a side hug.

"How'd she do?" I asked, gesturing with my chin to the stairs.

"Nightmares," Doc said with a shake of her head. "I didn't want to give her any sedatives because I don't know what's already in her system, but her vitals were all fine so there's nothing to worry about. She fell back asleep."

"Waverly, will you keep an eye on Sailor?" I asked, looking at my sister. "Maybe check on her every twenty minutes or so? See if she's awake."

Waverly nodded.

Brooklyn's cell phone trilled and she reached into her bag for it. "It's Jazz," she said before pressing a button. "Hey. Ah, wonderful. You guys are the best. Thanks. Yeah, see you in a bit." She hung up. "Jazz and Brielle said breakfast will be done in about twenty minutes and then they'll bring it over in the catering van."

"What would we do without you?" Joni called out.

"Live off slow-cooker meals," Brooklyn quipped. "Which there's no shame in, let me tell you."

"We better get out there," Mia said.

"Can I get a coffee refill before we go?" I asked.

"Hand me your cup," Brooklyn said. "I'm closest to the coffee pot."

The Old Ladies filed out of the living room, walked down the hallway, and headed to the back yard. Brooklyn and I brought up the rear.

Without a word, Brooklyn grabbed my hand and gave it a squeeze.

The brothers were already in the building they used for church. It was one large room with enough space for a table and chairs for meetings. It was also air conditioned.

The Old Ladies slid into empty seats next to their men. Rachel took the single chair next to Joni. There was a place for me between Savage and Duke. Duke placed his hand on my thigh and it comforted me instantly. Savage reached into a leather pocket on his cut and set down my engagement ring in front of me.

I raised my brows at him.

His grin was feral. "It was a pleasure getting this back for you."

"Do I wanna know?" I asked, taking the ring and sliding it back on my finger.

"Not even a little bit."

Colt sat at the head of the table and banged the gavel. He was brawny and lorded over the Tarnished Angels like a protective father. The murmur of conversations ceased and all attention turned to the president of the club.

"As you know, this is an unusual church meeting," he began. "But what I'm gonna talk about today affects every brother *and* every Old Lady." His gaze slid to me. "Willa. I can't tell you how sorry I am about what happened to you. I'm glad you're back home where you belong. I'm glad you're safe."

"Thank you," I whispered.

"I wish I could say this won't happen again," he went on. "But it *will* happen again. And again, and again. Waco has a problem, and it can't be ignored any longer. The Garcia cartel has set up a human trafficking ring in our own back yard. It's time to bring it down. It's time to clean house. Not just for the sake of our own, but for the community. Not everyone has been as lucky as Willa and Sailor—the other young woman with them…"

I thought of the girl that had been killed in the furniture truck. She was still nameless, her life snuffed out because someone had deemed her a commodity and she happened to be born beautiful.

"It's time to clean house," Colt repeated. "We're going to take out the Garcia cartel, completely. We'll need Mateo

Sanchez's help with muscle and firepower, but I can't even go to him with this until I know the club is on board. Because this thing we're about to do, this will bring violence to our front door. This will bring violence to our friends and families. If anyone here doesn't understand what's at stake, speak now, but understand this; a line has already been crossed. We've spilled cartel blood. There's no coming back from this without violence. My decision is to take it all the way, and I need your support to do it."

Colt looked at Rachel when he said, "This will bring death to us."

Rachel's mouth pursed.

Scarlett began to cry, which quickly set off a domino-like effect, triggering the other infants in the room to cry as well. Their mothers tried to comfort them, but to no avail.

"Take some time, think about it," Colt said. "We vote in an hour."

Chapter 40

THE GROUP WAS SOMBER as we left the shed. Duke and Savage exchanged a glance and then Duke guided me toward the picnic table.

"What do you think?" Savage asked me.

"I hate the idea of this happening to anyone else ever again," I said quietly. "I also hate the idea that people I love could get hurt or die."

"As far as I'm concerned, the vote is just a formality. We're already at war," Savage said.

I shoved against him, not liking what he'd said.

He wrapped his arm around me and hugged me. "You two talk. I'll give you some time."

Savage held out his fist to Duke who immediately bumped it. Savage released me and then headed inside, the screen door slamming behind him.

"War," I said quietly with a nod. "I vote for war. Even if... Even if it means I risk losing the people I love." My gritty eyes pricked with tears. "This can't keep happening. It just can't."

He placed his hands on my hips and brought me to him. "You're the bravest woman I know. And I'm honored you became my Old Lady. You honor me, Willa."

I pressed my cheek to his chest. And for a moment, we stood in the sunshine. And even though nothing was all right, everything was all right.

"Let's get some food," he mumbled against my hair.

"Five more minutes," I said.

His arms tightened around me. "Five more minutes."

The squeak of the screen door announced that we were no longer alone. "Food's here," Savage called.

"Be there in a bit," Duke said. "I'm holding my woman."

Eventually, we untangled. He took my hand in his and led me to the clubhouse. It was by no means boisterous, despite the number of people inside. It was as if the babies could sense the shift in mood and didn't even cry or fuss.

"Sit," Slash said to Brooklyn who was standing at the counter, making sure everyone had the food they wanted.

"I'll sit in a minute," she said.

"Sit now or I'm picking you up and making you sit," Slash said with a glare at her.

With a sigh, she took the plate he offered her and ambled over to the couch.

"The woman doesn't know how to rest," Slash grumbled.

"No rest for the wicked," Brooklyn called out to him.

Suddenly, he grinned and shot his wife a look full of heat.

"Anyone see Waverly?" I asked.

"Theater room with Sailor," Darcy said.

"Yeah?" I asked with a relieved smile.

"Fast friends," Darcy assured me.

I looked at Duke. "You mind if I go hang out with them?"

"Go for it," he said, loading his plate full of food.

Laughing, I pointed to the dish. "Seriously? That's all for you?"

"No. It's for you." He handed it to me.

I looked at the mountain of food.

"Let me feed you, okay?" he asked quietly.

Heart in my throat, all I could do was nod. I took plastic silverware and went downstairs into the theater room with the massive plate.

The girls were sitting on the floor. Sailor's back was to me and I couldn't see what had monopolized their attention.

"What are you guys doing?" I asked.

Sailor turned her head to look at me. "Playing cards."

"What game?" I asked.

"War," Waverly said absently.

I sat down on the couch. "Mind if I hang out with you guys for a little bit? There are a lot of people upstairs."

"Sure," Sailor said.

"How'd you sleep?" I asked her.

She shrugged. "Okay, considering." She shot a glance at Waverly who was reaching for her fork.

"Can Sailor stay over tonight?" Waverly asked.

"Oh, uh…"

"That's okay," Sailor hastened to say. "I can stay with my dad."

"You can't stay with your dad," Waverly stated. "You said he's out of town and won't be back for a few days."

Sailor bent her head. "I lied."

"Your dad isn't out of town?" Waverly asked.

Sailor shook her head. "He's home. Or I should say, he's in town. I just don't want to stay with him."

"Why not?"

"Waverly," I said. "Don't push her into talking."

"She's not pushing me into talking," Sailor protested. With a sigh, she announced to Waverly what she had told me in the truck, "My dad's a drunk."

"Enough said," Waverly responded. She looked at me, pleading with her eyes.

We didn't have the space, and everything was a cluster-fuck as it was. I didn't even have legal guardianship of my sister yet. Nothing was settled. But like hell I was going to let Sailor go home to a place with a parent who didn't even care that she'd gone missing.

"You call your dad?" I asked. "To tell him what happened?"

"I left a message last night—this morning, whatever. Doc let me use her phone and gave me the number for him to call back. He hasn't called yet."

"Some people really don't deserve to have children," I said before I could stop myself.

Sailor blinked, her eyes wide, but she nodded in agreement.

"You're welcome to stay with us as long as you need," I said. "Okay?"

"Okay," she whispered.

I'd figure out logistics later, with Duke's help.

The heavy thudding of boots trekking down the stairs alerted me that we had a visitor. "Colt's calling for us," Duke said.

Nodding, I stood up, taking my full plate of food with me.

"You didn't eat," he admonished as he followed me up the stairs.

"No. I was getting some things sorted."

"What things?" he asked as we made it to the first floor.

The living room had cleared out again, so we were alone. I set my plate on the counter.

"Stuff with Sailor," I said.

He peered at me for a moment. "You'll tell me more about it after church?"

I nodded.

"Okay, let's go."

He took my hand and we headed to the shed once again. Everyone was already there and I quickly sat down next to Savage so we could get on with the vote.

"All right. Let's vote," Colt said without preamble. "I vote aye. Mia?"

She let out an exhale and nodded. "Aye."

"Zip?"

"Aye," the VP of the Tarnished Angels replied.

Round the table we went. When it was Doc's turn to vote, she didn't say anything for a long moment. She was staring at Rachel, and Rachel was staring at her.

"Doc?" Boxer pressed.

"Nay," Doc murmured. She cleared her throat and said again, louder. "I vote nay."

"What the fuck, Linden?" Boxer lashed. "We talked about this. You were going to vote yes. Prez, she votes aye."

"Doc?" Colt pressed.

"I vote nay." She straightened her spine and met Boxer's gaze. "Nay, Boxer."

"You? Of all the people at this table, you know what these people can—"

"Yes," she agreed. "I know." She reached out and cradled his jaw with her scarred hand. "I *know*. I know more than anyone what war with the cartel will mean."

They stared at one another so intensely, it was as if they were entirely alone. They had a silent conversation with their eyes, until finally Boxer nodded. He turned his head ever so slightly and kissed her palm. "Doc votes nay."

The ayes swept the rest of the table; even Rachel voted aye.

Doc was the only one against.

"The aye's have it," Colt said, his expression grim. "We go to war."

The brothers beat and smacked the table.

Colt went on, "I'll speak with Mateo Sanchez, but we also need more Tarnished Angels. The Coeur d'Alene boys don't have enough men to spare."

Zip rubbed his jaw. "Spearfish has some brothers. Viper's getting out of the joint in a few weeks. He's probably itching for a fight."

"He's been locked up in the pen for five years." Gray said. "He's been doing nothing *but* fighting."

"Spearfish?" I whispered to Duke.

"South Dakota," he clarified. "There used to be a big chapter there, but it fell apart when their president died a while back. There's a few brothers still there, but they're lost right now. Kind of like Nomads—like Slash."

I nodded.

"Yeah, I'll make a call," Colt said. "Four or five extra guys would definitely help. And as the brothers and I have discussed recently, we've decided to patch in Crow and South Paw, effective immediately. We'll need new prospects." He banged the gavel and rose from the table. He took Scarlett from Mia and cradled her in his big arms.

"You want to tell me what you need to tell me?" Duke asked me.

I nodded and gestured to the door. We headed outside and I walked to the edge of the fence, far enough away so that we couldn't be overheard.

"Sailor might as well be alone in this world, for all her dad cares about her," I said.

"Yeah." He nodded. "He sounds like a real piece of shit."

"Pretty much. I told her she could stay with us, as long as she needed. Just kind of a safe place, you know? I know we don't have a lot of space right now in Mia's rental, but it doesn't matter, Duke. She needs people. She reminds me so much of—"

He placed a finger against my lips. "You don't have to convince me of anything. I'm good with it."

I kissed his finger and then grasped it in my hand. "You are?"

"Yeah." He smiled. His phone trilled in his pocket and he quickly fished it out to answer it. He put it to his ear. "Hello?" He paused for a second and then his smile widened. "Great. Yeah, I'll tell her. Thanks."

He hung up and put his phone back in his pocket.

"Who was that?"

"The realtor. It's official. We close in a few weeks."

"Really?" I blinked, feeling tears blooming in my eyes. "It's really happening?"

"Yes."

"Duke." I launched myself at him. He picked me up and swung me around.

He eventually put me down, but he didn't release me. He buried his face in the crook of my neck and said, "I'll make this go away for you, Willa."

"Make what go away for me?" I cradled the back of his head with one hand, threading my fingers through his brown locks.

"The horror of the last few days."

I gently tugged on his hair, forcing him to look at me. I

brushed my thumb along his cheek, the roughness of his stubble tingling my skin.

"You came for me, Duke," I said, my eyes earnest. "That's what I'll remember first. That's what I'll remember if it ever gets dark. You came for me."

"I'll always come for you. Always."

Chapter 41

"Sailor," Doc said, holding out her cell. "It's your father."

Sailor glanced at the phone for a moment and then took it and put it to her ear. "Hello? Hi, Dad. I'm—"

She turned and left the living room, heading out back for some measure of privacy. She returned not five minutes later, her eyes desolate as she handed Doc her phone.

"Ready to get out of here?" I asked. I didn't know the specifics of the conversation she'd had with her father—but I could guess.

She nodded but didn't meet my gaze.

Sailor, Waverly, and I left the clubhouse in my car—which had been retrieved from the junk yard by Crow.

I knew how Sailor felt. No matter what I did, my mother spared me very little attention. When Waverly came along, I thought at least the new baby would get the love and care she deserved. Nope. Angel ignored us both. Without love and attention from my own mother, I instinctively lavished it on Waverly, not only to care for her, but to receive love back. I saw her first smile, her first laugh. Her first word had been an attempt to say my name. Moments my mother could never appreciate belonged solely to me, and all I had to do was love Waverly. The fact was, my sister filled the gaping hole in my heart that my mother had left behind.

I turned in the opposite direction of the house.

"Where are we going?" Waverly asked.

"We're stopping at the store," I explained, looking in my rearview mirror to see Duke and Savage trailing me on their motorcycles. They weren't going to let me out of their sight for a good long while, if ever again. At the moment, I didn't mind. I needed to feel safe. Protected. Cared for.

Sailor didn't appear as though she'd heard me. She was staring out the window, lost in thought.

"Are you a chocolate person, Sailor?" I asked.

"Hmm?" She finally looked at me, meeting my gaze in the rearview mirror. "What did you say?"

"I asked if you were a chocolate person."

"Yeah."

"What about ice cream?" I added. "Cookies?"

"It's all good with me," she said, listless. She looked out the window again.

I glanced at Waverly. "I know it's a school night, but why don't you call Jessica? Ask if she wants to spend the night."

"Spend the night where?" Waverly asked.

"Our place, of course."

"Our place? Our place can barely hold the two of us and all our crap," she said.

"You three will take the fairy fort. Duke and I will sleep on an air-mattress in the office."

"You sure?" she asked.

"I'm sure," I said.

"What's the fairy fort?" Sailor asked.

Waverly smiled even before she began to speak. "When

I was little, Willa made us a fort out of chairs, sheets, and twinkle lights. When we moved to our new place a few weeks ago she made another one in our bedroom. You'll see. It's kind of ridiculous, but it's fun."

"Don't let her tone fool you," I said to Sailor. "She still believes in fairies and magic."

"I don't need fairies and magic," Waverly protested, looking at me. "Why would I need any of that when I have you?"

I reached over and took her hand. She gave mine a squeeze before letting go.

"I'm jealous of you guys," Sailor said. "I wish my dad…was a better dad."

"Yeah." Waverly sighed. "Your dad…wow."

"You're not mad at your mom? For leaving?" Sailor asked.

"I used to be," Waverly said slowly. "And then I realized something…"

"What's that?"

"Every time she was around, it was harder. She's like this giant vortex of need and desperation. She needs to be loved constantly, and searches in all the wrong people for it. The whole time she had two daughters who loved her no matter what, but she couldn't see it. I loved her even if she forgot to pay the electric bill, or forgot to go shopping so we got stuck eating baked beans out of a can. I didn't care about any of that because she was *there*, and she was our mom. For years I let her off the hook…but somewhere along the way, I just stopped being disappointed when she fucked up because I realized she couldn't help it. She did the best she could. Was it enough? No. But she's my mother, and I love her, even if I know that we're better off without her in our lives."

"You realized all that?" Sailor asked. "Wow."

"Yeah, wow," I repeated. "I wish I'd gotten Zen about it sooner. Would've made life easier." I pulled into a parking spot and cut the engine.

"It's different for you, Willa. You had to take on Mom's responsibilities even though you weren't supposed to be a parent yet. I needed looking after, and you did it. This is a textbook case of child abandonment by an incapable parent and one of the siblings rising to the occasion and raising the younger child."

"Textbook case?" I repeated.

Waverly nodded. "It's in a psych book I'm reading."

"Your school teaches psychology?" Sailor asked.

"Nope. I'm reading this on my own. I'm dropping out of school, actually."

"*You're dropping out?*" Sailor asked with her mouth agape. "Oh God, I'd *love* to drop out of school!"

"She's not dropping out." I rolled my eyes. "We're going to home school and she's going to get a GED as soon as I become her legal guardian."

"That's *so* cool," Sailor said.

Duke and Savage pulled their bikes into the spots next to my car.

"We didn't plan on a detour, babe," Duke said as I got out. "What's up?"

"Can't have a girls' night without obscene amounts of sugar."

"I got this," Savage said, walking with Waverly and Sailor toward the grocery store entrance.

When they were far enough away, I turned to Duke and said, "It's weird, you know?"

"What is?"

"How the world keeps turning whether or not you're a part of it. People drive down the road going to work; their lives are completely the same regardless of what happened to you…and then you try to do something normal like go to a grocery store, and for just a moment you forget you were held in the back of a furniture truck bound for Mexico, never to be seen again. Is it okay to forget, Duke? Is it okay to block it out entirely? To pretend like it never happened?"

"You could," he said. "But you won't."

I sighed. "No, I won't. And if I won't, then what does that mean for Sailor? She doesn't have anyone to work through this with. She's completely alone at sixteen. I care, but I don't know what to *do* about it. I want to help, I want to be more, I want to do more, but what?"

"You are helping," he said. "You're taking care of your sister. You're being there for Sailor."

"It's only going to get more dangerous, isn't it? I mean, this thing with the cartel heating up. When it finally goes hot, it's going to be horrible, isn't it?"

"That won't happen for a bit. At least on our end. There are things that need to be discussed, people need to be called, plans made. The cartel knows by now their guys are gone, but it's going to take them a little while to react. But when they do…fuck, Willa."

"Is Sailor going to be safer if she distances herself from us?" I asked baldly.

"If I said yes, what does that mean for Waverly? For Silas? Cam? Lily? The babies?" He shook his head. "It's shit either way. But if she's with us, we can protect her. She won't be alone. She won't be as vulnerable. And there's another thing…we don't know if Sailor was watched before they took her and they know who she is, or if it was random based on her appearance and she was just in the wrong place at the wrong time. With us, at least no one can get to her."

"I'd never forgive myself if something happened to her."

"You can't control everything."

"But I *want* to." I sucked in a breath of air. "I know what I voted for. I know I said yes to something horrible. But it's the only choice I *could* make… Duke, how much blood is going to be spilled? Really?"

"We can't know," he said quietly. "And blood is being spilled anyway. Innocent blood. Blood from people that were born and raised in captivity who don't even have birth certificates so that when they die no one asks questions because no one even knows they exist."

"*Oh my God*, seriously?"

"Seriously. And it's so much worse." He took a step closer. "Willa…" He cradled my cheeks in his hands. "There are women who've been put into breeding mills like animals. You don't even want to know what they do with the children born in those conditions. I can't discuss it all with you, but I will say this: when the club found out about what was really going on we decided we had to do something. The cartel snatching you was the final straw. We can't wait any longer. The things they're doing…"

My eyes widened.

"If you knew the true horrors…your entire world would change."

"Why did you tell me?" I whispered.

"Because you're strong enough to hear it. Because that's what we saved you and Sailor from. There's dark shit in this world, Willa. Maybe I was put on this earth to help get rid of some of it. There's dark shit, but there's light too. The Tarnished Angels *are* that light."

"I don't understand…" I said. "Why is the club dealing with this? What about the police? I mean this is insane… what about the military?"

"The things we have to do aren't even remotely legal. There's no law enforcement agency in the world that can do what needs doing. Besides, a lot of those guys are already on the cartel's payroll and the military isn't allowed to operate on American soil. The club is a tight-knit community. It's why we put the guys through hell waiting to patch in. By the time someone becomes a brother, we know exactly who they are and what they're capable of. The club is the only thing that can protect Waco."

I looked down at the grease-stained asphalt of the parking lot. "I didn't mean to have this kind of conversation out in the open like this."

"Doesn't matter where we have it. It doesn't change the truth of it. The world isn't the pretty little lie they've sold you."

I nodded slowly. "Yeah. You're right about that."

Duke took me into his arms. I buried my face in his shoulder and said, "I'm just one person. Trying to change the world is a heavy endeavor—too much for one person. But I can change Sailor's world."

"We," he corrected. "We can change Sailor's world."

I pulled back to look at him. I didn't even need to say anything, we spoke without words, a language we knew by heart because we'd known each other so long.

I could hear Sailor and Waverly's chatter across the near empty parking lot. Savage stood near them, shooting them looks and rolling his eyes.

Duke didn't drop his arms from around me and I didn't move away.

Sailor came to a stop and wrinkled her nose at us. "Are you guys always like this?"

"Like what?" I asked in amusement.

"In love and stuff," Sailor said.

"Worse," Savage mocked. "They're *much* worse. Right, Waverly?"

"Right-o," Waverly agreed with a nod. "If this pint of ice cream doesn't make me puke, they sure will. But Duke makes my sister happy, so I'll allow it."

~

After we got home and the groceries were organized in the fridge, Duke looked at Savage and said, "I've got to take care of something. You in?"

"Yup." Savage looped an arm around Waverly's shoulder. "Later, Little Punk."

"Get off me, delinquent." She zipped out from underneath his arm, grabbed Sailor's hand, and dragged her toward the bedroom.

"What thing do you have to take care of?" I asked as Duke grasped my hip.

"A thing." He shrugged and then kissed my lips. "Don't worry about it. You're staying here, right? You're not going anywhere?"

I frowned. "No. I'm not going anywhere. Why?"

"I just want to make sure you're safe," he said gruffly. "You're safe if you stay here."

"I'm not going anywhere," I promised.

He kissed me one final time before pulling away.

"And I like you both as friends, so I'm just going to hug you instead of letting you suck on my tongue," Savage said, embracing me.

"You're such a class act," I said as I squeezed him tight.

I made sure the door was locked and then I leaned against it.

"You were right, the fairy fort is ridiculously cool. Even

though we're totally too old for it," Sailor said as she and Waverly came back into the living room.

"Totally too old for it." Waverly shot me a look and winked.

"You guys don't have a couch," Sailor remarked.

"We'll get a new one when we move into the house," I said in way of explanation. "The closing is official. It's ours."

"Oh, fuck yes!" Waverly yelled.

"Waverly," I said with a sigh. "The cursing, seriously?"

"That's okay, I have a sailor mouth," Sailor quipped. "Get it, because my name is Sailor?"

"Yeah, it's not funny if you have to explain it," Waverly teased.

"It's still funny," Sailor assured her.

I shook my head at their easy comradery. "You guys dive into the chocolate. I'm blowing up the air mattress and taking a nap. Only wake me if the house is on fire."

Chapter 42

THE SOUND of the front door shutting was enough to rouse me from my nap. I didn't move my body, instead only turning my head slightly.

Savage only had one decibel, and it was loud.

I reluctantly sat up and took a moment to get my bearings. I wondered how long I'd slept for, but I hadn't taken my phone to bed with me and didn't know the time.

"Sleeping Beauty," Savage greeted when I popped into the living room.

"Not so beautiful," Waverly teased. She touched the corner of her mouth and inclined her head to indicate she was referencing mine. "Drool."

"Shut up," I grumbled, hastily turning and stumbling to the bathroom. As I was splashing cool water on my face, there was a knock on the door.

"It's me," Duke said.

"Come in." I snatched the hand towel from the rack and dabbed my face.

Duke opened the door and came in, despite the small bathroom.

"I can't wait to move into the new house," I said. "We need the room."

"Can you hold out for two weeks?" he asked, cradling my jaw.

I tilted my head up toward his. "Two weeks? What happens in two weeks?"

"We officially close and get the keys."

I smiled. "I can wait. It'll be tight for a bit, but we've done worse. *A lot* worse."

He left the bathroom first and I trailed after him. Sailor and Waverly were still sitting at the kitchen table while Savage stood by. It was awkward in the house without a couch. They'd blown up the other air mattress and set it in front of the TV.

"Hey, Sailor," Duke said, reaching into his pocket and pulling out a cell phone. "Think fast." He tossed it at her and she caught it.

"What's this?" she asked in confusion.

"A cell phone. Obviously," Duke said lightly.

"Yeah, but why are you giving it to me?" Her brow was marred, and she turned the phone over.

"Family plan, kid." Duke looked at me and winked, and then glanced back toward Sailor. "We put you on it."

"Oh." Her voice sounded thick. "I—uhm—are you sure?" She peered at me when she asked the question.

I swallowed my own emotion. Duke had blindsided me with this—in the best possible way. "Yeah, Sailor. We're sure."

"We paid your dad a visit," Savage announced. "Told him you were going to be spending a lot of time over here with Waverly. We said we'd make sure you got to school and everything. But if you want to get your clothes, I'll take you over there to pack."

"I'll help," Waverly said, jumping up. "Give me your phone."

Sailor handed it over. Waverly quickly typed a few things and then handed it back to her. "I put my number in your favorites."

"Thanks," Sailor croaked. She cleared her throat. "Yeah, I'd love to get my stuff."

"We can swing by Jessica's to pick her up," Savage suggested. "And you can show Sailor your furniture."

"Good idea!" Waverly said in excitement. "You'll love Jess. She's a rebel, too."

The two of them headed to the front door.

"How are you getting to her dad's place?" I asked. "You need my keys to take her?"

"Nah." Savage shook his head. "Acid's coming. He's borrowing Joni's SUV."

"Acid's coming?" Sailor whispered to Waverly.

Waverly shrugged.

I looked at Duke. "We're going to need a few more vehicles if we're going to have two driving teenagers."

He rubbed his jaw. "Yeah, it's looking that way."

"While we're putting in for things we want, I'd like a pony," Savage quipped.

"How about a spare room at the new house," I drawled. "We'll get the horse later."

Savage's levity vanished. "You're offering me a room? In your new home?"

"Our home," I corrected, stepping toward Duke and wrapping an arm around his waist and nuzzling into him. "You didn't think we'd have a house and not have a room for you, did you?"

Savage looked at Duke. Duke nodded. "Yeah, you idiot. You're family. Nothing's changed."

"Everything's changed," Savage protested.

"Not this," I said. "Not us. Never us."

Savage marched over and embraced us. "You guys, I don't even know what to say."

"There's a first," Duke quipped.

~

"It's oddly quiet in here without them," I said opening the fridge and pulling out a beer. I handed one to Duke and he took it. "I don't think I like the quiet that much. Gives you too much time to think."

He cracked open the beer and took a sip. "You need something to get into your head and blow out all the thoughts swirling up there. A couple of hundred miles on the back of my bike, the wind on your face, the sun at your back, you'll be thinking clearly in no time."

I nodded and took a drink. The light glinted off my engagement ring. The engagement ring that suddenly felt wrong on my finger.

Anxiety spilled through my chest, circled through my veins, pumped through my heart, and filled every crevice of my body.

I hastily set the bottle of beer down but missed the edge of the counter and it hit the floor, spilling immediately. But I didn't care, I was too busy clawing at my finger trying to get the ring off.

"Willa," Duke called. "Willa, hey."

"*Off*," I gasped. "I need this off…"

I nearly ripped the ring from my finger and then I sank to the floor. I pressed against the cabinets and set my forehead on my knees, trying to breathe air into my lungs.

Nothing was working. I couldn't make sense of my thoughts. My insides were ready to burst out of my skin, like they wanted to run far away and seek shelter.

"Willa. Look at me."

I forced my knees from my chest and peered at him. Duke had sat down in front of me, and he'd stretched his legs out enough that even though they were still bent, they were on either side of my body, like he was caging me in.

Protecting me.

He reached out and gently grasped my throat, stroking a thumb along the column of my neck. He took my hand and put it on his heart and covered it with his own.

"Breathe with me. Yeah, like that."

There was only a bit of pressure around my neck from his fingers. I focused on the feel of them, the sensation of his skin on mine.

His eyes were dark as they focused on me.

"There you are," he said faintly.

"Here I am," I whispered.

Duke released my throat.

"I think I had a panic attack," I said without any trace of emotion, like I was casually making an observation from outside my body.

"Yeah, I think you did. So, you don't want to marry me after all…"

I frowned. "What? What do you mean?"

He gestured with his chin to the diamond ring on the floor next to me.

"Oh. *No.* That's not it at all."

"No?"

I shook my head. "It's—I looked at it, and immediately remembered that it had been taken from me, and only returned because Savage found it on one of the creeps who kidnapped me."

Duke's expression softened. "And now you see it and remember."

I reached out and cradled his cheek. "I want to marry you. But please don't ask me to wear that ring again."

"Your ring, your choice. You want a different ring? I'll get you a different ring. Whatever you want."

I dropped my hand from his face and scooted closer. I pressed my face to the crook of his neck. "Only you, Duke. I've only ever wanted you."

He held me close, running one of his hands up and down my back.

"I can't believe seeing my beautiful engagement ring is what sent me over the deep end. I stupidly thought…"

"What?"

"That I was strong enough to process everything that happened to me. I didn't realize I'd break down."

"You just went through something that no one should ever have to live through."

"I'm alive," I pointed out. "Sailor's alive. The other girl…" I let out a sigh. "Any idea who she is?"

"Not yet. It's all over the media, but they're not sharing her info yet," he said.

"Can you imagine?" I asked quietly. "You're a mother or a father, and your daughter goes missing…and you have no idea what happened to her. So, you imagine the worst, but you don't get any closure. That would tear me up inside."

"Her family will get closure, eventually," he said. "They have her body. She didn't just disappear."

"Sometimes you don't get your happy ending."

"Sometimes you do."

"Sometimes you do," I agreed.

We were silent for a long moment and then Duke said, "Shit's going to be crazy in the next few weeks. I won't have a lot of free time and I won't be able to leave town unless it's for club business."

"Okay?"

"Prez gave me a few days off," he said. "So we can have a quick honeymoon."

"I don't need a honeymoon."

"Willa," he said, gently maneuvering me so I was forced to look at him. "Why do you do that?"

"Do what?"

"Not expect anything more than the bare minimum?"

"It's not the bare minimum. You just said things with the club and the cartel are going to heat up. I get that you have to be in town. I don't want to make it harder on you than it already is. That's all."

"I'm taking you on a honeymoon," he commanded. "And you're going to enjoy it."

"I'm going to enjoy it?" I asked with a raise of my brows.

"Damn right you're going to enjoy it. We'll be naked most of the time. Why wouldn't you enjoy it?"

I smiled. "Where are we going on this quick honeymoon?"

"It's a surprise. Don't worry about anything. I've got it figured out."

I let out a sigh and snuggled up against him again. "It's nice, you know? Letting someone else do the figuring."

"I've got you," he whispered.

"I know."

Chapter 43

"Where's your ring?" Brielle asked.

"It's a little loose," I lied. "I didn't want to lose it so I took it off."

"Oh." She wiggled her toes in the scented foot bath.

Jazz leaned back in her spa chair and closed her eyes. "I'm glad you let Brooklyn convince you to get pampered for your non-wedding wedding."

"It's very low key," I said with a glance at Brooklyn who was peering at me with an expression I couldn't discern.

"I don't know what's with you Old Ladies," Jazz quipped. "Such chill weddings."

"My wedding is going to be an all-weekend shindig where people go home fucking wrecked," Brielle said. "And reeking of booze."

"And sore feet from all the Irish dancing," Jazz said, finally opening her eyes.

Two spa attendants came and announced that it was time for Jazz and Brielle's massages. The two of them dried off their feet, slipped into spa slippers, and trekked after the attendants.

"What's the real reason you're not wearing your ring?" Brooklyn asked once we were alone.

I sighed. "Can't hide anything from you, can I?"

She shook her head.

"It reminds me of what happened…and I just…I can't have it on."

"Yeah." She rubbed her own wedding ring. "I get that."

I glanced in the direction Jazz and Brielle had gone. "It's weird. They don't know what I went through. And I can never tell them."

"The curse of being an Old Lady." She smiled sadly. "There are more good things about it than not, but yeah, not being able to share openly with people who aren't in the club…that's hard."

"I just don't want to feel like I'm lying to them," I said.

"The thing about Jazz and Brielle," she said, "is that they *know* there are things I can't share with them. So, they don't ask anymore. Or if they do ask, I just say it's club business and they immediately back off. It's not ideal, but it's better than outright lying to them."

I nodded thoughtfully and gently swirled my soaking feet in the warm foot bath water. "You voted yes. For war."

"I did."

I glanced at her swollen belly where her hand rested protectively on top of it. "Are you scared?"

"Scared? Of what?"

"Losing Slash. Your child growing up without a father."

"Of course, I'm scared, but how could I vote any other way? How could I look myself in the mirror and say I chose fear and hiding over attempting to make the world a better place? Will the club succeed? I don't know. It's the cartel. They don't just back down. They don't just go away. They're ruthless in a way that people don't understand. They make examples of their enemies… But what happened to you, what happened to Sailor—what happened to that poor girl whose name we still don't know…there's doing what's right and doing what's easy. They aren't usually the same thing." She tilted her chin. "Are you re-thinking being with Duke?"

"What? No! Not even a little bit. There is no me without Duke. My life would be…empty."

"And kids?" she pressed. "What about them? Do you still want them?"

I paused for a moment and then nodded. "Yeah, I really do. Even with all this—I still want them. Does that make me terrible or selfish for wanting to bring someone into a dangerous world?"

"Does it make me terrible that I stayed with Slash even though I knew he was a biker and that his life was dangerous?"

"I guess the world is a dangerous place for all of us, and we just have to know that. I don't want to live in fear, Brooklyn. But I don't want to be stupid, either."

"That's a fine line," she quipped. "But if you love Duke and he loves you back, and you're willing to be with him to the end, then that means living with whatever life throws at you. Only you can decide what that means or if it's worth it."

"I guess I was just hoping for a few moments of peace, you know? Some sort of calm, some sort of stability."

"You live in a biker's world now." She smiled. "It's rarely calm. But damn if it isn't exciting."

∾

It was a strange existence. Knowing that marrying Duke was what I wanted, but also being plagued by an immeasurable amount of anxiety at the same time. Not about our marriage or relationship, or even the kids we were going to have. It was a more generalized anxiety about the situation as a whole.

Everything was right, everything was perfect...

But I'd learned throughout my life that perfection never lasted.

Jazz and Brielle's hushed laughter pulled me from my thoughts. I envied them. Their innocence, their naiveté. Their ability to laugh and be carefree despite the darkness in the world—darkness I'd witnessed first-hand. I looked at them and realized that what the club was about to do was for them, too. Waco would be safer for my friends because of the club.

Brooklyn was in the bathroom, and the three of us were waiting for our toenails to dry. I suddenly realized that we were in a private room in the spa and that the door was closed.

We were alone.

Unprotected.

I forced myself to take a deep breath. And another. But it didn't help. At any moment, cartel men could storm into the room, snatch the three of us, and cart us off just like they'd done with—

My heart squeezed in my chest and my throat constricted. I struggled to get air into my lungs.

"Willa?" Jazz asked. "Willa!"

Brielle hopped out of her salon recliner and rushed to my side. "Willa, what is it?"

"Panic...attack," I wheezed.

"Panic attack." Brielle peered at Jazz. "I don't know what to do. She looks like she's gonna pass out."

"Willa," Jazz said in a calm tone. "What color are the walls?"

Brielle shot Jazz a glance, but Jazz kept her eyes on me.

"Walls?" I gasped.

"Yes, what color are the walls?"

"C—c—cream," I squeezed out.

"Good." Jazz nodded. "What do you smell?"

"L—lavender," I said. "Tea tree oil…from the massage lotion."

"Yes. What do you hear?"

"Music—something Enya-like, without being annoying."

The door to the private room opened and Brooklyn entered, tying the sash at her waist. She looked at me and then to Jazz. "What's going on?"

"I had a panic attack," I said. "And Jazz calmed me down."

"Jazz distracted her," Brielle explained. "Kind of genius. I had no idea what to do."

"We do it with my mother," Jazz said. "When she's having an episode and she needs to be grounded."

"Oh," I said in understanding.

"So, you have panic attacks," Brielle said slowly. "Is that—is this new? I mean, we've hung out a bunch and you've never…before, I mean."

I glanced at Brooklyn.

Brooklyn's expression hardened.

"What's going on?" Brielle demanded. "This isn't—are you having second thoughts about marrying Duke?"

I shook my head no.

"Then what is it?" Jazz asked. "Because if you're not panicking at the thought of marrying him, then what is this about?"

"Club business," Brooklyn finally said.

Jazz raised her brows. "Club business?" Her gaze bounced between me and Brooklyn. "Our friend is having panic attacks, and you think saying *club business* will make me drop the issue this time?"

"Does Doc know about your panic attacks?" Brielle asked.

"No one knows. Well, you three. And Duke. I had one in front of him a couple of days ago." I leaned back in my spa chair and sent another look to Brooklyn.

"Okay, stop doing that," Brielle commanded, her blue eyes narrowing in annoyance. "You guys are having a conversation without including me and I really don't like it."

"You and Jazz do it all the time," Brooklyn pointed out.

"Let's not get sidetracked," Jazz stated.

"I can't tell you," I said quietly. "I'm sorry. It's for your own safety. Please just let this go."

Jazz raked a hand through her dark hair. "I don't like this...but okay."

"I know you're mad at me," I said. "For not being able to tell you everything."

"Goes with the territory, I guess," Brielle said, wrinkling her nose. "I just want to know you're okay."

"I'm okay," I said.

"Are you lying?" Jazz demanded.

"I'm okay," I repeated, reaching out to grasp her hand. "And getting better every day. All right?"

Brielle took my other hand and gave it a squeeze. "All right."

There was a knock on the door and a moment later an attendant walked in, carrying a garment bag.

"What's that?" I asked her.

She smiled. "Phase two."

Chapter 44

Two HOURS later I was wearing a wedding dress I'd borrowed from Joni. It fit me perfectly, and I smoothed a hand down the skirt as I was being escorted to the limousine outside the spa. The driver opened the door for me and waited for me to climb in.

Brooklyn, Jazz, and Brielle smiled as they watched me get in.

"Where am I going?" I asked them.

"It's a surprise," Brooklyn said.

"My sister?" I pressed. "I can't get married without my sister."

"You won't get married without your sister," Brooklyn assured me.

"Savage?" I added.

"Not him either," Brielle said. "Trust us. Enjoy the limousine ride, and everything that comes after it."

"She means, please have sex in the limo after the ceremony," Jazz quipped.

The driver looked at her and lifted his brows.

"Oh please, don't be a prude." Jazz rolled her eyes. "Just raise the partition."

I'd never been inside a limousine, even though I'd gone to school with kids who rented them for prom. I wasn't from that side of the tracks, and it showed. As I slid across the smooth leather, I thought of my prom night. Savage, Duke and I had scored some beers and had drunk them after sneaking through the barricade to the top of the town water tower.

"There's a bottle of champagne pre-chilled for you," the driver said after he'd climbed into his seat, ready to drive us away.

"Thank you," I murmured. "Will you tell me where we're going?"

"As your friend said, it's a surprise."

I reached for my purse and found my cell phone. I called Duke, who answered immediately.

"Hey."

"Hey?" I repeated. "That's how you greet me on my wedding day?"

"It's Willa," Duke said to someone. "And she's pissed."

"I'm not pissed," I snapped. "I'm confused and I don't like to be surprised with an impromptu wedding."

The partition between me and the driver began to rise, the sound of an electric motor filling the cabin.

With a sigh, I tried to check my attitude.

"It's not impromptu, whatever the fuck that means," Duke said.

"It means without planning," came a female voice in the background.

"Is that my sister?" I demanded.

"Yeah, that's Waverly," Duke said. "You want to talk to her?"

"Yes."

A moment later, Waverly came on the line. "Hello?"

"Don't *hello* me. What's going on?"

"You're getting married."

"Yeah, I got that much."

"We're all waiting for you. We took care of everything. Try and relax."

"It was thoughtful of you guys," I said softly, "but *I* wanted to plan my own wedding. It would have been nice to be involved."

"I'm sorry." Waverly sounded contrite. "But I wanted to make sure you had a beautiful wedding and you weren't just slapping shit together in order to make it legal. You never do anything nice for yourself, so we took it upon ourselves to make it nice for you."

I sighed. "Will you put Duke back on the phone?"

"Sure."

"And Waverly…"

"Huh?"

"Thanks."

"No sweat. Drink the champagne, unless you're pregnant, then don't."

"I'm not pregnant," I protested.

"You sure? You're kind of ornery. It would make sense if you were pregnant."

"I could just be a bitch. You ever think of that?"

"I did, briefly, but my guess still stands."

"*I'm not pregnant!*"

"Is Willa pregnant?" came Savage's voice on the other end.

"Am I on speaker phone?" I demanded.

"Yes," Waverly said.

"I'm not pregnant," I insisted.

"Too bad," Savage muttered. "Get busy on my namesake."

"What makes you think Duke and Willa are going to name their kid after you?" Waverly asked.

"We have a deal," Savage said.

"You two, go fight over there," Duke said. "And let me talk to my woman in peace."

"Peace? What peace? Sounds like she's ready to cut your balls off right now," Savage quipped.

"Go away," Duke commanded.

"Is that any way to talk to your best man?" Savage demanded.

"Go," Duke barked. After a moment he said, "We're alone now, I promise. And I took you off speaker. Are you really pissed about this? The truth, Willa."

"No," I said quietly. "I'm not pissed. I'm… You know I want to marry you. That's not what this is. It's—shit, Duke. I know you can't control every aspect of your life, and normally, I don't even try to. It's just…"

"You were kidnapped and now you don't ever want to be out of the loop or out of control ever again."

I exhaled. "How did you—Jesus, Duke. You hit the nail on the head, more than I could even put into words."

"All you have to do is marry me. Everything else we can figure out."

"What's there to figure out?" I demanded. "I want you, you want me." I paused. "I had another panic attack. In front of the girls this time."

"You did." It was a statement, not a question.

"I didn't tell them anything. I know I can't. For their safety as well as the club's."

"Sorry you have to shoulder that burden, Willa."

"Will you do me a favor?" I asked him.

"Yeah."

"Clue me in next time you want to change our lives," I joked. "So I can prepare for it."

"You don't always get time to prepare, babe."

"When it comes to weddings and buying houses? Yeah, those are the types of things I want to be privy to before you pull the trigger."

"We bought the house, and we're about to get married. What other thing can I even do that might send your world for a spin?"

"I'm not sure. When I figure it out, I'll let you know."

We hung up and my annoyance had completely vanished. I leaned forward and knocked on the closed partition. A moment later, it slid down to reveal the driver's profile.

"Ma'am?"

"What's your name?" I asked.

"Al."

"Al. Nice to meet you. I'm Willa."

"Nice to meet you," he said.

"You're still not going to tell me where I'm going, are you?"

"Correct."

I sighed. "Figures."

"I *can* tell you that you're going to love it, though."

"You're just saying that because it's your job."

He smiled at my disgruntled expression. "Word of advice? Sit back, relax, and have a glass of champagne. We'll be there before you know it."

We arrived at the Fort Worth Botanic Gardens. Waverly was waiting for me at the entrance, dressed in one of her amazing outfits—a refurbed black 80s lace prom dress with a full skirt and a corset-type bodice glittering with huge, fake rhinestones. Her red hair had been styled in sleek side ponytail and her makeup was elegant and classic, a perfect contrast to her almost garish dress.

Somehow, Waverly made it work.

"Never change," I told her.

She cocked her head and peered at me with a quizzical expression. "Okay. You look incredible. Like, Grace Kelly level incredible."

"Watching those old movies paid off, didn't it?" Grinning, I lifted the hem of my dress and showed off the heavy boots I was wearing.

"Okay, a *biker* Grace Kelly. The humidity decided to take a break for your wedding," Waverly said. "It seems like good fortune, doesn't it?"

"It does, indeed," I agreed.

My sister and I walked through the gardens with her leading the way. I had no idea where Duke was, and Waverly wasn't saying.

Finally, we came to a wooden bridge over water. Duke and Savage were standing with a man I didn't recognize, but he was dressed in a blue button-down and black trousers. His dark hair was swept off his forehead and his smile was genuine when he saw me.

Duke had his back to me, but Savage said something to him. My fiancé turned and his face slackened in shock, but then a deep grin pulled at his lips, making his dimples pop.

He was wearing his leather cut, but he'd attempted formality with a black button-down. No sign of a tie.

Waverly's hand dropped from mine and I reached out to grasp Duke's.

"She's all yours," Waverly said. "Take care of her, or you'll answer to me."

"And me," Savage said with a devilish wink.

And there, in the late afternoon sun, among the bees and the flowers, I married my best friend.

~

"Well?" Duke asked, his fingers linked with mine—with my newly adorned ring finger.

"Perfect," I admitted as I snuggled into his shoulder. The partition in the limo was raised and Duke and I had privacy. Waverly was on the back of Savage's bike and they were meeting us at the clubhouse, giving Duke and I time as a newly married couple.

"And the ring?" he pressed.

"Also perfect. I hate to say it, but it fits my personality more than the beautiful diamond solitaire."

My new ring was a thick rose gold band that almost touched my first knuckle and it was engraved with *till death*. It was more poignant, more significant especially knowing what was coming in our world.

Duke's hand rested on my thigh, squeezing it. "It's done, Willa. Ansel Prescott will take care of the paperwork, we'll have a quick day in court, and we'll be able to rest easy that we're Waverly's legal guardians."

Tears gathered in my eyes. "Thank you, Duke."

"For what?"

I lifted my head and stared at him. "For everything. For this wedding. For this ring. For marrying me. For waiting for me until I was ready."

His mouth quirked up into a half smile. "You were worth the wait."

"I was stupid and scared," I protested. "And now we don't have to wait."

"Wait for what?"

My fingers went to the zipper of his trousers.

He raised his brows. "Al's not very far away, babe. You sure you want to do this?"

I angled my body so I was sitting next to him and gently removed him from his pants. I gave him a loving squeeze. "I'm sure. You just have to make sure you're quiet."

My head lowered to him. I tongued his crown and smiled when his breath caught. "Make sure you keep your hands to yourself, Duke. I don't want you messing up my hair."

"I'm messing up your lipstick," he muttered.

"Hush," I said. "I want to have my way with my husband in the back of this limo." I took him further into my mouth until he hit the back of my throat.

I sucked him deep, as deep as he could go, nearly choking me. His hands were clenched at his sides and when I looked up to gauge his reaction, his jaw was tight and his eyes were dark with desire.

He reached for me, sliding his hand underneath the skirt of my wedding dress. Duke's fingers tantalized my core, petting me through the lace of my panties.

I leaned into his touch, wanting more.

"So wet," he murmured. "So fucking wet for me."

"Always," I mumbled around his shaft.

"Come here," he growled. "I need to be inside you."

I climbed onto his lap and spread my legs. I lifted my skirt so I could watch us. He slid my panties aside and teased my entrance with the crown of his shaft, painting us with my desire.

I sank down on top of him, letting him fill me completely. I bit my lip to stifle a moan as I rocked against him.

He cupped the back of my neck and our lips met in a ferocious kiss. Duke thrust his tongue into my mouth and I sank down onto him, taking him all the way inside me.

The limo hit a speedbump, causing Duke to lurch up into his seat. His free hand went to my hip, keeping us connected.

I clamped around him and gasped.

The hand that Duke had been cradling my neck with was suddenly between our bodies, touching me, sifting between my folds to find the place that had me shuddering around him.

"Duke," I whispered.

"I know, baby."

He pressed his thumb against me and I clung to him, wanting to scream, but knowing I couldn't if I wanted this to remain between us.

My skin tingled and goosebumps broke out up and down my arms. Pleasure snaked between my legs, swirling in my belly.

"I'm close, Duke," I mumbled as my lips tasted his again.

"Good." He exerted more pressure and I leaned over and sank my teeth into his neck to keep from yelling.

"Shit," he rasped, rolling his hips and then slamming up into me.

I quivered around him, gasping for breath as my orgasm tremors stilled.

"You bit me," Duke huffed.

I lifted myself up and stared into his eyes. "I bit you."

He grinned. "I liked it."

"Yeah, I'll bet you did." I made a move to slide off him, but his hands on my hips stopped me.

"Not yet."

I curled into him, my eyes drifting shut as his arms went around me.

"We're ten minutes out," Al said through the intercom. "In case you guys wanted to make yourselves presentable."

I groaned into Duke's neck. "He knew what we were doing back here."

"Of course, he knew. I paid him to give us a heads up."

"You think of everything, don't you?"

Chapter 45

THE LIMO CAME through the clubhouse gate and parked. Al opened the passenger side door for me and to his credit, gave me no look of judgement.

Hand in hand, Duke and I walked toward the clubhouse where an old green pick-up truck was parked across the lawn. An enclosed trailer was attached to it.

"What is that?" I asked.

"That is what is getting us to our honeymoon destination," Duke explained. "My bike is in the trailer, which we'll take on day trips."

"Where are we going?" I asked.

"Colorado Springs. I'm taking you to the top of Pikes Peak, Garden of the Gods, and some other cool shit. Weather's perfect."

"I've never been to Colorado."

"I know."

"It's on my bucket list."

"I know that, too."

The front door to the clubhouse opened and Savage and Waverly came out, still dressed in their wedding attire.

"You beat us back," I said in surprise to Savage and Waverly.

Duke looked at me and winked. "I had Al take us the long way."

"God, that truck is so cool," Waverly said with a sigh. "It would be a perfect vehicle to cart around furniture."

"You like it?" Duke asked.

"I really do." Waverly came down the steps and glided her hand across the hood.

"It's yours," Duke said.

Waverly's mouth dropped open. "What?"

"It's yours," Duke repeated. "After we get back from our honeymoon, and you get your license, it's yours."

"You're shitting me," Waverly said.

"Will this truck even make it to Colorado?" I asked in genuine concern.

"This baby's only got about three hundred thousand miles on her," Savage commented. "She's nearly broken in."

"Can I sit in the driver's seat and have a moment?" Waverly begged.

"Have at it," Duke said. "Keys are in the ignition. Take her around the lot."

"But the trailer's attached," Waverly pointed out.

"So what? Gotta learn to drive with one of those, too. For when the furniture is too nice to be in the bed of the truck," Duke said.

"You are the best brother-in-law ever!" Waverly stated, jumping toward Duke and embracing him in a side hug.

"Keep an eye on her," Duke said to Savage. "I'm taking Willa inside to change and then we're going to get on the road."

"The clubhouse is quiet," I said as we headed to Duke's room.

"You didn't want a party, did you?"

"No. It was the right call, having the wedding be small and intimate." I presented him my back.

He closed the door and then unzipped my dress. I stepped out of the gown and placed it on Duke's bed.

"You've got to stop," I said.

"Stop what?"

"Stop spending money like you've got it to burn." I turned to face him. "You bought us a house. You paid for a wedding, and now a honeymoon and a truck for Waverly. It's a lot."

He sauntered toward me and placed his hands on my hips. "I can't believe you're trying to have a normal conversation with me while you're wearing garter belts and biker boots."

"What can I say, I'm a woman with many sides." I grasped the lapels of his leather cut. "Seriously, Duke. Level with me."

"We're technically on our honeymoon, and you want to talk about important shit?" He slipped his hand between my legs.

I hissed and clamped my thighs shut. "I know you're trying to distract me with sex, and normally it would work, but…"

With a sigh, he removed his hand. "The house I got a good deal on, so don't worry about that. The wedding wasn't expensive because you didn't want a big fancy thing —but if you had—I'd have paid for that too. As for the truck, it belonged to Mia, and Colt hates it when she drives it, so she sold it to me for a very reasonable price."

We stared at one another and then I said, "I'm not stupid. I know how you make your money. I just didn't know how *much* you were making."

"I make enough to take care of you, Waverly, Sailor,

and however many kids you feel inclined to have. You don't have to worry, and you never will. I promise you that."

"Okay." I nodded. "I won't worry."

"Now turn around and hold onto the dresser like a good girl and let me fuck you again."

Two hours later, Duke reached over and took my hand in his. "They'll be fine."

"I know," I said absently. "But I still worry."

He briefly took his eyes off the road to glance at me. "What has you worried? Sailor and Waverly are crashing with Darcy and Gray. It'll be hard to get into trouble with Lily and Cam close by."

"But teenagers are teenagers. Remember us when we were teenagers? We found a way to get into trouble all the time."

"We had no parental supervision, it was different," he pointed out.

"What if they get kidnapped?" I blurted out.

"Acid and Savage are training them."

"*Training them*? What do you mean *training* them? Training them how?"

"Training them on how to get out of…situations…if they should arise. Teaching them how to be alert, what to look out for. And…"

"And…?"

"Target practice. They're learning how to defend themselves with knives, and if they get their hands on one, a pistol."

"Shit," I muttered.

"I should've told you that before we left."

"Yeah, you should've," I agreed. "You better teach me when we get home."

He looked at me and smiled. "I already had plans to."

I let out a breath. "No sisters of mine will be victims."

"Sisters, huh? No, no they won't. And after I'm done teaching you, you'll never feel like a victim again."

We stopped for gas station barbecue. I took photos of the sign out front and made a note in my phone. "I want to remember everything," I explained.

Duke merely smiled.

We got back on the road for several more hours, stopping when it was close to eleven. We stayed in a cheap motel right off the highway. It was clean and had a short notice vacancy, which was all we cared about.

I washed the makeup off my face and changed into one of Duke's T-shirts that I found packed in the two duffel bags that were in the back seat of the truck.

Duke was asleep by the time I climbed into bed. I turned off the lamp and cuddled into his side, marveling at the fact that I was falling asleep next to my husband.

Husband.

Such a strange word.

Duke was more than my husband. He was my best friend. My protector. My savior.

I fell asleep with a smile on my face and woke up to Duke sliding into me from behind. We moved as one and I reached around to grasp his neck, wanting to meet his lips.

My release was quiet, but powerful, leaving me limp. Duke pressed a kiss to my shoulder and gathered me close, keeping us connected.

"The first morning we're alone, and you don't scream my name," he murmured.

"Guess you'll have to do better tomorrow morning," I teased.

We showered and got back on the road. By eight o'clock that night, Duke was driving the truck up a mountain, not stopping until we reached a small cabin with an A-shaped roof and large windows to look out over the terrain.

He parked the truck and turned off the engine. "Let's grab the bags and get inside."

"This is incredible," I said. "How did you find this place?"

"It belongs to Ghost," he said.

"Ghost? Slash's friend?"

Duke nodded. He grabbed the duffel bags from the back and shut the door. "Temperature is dropping. Let's get inside."

The cabin was cozy. It was all one room, with a wood burning stove in the corner of the living room and a ladder that went to a loft bed. There was a leather couch with a tartan wool blanket and an ample supply of wood for the time we were there.

"Very rustic," I said. "Do I have to poop in the woods?"

"It's got modern amenities," Duke assured me. "A bathroom with a real shower and toilet. All the good stuff. You didn't really think I was going to take you to a place on our honeymoon that had an outhouse, did you?"

"No." I snorted in humor. "I never thought that."

The refrigerator was well stocked and there was a bottle of scotch on a coffee table made from a giant slab of wood from an old tree. I grabbed the bottle and sat on the couch.

Duke lit a fire, and as the smell of burning softwood scented the air we got comfortable on the leather couch in front of the stove. I cracked open the bottle of scotch and had a tiny sip, straight from the bottle.

"That's fucking delicious," I said, handing it to Duke.

"It should be. It's SINNERS." He took a long swallow and tried to give it back to me.

I shook my head. "I'm good."

He raised his brows. "You're going to make me drink alone?"

I cocked my head to the side. "We're going for a baby, aren't we?"

His eyes darkened. "We are."

"Just thought it would be better if I abstained…moving forward, I mean."

He set the bottle of scotch onto the coffee table and then grasped my legs, hauling me close. "You're still good with that life plan? Even after…"

"Even after my kidnapping?" I finished for him.

"Yeah, that. I thought for sure you'd want to press the pause button on kids."

"I'm an Old Lady," I reminded him. "Is there ever a good time to have a baby with a biker?"

"Some times are better than others," he pointed out. "Shit with the cartel…"

"There's always going to be something." I took a deep breath. "I don't want to stop living my life because some-thing bad *could* happen. Something bad already *did* happen, you know? The world isn't safe, but you make it as safe as you can for your family. For us. We can't stop living for fear of the bad. We have to live for the good. You taught me that."

"You sure? Because I can wait if you want to wait."

I swallowed and ducked my head.

"There's more, isn't there. That you're not saying. What is it?" He reached underneath my chin and forced me to meet his gaze. "You can say it."

My lip wobbled. "I want a piece of you in this world with me…in case you…in case this war—"

"In case I die," he said baldly.

I nodded.

He skimmed his fingers along my jaw. "I'm not going to promise you that I'll live. No one can make a promise like that without it being a lie."

I nodded again, tears gathering in my eyes. "Yeah, I know."

Duke leaned in to kiss me, soft, tender, wanting.

I kissed him back with fervor and then said against his lips, "Make love to me, Duke."

Chapter 46

We slept in and got a late start on the day. Duke took his bike out from the trailer and we dressed appropriately for the new climate in Colorado. He straddled his motorcycle and I got on behind him, wrapping my arms around his muscled body. I scooted as close as possible and then we took off.

He drove us to Garden of the Gods, where we saw beautiful rock formations in different shades of reds and pinks. We ambled hand in hand without any purpose except to be outside and enjoy one another.

"I've never seen the sky so blue or so clear," I remarked.

"Perfect weather, too," Duke said.

We both turned to one another and said at the exact same time, "No humidity."

Duke's cell phone rang and he fished it out of his leather cut. He glanced at the screen. "It's Prez."

I nodded.

He had to take the call. Club business didn't stop just because we were on our honeymoon. While he was on the phone, I wandered over to a large rock where a group of school children were taking turns pretending to hold it up and snapping photos with their phones.

Their excitement was endearing.

Duke finished his call and approached me. He saw me watching the kids and he wrapped an arm around my shoulder, hooking me into his side. "Let's get out of here."

I nodded, knowing where his mind was at.

We hopped on his bike and Duke drove us up a winding mountain path, far away from people. He parked the motorcycle behind a large boulder. The air was fresh, and when I stepped off the bike, I inhaled a deep breath, trying to take it all in.

"Look at that view!" I exclaimed, marveling at the mountains.

"I am," Duke said gruffly.

I turned to find him staring not at the picturesque scene before us, but at me. And his gaze was hungry.

"Oh," I breathed. "I see."

He grasped my hips and guided me back to his bike. His fingers released the button of my pants, pushing them down, along with my panties, so they gathered at my ankles. Duke took my hands and placed them on the leather seat.

"Don't move."

His belt buckle clanged as he undid it, and then I felt him behind me. He glided his hands over my skin, down the back of my thighs to spread my cheeks. He slid a finger through my folds, causing me to shudder. I wanted him deep inside me.

We were hidden from the road because of the boulder outcrop and I was grateful for the privacy. All I cared about was the scent of the mountains, the hardness of

Duke pressing into me, the feel of the soft leather motor-cycle seat beneath my hands.

Duke slammed into my body, but I was ready for him. I was wet and aching, and even though we'd made love the night before, I couldn't get enough of him.

He reached around me to touch me between my thighs, stroking and pressing until I was shuddering around him.

Duke gripped my hips and thrust like an animal possessed, like he had no choice but to follow his baser instincts.

He moved his hand out from between my legs and gripped my hair, giving it a sharp pull.

"I want to fuck you like this always," he growled at my back. "I want you like this, but naked, and I want to come on your back. I want to paint my cum all over your skin. I want to be everywhere inside you."

"Oh, God," I gasped, his words causing another tremor to spark between my legs.

"Yeah, that's it. You like it when I talk this way, don't you?" He let go of my hair, but only so he could grasp my throat in his large hand, his thumb resting just below my ear. He squeezed slightly, exerting just enough pressure to heighten my senses.

My body froze and then another orgasm obliterated me. As wave after wave crashed through me, Duke continued to drill into me until he shouted his own release.

My arms were wobbly and barely held me up. Duke slipped out and I felt his essence on my leg. Without thought, I painted my fingers with it and pushed it back inside me, hoping we'd made a baby.

~

The late spring snowstorm blew in after we'd made it back to the cabin. Sight-seeing apparently didn't hold nearly the same appeal when I could sightsee my naked husband's tattoos and trace them with my tongue.

Which I did, before we both collapsed onto the bed in a sweaty mess. He lifted his arm and I snuggled into his side. His fingers trailed up and down my arm, sending another round of goosebumps along my skin.

"I think we did it," he said quietly.

"Did what?" I asked, turning my face so I could gently bite his chest.

"I think we made a baby."

I snorted. "Too soon to tell."

He fell quiet and I lifted myself up on my elbow to stare at him. "Unless there's something you know that I don't?"

Duke grinned. "Nah. Just hoping, I guess."

"Wish it into existence, hmm?"

"Wishing has nothing to do with it. I gave you enough seed to make an army."

"Charming," I muttered with a laugh as I sat up. "I'm hungry."

"Me too." His finger brushed my nipple.

I batted his hand away. "Feed me before I faint."

We got out of bed and Duke slid on a pair of flannel pants but left his chest bare. The cabin was overly warm due to the combination of our aerobic exercises and the roaring woodstove.

I threw on Duke's shirt and padded to the kitchen after him.

"Snow's still coming down," he said as he opened the fridge.

"Hard too, from the looks of it. Good thing we got your bike into the trailer." I wrapped my arms around him and laid my cheek against his body. "I almost wish we didn't have to leave."

"You don't want to go back?" He turned, forcing me to release him. I stepped away and then hopped up on the counter.

I shrugged. "I mean, yeah, I miss my sister and Savage. But this has been a nice reprieve. Where it's just us, there's no one else to worry about or think about. It's just you and me and…what *we* want."

Duke turned back to the fridge and pulled out a glass container. "Leftover stew?"

"Sounds good." I made a move to jump down, but he stopped me.

"I'll get bowls." He trekked around the kitchen while I looked on. "You didn't ask what Prez called about."

"Was I supposed to? It's club business, right?"

"Sort of. Not anything you can't be privy to though." He parceled out the stew into two bowls and put one into the microwave. "You know the land behind the clubhouse?"

"Yeah."

"The club bought it. Deal went through."

"That's cool."

"Yeah. Prez has been wanting to expand for a while. Club's growing and we need the space."

"Sure, makes sense."

The microwave beeped and Duke opened the door and touched the bowl. "Not too hot," he said as he stuck a spoon in it and handed it to me.

"Thanks." I held the dish in my hands. "Is that all? I mean, for the news about the club?"

Duke shook his head. "The clubhouse is gonna go through some changes."

"Changes? What kind of changes?"

He rubbed his stubbly jaw and said, "It's going to start looking more like a compound over time. We're beefing up security."

"Are we talking armed guards here?" I asked.

"At some point, yeah."

"Okay." I took a bite of stew.

"Okay? That's it?"

"What do you want me to say?" I inquired. "The club wants to ensure we're protected. As far as I'm concerned, that's all there is to it." I set my bowl of stew aside, leaned back against the counter, and spread my legs. "Let's make the most of our honeymoon before we have to go back to the real world."

Duke dropped to his knees. "Dessert before dinner. Just the way I like it."

Chapter 47

"I *DO NOT* LIKE THAT," I stated. "I do not like that at all."

"What?" Mia asked, looking around the back yard of the clubhouse.

I gestured with my chin in the direction of Sailor and Waverly, who were sitting on top of the picnic table, their heads together, as they were clearly attempting to have a private conversation.

"I don't get it," Joni said, adjusting the newborn to her other shoulder. "What's not to like?"

"They're conspiring," I stated. "I just know it."

"Conspiring about what?" Allison asked.

"Something to do with boys," I remarked. I took a sip of my soda.

"Waverly already has a boy," Brooklyn said.

"But Sailor doesn't, and she's a knockout," I replied.

The Tarnished Angels brothers came out of the building they used for church. My eyes swept over them, landing on Duke.

I absently touched my wedding ring.

"Married looks good on you," Brooklyn said with a smile, her hand resting on her belly.

"Feels good, too," I admitted. "Even though we have two teenagers in the rental. It's hard trying to make a baby without privacy."

"When do you move into the new house?" Rachel asked.

"Soon," I said. "We should get the keys in a few days. Until then, we're doing it in the truck daily."

Mia nodded. "You learn to get creative."

"And fast," Allison added. "In between baby naps."

"Quickies become the norm," Darcy added. "I miss slow and low."

"I need a refill," Rachel announced, quickly leaving the group of Old Ladies; sans Doc, who was still in Scotland.

"Damn," Mia murmured.

"She didn't need a refill, did she?" I asked.

Joni shook her head, her eyes sad.

"I've had sex in that truck," Mia said, obviously trying to turn the conversation away from Rachel's heartache.

"With Colt or someone else?" Brooklyn asked.

"Just Colt," Mia assured her. "I think Scarlett was actually conceived in that truck."

"Maybe the truck has superpowers," Darcy said.

"Don't tell me that. We're giving that truck to Waverly," I quipped. "And I don't trust teenagers not to fool around."

I went back to watching Waverly and Sailor while the Old Ladies talked about baby sleeping habits. Acid strode by the table they were at, and I watched as Sailor gazed at him with longing.

Fuck.

Savage sauntered toward us and wrapped an arm

around my shoulder, giving me a hug. "What are you ladies talking about?"

"Chapped nipples," Joni dead panned.

"Yeah, can't help you with that," Savage said.

"Damn, I thought for sure that would make him uncomfortable," Joni quipped. "Alas, he is unshakable."

"Have you met the South Dakota boys?" Savage asked me.

I shook my head. Duke and I had been running late, and the moment we'd gotten to the clubhouse he'd headed off to church.

Savage tugged me in Duke's direction. He was standing with two men I didn't know, but before we made it, Waverly and Sailor intercepted me.

"Can Sailor and I leave?" she asked.

"I'll meet you over there," Savage said, nodding his chin at Duke.

I turned my attention back to my sister. "You're bored."

"Yup."

"You want to go hang out with your boyfriend, don't you?"

"Yup." Waverly grinned.

"He's already on his way to pick you guys up, isn't he?"

"Busted," Sailor said with a laugh.

"You guys can go. But have him drop you off here at ten."

"We're not going home?" Waverly asked.

I tugged on her ponytail. "No. We'll crash here."

"Where?" she muttered. "There's a billion bikers here."

"We'll find room," I assured her. "Your phones are charged?"

"Yep."

"Okay. Safe."

"Always," she assured me with a hug.

I walked toward Duke and Savage, who were talking with a few of the South Dakota boys.

"Sorry about my delay," I said as I came to Duke's side. "Sailor and Waverly just left for a few hours. I told them to be back at the clubhouse by ten."

"Willa, this is Raze." Duke gestured to a dark-haired man who was burly and barrel chested. He had a strong jaw covered in stubble and when he smiled, his eyes crinkled.

"Nice to meet you," I said.

"Same. You're Duke's Old Lady?" he asked.

"Yes. Recently." I held up my hand to show the ring.

"Congrats," Raze said.

Duke introduced me to Viper, the other man standing with them. He towered over everyone, something uncommon for a group of big men. His jaw was clenched and his dark eyes seemed to swallow the afternoon sunlight. He was massive and looked like he was a professional body builder.

"Viper," I stuttered. "Nice to meet you."

He grunted in reply and then without a word, stalked away.

"Don't mind him," Raze said, his expression sobering. "He's had a rough couple of years. It takes a crowbar to pry two words out of his mouth."

I frowned and looked after the man who'd just left the group to go stand with three other men who were part of the South Dakota chapter of the Tarnished Angels. The Old Ladies noticed him, but Mia was the only one to hold up her hand and wave.

"Who are the others?" I asked.

"Kelp, Smoke, and Bones," Raze said.

"Smoke and Bones seem pretty self-explanatory road names, but Kelp?" I queried. "What's a Kelp?"

"You'll have to ask him," Raze said with a wink. "Heard about what happened to you by the way. Sorry about that, Willa. It's good we're here for a while. There's a lot that needs to be done."

I didn't know this man, but I was touched.

"Thanks, Raze. We're glad you guys are here too."

"Even Viper," Savage quipped. "Surly fucker."

"He should've been named Beast," I muttered before I could stop myself.

A crack of laughter escaped Raze's mouth.

The afternoon turned to evening and we lit a bonfire. Lily, Cam and Silas swarmed around their parents, demanding food. Colt finally caved and ordered pizza, much to Brooklyn's consternation.

"Woman," Slash growled at Brooklyn. "You aren't responsible for food at every event."

"Yes, I am," Brooklyn said, tearing up. "It's my thing."

We crowded around the bonfire, enjoying pizza right out of the box. Duke and I shared a few pieces while he drank a beer. I watched the bikers interact with their women, taking the moment in as I realized things were going to change soon.

Slash was doting on Brooklyn, making sure she was comfortable and that she had everything she needed. Zip held his newborn son, attempting to keep conversation going with Torque, despite his attention moving constantly back to the love of his life, Joni. Darcy sat on Gray's lap, whispering something in his ear that made him laugh. Torque stood over his wife, resting his hand on her shoulder while their son slept against her. Colt had his arm around Mia and they were talking to Bones and Kelp. Baby Scarlett was asleep in her arms.

Rachel was sitting with Raze and Smoke. She was smiling and laughing, but it was clear her mind was somewhere else.

Savage and Acid talked with the newly patched in Crow and South Paw. They were brothers now, part of the club, sworn to protect the innocent at all costs, even if it meant their lives.

Viper sat alone on the picnic table, holding a bottle of liquor. He was staring off into the distance, every now and again sipping from the bottle. No one approached him, not even members of his own club. He was not amicable and didn't appear as though he cared about anything.

I sat on a log in front of Duke. He was resting in a camp chair at my back. I turned and leaned against him for a moment before getting up.

He looked at me in confusion.

"Bathroom," I said quietly.

I went into the clubhouse up the stairs and used the restroom. I pulled my panties down and a pang of disappointment shot through me as I saw my underwear. I grabbed a pad from underneath the sink, glad the Old Ladies thought to keep feminine products on hand.

As I was washing my hands, there was a knock on the bathroom door. "Willa, it's me."

I opened the door and frowned at Duke. "What are you doing?"

He slipped into the bathroom and shut the door. "You used the code word for *meet me in five minutes for secret dirty sex.*" Duke grinned and moved toward me.

I put my hand on his chest and his smile slipped.

"Are you okay?" he asked, covering my hand with his.

"I'm fine. I just—not in the mood."

"Not in the mood. You're always in the mood."

I bit my lip. "I got my period."

"You think that would stop me?" He cocked his head to the side. "I still want you."

"That's nice," I said with a sigh. "But it's not that."

"Then what—oh. It means you're not pregnant."

"Yeah." My brow furrowed. "I'm more bummed than I thought I'd be."

"Hey," he said softly, grasping my chin and gently forcing my gaze to his. In my boots, we were nearly the same height. "It'll happen when it's supposed to."

"I know. But I was kind of hoping we'd already done it. You know?"

He flashed a grin. "We'll just have to try harder. Night and day; day and night."

Duke moved ever so slightly, backing me up so I hit the sink. He wedged his thigh between my legs.

"Whatever I have to do, Willa. Don't worry. You can count on me."

I chuckled. "Yeah, I know I can." I brushed my lips across his. "Thanks for cheering me up."

His hands moved to cradle my cheeks. His tongue slipped into my mouth and he pressed his thigh against my cleft. When he pulled back, he rested his forehead against mine.

"Come on, let's blow off the party," he said.

"Where are we going?" I demanded.

"I'm taking you to La Creperie for dessert."

"Now that'll cheer me up."

I let Duke lead me downstairs and outside to his bike.

"Hey," I said, pausing when he gave me a helmet.

"Yeah?"

"I love you. Like, *really* love you."

He reached out to grasp my hip and pull me toward him. "I don't know what I did to deserve you, but I'll spend the rest of my life grateful I have you."

My mouth quirked into a smile. "Funny. I was thinking the exact same thing about you."

We kissed gently under the stars, and then I climbed on the back of Duke's bike, my arms wrapped around him as we sped off into the night.

Our future was unknown, but at that moment, I had everything.

Epilogue

A couple of weeks later

Duke

"You're late," Savage stated as I slid into the booth across from him.

"Figured your hand would be up some chick's skirt to pass the time while you waited for me," I quipped.

Savage took a drink of beer from his half-empty pint glass. "I was giving you five more minutes before I made a move on the blonde."

"Which one?" I asked.

"That one." He gestured with his chin to the bar, but then waved his hand toward the pool tables. "Or that one. Not like it matters much. They're all the fucking same anyway."

He stared morosely at the table, his fingers drumming on the scarred wood.

"Shots?" I asked.

"Yeah, might as well."

"Let's make it bourbon," I suggested. "Or will that light your fighting fuse?"

"Fight or fuck." He sighed. "It's all the same to me."

I got up and went to the bar and made small talk with the new bartender at Shelly's. While I waited for her to pour the drinks, I turned to look at Savage. A woman had approached the table, but he hardly spared her any attention, and after a moment she left.

Very un-Savage of him.

"How's married life," Savage asked when I returned to the table.

I set the drinks down and sat. "You don't want to hear about married life."

"Nah, not really." He grasped his shot glass. "But is it different?"

"Different? What do you mean?"

"I mean, it's Willa. She's your wife now. That's kinda weird…"

"For you, maybe. Not for me."

We raised our shots in silent toast and downed them.

"So, it's not gonna change everything, right?" he asked.

"Change everything, how?"

"Well, you're a husband and shit. A family man."

"So that means, what? She's gonna bitch at me to take out the trash? Yell at me for leaving my dirty clothes on the floor?"

He shrugged. "I don't know. Maybe."

"Okay, what the fuck is up with you?" I demanded. "You're being a surly dickhead tonight. Are you having an existential crisis or something?"

"I don't know, man. It's fucked up. It's a mood. It'll pass." He shook his head and then downed the rest of his beer. "So, level with me. Married life. All it's cracked up to be?"

"Better," I admitted.

"She still fucking squirrelly about being committed to you?"

"Nah, she's settling down."

A few days ago while Willa was signing a legal document to finish the process of legally adopting Waverly, she'd messed up her signature. She'd written her maiden name, not my last name, and she'd gotten upset about it. Like *really* upset. Upset enough that I wondered if it was hormone related, and if she might be pregnant.

But I hadn't asked.

She didn't need that kind of pressure from me. Besides, I was having a hell of good time trying to knock her up. I'd made it my mission to fuck her at least once a day. Sometimes twice, and always with purpose.

"You look happy," Savage noted.

"I am happy."

"This shit with the cartel…"

"I try not to think about it too much."

"It's gonna get bad…"

"Yeah."

"Bloody."

"Yep."

"There's gonna to be total fucking carnage."

I nodded. "You're not going to do anything stupid, are you?"

"Stupid? Stupid, how?"

"Stupid like being reckless because you're in the middle of an existential crisis."

"It's not existential."

"What is it then?"

"Boredom," he muttered. "Fucking boredom."

"I don't get it. You're with a different woman every night. How can you possibly be bored?"

"But they're *all the same*, Duke. You don't get it. Willa's been the one for you since we were kids."

"Are you saying—do you want what we have?"

"I don't know. I just know everything and everyone is just—I'm bored."

I groaned. "When you're bored, you go looking for trouble. And if *you* get into trouble, Willa will kill *me* for not keeping you out of trouble."

Savage smirked. "You're right. Nothing has changed. Willa still has you a on a leash."

"If you're looking for a fight, you're about to get one."

My phone vibrated and I pulled it from my leather cut.

WILLA

> I'm going to bed. Be safe driving home.
> Flick Savage's ear for me. Love you. X

"The old ball and chain?" Savage inquired.

I set my phone aside, leaned across the table, and flicked his ear. "That was from Willa, you dipshit. And she only texted to say she was going to bed and to be safe getting home."

Savage made annoying kissing sounds.

"Ah, I get it," I said finally.

"Get what?"

"You're jealous."

"Fuck you."

"I knew it. You're jealous that I get to go home to my hot wife, and that she cares enough about me to want me to be safe."

I wouldn't brag to him about the fact that I'd get to

crawl in to bed next to her and then slide into her raw, without a condom. We kissed and told about one night stands; those nameless women didn't matter. But there were things that were meant to stay between a man and his woman once it got serious.

"She is hot," Savage said. "I'll agree with you about that."

If any other man called my wife hot, I'd be ready to lay him out.

But this was Savage. There was no jealousy about Willa on his end. There never had been.

"What do you need, brother?" I asked softly. "I mean, really?"

He cracked his knuckles. "I need a good fight."

With a sigh, I downed the last of my drink. "Let's get to it then."

Two hours later, I was turning down the street toward home, toward Willa. My jaw was bruised, my knuckles were scuffed, and adrenaline was still coursing through my veins.

It felt good. Really good.

I parked my bike and cut the engine. I took a deep breath as I got off the motorcycle, wincing from my battered ribs.

Over the years we'd fought each other to blow off steam, but never with the intention of actually hurting each other. It was better that Savage fight me rather than go out looking for trouble, and we both knew it.

Speaking of trouble...

I saw Dylan sneaking out from around the back of the house. He didn't see that I was waiting for him out front.

When he turned and saw me, he stopped dead in his tracks. "Hey, Duke."

"Dylan." I chin nodded. "Little late, isn't it?"

"Not that late." The kid stood taller as if it would somehow protect him.

"You ride your motorcycle here?"

"Yeah."

"Where is it?" I pressed. "Because if you were invited to girls' night—which is what Willa told me was going on —that would mean you would've parked your bike right outside the house. And it's not there."

When he didn't reply, I said, "Let's go for a walk."

"I should really get home," Dylan said. "It being late, and all."

"I wasn't asking. Let's go."

His mouth pinched into a line, but he reluctantly nodded.

"Now, tell me what you're doing sneaking out of my house," I demanded.

Dylan was tall—not as tall as me—and had the build of a runner. Lean and sinewy. "You want to explain why you're sporting a fat lip?"

"Watch it, kid. And before you say another word, you need to understand that Waverly is *my* business. She's my family now, and under my care. So think very carefully about what you say before you fuck around and lie to me."

"I was hanging out with Waverly in her apartment."

"No shit. But you know you're not allowed in her apartment at night," I stated.

"We were just hanging out, I swear it," Dylan said.

"Dude, stop. I was a teenager once. I know how it goes."

"But you don't know me," he stated. He halted, forcing me to stop walking. "I want her. I do. But I also love her.

439

She's not ready, and I'd never do anything to hurt her. All I want is to love and protect her. And I *have*—"

My jaw clenched, as did my fists. "You were the one."

"The one what?"

"The one who broke Cal's fingers. It was you."

"No, it wasn't me. It was a mugger."

I smiled as he failed to backtrack. "Give it up, kid. You let it slip… *And I have…*"

Dylan paused a moment and then a slight grin spread across his face, but then he got serious. "Are you going to stop me from seeing Waverly?"

"No. I know what it's like to fall hard and fast for a Gravestone woman. I can see that in your eyes. You're done for."

"You won't tell Willa?"

"We're men. You have my word. I won't tell Willa. But you can't keep sneaking in and out of Waverly's apartment. If you want to hang out with her, you come to the front door, you hang out, you leave—also through the front door. Got it?"

"Got it."

We walked until we were at Dylan's bike, which he'd parked far enough away from the house that there was no chance of his engine being heard when he started it up.

"How'd you do it," I asked.

"Do what?" He straddled his motorcycle.

"How did you get away with smashing Cal's fingers? How did the cops not tie you to it?"

"My uncle. He knows the owner of the gas station where it happened. He called a favor in and suddenly the surveillance tapes accidentally got wiped."

"Your uncle knows people," I said. "The right people."

"Yeah. He does." Dylan strapped his helmet on. "We good?"

"We're good. Come to dinner later this week, yeah?"

Dylan nodded. He turned on his bike and then zoomed off into the night. I stood there and watched his taillights disappear before turning around and heading home.

I let out a small laugh as I walked.

The house was dark and quiet. I walked slowly through the front room, still getting used to the layout. We'd just moved in and we didn't have enough stuff to fill the place and make it look like it was lived in. That would take time. Truth was, I didn't give a shit about it, and I was letting Willa handle it. Whatever she wanted, she got.

I crept up to the second floor and turned the knob of the bedroom door.

"You're not as quiet as you think you are," Willa muttered.

"Sorry, babe."

A moment later, a lamp on the bedside table turned on. "It's the boots." She flipped over and flopped down on her back, but then quickly reared up, brushing her tangled blonde hair away from her face. Even watching her do something as simple as that was sexy.

I wanted her all the time.

"What happened to your face?" she demanded, scrambling from the bed and coming over to me.

"Savage," I quipped and smiled. My lip immediately split and began bleeding again.

Cursing, she moved toward the bathroom. I reached out to grasp her wrist and pulled her into me. She smelled like Willa. I'd know her scent in the dark; I'd know her anywhere.

She was wearing one of my T-shirts and a pair of panties, her long legs and perfect skin on display.

"I was just going to get the First Aid kit," she said softly.

"Leave it. It's all superficial."

I released her wrist and stepped back, just so I could remove my leather cut and lay it on the chair in the corner. I stripped out of my shirt and tossed it to the floor, and when I did, I caught her look as she saw my chest.

She wanted me.

Willa bent down to pick it up but didn't give me any grief about not throwing it in the hamper.

Her eyes scanned me. "Your ribs are bruised."

"Yeah."

"What was the fight about?"

"We're fine," I assured her. "Savage needed to take out his frustration on someone who wouldn't pull a knife or gun on him."

She frowned.

I sat on the edge of the bed and leaned down so I could remove my boots. When I grunted in discomfort, Willa dropped to her knees and batted my hands away.

As she unlaced my boots, I explained what Savage had told me.

"Bored? Seriously?" she asked. "How the hell is he bored? He fucks different women constantly, he's in a biker club, and we're about to go to war with a cartel…"

As she talked, I began staring at her nipples as they poked gently through the shirt she was wearing. Willa had great tits. She had great *everything*.

"Duke?"

"Hmm?"

"Answer me."

"What did you ask?" I lifted my gaze to hers.

"You really weren't paying to attention to a word I said, were you?"

"Babe, you're on your knees in front of me and you're giving me a peep show. Damn right I'm not paying attention to what you're saying."

She snorted and tossed my boots aside before rising. "Need help with your jeans?"

I nodded.

Her fingers deftly undid my fly. I lifted up and she slid them down my legs. "Boxers, too, babe."

She pulled them off, so I was completely naked. My hand snaked out to rest on the curve of her hip and I pulled her closer, and then I buried my head against her.

Her fingers sifted through my hair.

"I know how you roll after a fight," she murmured, humor in her tone. "You're in dire need of a good fuck."

I wheezed out a laugh. "I'm shot to hell, but I still want to be inside you. Climb on top, and ride me, baby. I need it."

Willa removed her fingers from my hair and stepped back. She quickly pulled off the T-shirt and flung it aside. My eyes tracked her movements when she shoved her panties down her legs, stepping out of them. It was like staring at a super model in the prime of her life, and blood started pumping to my groin.

She came to the bed and leaned over, putting her ass in my direct eyesight. I stole a hand across her cheek as she settled pillows against the headboard.

"Up you go," she said.

I squeezed her ass and then released her. With slow maneuvering, I inched my way across the bed and rested against the pillows.

Willa swung her legs over my body, scooting up my lap. She bent toward me so her breasts swung in my face.

I captured a nipple between my lips and sucked on it.

She let out a low moan, shoving her breast deeper into

my mouth. Willa rocked against me, and I felt her slickness along my dick.

"You ready, baby?" I whispered, her nipple popping from my mouth.

"Hmm." She lifted herself up and slipped her hand down to grasp me. She angled my cock to her entrance and slid down on top of me, squeezing as she went.

We both groaned as I filled her, and I felt myself hit the back of her and begin to stretch her out.

I watched as her eyes rolled back into her head, her cheeks flushing with desire. I grasped her hips, loving the visual of her grinding against me. She was already wet, but I knew she would start to cream soon and I wanted it, so I pushed myself deeper into her as far as I could go.

"Yeah, baby," I gritted out, pleasure within me.

Our bodies were in tune, and it never took long to make Willa come. I was amped up and had to focus on lasting to make sure I pleased her before I came.

"I'm close," she whispered.

"*Thank God*." I snaked a hand between us, finding that perfect little bud between her legs, and running my fingers over her slickness. I toyed with it, and a few moments later she clamped around me hard, and then came with a strangled cry.

Her orgasm fueled my own. I gripped her hips and speared up into her slick body so her folds were all the way at the base of my cock, and I let go. "Fuck," I shouted, spilling myself in her.

She leaned down to put her face close to mine and then we held on to each other until our heart beats settled and our breathing slowed. She eventually climbed off me, scampering to the bathroom, her hand between her legs to keep from spilling my seed.

I laughed and pain lanced my ribs.

"Shut up," she said without any heat. "Do you have the energy to shower?"

"Only if you shower with me and wash my sensitive parts."

She popped her head out of the bathroom and grinned at me. "Didn't I give them enough attention?"

"I'm injured. I need help washing," I jested. I eased my legs off the bed and set them on the floor. I joined her in the bathroom and leaned against the sink counter.

"In you go," she said after adjusting the temperature.

I stepped into the shower and stood underneath the spray. I groaned at how wonderful it felt.

"Which is better?" Willa asked as she got in. "Sex with me, or the hot water?"

"Right now, it's a tie."

She snorted and reached for the soap. "Turn."

I turned and then felt her hands on me.

"I'd like to hear more about your night," she said. "I mean, I know you mentioned Savage was in a mood. But, is there anything to be worried about? Or is this just one of his spells?"

"It's possible," I admitted. "I'll keep a close eye on him. Could be the stress of what's coming with the cartel. The changes between us…"

"Why didn't he come back here after the fight? He has a room."

"Hook-up. He's not going to bring some random woman to our home to fuck."

"Valid," she said. Her hands moved to my arm and she began to wash my skin.

"Tell me about your night," I commanded.

"Hung out with Waverly and Sailor," she said. "Waverly went to bed early, though. Had a headache."

I bit my tongue.

Little liar.

"How's Sailor doing?" I asked.

"Better." Willa squatted and began to wash my calves, and when she did, I immediately wanted to fuck her again. "Doc prescribed her some gentle sleep aids—to help with the nightmares." She brushed her hand on my hip, signaling me to turn.

"Do you need a prescription?" I asked baldly, my mind returning to the seriousness of the conversation.

"No."

"You sure? You haven't slept the night through since it happened."

She swallowed and peered up at me, blue eyes wide. "I know. Doc said she'd prescribe me something, but I don't want to take them. We're trying to get pregnant."

"We could wait," I said gently, reaching down to grasp her elbow, forcing her to stand.

"Wait until what? The nightmares subside? They might never go away, Duke. I want a baby."

"Okay."

"I do," she insisted. "And I don't want anything getting in the way of that. Even if what's getting in the way is my own mind plotting against me."

"You sure?"

"Duke, you were the one who pressed for a family," she said in exasperation. "And for the record, I've seen you with Mia's daughter. You were terrified of holding her last I checked. What made you decide you wanted a kid if you feel that way?"

"Yeah, I was terrified of holding Scarlett," I admitted. "But when you and I finally got together, I started to think about a family with you. I've thought about it a lot actually. You know that. A baby with you doesn't scare me, because it's *you*."

Her eyes softened.

I rinsed the soap from my skin and then turned off the water. She climbed out of the shower first and handed me a towel.

By the time I dried myself, she'd changed and was settling back into bed. She pressed a hand to her mouth to cover a yawn. Willa snuggled under the covers and watched me move to the dresser. I opened the top drawer and pulled out a pair of gray sweatpants.

I climbed into bed shirtless and turned off the lamp. I reached out for Willa, and she immediately scooted closer and put a hand on my chest. She made me feel like a god when I was around her.

Her breathing began to slow, and she fell asleep.

An hour later, I was wiping away her tears and cradling her in my arms as the screams from her nightmare turned to whimpers.

"You're awake," Willa said the moment I entered the kitchen.

I grunted and headed for the coffee pot. I filled a cup and then took a seat at the kitchen table next to her. "So are you."

She sipped her coffee.

"You sure you don't want the sleeping pills?" I asked as I reached for her plate of toast and took the crust that she'd discarded.

Willa paused. "Another nightmare?"

"You don't remember?"

"No. Sorry," she muttered.

"Why are you apologizing?"

"Because my nightmares affect you—and your sleep —too."

"Fuck that. I don't care about that. I care about *you*."

She took another sip of her coffee. "I'll go see Doc today."

I nodded.

"Where are the kids?" I asked.

"Still sleeping, I imagine." She grinned. "Letting them bunk together in that apartment was either pure genius or the worst idea we've ever had."

"It's great for you and me," I quipped. "We get a lot more privacy."

"Want some pancakes?" she asked.

"I'd love some pancakes," I said with a smile.

She got up and began moving around the kitchen. While she was in the middle of flipping the first pancake, the back door opened and Waverly and Sailor strolled in.

"Pancakes!" Waverly said, moving toward her sister and laying her head against Willa's shoulder.

"Who said I'm making any for you?" Willa teased.

"Just because Sailor and I live in the guest house doesn't mean we can actually fend for ourselves," Waverly said.

"Morning, Duke," Sailor said, her eyes skittering from me to the coffee pot. "Rough night?"

"Rough—oh, you mean the split lip?"

She nodded.

"Savage and I wailed on each other," I explained.

"For what purpose?" Waverly asked. "Was he being an asshole again?"

"Waverly," Willa said with a sigh.

"Seriously, Willa. I curse. You curse. We all curse."

"He needed to blow off some steam, so we used each

other as punching bags. No harm, no foul. All good between old friends."

Willa snorted. "Tell that to your ribs."

"Coffee refill?" Sailor asked me.

"Sure thing," I said, pushing my cup toward her. The poor kid still acted like a guest, asking permission to use the fucking washing machine and shit. Didn't blame her though. It was a weird situation for anyone. She was also really young and it would take her a while to settle in.

"Why are you calling it a guest house when it's not actually a guest house?" I asked Waverly.

"Because calling it a one-bedroom apartment and shop doesn't roll off the tongue, and it's easier to explain to people when you just say you live in the guest house," Waverly said.

"We're out of coffee," Sailor announced.

"There's another bag in the pantry," Willa said. "But make sure you mark on the whiteboard that you took one, so we know what to get when we go grocery shopping."

Sailor nodded.

Waverly moved closer to Willa's side and said something to her, but I couldn't hear what they were saying. The front door opened without warning and a moment later Savage and Acid tromped into the kitchen.

"Just in time," Savage said, setting a plastic bag onto the counter.

"Nice shiner." I smirked.

"She's a beaut, isn't she?" Savage grinned back.

"You guys are so effing weird," Waverly huffed. "Who beats each other up and then acts like nothing happened?"

Savage looked at her and then at me. "We do. That's just how we roll. Willa, babe, is that first stack for me?"

"You're at the end of the line," she quipped. "I'll feed Acid before I feed you, if I choose to feed you at all."

"Just coffee for me, thanks," Acid said. "But your pot is empty."

Sailor popped out of the pantry holding a massive bag of coffee and came to a halt. Her gaze locked on Acid's.

"Morning, Blondie," he said to her.

Her cheeks flamed with color. "What are you doing here?"

"Self-defense lessons, remember?" he asked.

"Oh." She swallowed, and as if suddenly remembering why she'd gone into the pantry in the first place, she finally headed to the coffee pot.

"First batch is done," Willa said. "Waverly, take this to Duke, please. And set the table, yeah?"

"On it," Waverly said as she brought me the plate, butter, and syrup. She buzzed around the kitchen getting napkins and utensils.

"Hey, asshole, why don't you make yourself useful and help her," I said to Savage.

"Don't you dare," Willa warned. "Sit. Let me take care of you."

Savage grinned. "I knew you'd cave." He wrapped Willa in a hug and then came over to the table, pulling out the chair next to me.

"Dylan's coming over," Waverly said, setting her cell aside. "So is Jessica."

"Think your house just became the unofficial official youth hostel," Savage said, reaching for one of my flapjacks.

I let him have it. "You okay?" I asked, pitching my voice low so no one else heard us.

"Hmm. Yeah. I'm good. Thanks, brother."

"You'd tell me, if you weren't?" I probed.

"Fuck no. Don't worry about me, Duke. That's Willa's job."

"Babe?" I called out, entering the house.

It's too quiet.

I headed into the kitchen, but Willa wasn't there. Her car was in the driveway, so I knew she was *somewhere*.

I went to her office door and gently knocked.

"Come in," she called out.

I opened the door and stepped inside. Willa sat in a swiveling office chair behind the up-cycled desk Waverly had made for her. She was looking out the window.

"You working?" I asked. "I can come back."

"Not working," she said.

Her voice sounded strange.

"Are you okay?" I asked, stepping further into the room.

"Yeah, I'm okay." She lifted her mug to her lips.

"For fuck's sake, you're scaring me. Will you turn around?" I demanded.

"I'm watching the horses," she said.

I marched over to her desk, noting the prescription bag sitting near the edge of it.

"Doc prescribed you sleeping pills?" I asked.

When she didn't reply, I reached for the bag and pulled out the prescription bottle.

I glanced at the label.

Willa turned in her chair, a soft smile playing about her lips.

"Is this—" I swallowed "—for real?"

She nodded.

I set the bottle of prenatal vitamins back onto her desk and crouched down next to her. I placed my hands on her thighs. "You're pregnant."

"I'm pregnant."

"With my baby."

She snorted. "Who else?" Willa set the mug aside and then plowed her fingers through my hair. "We're having a baby, Duke."

I wrapped my arms around her middle and lay my head in her lap, realizing my dreams were coming true.

The front door opened, and the sounds of boisterous teenagers and my best friend's laughter filled the old home.

I pressed a kiss to her belly and sighed.

Life.

Life filled this home.

My life was in this home. My reason for living. My family.

My Willa.

Additional Works

The Tarnished Angels Motorcycle Club Series:

Wreck & Ruin (Tarnished Angels Book 1)
Crash & Carnage (Tarnished Angels Book 2)
Madness & Mayhem (Tarnished Angels Book 3)
Thrust & Throttle (Tarnished Angels Book 4)
Venom & Vengeance (Tarnished Angels Book 5)

SINS Series:

Sins of a King (Book 1)
Birth of a Queen (Book 2)
Rise of a Dynasty (Book 3)
Dawn of an Empire (Book 4)
Ember (Book 5)
Burn (Book 6)
Ashes (Book 7)
Fall of a Kingdom (Book 8)

Others:

Additional Works

Peasants and Kings

About the Author

Wall Street Journal & USA Today bestselling author Emma Slate writes romance with heart and heat.

Called "the dialogue queen" by her college playwriting professor, Emma writes love stories that range from romance-for-your-pants to action-flicks-for-chicks.

When she isn't writing, she's usually curled up under a heating blanket with a steamy romance novel and her two beagles—unless her outdoorsy husband can convince her to go on a hike.

Made in the USA
Middletown, DE
18 June 2024

55971852R00274